Worlds of
Edgar Rice
Burroughs

Worlds of Edgar Rice Burroughs

Edited by
Mike Resnick
and
Robert T. Garcia

BAEN

WORLDS OF EDGAR RICE BURROUGHS

All stories copyright © 2013 by ERB, Inc., except for "The Forgotten Sea of Mars,"
copyright © 1965.

A Baen Books Original

Baen Publishing Enterprises
P.O. Box 1403
Riverdale, NY 10471
www.baen.com

ISBN: 978-1-4516-3935-3

Cover art by Dave Seeley

First Baen printing, October 2013

Distributed by Simon & Schuster
1230 Avenue of the Americas
New York, NY 10020

  Library of Congress Cataloging-in-Publication Data

Worlds of Edgar Rice Burroughs / Robert Garcia & Mike Resnick, editors.
  pages cm
  ISBN 978-1-4516-3935-3 (trade pb)
1. Fantasy fiction, American. 2. Science fiction, American. I. Garcia, Robert T. II.
Resnick, Michael D., editor of compilation. III. Burroughs, Edgar Rice, 1875-1950.
  PS648.F3W69 2013
  813'.0876608--dc23
                        2013025696

Printed in the United States of America

10 9 8 7 6 5 4 3 2 1

⊹⇋ Contents ⇌⊹

To Joan Bledig,
Keeper of the Flame.
This one is definitely for you.
—Mike and Bob

Worlds of Edgar Rice Burroughs

Introduction

Welcome to the worlds of Edgar Rice Burroughs—and we do mean *worlds*.

Everyone knows about his most popular creation, of course. Tarzan, Lord of the Jungle, starred in twenty-two books during ERB's lifetime, and two more that were published after his death. He's been starring in movies since the silent era beginning back in 1918, he's had his own TV show, he was even the star of a Broadway musical and he had his own long-running comic strip and comic book.

But ERB's reputation doesn't rest solely with Tarzan. He also created the almost-as-influential Mars series, in which John Carter, an Earthman who becomes the Warlord of Mars, and his friends starred in ten books while Burroughs was alive, and part of an eleventh that was published, along with a John Carter novella written by his sons, after Burroughs died—and these books influenced such writers as Leigh Brackett, Otis Adelbert Kline, Lin Carter, and many, many others.

Not bad for one literary lifetime.

But there's more. *Lots* more.

Not content with setting adventures on Mars, Burroughs created another hero, Carson Napier, a kind of Wrong-Way Corrigan of space, who set out for Mars, somehow wound up on Venus, and stayed there for four books while ERB was alive, and part of a fifth that was published posthumously.

And for those who didn't want to fare that far afield for their fantastic adventures, Burroughs created Pellucidar, the strange world that exists at the Earth's Core. It was discovered by David Innes and Abner Perry, but eventually even Tarzan made it down there, and seven books were devoted to it.

Forty-five books about his four worlds. That would be a half a dozen careers for most writers, but Burroughs was just getting started.

He served in the cavalry in Arizona, and it turned up in his two novels about Shoz-Dijiji, the War Chief of the Apaches. (And he gave equal time to the other side, with *The Deputy Sheriff of Comanche County* and *The Outlaw of Hell's Bend*.)

He was back in space—*deep* space—for his tale of Poloda, a planet that exists *Beyond the Farthest Star*.

And he came a little closer to home with his novel, *The Moon Maid*.

For those who like their heroes to wear more than a loin cloth and to look and act like you and me, he wrote *The Mucker*.

There was more, of course, but these constitute his major worlds and his major achievements, and we're proud to present at least one story about each of them.

Edgar Rice Burroughs was, and is, a national treasure. Tarzan became an instant icon with his first appearance in the October, 1912 issue of *All-Story Magazine*. By the 1920s, the best-selling American author in the world was not Hemingway or Fitzgerald, but Edgar Rice Burroughs. He became a success at something that had eluded Mark Twain and others: publishing and distributing his own books. Two cities—Tarzana, California and Tarzan, Texas—are named for his most famous character. More than a decade after his death in 1950, when most of his titles had fallen out of print, there was a massive paperback revival, and he was a bestseller all over again. Fanzines arose that were devoted exclusively to his work, and the Burroughs Bibliophiles have been convening regularly since the early 1960s.

When we finally decided to create an anthology of original stories, using his characters, we approached some of the top science fiction and fantasy writers in the field, and we were overwhelmed by their enthusiastic response. Most had been waiting their whole lives to write a Burroughs story, and now that we'd received permission from Edgar Rice Burroughs, Inc., nothing was going to stop them.

And nothing did.

So read, enjoy, and marvel at some new takes on the many worlds of Edgar Rice Burroughs.

—Mike Resnick & Bob Garcia

Usually when you think of Tarzan you think of a bronzed, godlike figure in a loincloth, swinging through the trees or engaged in mortal combat with Numa the Lion. But Edgar Rice Burroughs gave him no such limitations, and neither does Hugo-winning writer and editor Kristine Kathryn Rusch. Burroughs pitted Tarzan against the Germans in World War I, and against the Japanese in World War II. Ms. Rusch takes us back to that earlier conflict in this story.

—Mike

Tarzan and the Great War

Kristine Kathryn Rusch

The little man who carried the telegram had no teeth, yet he looked familiar. It had been years since Tarzan had been to Algiers, and then he had not spent a lot of time with the locals. Yet this man seemed to know him.

"Excuse. Tarzan?" the man said in bad English. It was clear he did not know if Tarzan was the person he sought.

"I am Tarzan," he said. "And I speak French."

He wondered how the little man had missed that. Tarzan had been speaking French at a nearby table in an outdoor café, under a large canopy against the exceptionally bright sun.

The canopy had not been for him—Tarzan did not need or crave the shade the way that Europeans did—but it had been for his companion, a French expatriate who claimed he knew where Tarzan's missing wife, Jane, was. For several weeks, Tarzan had thought her dead, but later learned that she had been spared.

He had spent a long time searching for her and had come no closer to her. But he knew he would eventually find her, and the men who took her would pay.

Unfortunately, the Frenchman he had spoken to hadn't known

anything. That became clear after a moment's conversation, when the Frenchman had not used Jane's name at all. The Frenchman had tried a gambit: *I may know where your missing wife is,* apparently something many men in the middle of this Great War needed to know.

The Frenchman had expected payment first, and Tarzan had set a gold piece on the table. The crowd of people, constantly moving through the narrow streets of the Kasbah, didn't seem to notice the gold piece's shine, which relieved Tarzan. Still, he kept his forefinger on the gold piece, figuring anyone who would try to steal it would suffer a broken wrist before he knew what happened.

The Frenchman had eyed the gold piece as if he wanted to steal it himself as Tarzan pressed the Frenchman for more details about Jane. Since he had none to give, Tarzan pocketed the gold piece and sent the Frenchman on his way.

Now a native Algerian stood before him, clutching a ratty piece of paper.

"I have for you a telegram," the Algerian said, his French soft and accented. "You are Jean C. Tarzan, no?"

Tarzan started. He hadn't used that name for years. He had taken it as his name during his first travels outside of Africa. Then he had known he was Lord Greystoke, but he could not admit it without ruining Jane's marriage with his cousin, William Cecil Clayton, who had taken on the role of Lord Greystoke when the family believed that Tarzan's father had left no heirs.

(It was, of course, more complicated than that, but, Tarzan had learned, all things concerning his family were complicated.)

Tarzan hoped his surprise at the old name did not show. "I am Jean C. Tarzan," he said.

"Ah, *monsieur,*" the little man said with great relief. "I have been holding this telegram for you for months. I have searched for you all over the city, and could only hope you had already received the news."

For a moment, worry ran through Tarzan. Could this be bad news of Jane?

Then he realized no news of Jane would come to him through that name. If someone were sending him bad news about her, it would come through proper channels, addressed to John Clayton, Lord Greystoke.

"You read the telegram?" Tarzan asked, knowing that operators prided themselves on translating the dots and dashes, but did their best to forget the messages.

"I did, *monsieur*, I am sorry," the little man said. "I memorized it in case something happened to the paper."

Now Tarzan could not ignore the message. His curiosity was piqued. Who would try to reach Jean C. Tarzan with an important message? Jean C. Tarzan had existed only for a short time in the years before the war, and had vanished after only a few months.

He took the gold piece he had planned to give to the Frenchman and handed it to the little man. The little man looked at it as if it could bite him.

"*Monsieur*, I am well paid at my work. I am doing this for you and for the Allies!"

Then he handed Tarzan the paper, nodded his head, and made his way through the crowd. Quickly he disappeared down a hill leading to the sea and the French section of the city, the blazing sun on the white buildings making it impossible to see anything other than movement.

Not for the first time, Tarzan silently cursed the civilized world. White buildings might remain cool inside, but a man could not see anything in this sea of people and brightness. He wished he could return to the jungle, where everything was clear.

But he needed word of Jane, and that word would come from men, who congregated in cities.

Until then, he would follow whatever leads he could, and find them where he may.

He opened the crumpled paper and read the smeared French. The telegram came from the War Ministry to Jean C. Tarzan.

We are reactivating your status. Contact Aiden Mireau regarding assignment. Do not trust local French officials. Urgent.

He stared at the words, then read them again. He had worked for the War Ministry well before the war, and he had operated out of Algiers, solving many a case and stopping many a problem. But he had disappeared after the Gernois incident.

The date on the telegram was curious: he had not been part of the ministry for so long that he had no idea why they thought he would help them.

Still, he could not ignore this. Contact with Europeans,

particularly those who had a stake in the secret underbelly of foreign affairs, might lead him to Jane.

He would find this Aiden Mireau and discover what it was the War Ministry wanted him to do.

It was a ridiculous job, or so Arthur Beaton had thought before he arrived in Africa all those months ago. Since then he had tracked this so-called Lord Greystoke all over the continent, hearing rumors that the man had killed Germans with his bare hands.

Beaton, a loyal Englishman to the core, was quite happy with the German deaths. The war had become ugly and, many believed, unwinnable. He had been unable to serve due to age, but that hadn't stopped the British government from sending him on this mission—to find the faux Lord Greystoke, strip him of his title, and confiscate the money from the Greystoke estate for England herself.

This last Beaton had learned only because he was a good investigator. The British government had thought it no concern of his what would happen to the funds. But Beaton had thought the timing odd, so he had looked into the rationales behind the orders before taking the case. Had it been peacetime, he might have been more trusting. Or even if the orders had come several years ago, when this faux Lord Greystoke had appeared on the scene.

Then the longtime heir, William Cecil Clayton, would have lodged a complaint. But now the estate would go to some sixteenth cousin twice removed, and Beaton had no idea why the government would interest itself in such matters during wartime. Not until he learned about the vast wealth of the estate did he understand.

Things had become quite desperate after years of war. The government needed men and materiel, but more than that, it needed funds to pay for the men and materiel, funds from defunct estates and potential nonloyalists like this faux Lord Greystoke.

Even after Beaton discovered what the job entailed, he believed in it. He certainly thought that some sixteenth cousin, twice removed, a sixteenth cousin from the merchant classes, speaking with an accent bred in public schools, would be preferable to the faux Lord Greystoke, who had once told friends he had grown up in Africa "among the apes." Tales of his uncouth behavior had disgusted Beaton, and made him even more willing to take the assignment.

But all of these months tracking down the man who had lost his home and his wife to German soldiers, and who had thwarted some German attacks, seemed a bit much.

By the time Beaton had arrived in Algiers on the heels of faux Greystoke, he felt a begrudging admiration for the man. In Beaton's personal opinion, England needed such a man on her side.

Still, Beaton had a job to do, and he was not one to give up when success was so close at hand.

He could see the faux Lord Greystoke on the other side of the road. Beaton had taken a spot underneath an archway in one of the old buildings of the Kasbah. His white straw hat never gave him much protection from the harsh sunlight, even if the temperatures here in Algiers weren't as brutal as they had been deeper inside the continent.

The Mediterranean Sea had a moderating effect, although its salty scent could not penetrate the odors of tobacco, incense, and roasting meat that seemed part of the Kasbah itself.

Beaton had been watching the faux Lord Greystoke all morning, and the man seemed a lot more civilized than Beaton had been prepared for. He clearly spoke several languages, seemed at ease in the crowded streets, and sipped tea while he awaited his companion, a rather shady Frenchman whom Greystoke had dismissed almost as soon as the man arrived.

But it wasn't the Frenchman who caught Beaton's eye. It was the rumpled little man who wore the robes of an Algerian, but who had come from the colonial part of the city, who had gotten his attention. That little man had watched Greystoke for nearly an hour before approaching him, and then had spoken to him only briefly, handing him a piece of paper that seemed to have perplexed Greystoke greatly.

Greystoke had read the paper several times before stuffing it into his pocket. Then he had stood near his table as if trying to make a decision.

He was an excessively tall man, with olive-colored skin darkened by the sun, and black hair in need of a trim. If the women around him were any judge, he was stunningly handsome. Certainly not the kind of man who could easily blend in, especially here, where most men were not as tall and not as muscular. Greystoke was, if anything, the epitome of British manhood, and Beacon felt increasingly strange about having to challenge the man's heritage.

Still, as Greystoke stepped purposefully away from the outdoor café, Beaton followed—at a discreet distance, of course. Following such a man through the streets of the Kasbah should have been difficult, but was not, because the man towered over everyone.

Beaton did have to hurry to keep up. Even here, in the tight confines of the city, Greystoke traveled swiftly, as if the crowds parted before him just because they saw him coming.

Aiden Mireau was easy enough to find. He had an office in the Grand Post Office, one of the last buildings built in Algiers before the war. Tarzan remembered when it was new and controversial, at least among the Algerians. The French thought it lovely and perfect, the white sides and the Moorish arches a tribute to the African peoples. The people of Algiers just saw it as another reminder of the Europeans who had captured and held their country for so long.

Tarzan had learned the hard way that these small battles among peoples that, to him, had more in common than not, were extremely important. They could rupture into worldwide war, sucking in every corner of the globe and leading to the destruction of families like his own.

Before, when he had acted as Jean C. Tarzan, he had thought such things minor blips in a lifetime. Now he knew they could destroy a way of life. He kept telling himself that once he had Jane back, he would rebuild the plantation and retreat to his mountainside, never to leave her alone again.

He told himself this, but part of him thought it would not come true.

Tarzan stepped inside the large building. Despite the number of people inside, the central hall was cool. Arches created both a sense of division and of openness. The windows, with the arch pattern in their shape and in the glass, let in just enough of the bright sunlight to add to the illumination provided by the gigantic chandelier that hung from the very high ceiling.

He slipped around the crowd, going to the directory near the grand staircase. Aiden Mireau's office was listed alphabetically, like all the office holders here. But unlike most of them, nothing identified Mireau as a representative of the French government.

Tarzan found that curious in and of itself.

He took the steps two at a time as he headed to Mireau's office, not realizing that three different men watched him from the floor below.

The first man always watched the stairs. He kept track of the Europeans who were coming and going. He had never seen the tall broad-shouldered athletic man before. That man looked formidable.

The first man hoped his compatriots on the upper levels kept track of where the athletic man was going.

The second man had tailed the athletic man from the Kasbah, careful to keep his distance. No one looked out of place in the Grand Post Office, but it was more common to see men in European dress than Algerian garb. And the second man wore robes. He blended in, but he didn't believe he would if he went to the official floors.

Still, he knew that Mireau had an office here and was involved in things that might change Algiers forever. The second man watched warily, wondering what the athletic man would do, and if he would be useful.

The third man who watched the athletic man go up the stairs was Beaton. Beaton watched faux Greystoke read the directory, so Beaton knew Greystoke was meeting someone. Only the French had offices here, and that made Beaton uneasy. Greystoke had odd allegiances for an English lord, and that alone made this worth pursuing.

Although Beaton didn't know quite how to do so.

He would bide his time, watch, and take all actions under consideration. That was all he could reasonably do.

Aiden Mireau did not have a secretary. Nor did he have an impressive office. He had a room on the top floor, tucked behind the edge of the arches. The floor was hot, and Mireau's office hotter still. It smelled faintly of sweat and whiskey. It had one window that clearly did not open, and a narrow battered desk that might have been new when someone tried to squeeze it through the door.

The man behind the desk was small, balding, and completely forgettable. Adrian Mireau looked like a bureaucrat. His clothing was cheap and ill-fitting. He had draped his suit coat over a nearby chair, and his wrinkled linen shirt was dotted with sweat.

He smoked a cigarette as he shifted papers back and forth. He did not look up as Tarzan entered the room, but waited for Tarzan to introduce himself.

Tarzan did so in French, using the name Jean C. Tarzan.

"Close the door," Mireau said without looking up.

Tarzan looked down the hall before he closed the door. He saw movement near the stairs. Men on each floor kept track of comings and goings. He knew that he had become part of today's list. Usually such things did not bother him, but too many strange things had happened on this day. He made note.

He turned toward Mireau to find that man looking at him.

Mireau's face was as rumpled as his clothing. He looked gray and tired, a man who had long exceeded the end of his rope.

"Jean C. Tarzan," he said. "I was beginning to believe you were a phantom."

"I received this just today," Tarzan said and handed him the crumpled telegram.

Mireau glanced at it, then sighed. He handed the paper back. "What have you been doing during the war?"

Tarzan decided he would tell only part of the truth. This man did not need to know everything.

"I retired from the War Office and married. My wife and I settled on some land in rural Africa, where we stayed until Germans destroyed our home."

"And your wife?" Mireau asked.

Tarzan shook his head, unable to lie about this. But Mireau clearly took that gesture to mean that Jane had not survived.

"My condolences," Mireau said. "So you returned to Algiers to resume your work?"

"I do what I can to stop the Germans," Tarzan said.

"But you did not contact the War Office," Mireau said.

It took Tarzan a minute to realize that Mireau was not repeating what he understood; Mireau was making certain that Tarzan had spoken to no one in the French government.

"I had not given the War Office any thought until I got this telegram an hour ago."

"It is several months old."

"I am aware of that. The man who delivered it worked hard to find me."

Mireau's eyes narrowed. Then he nodded at a nearby chair. "Would you like a drink?"

Not in the middle of the afternoon. Tarzan had never gotten used to that custom. He declined, and then peered at the chair. It was too small for him. He knew without trying that he could not sit in it.

So he remained standing.

"I am to talk with you," Tarzan said, wondering if he should have come. Mireau had not volunteered anything when Tarzan mentioned the Germans.

"Yes," Mireau said. "I would like to see your papers."

"I don't carry papers," Tarzan said. At least not in the name of Jean C. Tarzan. But he didn't add that.

Mireau stubbed out his cigarette. "I would normally ask you to leave if you did not have papers, but I have read your files, Mr. Tarzan, and those of your superiors, and I know what an unusual man you are. I doubt there are two men who look like you in all the world."

Tarzan smiled thinly. "The portraits of my ancestors show that my looks are not that unusual."

"Around here they are, *monsieur*," Mireau said. "And on that basis, I will ask you this: would you be willing to take an assignment off the books for the War Office? We have need of someone with no ties to officialdom."

"I am not sure whom you are, sir, nor do I know who you represent," Tarzan said.

Mireau smiled thinly. "There are official diplomats and *charges d'affaires* in each major city. Then there are men like me, who handle the—shall we say—darker side of diplomacy."

Tarzan had met such men before. They had fewer scruples, but they seemed to be loyal to their countries. Tarzan had no such loyalty to France, nor to England, but he did feel such loyalty to the jungles here in Africa. So, for that reason, and because he hoped to ask in a roundabout way about news of Jane, he asked, "What do you need me for?"

"You know the war is going badly for the Allies," Mireau said.

Tarzan waited.

"We believe that a small group of our own people is selling information to the Germans."

Tarzan shrugged. "Arrest them."

"It is not that easy," Mireau said. "A network of spies works Algiers, and the head of that network is making a small fortune by ruining the war effort. Track the money, perhaps get involved in the network, and we will—"

"I am not a subtle man," Tarzan said. "And I do not plan to stay in Algiers long enough to infiltrate any group."

Mireau tilted his head back and stared at the ceiling for a long moment. Then he sighed and sat up. "You are our only hope."

"I'm sorry," Tarzan said. "I'm not the man for you. Perhaps someone else will be able to help you."

He turned and as he grabbed the door knob, Mireau said, "Perhaps there is a different way to do this. You are looking for news of the Germans in Africa. These men would have that news."

Tarzan turned around slowly. "You do not want me to find these men so that you can arrest them."

"We are at war, *Monsieur Tarzan*," Mireau said. "Finesse belongs to peacetime."

"I am not an assassin," Tarzan said, and left.

Tarzan stepped into the hallway, noting that it was just a bit cooler out here. That office had felt stuffy and uncomfortable, and not just because of what Mireau had asked him. It was an unhealthy place to be, the opposite of the life Tarzan preferred.

He scanned the hallway and saw no one, nothing that caused that movement he had seen when he closed the door. Of course, the door was a thin one, and someone might have heard his voice as he got closer to it.

He didn't like the feeling he had, as if he were being watched. Better to get out of here and find out information on Jane on his own.

He hurried down the stairs, wanting out of the Grand Post Office. Even the bright streets were better than this place.

He was halfway down when he heard a gunshot. It had come from behind him.

He pivoted, knowing the shot had something to do with him. He ran back up, keeping his eyes peeled for any more movement, knowing that someone could be staring down the sight of a gun at him even now.

No one ran past him, but the hallway smelled of gun powder. The door to Mireau's office was open, even though Tarzan had closed it behind him.

Mireau sat back in his chair, a bullet hole in the center of his forehead, blood against the back wall. He still clutched the whiskey he had poured before Tarzan had left.

Tarzan cursed. He heard footsteps on the stairs as others hurried up, but no one had come from this floor.

He told himself that Mireau's death had nothing to do with him, that the man had worked—in his words—on the "darker side of diplomacy" for a long time, and someone could have killed him for that.

But still, the timing was suspicious. Tarzan did not go inside the office—he knew better because the footsteps on the stairs were getting closer. Someone could arrest him for the murder, even though he did not hold a gun.

Instead, he walked through the hallway, looking for the cause of that movement earlier.

Toward the back, the hallway was covered with dust, caused by construction that clearly continued. There were no footsteps in that dust, nor was there any indication that someone had leaned against the wall. But closer to the stairs, he saw one sandal print, and a stubbed-out cigarette butt. The sandal print was smaller than Tarzan's shoe print—not that such a thing was unusual—but it was small enough that it *seemed* unusual.

The footsteps on the stairs grew closer—the sound of stomping, really, and labored breathing. Only one person was coming the entire way up the stairs, and Tarzan thought that unusual too.

If he went down now, he would be the only suspect in this murder, which he suspected he was meant to be. If he waited, he could shadow the other man down, and perhaps no one would notice him.

Or maybe he could find another way out of this building—after the other man had left.

Tarzan stepped into the shadows and waited for the man to finish his climb up the stairs.

Arthur Beaton was too old to run up a flight of stairs, let alone several flights. Halfway up, his breath came in short bursts, and he got lightheaded. Still, he didn't want to stop.

No one else seemed alarmed that a gunshot resounded through the Grand Post Office. He would have thought it his imagination if it hadn't been for the fact that two men near him peeled away from the walls and headed calmly outside.

Several others walked out as well, not like men who had finished whatever task they had to do in a post office, but like guards at the end of a long shift.

For one second, he debated following them, and then he remembered where he was.

He was in Algiers. The local law had its own agenda and the French colonial government only cared if one of its own died. Beaton wasn't certain if the French would consider faux Greystoke one of their own, but he didn't want to risk it.

If Greystoke were dead, Beaton wanted to see it for himself, so that he could report back to the English government.

He knew that the body could be moved or tampered with immediately after the killing. He also knew he was running toward trouble, not away from it, so he pulled out his own gun.

Although he was beginning to question the wisdom of that move as he got closer to the top, and his breath was getting even harder to catch. Soon he would double over wheezing, and he didn't want to do that.

But the heat up here wasn't helping. Neither was the fact that the last time he had run might have been in the previous century.

Finally he reached the top of the stairs and forced himself to breathe properly—not that he really achieved it. He was wheezing. He just hadn't doubled over.

He kept his gun extended, noting the scent of cordite. He was about to follow that smell when someone pulled him into the darkness.

Tarzan gripped the man's gun arm, keeping the weapon pointed away from him. But he did not let the sweaty European's gun go down, just in case someone else came up the stairs.

Tarzan used the man as both a shield and a weapon. He couldn't do much else, considering how hard the man was breathing. Tarzan had seen men this red-faced and short of breath before, often before they fell down in a fit of apoplexy.

Tarzan didn't want the man to die, but he also didn't want the man to turn on him, either.

No one came up the stairs. The man stopped wheezing, but he was still breathing hard.

Tarzan turned him around and took the gun. He emptied it of bullets.

The man looked familiar. Tarzan had seen him on the street for the past twenty-four hours. Even though Algiers was a French colonial city, Europeans did not go to the Kasbah in large numbers and almost never alone. This man had been near Tarzan's hotel, near the cafés where he dined, and now here, in the Grand Post Office on the top floor, right after Mireau had been shot.

It was clear, however, from the man's breathing that he had not been anywhere near Mireau when Mireau died.

"Who are you?" Tarzan asked in French.

Sweat dripped off the man's bright red face. Still, he managed to straighten just a little. "Arthur Beaton."

"Do I know you, Arthur Beaton?" Tarzan asked.

"I really prefer talking in English," Beaton said in that same language.

"As you wish," Tarzan said, still looking around the floor, trying to see if anyone else joined them. "The question remains. Do I know you?"

"Er, can that wait?" Beaton asked. "I heard a gunshot."

"You did," Tarzan said. "Someone shot Aiden Mireau. He's dead."

"Aiden Mireau?" Beaton asked. "Surely, you jest."

Tarzan hated that phrase. He'd heard it ever since he had contact with the British, and it was always used in cases like this.

"Surely, I do not," he said.

"Oh, good heavens." Beaton actually looked distressed. "Why would you kill him?"

"Me?" Tarzan asked. "If I killed a man, I would not do so with such an unreliable toy."

He shook the empty gun at Beaton, who cringed, even though he had watched Tarzan empty the chamber.

"If there's a killer up here, I would like my unreliable toy back," Beaton said.

Tarzan did not let go of the gun. "You've been following me."

Beaton licked his lips. "It's—um—not relevant at the moment."

"It is to me," Tarzan said.

"It's complicated," Beaton said. "May I see Mireau?"

Tarzan had no idea why this little man would want to see Mireau, unless he had something to do with the crime. "As you wish," Tarzan said, and led Beaton to the door. He kept his hand on the Englishman, figuring if someone came up the stairs ready to make an arrest, Tarzan would give them Beaton along with the gun. It would take them a while to figure out that Beaton hadn't fired his gun at all.

Beaton had to struggle to keep up with Tarzan, even though Tarzan kept his gait short. They reached the door. Beaton took one glance at Mireau, and then closed his eyes for a brief moment.

"Was he like this when you found him?" Beaton asked.

Tarzan could answer the question two ways. He had found Mireau twice this day, first when he had initially come up here, and then when he came back after the gunshot.

Tarzan chose to answer it a third way. "What does it matter to you?"

Beaton let out a small breath of air. "If Mireau was alive when you first came up the stairs, then perhaps someone overheard your conversation and killed him."

"Or perhaps the killer had waited until I left before doing this," Tarzan said.

"The killer could still be up here," Beaton said.

"I have not found anyone," Tarzan said.

Beaton gave him a curious glance. "You looked?"

"Why did you think I wouldn't?" Tarzan asked. "No one passed me on the stairs."

"They wouldn't," Beaton said. "Places like this have many hidden rooms. Someone could be listening to us even now."

Tarzan thought for a moment. How important was it for him to find Mireau's killer? He wasn't even sure he could answer that for himself. The man had wanted him to murder men he had never met, for a reason he wasn't sure he believed in.

But then, perhaps someone was trying to frame him for this murder.

"I think I saw his compatriots leave," Beaton said. "I could—"

Tarzan raised one finger, silencing Beaton. Then he shook his head. If someone was listening in, then Tarzan didn't want Beaton to admit he knew what the killer's companions looked like.

"I'm sure they wanted me to take the blame for this," Tarzan said. He glanced at the closed window in Mireau's office. Tarzan could leave by the roof.

"I wouldn't consider it," Beaton said. "The French invented the art of the fingerprint, and theoretically yours are on file."

The "theoretically" caught Tarzan. That was an odd word to use.

"If we walk down together, they might think nothing of it," Beaton said.

Tarzan wasn't sure he could trust this man, but he did want to know why he was being followed. And he also wanted to know why he was being used.

"Good idea," Tarzan said. "But we will do it my way."

They went down the stairs. Tarzan let go of Beaton's arm on the second landing.

"Go the rest of the way without me," Tarzan said.

"But I thought—"

"I know," Tarzan said, unwilling to explain that if someone had set him up, he would be arrested whether he came down with Beaton or not. Tarzan was extremely recognizable, as this day had already proven. "I will meet you at the hotel."

Beaton nodded, inadvertently confirming his identity as the man in the straw hat near the hotel. "I would like my gun," he said.

Tarzan smiled. "I'm sure you would."

Beaton was shaking as he made his way down the stairs. Something awful had happened here, and Greystoke believed it was because of him, that they wanted to blame him.

Beaton was shocked that the dead man was Aiden Mireau. Beaton had known Mireau's name for years. Mireau was one of those men one contacted if one got in trouble near French Algeria. Mireau could get any European out of Africa on a moment's notice. He knew everyone and everything, and used his knowledge to help the Allied cause.

Beaton had never met Mireau, but he had always believed that he could contact Mireau as a last resort. Now that option was gone.

The run up the stairs, the encounter with Greystoke, and the sight of Mireau had left Beaton feeling spent. He wasn't used to the heat or the exertion, and it had been years since he had seen a dead body.

Plus, Greystoke seemed both civilized and uncivilized at the same time. His English and his French were flawless, but there was something in his eyes that suggested a wildness. Besides, he had easily disarmed Beaton and could have shot him, or tossed him down the stairs had he wished. The man was freakishly strong.

Not many men made Beaton wary, but Greystoke did.

Beaton was so shaken it wasn't until he reached the main floor of the Grand Post Office that he realized he had given himself away. Greystoke clearly knew Beaton had been following him, because Greystoke had not specified which hotel, yet Beaton had nodded.

Now the choice was his: How did he play this next part? Or did he "play" it at all?

Tarzan went down the hall on the next floor. There were cupolas on the roof, and there was no obvious way to get to them from the upper floor, which meant that the route was either hidden or the access was one floor down. He doubted, with such an obvious design feature, that the access would be hidden.

When he reached the end of the hall, he saw that he was right. A narrow door with a sign above it reading "staircase" and "private" in French stood directly beneath the part of the roof where the cupola stood.

He tried the door; it was locked. So he slammed his shoulder against it, easily breaking the flimsy lock. The resounding bang should have brought people out of their offices, but no one so much as looked.

There was a lot of ignoring going on in this building. He did not know if that was normal or if it was because of Mireau's death.

At the moment, Tarzan didn't care. He closed the door and walked silently up the stairs, noting another entrance one flight up. That entrance hadn't been obvious from the top floor. Beaton's statement about hidden rooms, then, was absolutely correct.

Had someone stood in one of those rooms, heard Tarzan turn down Mireau, and then killed Mireau? It seemed likely.

Tarzan went up one more flight into the cupola itself. It was two stories high, and the second story had narrow windows, almost like gun turrets. The French thought of everything.

Including a door onto the roof. Tarzan opened it and stepped into the blazing sunlight.

He blinked once, waiting for his eyes to adjust, when he sensed a movement to his left. He feinted right as a man tried to knock him aside. Tarzan shoved him, using the man's own momentum, and the man stumbled sideways, tripped, and fell, screaming as he tumbled off the roof.

Tarzan turned and found himself face to face with another man, holding a gun.

This man wore European garb. He was nearly as tall as Tarzan. Tarzan had not ever seen him before.

"It seems, Mr. Tarzan," he said in French, "you have become quite the maniac, going on a killing spree that has resulted in the death of several agents. I'm sure the authorities will be up here shortly because you tossed my man off the roof. I will be a hero for killing you."

"You killed Mireau," Tarzan said. He did not look at the gun. Guns did not frighten him.

"He got too close," the man said. "You gave me an alibi. Thank you."

"Tell me the names of the men you work with, and I'll spare you," Tarzan said.

"I believe you told our friend Mireau that you are not an assassin," the European said.

"I defend myself," Tarzan said.

"Not against a gun," the man said and fired.

Tarzan leapt to the left a half second before the shot. Talkers always telegraphed their next move. Before the man could shoot again, Tarzan tackled him, and knocked the gun aside. It skittered across the roof.

Tarzan dragged the man to the edge, then held his torso over it. The man kicked ineffectually.

"Tell me who you work with," Tarzan said.

The man looked down. His compatriot remained on the dirt street below, his legs at an odd angle, his back clearly broken. From this height, Tarzan couldn't tell if he survived the fall or not. It didn't matter, though. He would clearly never be the same.

The man looked at Tarzan, eyes wild.

"Tell me," Tarzan said.

"No one," the man said.

The man's hand gripped the side of the building. Tarzan leaned on his fingers until he heard a snap.

The man screamed.

"Now," Tarzan said. "The names."

The man gave him a rapid list of French names. Tarzan nodded once. "And what of the Germans? Do you know one named Obergatz?"

"No," the man said. Tarzan leaned on his wrist. "*No! No!*"

The man's eyes told the truth. He did not know, which meant he had no idea what happened to Jane.

"Who do you work with among the Germans?" Tarzan asked.

"Whoever pays the most," the man said.

"And who would that be?"

"It's never the same," the man said. Then he listed several more names.

Tarzan memorized all of them.

"Please! Please! Do not kill me!" the man said.

"You didn't give Mireau the opportunity to beg for his life," Tarzan said.

The man's mouth opened in fear. Tarzan gripped him strongly, then swung him forward as if throwing him off the roof.

The coward fainted.

Tarzan brought him onto the roof proper, then ripped pieces of the man's shirt, and tied him in place. He removed the remaining bullets from the gun, pocketed them, and placed the gun just out of the man's reach.

The authorities would find him soon, and they would decide what to do with him. If they did not arrest him, Tarzan would make sure the man paid for Mireau's death.

First, he had some business to finish. He went to the far end of the roof. Three buildings stood nearby, but were not attached. He missed trees, vines, branches, easy ways to travel from one high place to another. But heights did not bother him, and neither did taking a running jump—which he did.

He landed on the next roof down, then jumped onto one more, before using an interior staircase. When he reached the bottom, he walked but not to the Kasbah where his hotel was.

Instead, he went to the telegraph office.

The little man sat at his desk. He had a light jacket draped over the back of his chair, apparently in deference to the French government that he worked for. He reached for the jacket when Tarzan entered, then saw who was there, and grinned his toothless grin.

"Can you send three messages for me?" Tarzan asked. "I need them to remain confidential."

"I am trustworthy, *monsieur*," the little man said.

"I know that," Tarzan said. "You have already proven it."

But still, he worried that someone else might not be.

He sent the cables back to the office that had initially contacted him. He signed all three missives, *Jean C. Tarzan*.

In the first message, he said he regretted to tell them of Mireau's death. Then he said that he would provide the information they sought and nothing more.

In the second message, he simply listed the French names that the man on the roof had given him.

And in the third message, he wrote, *These Germans have paid for the services we discussed.*

He figured the Allies could take care of everything—or not.

The fates of nations were not his concern. He had to continue his search for Jane, and then he would retire to his jungle.

He paid the little man five times the cost of the cables.

The little man scowled at him. "I do not take tips, *monsieur*."

"I am not giving you a tip," Tarzan said. "I am paying you for your service in the war effort."

The little man smiled. The smile, even without the teeth, was infectious. "My pleasure, monsieur," he said. "My pleasure."

Tarzan did not have to return to the hotel. He had left clothes there, but clothes were easily replaced. He now knew that Algiers did not have the information he so desperately wanted.

He didn't have to see Beaton, but he was curious why the Englishman had been following him. So he walked back. Along the way, he heard discussion of the deaths at the Grand Post Office, and relief that the man who had caused them had already been caught.

Algiers did not like even a hint of the war at its doorstep.

The hotel he had chosen was shabby and nondescript. It had a café that wasn't very good.

Beaton sat at a table near the hotel's main door, nursing a glass of tea. He looked relieved when he saw Tarzan.

"Milord," he said as he stood.

So this man did not confuse Tarzan with his old identity, Jean C. Tarzan.

"Everything's taken care of at the Grand Post Office," Tarzan said.

"And they do not blame you for Mireau?" Beaton asked.

"They have their killer," Tarzan said.

"Will you tell me what that was about?" Beaton asked.

"Government business," Tarzan said. "Now, tell me why you're following me."

He hovered, ready to leave at a moment's notice. But Beaton waved at the only waiter and ordered another glass of tea.

"Sit," he said. "This will take a little while."

Beaton had sat in the heat of the day, waiting for Greystoke to arrive. After two hours, he believed that Greystoke had left, and then Beaton had to decide if he would try to find the man again.

Then Greystoke showed up, looking a bit dusty, but no worse for wear.

By then, Beaton had made his decision.

"The British government would like your fortune to fund the war effort," Beaton said.

Greystoke frowned. "What does that mean?"

"It means that they had an expert who would claim there was no way that the baby handprint in your father's diary could have been your father's son. They decided that they would declare the fingerprint void. And then they would confiscate your lands and holdings. I was to notify you of all this and figure out what your holdings were here in Africa."

Greystoke's face reddened. "They thought I would submit to this?"

"There are rumors in London that you are a savage, milord."

Greystoke's eyes narrowed. "Do you believe the fingerprints valid?"

"I did not at first," Beaton said. "I did think, however, that someone in your family would have protested long before now. Still, I needed the work. I decided to decide when I saw you."

"You called me 'milord,'" Greystoke said.

"I did indeed," Beaton said. "You have conducted yourself extremely well, even *in extremis*. I think the British aristocracy should be proud to have you in its ranks."

"They can still pursue this," Greystoke said.

"They can," Beaton said. "But they won't. First, I can guarantee that it will take me many months more to find you. And when I do, you will tell me that you would take this matter to the courts. And by the way, if it does come to that, go to the French for your fingerprint analysis. As I said earlier, they invented the science. They know it best."

Greystoke studied Beaton. "Is there a reason you're doing me this favor?"

Beaton smiled. "I realized when I heard that gunshot in the Grand Post Office that you could have been killed. And honestly, my reaction surprised me, milord. I was saddened. I believe we need you. You are no savage, sir."

Greystoke smiled in return. The smile was warm, but it sent a shudder through Beaton all the same.

"Apparently, you met me on a good day," Greystoke said.

Then he drank his tea in one gulp and walked away.

Beaton did not follow him. Beaton did not watch which direction Greystoke took.

The war would continue, and Greystoke would continue to fight Germans as he searched for his wife. Greystoke had not enlisted, he was not fighting in trenches in France.

He was much more effective here, in Africa, destroying Germans in his hunt for information.

And if anyone pressed Beaton later on why he had made this decision, he would say simply he knew no one else who could face the enemy single-handedly and triumph.

He would say honestly that he had never met another man quite like John Clayton, Lord Greystoke, the man whom they called Tarzan.

—⟩⟨— END —⟩⟨—

Among the hideous creatures in Pellucidar, ERB's world at the earth's core, are the Sagoths, which the Emperor (David Innes) describes as "barely sapient gorillas." Leave it to bestseller Mercedes Lackey to come up with a tale of Pellucidar that is narrated by, of all things, a Sagoth—and a Sagoth that possesses all the hopes and emotions of any of its human counterparts. So join her as she relates the story of Mirina, known as The One Who Fell.

—Mike

The Fallen
A Tale of Pellucidar
Mercedes Lackey

I am Mok, son of . . . well, I do not know who my father was. My mother was named Lur, but there are many Lurs among the Sagoth that I grew up among, and I doubt that I could single her out were she to stand before me now.

Oh yes, I am a Sagoth. Surprised? Shocked that such as I, of a race that, as a whole, can barely reckon up the fingers and toes, a race that the Emperor calls "barely sapient gorillas," should be writing this? I can tell you, not nearly as shocked as the Emperor was when I was brought before him. His friend, Abner Perry, thinks that I am the result of some meddling by the Mahar, and I am not inclined to argue with him. The Mahar were wont to meddle in the breeding of the lesser creatures, trying to make humans fatter and more docile, for instance, so why not meddle to make my kind fit for more than understanding a few orders at best? Abner Perry calls me the Pythagoras of my kind. I think he is greatly mistaken, but then again, compared to my fellows, perhaps I am.

This makes me lonely. I do not find the females of the human kind to be attractive, and it would be a strange human female who would yearn for me, yet the females of my own breed, while drawing me to them with their broad jaws and hairy bosoms, repulse me at the same

25

time with their stupidity. So Loneliness is an old and familiar companion, and perhaps that is why I was fit to play the part that I did—

But I am ahead of myself, and this is not my story. It is the story of Mirina, the One Who Fell. So let me begin the tale at its true beginning.

It was a perfectly ordinary day in the land of Thuria, the Land of Awful Shadow—the only place in all of this world that has anything like darkness, because of the great orb that the Emperor, David Innes, calls a "moon" that hangs between Thuria and the source of our light. My friend Kolk, the son of Goork, who is King of the Thurians, and I were out upon the water with Kolk's son Dek. This might seem strange, since the waters of this world teem with terrible beasts, but Abner Perry had invented a boat he called a "whaler" and a weapon he called a "harpoon gun," and we were afire to test it. One day I will tell the story of how I came to be friends with Kolk and saved his son's life, but that is not today.

Suffice it to say that we were on the water with Perry's gun, and things were not going well for the great beasts of the waters. We had just dispatched our third, when a flash of light in the sky above us caught our eyes.

It came again, and we could see it was something white . . . winged, like a Mahar or thipdar, but not so big, and the wings were oddly made. It was not flying, it was falling—or rather, falling, then flailing with its wings as if trying to save itself, then falling again. The effect was somehow one of piteousness, helplessness—so much so that I think we were all moved by compassion at the same time. I do not know how that came to be, but I do know that the three of us, as one and without any consultation, turned our vessel toward the place where we thought the thing would fall and made all haste to be there when it landed.

We had not quite reached the spot when the creature—which we could see now looked like a human with wings!—gave a last convulsive attempt to save itself and plunged into the water.

Dek was over the side in a moment. He has long spent as much time with the peoples of the islands as with his own folk and is as much at home in the water as he is on the back of a lidi. We were roped for safety to the boat, of course—something I insisted on, since

I swim like a stone—so when he plunged over the side, I made haste to seize his rope and play it out so it did not snag and pull him up short. In no time he had reached the floating figure and was pulling it back through the water. But such commotion was bound to attract unwelcome guests.

And of course it did.

I saw it first, the hump rising above the waves as the thing moved swiftly toward us. I shouted and pointed with my chin, my hands and great strength busy hauling Dek and his burden in as fast as I could. There are many times when it is good to be a Sagoth, and this was one.

Kolk also did not hesitate. He sprang to Perry's gun, armed it with one of the harpoons that did not have a rope attached to it, and fired into the bulk of the beast before it could submerge and come up beneath his son.

The goal must have been to distract it from its quarry, and if so, the ploy worked.

A nightmare head, all jaws and teeth, broke the surface. Its neck was not long enough to permit it to bite at the iron harpoon impaling its side, so, after a futile attempt, it turned its fury on the boat.

By now Dek was aboard and pulling the fallen creature aboard with him—no easy feat, since the creature's long wings were impeding his progress. He no longer needed me, so I rushed to the other weapon aboard this little ship—the real cannon, a six-pounder, which I had insisted on being left charged. Not all the natives of the islands are friendly, and not all the beasts of the water could be dispatched with a harpoon.

As jaws twice as long as a human is tall opened to close on the prow of the ship, I turned that cannon into them and touched the match to the powder.

By good luck, my aim was true. I sent the ball crashing into what passed for the monster's brain, as well as shattering half of its jaw. It gave a terrific screech that deafened us, thrashed its whole body (barely missing the prow again) and sank into the depths.

Now we could turn to help Dek haul the winged stranger aboard.

I expected something like a stunted Mahar, or some other freak like myself. I imagine the others were assuming the same. Picture our shock to discover that it was a winged human, and a girl!

She was slender, scarcely half the height or weight of a typical woman of Sari or Thuria. Her hair was long, and hung down her back in a single tail I was to learn was called a "braid," and pale as the moonflower. Her wings were not naked and webbed like those of the Mahar and thipdar; instead they were covered with things that appeared to be large feathers, like a bird. Strangest of all, she was wearing not a garment of leather, but one of some other substance, more light and flexible than any leather I have ever seen. In fact, it was like the coverings that David Innes and Abner and the other men of the outer world sometimes wear. David had told me that this stuff was called "cloth."

We had never seen such a strange creature in all our lives.

I thought at first the fall had killed her, but Dek cried out that she was breathing, and we must get water. I was a little afraid—there was no telling what manner of fair-faced monster this girl might be—but I obeyed. I went to the stern and got one of our waterskins and brought to it to him just as the girl opened eyes of a color of blue I have never seen before nor since.

She gasped on seeing Dek, and her face went white, then red, then white again. Dek for his part was oblivious to this and merely seized the waterskin from me and urged her to drink.

This she did, as the pulse in her throat fluttered and I heard in my head that which I had never expected to hear from something shaped like a human—the soundless speech of the Mahar!

Do you not know me? How can you not know me?

Her words were addressed to Dek, not to me, but I was the one to answer. *He is Dek, son of Kolk, and we have never seen a thing like you before,* I replied, a little sternly—because if Mahar speech came from this creature, then it must *know* the Mahar, and converse with them. And that meant it might be an enemy, an agent of those awful creatures that feed on human and Sagoth and regard us as we regard insects.

Startled, she turned her head to stare at me. I saw nothing in her face to indicate subterfuge, only bewilderment and fear, and something I could not read, then. *But he has been in my dreams all of my life! How can he not know me? Why does he not speak to me himself?*

I softened my tone, though I remained stern. Clearly she did not know my kind, for she showed no surprise that I could speak beyond simple words. *He is a human, and he cannot hear the speech of the Mahar. What are you, and where have you come from, and what do you intend here?*

At the mention of the Mahar she turned paler than before, if that was possible. Dek was glancing from her to me and back again, sensing something was going on between us, but not able to hear it himself. "What's going on, Mok?" he demanded.

"Somehow this girl-creature speaks the speech of the Mahar," I explained. "I am questioning her." At that both Dek and his father held their peace.

Faced with my intimidating face and stern voice, the girl trembled, but answered my questions unflinchingly, and I pieced together her story. And if I had not spent the majority of my life in the company of the Emperor and Abner Perry, who found me as a child, I would never have believed it.

"She comes from there," I said, nodding upwards with my head to that thing that loomed above us, that Innes and Perry called a "moon." Dek gaped but did not look as if he disbelieved me. Kolk shook his head but did not interrupt. "She says that as we have driven the Mahar from here, it is there that they have fled to. Her people have seen them, streaming to the surface from what she calls 'the land above' in a vast migration. There were always *some,* but now there are legions more."

"But how did she get h—" Dek began, then flushed with embarrassment when he remembered her wings.

"She says she was pursued by a Mahar, and determined to die rather than be taken," I related. "She had no expectation of reaching here—and did not want to, since her people regard the *land above* with terror, as the place from which the Mahar are coming. She knew that the higher she flew, the colder she would become, and she expected to die from it. But instead, at some point, she reached a place where the land no longer called to her from below, and our land called to her from above . . ." I rubbed my head at this point, because the girl's thoughts were as confused as to this point as mine, and were mostly full of how cold it had been. "Then she began to fall, but toward us, not toward her home. As she grew warmer, she tried to fly again, but succeeded only in checking her fall. The rest you know."

I said nothing of what she had said of Dek. Instead, I turned back to her. *Can you hear the sounds we make when our mouths move?* I asked.

She answered in the affirmative, but her hands fluttered at her throat. *We do not make such noises, my people.* So she was mute but not deaf.

You had best learn how to understand the noises then, I told her, *for I am the only one who can speak to you in this way—or at least, the only one who is not a beast that would probably kill you.* "She cannot speak aloud," I added. "So I suppose I will have to stay with her for now."

Dek's face showed his relief. "Well, good. I cannot imagine anyone I trust more with such a task."

Kolk finally spoke. "It is good that the Emperor and Perry are here," he said. "Surely they will know what to do with her."

And so it was decided. We would take her to the Emperor. And at some point as we sailed the whale-boat back to shore, it was also decided that we would call her Mirina.

David Innes was intrigued, and delayed his departure by some sleeps in order to study the girl—once she recovered, that is. She had taken a terrible fall, after an even more terrible journey from her world to ours, and she was some time in growing better.

In some ways, she did not grow better at all. I understood this, and so, I think, did Innes. We have both grown used to being the only ones of our kind among strangers. I could see the loneliness growing in Mirina's eyes, and a desperation as she came to understand that Dek really had no notion she had ever dreamed of him once, much less many thousands of times.

Yes, thousands, for it seems that they sleep up there in the sky, much more often than we do. And not just when they grow weary, but are asleep as much as they are awake. Innes says this is because they have something called *time*, because their world turns so that half of it is always in darkness and half in light, and that life is like that on the Outer World where he is from. This has always seemed so strange as to make my thoughts spin, but I can look at the *moon* above us and see it turning, so I know this to be true. Our *timelessness* troubled the girl, though not as much as her loneliness, and another thing of which I will tell you.

When she finally grew well enough, she made the attempt to fly, only to find she could not even raise herself a little bit above the ground. Her wings beat gallantly against the air, yet nothing happened.

This nearly broke her, I think. She collapsed in a heap and covered her face with her hands and her head and body with her wings, and wept soundlessly as her poor, frail little body shook with sobs. She could not understand it. When she tried to speak to me, all she could manage was, *So heavy! Why am I so heavy?*

It was Perry who explained it, though I did not understand the explanation, and neither did Mirina. Perry said there was something called *gravity*, which pulls us down to the land, and that the *gravity* of our land is stronger than the *gravity* of the moon. He went on at some length, and no one understood it. It was Innes that said, "There is so much more of our land than the land of the moon that it calls to everything upon it with greater strength." That seemed logical to all of us, and we nodded, though Perry looked at us with disgust and muttered something under his breath.

Mirina then took to two pursuits. One was to spend herself into exhaustion, beating her wings to strengthen them, for after all, the Mahar can fly, and fly to her land, it seems, so eventually she felt she should be able to do the same.

The other was to follow Dek about, when she was not beating her wings.

For his part, he did not mind, although I could see that in his head he regarded her as a charming child, well worth indulging, and not the well-grown woman I knew her to be. He taught her a simple language of hand-signals, he supplied her with a light bow and arrows, which she used to great effect, so they went hunting together. He watched, fascinated, as she demonstrated *braiding* and *weaving*. Braiding he found particularly intriguing, especially as it enabled him to keep his long hair out of his face. So he enlisted her help in making his hair controlled . . . and I would watch her face as she did so, and it nearly broke my heart to see how it pleased and hurt her at the same time to give such an intimate service to him. For of course I was always their companion, since I was the only one who understood her.

Why do you torment yourself in this way, with him? I would ask her. And the answer was always the same.

I will be miserable regardless. I would rather be miserable with him, than miserable without him.

So day by day, her wings grew stronger, and she grew sadder. I thought that in the end she would probably try to fly back to her home, and maybe die in the attempt. Maybe? Almost certainly—unless she would gain the help of one of Perry's gigantic floating bags. Then . . . maybe she could. I wondered if I should tell her about them. Perry had never made another, after nearly killing Dian the Beautiful, the Emperor's mate and beloved, when one ran away with her. But for this . . . for this he might make one.

Would that be a good thing, or a bad? Because the land does call to us ardently, and I was not at all sure that even with the help of a floating bag that she could escape the call. Even if she did, there would be the return to her own land, up there in the sky, and the Mahar that were living there and preying on her people. A perilous plummet that would be, even with stronger wings than she had before.

But before I could make up my mind whether to tell her or no, events were taken from my hands.

It happened, after the Emperor had left us to return to his land and mate, and Perry with him, satisfied with how well his boat had turned out, that Dek and I were out on one of those selfsame boats, with Mirina with us also, and three other men of Thuria. This time we were hunting in earnest, for the purpose of clearing the waters and making them safe to navigate for the canoes of our island allies. Mirina, light as she was, with her wings to help her balance, had a perch on the top of the mast and was serving as our scout.

We had just dispatched one of the great sea-creatures with surprisingly little bloodshed, our harpoon having gone through its head from eye-socket to eye-socket. Seeing an opportunity, we brought it quickly alongside and tied it there, making sure that no fluids leaked into the water to attract others of its kind. There was much good meat on such a beast, and the bones, the skin, all were of immense use to us. Even the ribs could be used to form the ribs of a boat. We had used such when they washed ashore, but now we had an opportunity to bring one home intact and not half-rotten.

So intent were we that we paid no attention to our surroundings until finally a shrill whistle from above penetrated the noise we were making as we worked. Several of us looked up.

Mirina was blowing on the alarm-whistle that Dek had made her from a bit of hollow bone and frantically gesturing to the stern.

And we saw it. One of the terrible, unpredictable storms, coming straight at us.

It killed us to do so, but we straightway cut the big carcass loose—though as the others sawed at the ropes, I took care to remove the fins and stow them belowdecks with our water. Mirina half-slid, half-fluttered down out the mast, for when that wind hit, she, with her wings, would be the most vulnerable of us all. Then we put on full sail to try to outrun it and get into shelter in the lee of one of our ally-islands.

But the storm was coming on too fast. Seeing this, Dek sent Mirina to huddle in the storage belowdecks, dropped all sail, and sent out the sea-anchor. He ordered all of us to rope ourselves to the boat, and just in time.

I cannot tell you how long the storm lasted. Dek and I stood at the tiller and kept her nose into the waves. The other three huddled down as best they could. Perry and that strange cannibalistic fellow who was so good at boat-building had sworn this craft could weather any storm, but I had never seen a storm such as this. I do know that it drove us right out of the Shadow and well into the part of the ocean where all is light very quickly, for the sky, which had been black, lightened into a sullen gray, and so it stayed.

It is good that we had my strength. I do not think Dek could have held the tiller steady without it. It is good that the ship had a tiller carved of the keelbone of a great sea-beast, for it was flexible and did not snap. Several times, a slender, white arm came from below the deck between us, at a little hatch, and Dek would stoop and take what Mirina offered—dried fish, dried meat, a waterskin. If we had not had those, I think we would have perished. The other men crawled to us and shared what Mirina sent up to us, then huddled down at our feet.

Then came a terrible moment, when a wave as tall as a mountain towered over us, blotting out the sky. The other men stared at it in horror as it threatened to fall upon us. But Dek and I held the tiller steady, and the sea-anchor held, and we somehow climbed the near-vertical face of that dreadful water, hovered for a moment on the peak, then slid down the other side with a speed that stole the breath from my body and made my heart stand still.

And that was the worst of the storm. Not long after, we got into a place of calmer winds, huge swells rather than waves, rain and lightning.

Dek was exhausted. He trembled as he stood there. I assured him I could hold the tiller while he slept, which of course I could and did, and he fell down with the others, pulling the canvas of the sail over the lot of them to shelter them a bit from the rain.

Mirina crept out from belowdecks. She was soaked, of course, from the times when she had opened the hatch, but she did not appear to feel the cold. She had brought me a great piece of fin, all meat and fat, which I devoured and did me much good.

Do you know where we are? she asked me.

"Not in the least," I answered aloud. "But this ship has that *compass* thing fastened in that box on the prow." I pointed with my chin, not wanting to let go of the tiller. "The prow would have to crack off before we lost it, and if that happened, we would be in such straits that losing the *compass* would be the least of our worries."

My home is there,—she said, and pointed up and to our stern. *I can feel it. So if we go that way, we will come to the Shadow and all will be well with you.*

Well! That was useful. I knew, of course, that every human and most Sagoth, when on land, knows exactly where the land of his birth is—and also any land he has visited in person. It is something born in us, but we lose it on the water. The natives of the islands can tell you each where his own island is as well, though they are lost on the land. But it seemed this child of the air was not lost, neither on land, nor on water. And she was right. If we followed where she pointed, we would come to the Shadow of her world and be home. Thus it would not matter even if we lost the *compass.*

I confess that I was much cheered by this, and restored by the food and this knowledge, I held course through the rain and thunder until at last the storm died and the men awoke. Then I imparted what Mirina had told me to Dek.

By now we could see we were deep among the islands. The *moon* was not visible; it must have been hidden behind one or more of them. These islands towered around us, looking like what Innes and Perry had told us they were, the tops of submerged mountains. We recognized none of them, and reckoned ourselves lucky that caution on my part had caused me to insist that we had sailed with water belowdecks enough for many sleeps. Food we could catch with our harpoon, and by fishing, but water . . .

Before I slept myself, I helped Dek haul in the sea-anchor and stow it, helped the men to rig the sail, and got the boat turned about and pointed in the direction Mirina wished us to go—which agreed with the *compass*.

We knew we were not out of peril yet. There are many strange races living on the islands. Some are peaceful and friendly. Some are wary and hostile.

And some are deadly.

Also, there were the great beasts of the sea.

No, we were by no means celebrating, except in that we celebrated going down the throat of the storm and coming out alive.

I flung myself down on the deck and slept, as Dek and the others made for home.

It was Dek kicking me in the ribs that woke me. A quick glance at the hurried preparations for combat told me why.

"Astern," Dek said, briefly, and took the tiller.

Now, the good thing about being a sailing ship with only four rowers is that most of the time the rowers do not need to work; the wind does it all for you. The bad thing about being a sailing ship with only four rowers is that when you are being overtaken by a dozen islander canoes of the sort with the pods on the side, and the wind is scarcely a breeze, then you know that the canoes are going to win this race. We Thurians did not know many folk with that sort of canoes— only one of our island allies had such, and these were too far to be our allies.

I glanced up. Mirina was hanging quiver after quiver full of arrows on the top of the mast at her usual perch. Good. She would be able to stay out of reach, at least until they swarmed us. What would happen to her then . . .

I got my sword and my club, and a tiny shield I fastened on my wrist. I was of little use with distance weapons. The rest armed themselves with their guns—alas, we had not brought much ammunition for them, since they were all but useless against the sea-beasts—and put spears, bows, and their swords at their sides in readiness. We turned to face the foe. There was no point in trying to race them, and our harpoon gun and cannon faced forward. We might as well use them while we could.

As soon as the first canoe was in range, we fired the cannon. It was both a lucky and a good shot; it hit the canoe squarely, and the thing exploded in flying splinters and falling bodies.

That took our foes aback; we could see them gesturing to one another vehemently, and the paddlers slowed or stopped. But they must have been made of stern stuff; before long the paddlers dug their oars into the water, and they came at us again.

But of course this had given us plenty of time to reload and aim, and the second shot hit another canoe before they had gotten properly underway. This time our attack was met with fierce howls of rage.

We got off two more shots, both scoring direct hits, before we knew there would be no time to reload for a fifth. But now they were in harpoon range, and Dek ran to that gun, taking careful aim before firing.

It was a terrible sight.

The harpoon not only struck the man he had been aiming for, it passed through him and impaled the second man in the canoe as well. Dek had used one of the harpoons that had no line fastened to it, as those were more accurate, so the two men thrashed together, screaming and bleeding, before they finally fell overboard, still pinned together.

This only enraged the attackers, but Dek managed to get off a second harpoon before they were on us.

But we had narrowed the odds against us, somewhat. There had been a dozen canoes, with two men to each; the cannon had taken four, and the harpoon one. That left but seven, with fourteen men to our four, plus Mirina, though to be honest, I did not think she would be of much use.

We began to hurl spears, but those were deflected by the bark shields the men put up as they came alongside. We four put our backs to the mast and prepared to fight as we were surrounded by canoes and their occupants swarmed the sides of the boat.

A strange sound came to my ears as they screamed and boarded us. I looked up. It was Mirina. She was flying!

Hovering, rather, using what little wind there was to help her stay aloft. And with a grim look upon her face, she was carefully sighting and loosing her arrows down into the mob around us.

Her bow was light, and her arrows, perforce, were just big enough to take down birds or hare. They were hardly man-killers, unless she got off a lucky shot.

But they *were* man-cripplers.

And she had the advantage of height and the knowledge that even if one of them got past us and up the mast, he could not reach her. She could take her time sighting, and pick her target—their arms, their necks, their heads. One arrow in a bicep made it hard to wield the club-like, shell-edged wooden swords they were using. Two made it almost impossible. They could not use their shields to protect themselves from her arrows without opening themselves to our swords.

But I could not watch her further, as we were fighting for our lives.

It was hard, bloody work.

Those curved, bark shields were effective. I had never seen the like. They were light, and flexible, so when you hit them, your blow rebounded, giving the man or one of his fellows a chance to strike at you while you were still recovering from what had happened. If it had not been for Mirina, I think we would have lost.

But her steady firing weakened the enemy. Shields drooped, giving us openings; men found their swords dropping from nerveless fingers. We were bleeding from a hundred shallow cuts, but they could not manage a fatal blow, while we slowly took them down, one at a time.

Finally someone realized that they were but five to our four, and the little archer above was showing no signs of running out of arrows. One of them yelled, and the remainder retreated to their canoes, cutting them loose and pushing off. In very little time, they were but specks in the distance.

Mirina dropped to the deck of the boat, heedless of the blood, spent.

She collapsed there, wings sprawling, body heaving with pants and shuddering with the pounding of her heart. Dek ran to her, seizing a waterskin on the way, and cradled her in his arms, putting it to her lips.

She had not even the strength left to drink, so he used a little of the water to gently bathe her face.

For a moment I feared that she had overtasked her strength, defending us, and that her frail heart would fail.

But then she took a deep and shuddering breath, and looked up at Dek. And that was when I saw it happen, when he *looked* at her for the first time, and saw, not the strange birdlike creature, nor the seeming-child. He looked at her and saw the woman in the slender body, and looked on her, not as a man looks on a child, but as a man looks on a woman.

She saw it, too, and her eyes widened. Her hands started to move in that language of signs, but he forestalled anything she might have "said" by kissing her.

Well, that is all that there is to the tale. The rest was commonplace; we heaved the bodies of our unknown enemies overboard, cleaned the decks of blood, and tied the captured canoes behind us, for they were exceptionally well-made, and more than made up for the loss of the sea-beast. The wind finally rose in our favor. Between the *compass* and Mirina's inner sense, we returned to our own shores, and Dek presented Mirina to his father as his mate. Nor did Kolk appear displeased with this.

And as for me . . . well, this tale has given me new hope. For if a man of Thuria can have his mate fall from the sky to him, a mate half-bird and half-girl, then surely there can be a mate out there for me.

After all, what in Pellucidar is less likely—a female Sagoth as intelligent as I—or a girl with wings?

 END

Amtor—ERB's Venus—is a watery jungle world, and its hero is blond Carson Napier, who set out for Mars but forgot to take the gravitational field of the Moon into account and wound up on Venus. The villains in the first book were (well-disguised) communists, and the villains in the third of the four books were parodies (but deadly parodies, paradoxical as that may seem) of the Nazis. Here Richard Lupoff, long-time Burroughs scholar and author of two nonfiction books about ERB's worlds, comes up with a new menace to our hero.

—Mike

Scorpion Men of Venus

Richard A. Lupoff
(dedicated to Dave Van Arnam)

Jagged-edged and venomous thorns tore at our clothes and deadly vines swung from the dripping limbs of towering deciduous pitcher-trees—seeking as if intelligently motivated—to capture Duare and myself. Armed only with machetes, their blades honed from Venusian ironwood trees, the courageous sable-tressed Venusian maiden and I beat back our vegetable attackers.

"I am weary, Carson," the lovely Duare gasped. "I do not know how much longer I can continue." For a moment she collapsed into my arms. Seeming to draw strength from our momentary embrace, she drew a deep breath and, uttering an oath in her native tongue, swung her weapon at a sinewy green creeper that had made its way across the jungle floor and was attempting to wrap itself around her ankle.

"Do not lose hope, O Princess," I encouraged her. "While yet we draw breath, there remains a chance that we will win free of our pursuers."

"Princess." Duare spoke with bitter irony. "What matters it be I princess or slave, should I be sawed to bits by blade-thorn bushes or, worse yet, captured by a pitcher-tree and digested alive!" She wiped perspiration from her brow, swung her blade once more at a clutching vine, and strode ahead.

Behind us we could hear the eager cries of the brutal Andaks of Kattara. Half-human, half-beast, each of these nightmarish monsters resembled a mad attempt to blend a human being with a gigantic arthropod. Imagine if you can a man with the claw-tipped limbs and deadly stinging tail of a monstrous scorpion. They had no voices in the sense which you would recognize as such. Instead they communicated by a combination of clicking mandibles and weird, ear-piercing screeches, and we could hear them now, a hunting party close on our trail.

"Press on, my Princess," I urged Duare. I took up a position with my back to her, ready to face the lead Andak, who seemed to have been sent ahead of his monstrous fellows as a kind of advance guard. Pushing aside a tangle of writhing vines, it stood facing me, its terrible mandibles opening and closing, its weird, faceted eyes blazing eagerness and hatred.

It reached for me with a pair of pincers that I slapped aside with my machete. The other pair of pincers snapped, snagging the sleeve of my garment. Ignoring the threat, I lunged with my fire-tempered weapon, wishing futilely for a steel-bladed sword, or better yet a firearm.

Straight for the monster's eye I lunged. The Andak dodged aside, and my blade passed harmlessly over its naked, scaly shoulder. Frustrated in its attack, it emitted a screech that all but stunned me, clearly a weapon with which evolution had fitted these monsters to use as they closed in combat with their enemies.

"Carson!" I heard Duare's scream of warning. "Beware! Above you!" I jerked my head and saw the Andak's deadly curving tail plunging downward toward me. This time it was I who dodged to the side. It drew its tail back, a few drops of its deadly venom dripping onto my arm, where they burned and hissed, emitting a sickening stench of death and instant decay.

In the throes of its continuing attack, the Andak had yanked its claw free of my sleeve. It reared back, its segmented, chitinous tail arching overhead in another attempt to strike at me. I barely managed to leap aside, my shoulder colliding with the trunk of a nearby *crann* tree, a Venusian giant roughly comparable to a Florida palmetto.

The Andak's tail swung toward me, and as I threw myself flat, it thudded into the trunk of the tree, the twin knifelike shafts that it used to administer venom to its prey trapped for the moment in the pulpy *crann* wood.

In response to the twin jolts administered to the *crann* tree by my shoulder and the monster's venomous tail, a green shaft no thicker nor longer than an ordinary lead pencil tumbled from a limb of the tree, landing on the back of the Andak. It was followed by another and yet another, until I saw that the green shafts were raining down upon it, burying their tips in its flesh until it resembled an Earthly porcupine or spiny sea urchin.

The green shafts, I realized, were Venusian *nathair culebras,* or tree snakes. Among the deadliest of the venomous creatures that infest the jungles of Earth's sister planet, they covered the body of the Andak and were soon squirming like the snakes on a Gorgon's head.

Even as the Andak writhed and emitted the ear-piercing screams of its death agony, I lost no time in grasping Duare by the wrist and half dragging, half-carrying her ahead. Our determination to persevere was quickly rewarded as we burst from the forest into a grassy clearing surrounded by towering *crann* trees and giant, wind-tossed ferns.

We made our way to the center of the clearing, believing for the moment that we had reached safety, but our relief proved to be short-lived, as the very ground beneath us began to move, at first with gentle tremors almost too slight to be felt, then with perceptible ripples, finally heaving itself as if it were the back of a giant beast and Duare and myself annoying pests of whom it was trying to be rid.

"Duare," I cried, "what is this? What is happening, O my princess?"

She had gone suddenly pale, her normally healthy olive-hued complexion becoming almost corpse-like in its pallor. "Carson," she gasped, clutching my arm and pulling me to the far side of the clearing. "Carson, it is a *fearmharr arrachtach*! We can't stay here. It means sudden death!"

"What do you mean?" I queried. "What is a *fearmharr arrachtach*?" Again I asked, "What is happening?"

"Never mind," she urged. "We must get away from here. Please, my beloved, our very lives are at stake!"

She pulled me toward the surrounding forest even as the grassy area beneath began to rise up in ridges and mounds that rippled and flowed together, forming erections as tall at first as a common house cat, then as high as our knees, then as our waists, rippling and shifting until, to my astonishment and horror, I saw one of them shaping itself into a perfect simulacrum of Duare and another into a duplicate of myself.

"Are they alive?" I shouted.

Duare shook her head. "They have the semblance of life but are mere simulacra of you and of me, O my Carson. They are dangerous. Do not trust them. Quick, we must get away."

"But the woods are full of hunting Andaks and deadly *nathair culebra* snakes!"

There we stood, trapped between the deadly advancing simulacra, which moment by moment seemed to be perfecting their resemblance of us. If you have never seen a perfect duplicate of yourself suddenly appear from the very ground beneath your feet and advance toward you with murder in its eyes, you can only imagine the horror that Duare and I felt at that moment.

Trapped between our murderous doppelgangers, the hunting scorpion-men, and the incredibly deadly *nathair culebras*, Duare and I stood, ready to meet our fates together. At that moment whatever gods there may be had at least granted us the final boon of permitting us to die together.

I took Duare in my arms and drew her lush, pulsing body against my own.

"My princess," I murmured, "I die happy for having found you and won your love!"

"O my Carson," she replied, pressing her lips upon my own, "my champion from a distant world, I will go anywhere with you, even unto the great beyond from which none return!"

At this moment a light flashed from above, and together Duare and I turned our faces upward to behold the most amazing sight of all the amazing sights I had beheld since my arrival upon Venus.

A giant dragonfly was circling above us. Its gossamer wings caught the diffuse gray daylight that the twin cloud covers of Venus permit to reach the surface of that planet. A beam of light of an intense ultramarine hue flashed down, brilliantly illuminating one of the simulacra that had mere seconds before threatened the lives of my glorious beloved and myself.

The *fearmharr arrachtach* threw its arms upward as if trying to reach the dragonfly and draw it down to the ground, then slumped and lay briefly at my feet. I gazed down into a perfect copy of myself, from my thick blond hair to my muscular arms and powerful torso to my heavy jungle boots.

The beast writhed once, twitched, tremored briefly, then subsided back into the grassy covering of the clearing. I stood, thunderstruck, as a simulacrum of the splendid Duare was caught in the ultramarine ray, duplicating the agony and ultimate demise of my own duplicate.

The process continued until the clearing had returned to its original innocent-seeming appearance. I looked skyward at the dragonfly and saw the ultramarine ray pointing at myself. There was no time to avoid its brilliance. As it struck my body, I felt an icy tingling, from the crown of my head to the soles of my feet. I looked down and saw myself bathed in a brilliant blue glow, but other than the frigid tingling I was unharmed.

The ray was withdrawn from my body and aimed at Duare.

"Do not be afraid, my princess. It will not harm you!"

Nor did it.

With a whirring of its mighty wings, the giant dragonfly circled lower and lower, finally settling to the grass.

Side by side, Duare and I advanced toward it. Duare reached to touch the creature's shell, then drew back her hand. Now it was she who asked me, "What can it be, O Carson? What can this thing be?"

"This is no insect," I replied. I turned to study the dragonfly. "This is a machine. The creation of some clever artisan, but it is not a living thing."

We advanced toward the head of the segmented, seeming beast. As we stood staring awestruck into its huge faceted eyes, one of them rolled back like a gigantic eyelid to reveal a cockpit and a set of controls, and seated at the controls a pilot clad in flight-suit, complete with helmet and goggles.

"Thank you," I stammered. "You saved us. But—who are you, and what does this mean?" Never in my time on Venus had I seen any sign of the technological development necessary to build so advanced a flying craft as this magnificent artificial creature.

Searching my memory for details of my studies of the insectivora of the world during my sometimes ill-spent college days, I recognized this machine as a remarkable mechanical recreation of *Odonata Anisoptera Synthemistidae*. Its four gossamer wings shimmered in the pearl-like glimmering of an Amtorian afternoon. Its six legs held it in precarious balance.

The pilot did not respond to my query, but instead gestured with one gloved hand to the compartment behind the cockpit. Nodding his head, this mysterious figure indicated clearly that Duare and I were to climb into the dragonfly and prepare for flight.

When you have been saved from a Hobson's choice between two forms of death each more horrible than the other by a total stranger who invites you to join him in a magnificent aircraft, you do not quarrel. Duare and I accepted this mysterious stranger's invitation with alacrity.

We climbed into the aircraft, and the pilot reached for a handle and swung the artificial eye back into place. He threw a switch, and the mechanical dragonfly raised and lowered its wings twice. Another switch, and I could feel the six legs flex, then straighten, and the artificial dragonfly was airborne.

Looking ahead over the pilot's shoulders we could see that the faceted false eyes of the dragonfly were transparent when viewed from inside the craft. By craning my neck I was able to get a view of the terrain over which we passed.

We crossed mile after mile of lush jungle, but eventually this gave way to a grassy savannah—not populated by any more of the deadly *fearmharr arrachtachs* that had menaced Duare and myself and from which this mysterious aviator had saved us, or so I hoped.

Giant beasts grazed on the rich plant life beneath us. Huge Venusian—Amtorian—mammals such as roamed the Americas before the last ice age gazed skyward to see this strange object passing overhead, then returned to their grazing, unconcerned.

We rose toward the planet's perpetual cloud cover and passed over a ridge of jagged granite peaks, then dipped again to skim the ground in the next valley. As if Nature had separated the two adjacent lowlands, this next savannah was populated by an even more astonishing array of beasts. If not dinosaurs, then surely these creatures were Amtor's analogs of them. I saw something that looked remarkably like a triceratops placidly grazing until it was surprised by the attack of a bonapartenykus—a feathered dinosaur whose fierce claws and teeth belie its otherwise benign appearance.

I would have been curious to observe the battle between these two giant beasts out of Earth's multimillion-year past, but the dragonfly continued onward, our pilot never taking his eyes off the controls and the passing landscape, totally ignoring Duare and myself.

Now we approached another range of jagged granite peaks. I had lost all track of time and had no idea how long we had been flying over Amtor's amazing landscape. But as the aircraft initiated its climb into the new range of mountains, I felt the temperature drop precipitously.

For the first time since arriving on Venus, I actually felt cold. The landscape visible over our pilot's shoulder changed continuously. We had flown over lush jungle, then over grassy savannahs, and now our giant dragonfly's four gossamer wings carried us ever higher, the terrain beneath rising into rolling foothills and the rocky scarps of towering granite mounts. At times I almost believed that we were passengers in a living organism, so convincing were the dragonfly's movements.

After a while I felt myself becoming dizzied by the changing world outside the dragonfly. The tropicallike vegetation that I had become accustomed to on Venus now gave way to some botanical analogs of Earthly evergreens. Tall, graceful trees that could have passed for northern pines towered into the air.

We rose above the snow line, and the pine-analogs rising from the wintry accumulation caused me to feel a pang of homesickness for the warm hearths and gaily wrapped gifts piled beneath decorated evergreens that I had known and loved as a child. There was a difference, however. The "snow" of Amtor, if snow I may call it, was not the pure white of Earthly snow. Instead, it showed swirls and ridges of color where the winds of this planet drove and shifted it. It was a remarkable substance. Seen from afar, as it was when I peered ahead from the dragonfly, the colors did blend into a dazzling white. But by looking straight down, or as close to straight down as the configuration of our aircraft permitted, I could make out glittering bits of crimson, cobalt, sapphire, and indigo blue, emerald, lime, and forest green, richest gold and vivid purple.

I must have clutched Duare's hand in my emotional longing for my home planet and the joys of childhood that I had experienced there, for she made a startled sound and turned toward me.

An encouraging expression crossed her face, and I told myself that I had found another love, another kind of love, here on Earth's sister planet.

Eventually even the pines disappeared and there was nothing but gray granite and white snow reflecting the diffuse light that passed through Amtor's double layer of clouds.

Without preliminary, a sound like the rattle of hailstones on a tin roof burst upon us. Outside the dragonfly's snug cockpit and cramped passenger compartment millions of brilliant gems were cascading onto the wings and body of the aircraft.

Above us a hole seemed to have opened in the lower of the planet's two cloud envelopes. A vortex perhaps two hundred feet in width had appeared, and within it whirled a sight both glorious and mystifying. Myriad specks of every imaginable hue circled, propelled by some atmospheric phenomenon.

Even more astonishing, through the glowing colors of this atmospheric whirlpool I could see the upper cloud layer. A similar gap had appeared there, filled with a similar array of dazzling illumination. For a moment I felt that I could actually see the sun, and again a pang of loss and longing clutched at my heart.

The colored motes that clattered off the wings and body of the dragonfly were falling like hailstones from the gaps in the two cloud layers. But the two cloud layers moved independently of each other, and soon the two whirlpools were no longer in alignment. In a short time the one above us, from which the seeming hail of colored crystals had come, closed like the iris of your eye. The hail ceased to fall.

I made mental note that the mystery of the colorful snow was solved. It was indeed a product of the cloud vortices of Amtor's double cloud envelope. Like Earthly precipitation, I inferred, it might fall as rain, as snow, or as sleet. At the right altitude and under the right conditions, there might even be a Venusian fog of almost hypnotically swirling colors.

Above us and not far ahead I saw still another incredible vision. From the impenetrable gray wall of jagged granite there rose a precipitous escarpment of ruddy red rock, and upon its peak a gigantic structure, one that must contain no fewer than a thousand rooms, towers, and courtyards.

As if sensing my reaction to this startling sight, our pilot pointed ahead and lifted the dragonfly even higher. We circled over the amazing structure. I shook my head in puzzlement, trying to identify the image which this titanic architectural achievement called to mind.

A gasp of surprise escaped me as I realized where I had seen a building of similar nature. As a young man I had traveled to the Orient. I had been one of the first Westerners ever permitted into the secret Kingdom of Tibet. There, in the holy city of Lhasa I had been welcomed into the Potala Palace, the capitol and abode of His Holiness the Dalai Lama.

And here, on an alien world millions of miles from Earth, I beheld a replica of that ancient structure.

A banner of strange design fluttered from a shaft rising above the highest point on this alien Potala. Our pilot dipped his head toward the banner; then the dragonfly spiraled slowly downward, settling finally in a broad flagstoned courtyard.

Our pilot peeled back the facetted canopy that covered the cockpit and climbed from the dragonfly. Duare and I followed suit. Our long flight had been conducted in nearly perfect silence, and our pilot maintained that silence as we were met by two Amtorians clad from head to toe in costumes of black. Their hair was swept up into peaks. Their faces were stolid and expressionless.

Our pilot turned toward Duare and myself, then spun on his heel and strode away, disappearing into a darkened doorway in the Potala.

One of the two Amtorians who had come to meet our party spoke in a clear but uninflected voice, in the language which is universally known and used on Venus. "You will follow me, please."

He and his counterpart—I realized now that one was male and other female—turned toward the Potala and began walking toward it at a steady pace. Before striding away from the dragonfly, I swept my hand across one of its winged surfaces, where a few of the glittering Amtorian hailstones had stuck. I picked up a handful of the little gemlike objects and dropped them in my pocket.

Speaking of pockets—I must admit, at this point, that Duare and I were a pair of very bedraggled travelers. We had trekked through the jungle for days following our escape from captivity in the village of the Zorangs, at the end of which we had fought and escaped from the semi-human Andaks with their scorpionlike caudal appendages, only to confront our grassy doppelgangers, the *fearmharr arrachtach*.

We were both exhausted, filthy, scratched, and scraped. Our clothing hung on us in tatters. Our boots had been through swamp and bramble. I stared at Duare and she at me, and we both burst into laughter at what we beheld.

And yet . . . and yet . . . to me this woman, her face streaked with dirt, knots and twigs in her tresses, her hands roughened and scraped . . . to me this woman was still the most beautiful creature on two planets.

We followed our guides into the great palace. After their initial invitation to follow them, neither spoke again until we had penetrated the great entry hall of the Amtorian Potala. This was floored with a substance that might have been polished marble or obsidian. It was lighted by cressets mounted every few yards along the walls, filled with an oily substance that burned without giving off smoke but a soft, orange-yellow illumination.

The walls on both sides were lined with cyclopean statues of grotesque figures that I inferred to be the ancient gods of Amtor. Each statue was different in color and configuration. Some were human, alternately magnificently heroic and distressingly deformed. Others were of beasts or, worst of all, monstrosities that combined the features of humans and other creatures, like the half-human, half-arthropodal Andaks from whom Duare and I had escaped only through the intervention of deceptively harmless-appearing green *nathair culebra* or Amtorian tree-snakes.

High on the shadowy walls of the great hall were window slits through which the silvery-gray glow of an Amtorian afternoon penetrated.

Duare and I followed our guides up magnificent stairways and down another hall lined with alcoves and side-passages leading to left and right. With a gesture by the male and female guides, we were directed to separate chambers. As I entered mine, I thought to leave and rejoin Duare, but my way was blocked by my male guide. On the other side of the hallway, illuminated by cressets of burning oil as had been the great hall below, I could see the female guide standing outside the opening to Duare's chamber.

Were these two black-garbed strangers our guides, our protectors, or our captors? Were we visitors to the Amtorian Potala, guests, or prisoners?

I found in my chambers a comfortable bed and a clear bath drawn in an obsidian pool. Only after lowering my tired limbs and aching torso into the refreshing waters did I realize what a sad state I had reached.

There was no way of knowing what fate awaited me now, but these facilities were at least encouraging. With my body cleansed and refreshed, I searched my new quarters further. There was an area of perfectly polished stone wall that would serve admirably as a mirror, and a piece of sharpened stone that I found served as a razor.

I returned to my bedchamber, where I found awaiting me an outfit of comfortable soft trousers and a blouse and footwear. No sooner had I donned these than my keeper, as I had come to think of him, appeared in the entryway to my bedchamber and spoke once more in his dull, almost lifeless voice.

"You will follow me."

Well, I figured, why not? What had I to lose by complying? What had I to gain by refusing to do so?

There were no doors as such in this Venusian Potala. Rather, each suite of chambers was entered through a series of turns and baffles that effectively sealed it from the main corridor, permitting neither sound nor light to penetrate.

We retraced our steps to the lower level of the Potala, then crossed the great hall to another grand chamber. The ceiling was beamed and towered high overhead. The stone floor was covered with some substance I could not identify but which made walking most pleasant. A fireplace had been built into one wall, and a great blaze sent multicolored shadows dancing and cavorting around the room as if they were living beings with wills of their own.

As in the grand hall of statuary, window slits set into the walls near the high, beamed ceiling of this room let in additional light from the mountainous realm outside while drawing the smoke from the fireplace and maintaining the quality of the air within.

A table had been set for a meal, but it was deserted.

Most startling of all, at the far end of the great room an elaborately carved chair, almost a throne, stood on a low dais. Seated upon it I beheld a tiny, wizened human being.

It was not easy to calculate his height, as he was seated and I was standing, but I inferred that he could not have been as tall as five feet. His head was completely hairless, and his almost abnormally large cranium and bulging brow bespoke a brain of exceptional capabilities.

His face was triangular in configuration, narrowing precipitously from the width of his brow to the point of his chin. His eyes appeared huge behind thick lenses. In the midst of all this day's strangeness, I almost laughed at myself for being impressed by the fact that he wore spectacles—the first such that I had seen since arriving on this weird planet.

He was garbed entirely in white, a high-collared tunic closed at the throat, sleeves reaching to his wrists, spotless white trousers, and even white shoes.

I stood speechless.

The apparition in white spoke in a high, shrill, almost effeminate voice, yet one that gave the impression that it could also embody unspeakable cruelty.

"Come," he commanded.

I complied, halting a few feet away from the dais upon which he was seated.

He said, "I have awaited your arrival." He raised a gnarled, nearly clawlike hand and gestured. Almost at once there was a sound from the entryway through which I had entered minutes earlier. Before I could turn, however, the tiny man rose from his throne and stepped from the dais.

He walked carefully, as would an aged man who feared to lose his balance and damage fragile, ancient bones. As he passed me he grasped me by the biceps. He had to reach up to do so, but his grip was most surprisingly strong. He guided me toward the elaborately set table. Hardly had we reached our places when we were joined by three more individuals.

One was the Princess Duare. Obviously her quarters had been as elaborately and tastefully equipped as had been my own. Her face bore no trace of the filth or the fatigue of our day's misadventures. Instead her olive-hued skin glowed with the purity of youthful beauty. Her hair had been carefully coiffed in a soft, graceful fashion.

She was garbed in soft, colorfully draped cloths that resembled fine silk. Their dominant shade was a deep vermillion set off with highlights of gentle yellow that seemed almost to live in the waving light of the oil-cressets and the great fireplace. The overall effect was suggestive of an Indian sari.

Unfamiliar symbols were woven into Duare's garments, vaguely suggestive of the signs of the Earthly zodiac, but how the Amtorians could have developed a zodiacal system without ever seeing the stars and planets was a mystery to me.

The other two figures were of similar stature and build, although clearly one of them was female and the other male. As all five of us took our seats, our almost elfin host reached for a glittering goblet that stood before his place. In the few moments that had passed since the completion of our party, unobtrusive, dark-garbed servants had filled goblets at each place.

"As is our custom," the tiny man rasped, "we will introduce ourselves to our guests, and they to us. But first, a ceremonial sip of our *fionbeior*." He raised his goblet and tilted it for the barest moment toward his mouth.

This must be some beverage, I thought. I am not a great imbiber, but in my wasted youth I will confess to spending many a happy hour with my compatriots, toasting and guzzling brews of various sorts. Our American government's so-called Noble Experiment of Prohibition has served only to give strong waters the added appeal of forbidden fruit, and as a daring young man I had been ever eager to strike a blow for freedom.

I took a hearty swallow of this Amtorian *fionbeior* and at once promised myself to be more cautious with the beverage. Not that it was unpleasant stuff. On the contrary, it was thoroughly delicious, but it had hardly had time to reach my stomach when my ears were filled with a rushing sound and my eyes filled with tears.

I lowered my goblet.

The elf laughed.

"Very well," he rasped, "I see that one of our guests has already learned a valuable lesson. I am pleased."

A peculiar expression gave his face the appearance of a grinning skull for the barest of moments.

"As is our custom," he resumed, "we welcome our guests by introducing ourselves. Then we shall ask them to do the same."

He nodded his head, as if approving of his own conduct.

"In my lifetime I have been known by many names," he said, "but for now you may call me simply Dr. Bodog. I am your host. You are welcome in my home. We shall all get to know one another well during your stay."

Clearly, he was addressing Duare and myself.

"And my children," he went on, nodding his great, hairless dome toward the man and woman who had entered the hall along with Duare.

"Yes," the man said, raising his goblet and taking a ceremonial sip of the *fionbeior*. I watched as everyone at the table emulated him. This time, I assure you, I was more cautious.

"My name is Oggar," he stated. His voice was deep and powerful, a suitable match for his heavily muscled frame.

"And I," his female counterpart intoned, "am called Istara." She nodded to us, sipped carefully at her *fionbeior*. She shot a mischievous glance at Duare and myself. "Do you not recognize me?"

She did look vaguely familiar to me, but I confess that I was unable to place her. Had I ever encountered her before today, here on the planet Venus? Or did she resemble some woman I had known on my native planet, or perhaps a movie star whose visage I had seen on the silver screen in years before?

She shook her had amusedly. "You were engaged in what seemed like an unpleasant encounter with some *fearmharr arrachtachs* when first we met. It was mere hours ago. My feelings are hurt that you do not recognize me."

I stared. Was she—was this beautiful young woman—the courageous and skillful pilot who had flown the mechanical dragonfly to Duare's and my own rescue from the attack of our grassy doppelgangers? Was it she who had aimed the blue ray at those creatures, disrupting their plan of attack and reducing them to the seemingly ordinary grass from which they had sprung?

"Yes," Istara insisted as if reading my thoughts, "it was indeed I." She laughed, a delighted, rippling sound of amusement. Her facial expression seemed to reach out to the others at the table, especially to Duare and myself, inviting us to join in her good-natured amusement.

I found myself grinning involuntarily. The joke had indeed been on Duare and me. Duare, however, did not seem to share my willingness to join in Istara's friendly jest. Instead, she glared angrily at Istara, as if resenting having been made a fool of.

Hoping to break the icy stalemate of the two women, I exchanged smiles with Istara, then asked this tall, blond, almost boyishly attractive, yet ineffably feminine woman, "Why were you silent, then, during our flight from the grass-men to the Potala?"

She shook her head, her soft tresses bouncing merrily. "There are some men who might resent being rescued by a mere girl. I could not risk a quarrel or even a moment's hesitation during the rescue. I hope you are not angry with me."

Of course I was not. Istara had saved Duare and me from dire peril. Unfortunately, I could not certify that Duare shared my feelings of gratitude toward Istara.

Our tiny host interrupted this exchange by tapping lightly on his goblet with a golden dining implement. "We have introduced ourselves to our guests," he rasped in his unpleasant, grating voice. "It is time for them to tell us who they are and why they are here."

"We are here because we were brought here, Dr. Bodog," Duare exclaimed angrily. "I am a Princess of the Realm of Vepaja, and I wish to know by what right you hold me here."

I noted that she used the Amtorian word for *me*, not *us*, and wondered what thought had provoked that choice of expression. Before I could speak, however, our host responded to Duare's demand with a smile.

A smile, I say, but somehow, I must admit, I found Dr. Bodog's smile more intimidating than reassuring. He had done nothing to harm Duare or myself that I knew of. He had, in fact, sent his daughter to rescue the two of us from our probable demise. And yet I could not bring myself to trust him.

Still, as black-clad, silent servants brought viands and placed them on the table, Dr. Bodog spoke, and I drank in every word, wishing, as ever any explorer who is a scientist at heart would do, to retain and understand all that this strange, wizened person had to say.

"This building, which you call a Potala, is both my home and my workplace. It has been the home and workplace of my family for—you will forgive me, but I wonder if should tell you how long. I do not wish to withhold this information, Your Highness." I noticed that he uttered the honorific in a tone of irony. "It is merely that I fear you will find the truth incredible, which would place us in a most uncomfortable position."

"Go ahead, Doctor." Duare spoke that last word in a tone to match that of our host. These were worthy debating foes, I realized. I had not previously realized that Duare had such skills, nor that she would react to Dr. Bodog with such scorn.

"Very well," he resumed. "My family had its origins on a continent that spanned a broad region in the greatest ocean of the planet whose orbit lies beyond that of Amtor."

"The Earth!" I exclaimed.

"The science of my people was far advanced. They had achieved great discoveries in the realm of optics and astronomy. It was their custom to study the celestial objects that filled the night sky of Earth. A sight, unfortunately, denied to denizens of Amtor."

During Dr. Bodog's narration, the silent servants had continued to bring delicious dishes—Venusian versions of venison, pheasant, brook trout, vegetables and spices. Of course none of these were exactly the same as their Earthly counterparts, but they were without exception delicious beyond compare. And I imagine I need not add that our goblets were kept filled with the local *fionbeior*.

I will say this for the diminutive doctor: despite his rasping delivery and the fact that I found something disquietingly untrustworthy about him, his story was fascinating. He told of an ancient civilization that spanned a huge continent located in the greatest of Earth's oceans. The astronomers of that ancient civilization had built powerful telescopes that scanned the night skies, searching out the wonders of the universe.

These people were the oldest humans in the world (Dr. Bodog claimed) and had colonized every continent. The high plateau of Tibet was an important outpost, and the Potala Palace, which later came to be the abode of the highest of high lamas, was the headquarters of their settlement.

Their astronomers had studied the planets of the solar system, searching for another habitable world. They had settled upon Venus.

Their name for it was Amtarra, Dr. Bodog stated, causing me to wonder if that was the original form of the word Amtor. Amtarra was almost identical in size and mass to Earth. It was closer to the Sun, indicating a warm, even tropical climate. And it was covered with clouds, implying a plentiful supply of water.

In short, Venus—Amtarra—Amtor—was very likely a suitable place for a human settlement. It might even harbor indigenous life-forms! The most brilliant engineers of Earth's incredibly ancient civilization set out to construct machines that might carry settlers to Amtarra.

At this point the astronomers announced a dreadful discovery. A huge planetoid, one of the countless miniature worlds that orbited between the fourth and fifth planets of the Sun, had collided with a smaller planetoid. Such events were not uncommon, of course, and at first the larger of the two objects continued on its way. But its orbit had been shifted, and in its new, irregular path, it was headed for Earth. Its arrival would occur in twenty years, time enough to build a fleet of machines that would carry hundreds of thousands of humans to Amtarra. The fleet would also be fitted to bring seeds for food crops and breeding stock of animals.

Was this, I wondered, the origin of the story of Noah's Ark?

Then disaster was piled upon disaster! Still another planetoid collided with the one headed for Earth. Its path was once more diverted. Instead of swinging around the sun, picking up more energy on each pass until, in twenty years, the planetoid would strike the Earth—it was now headed straight for our planet. It would arrive within a matter not of twenty years but merely of months. Engineers worked feverishly to complete the fleet of space fliers, but had barely got beyond the level of a prototype when they realized they were running out of time.

One of the engineers working on the project, the most intelligent and noble of all men on Earth (according to Dr. Bodog), hatched a desperate plan for the salvation of humanity. In the dead of night he smuggled his own wife and children aboard the prototype space flier and launched the craft on a trajectory for Amtarra.

The flight was successful, but there was no time to build any more fliers. Even as the prototype space flier sped past the moon, the engineer's wife turned to look back at the Earth and beheld the impact of the planetoid. It landed in the ocean just off the coast of the great continent. The explosion that its impact caused was terrible. Plumes of steam rose hundreds of miles into the air. Huge tsunamis swept the continents. The great land mass from which the space flier had lifted was pelted with fragments of rock and dirt ranging in size from grains of sand to boulders half the size of Earth's moon.

Only the highest peaks on the planet were not drowned. A relative handful of humans and other species survived on Earth. But the engineer and his family landed safely on Amtarra.

"And you see before you the last surviving descendents of those settlers," Dr. Bodog stated, indicating himself, Istara, and Oggar. And at this moment I thought I heard a distant, desperate cry of despair in a female voice.

Dr. Bodog, Istara and Oggar pointedly ignored the sound.

Duare exclaimed, "What was that?"

Dr. Bodog said, "I heard nothing. Did you hear anything, Istara, Oggar?"

The others responded negatively to the question.

Dr. Bodog addressed me. "And now, sir, if you will be so kind as to share your own story with us . . ."

"My name is Carson Napier," I told him. "I come from—" At this point I realized that I did not trust this man to know the location of my own home. "I come from Key West, Florida." I had been in that city and knew it well enough to deceive Dr. Bodog, should he query me about its layout and architecture.

"I left Earth on board an experimental space rocket, headed, I had thought, for the planet Mars." I looked at the others, wondering what they would make of my tale. Surely Dr. Bodog would comprehend, but to Duare, born and raised beneath the double cloud envelope of Amtor, the very concept of black space dotted with millions of suns and populated by planets comparable to her home would in all likelihood defy her ability to comprehend.

And as for Istara and Oggar—these two were utterly mysterious to me. Had they been born on Amtor? For that matter, had their father, the wizened Dr. Bodog, been born here? What did they know of the universe beyond the clouds that surrounded this world? I tried to explain as best I could the nature of the solar system and my attempt to travel to Mars, only to be drawn off-course by the gravitational attraction of Luna. How could my navigator have been so foolish as to overlook that? How could I have been so irresponsible as to accept his charts without insisting that we go over every calculation together?

Only sheer luck—at least if you do not accept the notion of divine intervention—had caused my rocket to veer toward Venus. Once beneath the clouds, I was able to bring my ship to a safe landing, only to have it swallowed by a pit of steaming quicksand from which I was barely able to escape with my life.

My adventures on Venus had been many and thrilling, and my love for Duare had sustained me through uncounted moments of peril and of fear, but I longed desperately to return to Earth and to share my story with the friends I had left behind.

Dr. Bodog gestured to one of the black-clad servitors who seemed always to hover in the room. He spoke a few words, too softly for me to make out, and the servitor disappeared, to return in a short time bearing a carefully crafted globe of the Earth. This he placed on the table between us.

I determined that this globe reflected the reality of the planet I had left not so very long ago, save that a huge continent stretched across the Pacific Ocean, from a point near Easter Island off the coast of South America nearly to the Indo-Chinese peninsula in Southeast Asia.

"Gone," I told Dr. Bodog. I indicated the continent which I now recognized as the legendary Lemuria. "Some islands survive, dotting the broad Pacific Ocean. Hawaii, New Guinea, Java, Sumatra. Otherwise, Lemuria is gone. The rest of the Earth seems to have recovered well from the catastrophe, and the Potala still stands in high Tibet. That is all that remains of your civilization."

"Strange names," Dr. Bodog grated. "Hawaii, Sumatra, Lemuria. You call the continent Lemuria, the ocean the Pacific." He heaved a sigh, and for a moment I pitied him. How old was he? A cold hand seemed to clutch at my spine. Was this tiny, wizened man the engineer he had spoken of? Had he saved humankind—in his own estimation— by stealing the prototype space flier and rescuing his own family in preference to the millions who must be sacrificed?

Had his wife been driven mad by the sight of the planetoid striking the Earth, and was the cry of pain and desperation I had heard that woman, prisoned somewhere in this replica of the Potala?

Our meal was completed by now. The fire that gave both warmth and illumination to the room had burned low and was guttering toward extinction.

"We have had enough for the evening," Dr. Bodog announced. "It is time for all to retire to our chambers and rest."

He stood, following which all the others followed suit, and wobbled determinedly from the room on his ancient, spindly limbs. As I strode after him, I could not help glancing at the windows high above. Amtor's eternal gray skies loomed. Night had fallen, but on Amtor there is never full darkness, as the double cloud layer diffuses the Sun's rays over all the planet.

I felt the presence of a woman at my side. Expecting Duare to be there, I extended my hand toward her and felt her take mine with a warm, surprisingly intimate grip. I turned and saw that it was not Duare but Istara who moved gracefully beside me. Casting a glance behind us, I saw that Duare and Oggar had also paired off.

What to make of this new arrangement I could not fathom, but that night, as I lay in my comfortable bed, I kept one eye peeled on the darkened passage that led from the outer hallway into my own chambers. Wearied by the day's activities and mildly fuddled by the heavy meal I had consumed and the strong *fionbeior* I had downed, I soon found myself in the cradle of Morpheus.

How long I slept I could not determine. How I wished that I had thought to wear my faithful Bulova watch when I left Earth so long ago! On Venus, with its indistinguishable transition from dim daylight to the glow of night, the whole concept of time had apparently not evolved as it had on Earth, with its clear differentiation of day and night.

I rose and made my ablutions, then donned a fresh set of Amtorian garments. Making my way through the passages of this Amtorian Potala, I soon found myself in the grand entry hall, surrounded by statues that loomed and leered eternally. I wondered if I ought to search for Duare. She had pointedly ignored me as we parted after our evening repast. We would need to make plans, at the very least, and I feared that our hosts, for all their seeming hospitality, had plans for us which did not bode well.

My meditation was interrupted surprisingly as I detected a slight, sudden perfume. Amtorian flowers, like those of Earth, attract insect pollinators with their scents . . . and, by one of the great ironies of Nature, those same scents are among the most beautiful in all creation to the human sensorium.

I turned to see the source of the delightful scent, a compound, it seemed to me, of the odor of mimosa, jasmine, and peach, utterly feminine and yet speaking (if an odor can be said to speak) of strength and individuality. There stood Istara, now garbed in what appeared a practical outfit of soft blouse and loose trousers similar to my own.

"Carson Napier," she addressed me, "I sense that you are looking for something. What is it that you desire?"

"Breakfast," I replied.

Istara laughed, and as she did so it seemed that I could hear holiday bells jingling merrily. "You are a practical man, I see. Well, we shall tend to that."

By some means which utterly escaped my comprehension, she summoned one of the black-clad servants and directed him to prepare a meal for us. She led me to a room smaller and brighter than the chamber where we had dined the previous evening.

I indicated to her that I was concerned regarding the whereabouts and safety of Duare, and she assured me that Duare was well and unharmed, and at liberty to go where she would in the Amtorian Potala.

Over a delicious repast reminiscent of Belgian waffles with maple-walnut syrup, she plied me with questions about Earth. These I answered as best I could. When I described Earth's gleaming ice caps, glaciers, and icebergs, and the wondrous creatures that populated them, polar bears at the north and emperor penguins and sea lions at the south, she shook her head in disbelief.

"I would love to see such things," she exclaimed.

We dined in silence for a little while, our food accompanied by a hot Amtorian beverage that I tried unsuccessfully to pretend was coffee. As I swallowed the last of it I was overcome by a silly impulse, yet one to which I gave way without hesitation.

"There's an old"—I realized that I did not know the Amtorian word for *song*.—"an old statement," I continued lamely, "that goes like this." And I sang, "Mid pleasures and palaces though we may roam, be it ever so humble, there's no place like home."

Istara clasped her hands to her cheeks, a look of astonishment on her face. "Carson Napier, what was that?"

"What was what?" I echoed, frowning in puzzlement.

"That." And she tried to mimic my singing, which is amateurish at best. Her own efforts, let us say, were not going to rival those of Connee Boswell, no less those of Amelita Galli-Curci.

"It's called singing," I told her, using the English word as there was no equivalent in Amtorian. "It's a way of making—" and again I was stymied. I tried again. "It's a way of making pleasant sounds with your voice, instead of with a piece of wood."

She shook her head in amazement. "Oh, how wonderful. Glaciers and penguins and—and singing. Singing! Oh, what a place must this Earth of yours be! And, Carson, Carson—"

She leaned across the table and took my hand, drawing me forward so that our faces were very nearly touching. "Carson, I must tell you something." She looked around. One of the black-clad servitors was still in the room with us. With a gesture she commanded him to clear the table.

As soon as he had exited the room, Istara leaned still closer. I could feel the softness of her tresses and smell the perfume of her hair. In a voice so low as to be almost inaudible she said, "My father, Bodog, has rebuilt the ancient space flier in which the ancient Lemurian settlers came from Earth to Amtarra. He—"

"Istara," I interrupted her, "how old is Bodog? How long has be been on Amtor? How old are you and Oggar? Where is your mother?"

She pulled away from me, drawing a shuddering breath. "I do not know, Carson. I have memories, unclear images of another life, another world. I have discussed them with my brother. He has similar memories. Were we born on Earth? Did our father bring us to Amtarra? I do not know how old I am."

For a moment she preened. Yes, even on Venus, the eternal female will play her part in the grand drama of life. "How old do I look to you, Carson?"

I took her hand again, studied it and her face. I said, "Twenty."

"Perhaps," she assented. "Or twenty thousand? I do not know, myself."

A silence descended upon us, then she rose and took my hand. She led me from the Potala. Soon we were strolling outside. There had been another of Amtor's strange "snowfalls" while we slept, and the ground was covered with myriad granules that shone in every color imaginable when viewed from close, but gave off a white glare from afar.

"He is going back!" Istara blurted suddenly. "He has kept the space machine all these years, never knowing if Earth was inhabitable, never knowing if he could return. He is mad, you know."

I said, "I have detected something disquieting about Bodog, but I knew not what."

"Yes," she repeated, "he is a genius, possibly the greatest genius who has ever lived, but he is quite insane. You saw his throne. Sometimes he sits there for days on end, commanding empires and armies to do his bidding. He fancies himself the rightful ruler of the universe. If he returns to Earth, his brilliance and his ruthlessness may well make him ruler of the world."

"We must stop him," I told her.

"Stop him, indeed. But how?"

"Have you tried to persuade him to give up his plan? He is comfortable here. Why not remain on Amtor?"

"It is no use. Oggar and I have both tried to convince him that his plans are futile at best, monstrously evil at worst. He only laughs, and if we persist he flies into a rage. Our mother tried to get him to abandon his plan, and he drove her mad with his cruelty and abuse. It was she whom you heard screaming last night, Carson. We all pretended to hear nothing. Oggar and I learned long ago what we must do. But we heard."

"Can you not simply overpower him?" I persisted. "He is a feeble old man. Oggar could crush him with one hand. Or you could use the blue ray that you used on the grass creatures."

"No." She shook her head. "You felt the ray. It is harmless against humans. It was so designed to be. And as for attacking him with our bare hands, he uses his servants as bodyguards. They are not fully human, Carson. Surely you can tell that. They are—not exactly alive. They are some sort of half-living beings, utterly without will of their own, subject to the command of any human but to that of my father above all."

I wracked my brain, trying to think of a way to defeat this self-styled rightful ruler of the universe.

"When does he plan to go?" I queried Istara at last.

"He has been delaying the trip because he does not know conditions on Earth. I do not know how long it has been since we traveled from—did you call it Lemuria?—to Amtarra."

"Many thousands of years," I told her. "Perhaps millions. On the present Earth, Lemuria is but a legend and Amtarra is known only as a mysterious, cloud-shrouded world."

She nodded thoughtfully. Then she spoke again.

"So you see, Carson, you were a godsend to Bodog. You will be his guardian, his guide and adviser when he returns to Earth. He truly thinks that he is the rightful ruler of the universe, and he plans to start by conquering the planet of his birth. He will want to take you with him, Carson. And—what will you say when he asks you to join him?"

I fear that I bit my lip in distress. I was torn between my desire to return to Earth and my fear that Dr. Bodog would cause misery once he took up his campaign of conquest. He was but one wizened elf of a manikin, but I knew that his bulging cranium contained the most brilliant and dangerous mind in two planets.

If I could return to Earth, perhaps even bring the lovely Duare with me, I might risk it. But then a further thought came to bother my shaken tranquility. Duare had become increasingly uninterested in me of late. She seemed drawn to Istara's brother, Oggar. And at the same time—I looked at Istara, drank in the beauty of her silken tresses, the grace of her tall, fit figure, the depths of her emerald-colored eyes in which I imagined I could see the nobility of her mind and her soul.

"I will talk to Bodog," I announced at last.

Istara led me back into the Amtorian Potala.

I found Dr. Bodog working in his laboratory. He had trained several of his black-clad servitors as research assistants. Their blank eyes and expressionless faces produced a *frisson* in me whenever I had occasion to look into the face of one of these strange beings. I inferred that they were living creatures of some sort, for some of them seemed to be male and others female.

They obeyed Bodog with a kind of zombielike intelligence. Were they born without will or personality, and did they spend their entire existence as victims of this weird living death, or did they have some degree of awareness of their condition? I wondered if they might actually rebel against their circumstance.

As for Dr. Bodog, while what little scientific knowledge I possess was chiefly in the fields of anthropology and sociology, I was sufficiently familiar with the physical sciences to achieve a general understanding of what the wizened Bodog was working on.

He was developing ray projectors. Probably the azure ray that Istara had used on the grass creatures was of her father's devising. But as I entered Bodog's laboratory on this day, it became clear to me that he was working on a device that would have a far different effect from the blue ray.

I watched as he trained an experimental projector on one of his assistants. A brilliant ray, golden in hue, sprang from a polished lens onto the black-clad servitor, this one a female. At first there seemed to be no effect on the female. I do not know if I ought even to call her a woman. Bodog held a cube of a dull black nature. A small cylinder no larger than a common light switch protruded from the top of the cube, which was itself not much larger in any direction than the length of a man's hand.

As Bodog moved the cylinder, the black-clad female moved like a marionette, raising and lowering a hand, standing on one foot then the other, twirling like a ballerina, lifting a piece of electrical equipment from one work bench, carrying it a few yards, then lowering it onto another. Finally she drew away from us and stood with her back to the wall, ready to respond to Bodog's control should he summon her again.

The scientist turned toward me. The corners of his mouth rose in an expression that was more a malevolent grimace than a true smile. Then he laughed: a mirthless, unpleasant sound. "You see, Carson Napier, with my electrical brainwave amplifier I can transfer my commands to anyone I choose. As I think, 'Raise your hand,' the subject raises her hand. As I think, 'Turn around,' she turns around. So far I can control only the gross physical movements of my subjects, but when I establish my new laboratory on Earth I will build more advanced and more powerful brainwave amplifiers. I will be able to control not just my subjects' physical movements but their very thoughts. Thus will I achieve my proper place as the rightful ruler of the universe."

And he let forth that horrifying parody of laughter.

At this point I let him know what Istara had told me of his planned

return to Earth. Since he had already mentioned his plan, there was no
need to conceal my knowledge of it.

"Yes," he grated, rubbing his hands and all but dancing a jig of
glee. "Tonight I will leave this planet and begin my return to Earth.
And you, Carson Napier, will be my right-hand henchman."

"On one condition, Dr. Bodog," I replied. "The Princess Duare
must accompany us. Will your space machine accommodate three?"

"Come," Bodog said. "I will show you."

So saying, he led me to another chamber. Here stood a strange
craft indeed. In no way did it resemble the bullet-shaped rocket in
which I had traveled from Earth to Venus, the rocket which now lay
hopelessly mired in a quicksand swamp, many miles from the
Amtorian Potala.

Bodog's craft was no larger than an ordinary automobile, like the
Stutz Bearcat that I had driven during my halcyon college days. A door
opened in its side, and Bodog led me inside the space machine. A
strange arrangement of shafts and wires filled much of the cabin.

"What propels it?" I asked, for I had seen no rocket tubes or other
means of propulsion on the outside of the craft, the overall shape of
which was peculiar, an array of panels connected at odd and
disquieting angles, seeming now to disappear out of the purview of
ordinary three-dimensional space, yet again to reappear at unexpected
places.

"Gravity, Carson Napier. My machine is powered by gravity."

"But gravity is what holds us to the planet. How can it propel us
hence?"

Again that horrid laugh, rising almost to a shriek of triumph. "It
is simple, utterly simple for a genius of my dimensions. All I need do
is bend the direction in which gravity pulls us. Do you see, it is as if a
sailor were to run a line around a stanchion and attach the end of it to
a heavy weight which lay beside him. The sailor pulls on the rope, the
stanchion bends the direction of force, and even as the sailor pulls the
rope toward him, the rope pulls the weight away from him!"

I shook my head in amazement. His concept was amazingly
simple, almost obvious, and yet it was a principle that only a genius
like Dr. Bodog could imagine. Too bad that this superb intellect was
the possession of a man of such sinister if not absolutely insane
intentions.

"Here," he said, leading me to a rack from which hung a row of peculiar garments. "We will wear these during our flight. They are of a special material that will protect us from the effects of the gravity bender, for otherwise our internal organs would become fatally disorganized."

He stared at me, then burst into his hideous, mocking laughter again. "Organs—disorganized. Do you see the joke, Carson Napier? *Organs disorganized*. No? Ah, well, never mind."

The suits were of a thin and flexible substance which would cover the wearer totally. Gloves and footwear were attached, as was a flexible helmet or head-and-face covering, leaving only slits for vision, and even these were fitted with protective lenses.

"My special fabric permits air to pass to and from the wearer," Bodog explained. "And the suits are of sufficient resilience that they do not need to be specially fitted for each wearer."

He clapped me on the shoulder with one of his skeletal but surprisingly powerful hands. "Tonight," he rasped, "we shall share a farewell dinner. I will leave Oggar and Istara in charge of my holdings on Amtor, and you and your Duare shall accompany me to Earth. Just think of the astonished expressions of Earthly scientists when they meet a woman who was born and raised on Venus!"

Dinner that night—or what passed for night on this cloud-shrouded world—lived up to Bodog's prediction. A fire had again been laid on the great hearth, and powders of Bodog's devising were added to create weird tinctures and forms that swayed and danced hypnotically. Istara and Oggar, Duare and I, sat on opposite sides of the table while Bodog, presided. Toasts were drunk in strong *fionbeior* while black-attired zombielike servitors brought course after course of exotic and piquant delicacies.

At the end of our meal, Dr. Bodog suggested that we each retire to our respective quarters. The three travelers—Bodog, Duare, and I—would in due course assemble at the space machine, which, Bodog explained, would by then have been moved to the courtyard outside the Potala.

I had very little to do in preparation for the flight to Earth. I cleansed myself and changed to fresh garments, then made my way to the courtyard. I encountered Dr. Bodog as I crossed the open area to the machine. Inside we found our special protective costumes and proceeded to don them. Duare, I saw, had preceded us and awaited us inside the machine.

With hardly a moment's hesitation, Bodog directed Duare and myself to seats where we were held by belts to prevent our being injured when the ship's machinery bent the force of gravity. Bodog turned a knob, and the little craft was filled with a weirdly harmonic humming.

My head began to whirl, and I felt as if I were being turned upside down. Through the windows of the machine I could see the Potala fall away beneath us—or was it above us? I looked up—or was it down?—and saw the ceaselessly roiling clouds of Amtor.

One of the planet's colorful vortices had formed and Bodog headed straight for it. We burst through and found ourselves between two layers of clouds. We sped horizontally until another vortex appeared above and ahead of us. Bodog directed our little craft to that swirling disk of light. We burst through it and suddenly there we were, in the blackness of space. I nearly wept at the beauty of the heavens that I had not seen for so long.

I will not detail the events of our trip Earthward. The little gravity-powered machine attained astonishing speed. Bodog called upon the ancient astronomical knowledge that he had acquired uncounted centuries before in the redoubts of Lemuria and ancient Tibet to navigate our course to Earth.

It had never occurred to me until now, how vast is the void between the planets and how easily travelers could become lost, to drift endlessly through space like the legendary Flying Dutchman.

I wondered where Bodog planned to land. Knowing his wild, almost insane ambitions, I expected him to make his return to the world of his origins in a dramatic fashion, and he did so in a manner that outdid even my wildest guesses.

It was January first, the first day of the new year. A championship football game was in progress in a great stadium in Los Angeles. It was halftime, and the players were resting in their locker rooms while bands played and cheerleaders pranced to entertain the gigantic crowd.

Bodog brought our little craft down precisely on the fifty-yard line, in this stadium packed with 100,000 cheering spectators. He opened the door and the three of us stepped out, still wearing our special protective suits.

Bodog removed his flexible helmet, revealing his naked pate and frightening countenance to the multitude. As the crowd became silent in its curiosity as to this strange display, I followed suit. And then Duare did the same. Duare, whom I had loved on Amtor—or thought I had loved. But in our days as Dr. Bodog's guests, she had shown her deep interest in Oggar, while I had begun to feel a deeper rapport with Oggar's tall and lovely sister, Istara.

And as she removed her helmet, revealing her face for the first time since our farewell dinner in her father's redoubt, I beheld the lovely and beloved features of my one true love, Istara of Amtor!

 END

This is the only reprint in the book. Due to a prior contractual arrangement, ERB, Inc. could not allow any new Mars stories to appear here . . . but we found a way around that.

In 1963, literally half a century ago, I wrote the following, a sequel to the tenth (and then final) Mars book, Llana of Gathol. *It was published in 1965 and circulated free of charge with ERB-dom magazine, which may have been part of the reason that ERB-dom became the only Burroughs fanzine in history to win the Hugo Award, back in 1966. A thousand copies were printed, and during the past decade I have seen them going for as high as $300 in convention dealers' rooms.*

This bears no resemblance to what I write these days. It so meticulously emulated ERB's style that it was my hope, when writing it, that if it were found in his safe (where so many posthumously published treasures were found), no one would doubt that he had written it himself.

—Mike

The Forgotten Sea of Mars

Mike Resnick

Prologue

The day breaks with surprising suddenness in Arizona, and as I stood on a bank overlooking the headwaters of the Little Colorado, I watched the starry heavens fade into the bright blue sky which marks the Southwestern day. I, like so many others before me, had a few weeks ago unplugged the phone, packed my gear, locked my house, and taken a temporary leave from the rigors of that phenomenon we call society.

Arizona had seemed to me the ideal place for the solitude and beauty I craved, and so I had rented a cabin that was once owned by a famous writer and set up housekeeping.

This day was to remain in my memory for a long time, although it began innocently enough. As usual I was off at daybreak, wandering through the hills and canyons, sketching, photographing, and generally exploring in my amateur fashion. I had borrowed a horse but could see no reason for making him carry my weight during the heat of the day and spent most of the time during my excursions leading him by the rope that was attached to his halter.

Returning to my two-room cabin just before twilight, I watered the horse and went inside to prepare my dinner on the primitive stove. The sun had set and the skies had turned dark long before I finished my meal, and as I peered through the window I could almost see the long-gone warriors of Geronimo seated in council or donning their war paint. I have always been a daydreamer, and so I turned, supporting my chin on my hands, and gazed at the Apache warriors. They were dancing now, all except one who was facing my cabin, and I could imagine the horror their martial war-whoops must have inspired in the breasts of our early cowboys and settlers.

Then one warrior, the one who had not partaken in the dance, began approaching, which apparitions are not supposed to do. I closed my eyes and shook my head vigorously. When I looked again, the Apache village had returned to the inner recesses of my mind, but the warrior was still coming toward me, and as he did so I thought I could hear the clanking sound of metal upon metal.

Finally, when he was within a few feet of the cabin door, he stopped, and in a strong masculine voice called out a single word: "Nephew?"

"Who's there?" I demanded, drawing my revolver. "Friend or enemy?"

"From the tone of your voice I assume that I'm not a friend," he answered in a calm voice. "You'll have to accept my word that I'm not an enemy."

I opened the door, my gun cocked, and was startled by the sight that greeted my eyes. There, not three feet away, stood a tall, handsome, clean-limbed man. His hair was black, his eyes gray, his face ruggedly handsome. He wore only a jeweled harness of unearthly design, and at his side hung a longsword, a shortsword, a dagger, and a strange-looking pistol. Immediately I holstered my revolver and, stepping forward, extended my hand.

"John Carter!" I exclaimed as he took my hand in his firm grasp. "It could be none other than you!"

"Then you know of me?" he asked pleasantly.

"Know of you? I was brought up on the Martian stories! But come inside and tell me what brings you to Earth."

"Nothing of great importance," he replied, following me into the living room. "I returned primarily to see my nephew. I met him in this very cabin once before, and I had hoped that he might be here again."

"Do you mean Edgar Rice Burroughs?" I asked, and he nodded. "I'm afraid he's been dead for a number of years."

A look of sadness spread across his face.

"I had feared as much," he said at last, "but this is the first chance I have had to visit my native planet since I saw him last." He rose and walked slowly to the door. "This shall, I believe, be my last voyage across the void which separates Earth from my beloved Barsoom, for I now have no ties to return to."

"No!" I said. "You must not deny us more tales of Mars; it would be too great a loss!"

He turned to me with a questioning expression on his face,

"Let *me* bring your adventures to the world!" I pleaded.

He shrugged his shoulders and sat down. "Why not?" he said with a smile. "Where shall I begin?"

"Let me see," I said. "I never found out what happened to Tan Hadron of Hastor. Did you ever see him again?"

"That," he replied, leaning back in his chair, "would make a most interesting and unusual story. Perhaps you would like to hear it?"

I assured him that I would, and here, in his own words, is the tale he told me that night beneath the cold light of the Arizona moon.

⊹⇒ I ⇐⊹
Rab-Zov

As you may recall, I had last seen Tan Hadron of Hastor when we were aboard the *Dusar*. The crew mutinied rather than return to

Pankor, and since we were the only ones with sufficient knowledge and skill to operate the ship, they kept Hadron as their pilot and Fonar as a hostage, and set me aground, little knowing that Tan Hadron's prowess with a longsword was among the best in all Helium.

During the ensuing war with Hin Abtol's forces I lost all track of Tan Hadron, all my energies and attention being required for the fighting at hand. Immediately after the combined forces of Helium and Gathol had emerged victorious, I determined to discover his whereabouts, for no trace of him had been seen after he had flown that crew of Panar cutthroats away from Pankor.

Under my guidance great numbers of search parties were sent to all ends of Barsoom in quest of Tan Hadron, but these efforts ended in failure, quite probably because Tan Hadron had been wearing the harness of a padwar in Hin Abtol's navy when last we parted, which was the equivalent of a death sentence in a majority of the nations of Barsoom.

I had conducted this search openly in the hope that, as often happens, whoever had the knowledge I desired might prefer to offer it anonymously, and sure enough, just when I was on the verge of admitting defeat, I received an unsigned note; I was told that if I desired to learn the whereabouts of my missing officer, I must be on the upper level of a certain boarding house in Zodanga, alone, at sunset two days hence.

Carthoris and Kantos Kan advised me against going there, as it seemed too suspicious a meeting place. Zodanga has long been a breeding ground of sedition and insurrection, but it was my only tangible link with Tan Hadron, and I decided to follow through on it, however dangerous the situation might seem.

I left Helium on the morning of the appointed day and set off for Zodanga, which lies about fifty-one hundred haads east of Helium and is located at Lat. 30°S., Lon. 172°E. As I was to be in the city but a brief time, I made no attempt at disguise, and, flying the colors of the Warlord of Barsoom, I soon gained the hangar on the roof of the boarding house. Having an hour or so on my hands before sunset, I took a short walk through the city.

Unlike most Martian cities, which contain numerous buildings and monuments from antiquity, Zodanga is almost entirely new, for Tars Tarkas and I had burned the city to the ground not so many years past, nor had the people of Zodanga forgotten that, as was evidenced by the hateful glares they threw at me as I progressed through the crowded streets.

I must have walked close to two miles when I looked up and saw Thuria, the nearer moon, racing across the heavens on her endless voyage. The sun was beginning to dip over the horizon, and I made my way back to the rooming house and ascended to its highest level.

The entire floor was comprised of one large sleeping chamber, and I was surprised to note that it was almost deserted. Three men were reclining upon their sleeping silks and furs, and a fourth was sitting in a chair of sorapus wood, reading a book.

The reader rose as I entered. I found his evil-looking face familiar, but I couldn't place it.

"Welcome, John Carter," he said with a smile on his thick, ugly lips.

"Have you the information I seek?" I demanded, advancing.

"Yes."

"Good!" I said. "Let me have it."

"Not so fast," he replied. "Are you prepared to pay for it?"

I had suspected something of this nature and had brought along a few diamonds from the mines of Gathol, which I now withdrew from my pocket-pouch.

"I trust this will suffice," I said.

He examined them carefully, taking his time, and finally handed them back.

"The price is not high enough," he said at last.

"They're a Jeddak's ransom!" I exclaimed. "What do you want?"

"Your life, John Carter," he said, and in that instant I recognized him.

"Rab-zov!"

"Yes," he said slowly. "The man whom you disgraced in the presence of Hin Abtol, Jeddak of . . . Pankor."

I was looking at him intently when his eyes left mine for just an instant and looked beyond me. Immediately I jumped aside and, drawing my sword, turned to face three armed men, the same three who had been feigning sleep when I had entered. I felt the old fighting smile of my Virginia ancestors come to my lips as I prepared to do battle.

They spread out a bit, and I backed into a corner to better defend myself, although I had no doubt as to the outcome. Regardless of their skill, I would win. I am, unquestionably, the greatest swordsman ever born; I say this not in a spirit of bravado, but as a simple fact, a fact which nobody who has ever seen me fight will deny.

My opponents were no mean antagonists themselves, but it wasn't long before the nearest of them dropped his guard for an instant and was sent off to join his ancestors. I then employed my rushing tactics and caught the remaining pair so off guard that the duel was over in a matter of seconds.

I turned back to Rab-zov, who had stood on the other side of the room all during the fight, never attempting to come to the aid of his comrades. I had not yet sheathed my sword, and in a single bound I was beside him, my point at his throat.

"Now," I said, "you will give me my information or your life. Which shall it be?"

"I shall tell you of Tan Hadron, although it will do you little good," he answered. "The entire building is surrounded, and fifteen of my men are just without the chamber."

I rushed to the window, and, sure enough, there was a group of men standing in the street, all wearing the insignia of Hin Abtol's army. So this was a plot on my life! I realized now why they had chosen Zodanga: it was sure to be friendly to any enemies of Helium.

"Was this all a ruse?" I asked, turning to Rab-zov. "Or does Tan Hadron of Hastor still live?"

"He lives."

"I have combed Barsoom's surface from pole to pole. Where is he hidden?"

"Tan Hadron of Hastor," he replied, "is not upon the surface of Barsoom, but is imprisoned far beneath it."

"You lie," I said, "for my men have returned from the buried sea of Omean just two weeks past and reported that they could find no trace of him."

"Omean, John Carter, is not the only submerged world of Barsoom. Just as it lies near the South Pole, so does Ayathor lie near the North Pole. It is in Ayathor that Tan Hadron is being held, although in a moment you will be unable to help him or anyone else again."

With that he clapped his hands twice, and fifteen armed men entered the chamber and slowly began advancing. I love a good fight, but there were no pedestals or nooks in which I might take them on three or four at a time, and not even John Carter could take on fifteen swordsmen without some kind of advantage.

They had great respect for my blade, and were still moving toward me very slowly, and in that I saw my only chance for escape.

Scarcely had the plan entered my mind than I was enacting it. Rapidly I grabbed the smirking Rab-zov, and, as I had done in Pankor, I held him high above my head. Then, extending my Earthly muscles to their fullest, I hurled him into the wall of oncoming swordsmen, and in the moment of confusion that followed I made a break for the window. The success or failure of my plan depended on whether or not the new Zodanga had the same type of ornamentation on its buildings as the old city had, yet even as this doubt crossed my mind I leaped upward from the window ledge, my hands came in contact with a smooth surface and slid rapidly down until, when I had almost given myself up for lost, I came to a great carved protrusion.

With a sigh of relief I began, systematically finding handholds and toeholds, to climb toward the roof, which was about twenty feet above me. Realizing that should Rab-zov and his men gain the roof before I did I would be no better off than before, I hastened my efforts, and a few seconds later the edge of the roof was within my grasp.

Here I paused, listening for Rab-zov, but as no sound came to my ears I cautiously raised my head until I could see across to the hangar.

And then, just as I was about to pull myself up, a hand shot out of the darkness and I could see the cold light of Cluros, the farther moon, reflected off the blade of a dagger.

⊰⊱ II ⊰⊱
A Unique Discovery

As I looked up from my precarious position, I found my new antagonist to be another of Hin Abtol's former officers. Rab-zov had evidently left him to guard the roof alone, and from my present plight it appeared that one man was quite enough.

I grabbed his wrist in an attempt to keep the dagger from reaching my breast, but that was the extent of my possibilities. I couldn't let go of the edge of the roof with my other hand without plunging to my death; I knew it, and my opponent knew it, too, for he began pummeling my face with his free hand,

"The Warlord!" he screamed. "Come to the roof! I have the Warlord!"

As he yelled to his comrades he turned his head in the direction of the ramp upon which they must ascend, and in that instant I managed to swing my body to the roof. He immediately turned back to me, redoubling his efforts, and the ferocity of this renewed attack rolled me halfway over the side again. But now I had the use of both my hands, and, still holding his dagger arm with my left, my right grabbed for his throat. There we remained, motionless, he trying to stab me or push me off the roof and I trying to choke the life from him. It was scarce thirty seconds since I had left the sleeping chamber, but I knew Rab-zov and his men must be on their way to the roof by now and would reach it momentarily.

I closed my hand more and more securely about his throat. He was weakening, but still that blade came ever closer to my heart. Then, with a final convulsive shudder, he died. Rising, I flung his lifeless body to the street below and raced toward the hangar.

Rab-zov and his men were emerging from the ramp, but my powerful Earthly muscles carried me to the hangar in great leaps and bounds that no Martian could ever hope to match. They began firing at me with their radium pistols, but it was dark and I reached my flier unscathed.

However, once aboard it, I couldn't make it rise, and realized that they had punctured the tanks which contained the Eighth Barsoomian Ray, the ray of repulsion. Running to another side of the roof, I saw a building some fifty feet away. Without breaking stride, I jumped the intervening space amid a barrage of fire from their pistols, and, keeping to the rooftops, I had soon covered half a mile.

Here I paused to strip all the insignia and jewels from my harness, for there were others in Zodanga besides Rab-zov who desired the demise of the Warlord. This done, I withdrew the red pigment given to me many years ago by the Ptor brothers and smeared it over every inch of my body until I appeared no different than any red man of Barsoom.

As I descended to the street, I decided to go straightaway to Ayathor. I was certain of its existence, for Rab-zov had thought I would soon be a dead man when he told me of it. There was a note of urgency attached to finding Ayathor, for if Rab-zov returned there ahead of me, I could count on a most unpleasant welcome.

Could I but gain access to a flier, I had no doubts that I could easily outdistance the Panars, for they would probably be using the slow, outmoded ships of Hin Abtol's navy.

Then, recalling the diamonds I had in my possession, I went directly to a public hangar, where I purchased a two-man flier, for I planned on returning with Tan Hadron or not at all. The man who sold it to me examined the diamond suspiciously, but his greed was greater than his sense of duty and shortly thereafter I was skimming rapidly across the dead sea bottoms of Barsoom, bound for the frozen North.

I set the directional compass toward Pankor and settled back to relax. This compass, invented by my son, Carthoris, is a most unique mechanism, allowing the pilot to set the pointer at any location in either hemisphere, after which he is not needed at the controls until the craft reaches its destination, whereupon he will be notified by the ringing of a small alarm. There is, in addition, a device which enables the ship to avoid mountains, other ships, or any similar obstructions.

It was not without an air of sadness that I looked out over the ochre, mosslike vegetation of the dying planet. Beneath me great oceans had once brought commerce to the now-deserted cities. As I flew over one of the cities now inhabited only by the great white apes and fierce green men who roam the sea bottoms in warring tribes, I could almost visualize the sailors of those long-forgotten days returning to their women after a prosperous voyage; and hear the vendors' calls in the crowded market places.

Traces still remain of the great coliseums where the cheering multitudes had given moral support to their favorite gladiators, and of the strongly martial architecture of the many palaces. Now the finely carved buildings are broken and crumbling, the streets are overrun with moss, and only the occasional screams of an ape permeate the cold night air.

It was a sad and lonely sight, this tribute to the youth and glory of Barsoom, but a rifle shot from the city soon awoke me from my reverie, and I quickly swerved out of range and continued on my way to Pankor. Pankor, I was sure, would be the logical place to begin my quest for the hidden city of Ayathor. Hin Abtol's warriors came from Pankor, Tan Hadron was the prisoner of a group of Panars when last we parted, and Pankor was sufficiently close to the North Pole to afford some means of ingress to Ayathor.

I checked to make sure that the ship was going at full speed, and then, covering myself with some furs which I had found on board, I lay down to sleep, exhausted from my efforts in Zodanga.

When I awoke it was midday, and the air had become cold. Looming large in front of me were the ice caps which surround Okar and Pankor, the two countries within the circumference of the snow-capped polar circle.

I had no knowledge of the location of Ayathor other than what Rab-zov had told me, nor were there any books or maps to aid me. Before Thuvan Dihn, Jeddak of Ptarth, and I had overthrown the tyrannical Salensus Oll and placed Talu, the rebel prince of Marentina, upon the throne of Okar, the yellow men of the North and their cities were widely thought to be a myth, due to their inaccessibility by land, and the Guardian of the North, that great magnetic pole which drew all the outside world's fliers to their destruction. Since that time, Pankor had been discovered, and the cities have been charted, but no maps of the surrounding territory have been compiled, as it is comprised entirely of fields of ice and snow.

Now, however, I wished that a more thorough survey had been made, for I was utterly at a loss as to my next move. It seemed likely that my red pigment would afford me safe entry into Pankor, but, once there, any inquiries I might make of Ayathor would probably show too great a lack of knowledge and could well result in the discovery of my identity. Nonetheless, there seemed naught else to do but take my chances in the plastic-domed hotbox city.

As I approached I became aware of a distracting patch of color—or rather an absence of it—in the distance off the starboard bow. As I was less than fifty haads from the city and well in advance of Rab-zov,

I swung to starboard and curiously approached it. As I drew nearer I found the distraction to be a large black spot of circular proportions, which of course made it stand out like a sore thumb against the brilliant display of ice-covered mountains.

A sudden gust of wind came from the northeast, and, rather than try to fight onward in my light flier, I descended to the ground to wait until it had passed. To my surprise, as I descended the spot gradually disappeared.

Now indeed was my interest aroused, and I took the flier up again. Sure enough, when I was about two thousand feet up the spot reappeared.

As my elevation increased, the spot became larger and rounder. Long before I reached it, I realized that by a fluke of chance I had discovered a shaft, the exact counterpart of Omean's shaft, and I knew that this polar opening must lead to Ayathor.

It was a beautiful job of natural camouflaging, for from the ground the shaft appeared no different from any of the myriad of glacial mountains surrounding it, and from the air it was probably unnoticeable from any great distance.

As I hovered over the mouth of the shaft, my conclusions were borne out, for it was indeed a hollow, cylindrical passage, although I could see no farther down than forty or fifty feet, so steeped in shadows was it.

I paused only long enough to direct my flier to the exact center of that yawning chasm, and then plunged into the Stygian darkness.

⊹⇒ III ⇐⊹
Ayathor

Downward, ever downward, I plummeted, until it seemed that I must each second come to the end of my descent. However, except for a slight increase in temperature, nothing happened. I must have been in the shaft for an hour before any change in my surroundings became noticeable. Then, of a sudden, I found that I could make out the walls of the shaft. The air was now warm, the light increased, and, a moment later, I arrived at the bottom of the shaft and broke out into the open.

I could perceive a light in the distance, and, looking down, I saw that I was flying but twenty ads above a dark, still body of water. As I approached the light, I found that it emanated from a fair-sized city located upon an island about two haads distant from the cylindrical passage from which I had just emerged.

I paused here to consider my situation. This forgotten world was seemingly composed of a great sea dotted by hundreds of islands. The walls exuded a soft phosphorescence which sent dull streaks of light across the placid waters.

One island appeared much larger than the rest, and it was upon this that the city was built. How far the sea extended I could only guess, for I could not see the horizon in any direction.

I drew nearer the city, and, when about a haad distant from it, I chose a deserted, rock-covered island and landed upon it. To approach the city in a strange craft would have been suicidal, and so I had no recourse but to leave the flier behind and hope it would still be there if and when I returned. Then, fixing the location of the shaft in my mind, I dove into the cold, foreboding waters.

I had determined to swim to the shore of the island which seemed farthest from the city's main entrance, but as I headed in that direction I saw great ripples in the water, and since I possessed no knowledge concerning what types of creatures had inhabited the long-dead oceans of Barsoom, I altered my course, taking no chances.

I had covered about half the distance to the shore when, suddenly, I felt a powerful, boneless hand grab hold of me. I drew my sword and hacked away at it, but before I could disengage myself I felt another hand, and then another, and I was pulled, slowly but inexorably, beneath the surface of the sea.

The water was ink-black; I couldn't see what manner of creature it was that had attacked me and so had no idea where a vulnerable spot might be. There was nothing I could do but slash frantically and hope that I might disable it enough to allow me to regain the surface.

This was not to be, however, for my blade seemed only to enrage the thing. It pulled all the harder, and I was drawn farther and farther into the depths of the hidden sea. There were hands all around my legs now, so many that I felt certain that more than one of the creatures was attacking me. My lungs were bursting, and I knew that I had but a few seconds of life left in me if I could not escape its clutches and return to the surface for air.

I had not stopped slashing and hewing with my sword, and I suddenly felt it swish cleanly through the water as I severed one of the thing's hands. This seemed to infuriate it, for it now brought its great fangs into play. Despite the pain, it was with a sense of relief that I became aware of two powerful jaws closing about my leg. Here at last was a target which might prove fatal!

Using the flat of my blade, I glided my sword swiftly over the scaly face until I came to a bulging protrusion. This, I knew, must be an eye, perhaps the only one. Immediately I ran my point through it.

The creature, trembling with pain, lessened its grip on my leg. Then, drawing my shortsword, I began stabbing, a sword in each hand, at where I thought the jugular vein must be. It released my leg with all but one of its hands and began writhing in agony. In another second I had decapitated it, and yet that hand hung grimly on, and I was like to have been torn apart by the headless body's convulsions.

Working furiously, I severed the hand and, keeping clear of the thrashing body, rose rapidly to the surface. Gasping and panting, I examined my leg and found it to be only superficially wounded. I was about to resume my journey when I saw a ripple, and then another, converging upon me. Mustering every remaining ounce of strength within my exhausted body, I swam as fast as I could toward the city, knowing all the while that I could never hope to escape these sea-things in their own element. It was only a matter of time before they reached me, and, once caught, I knew that I could never survive another underwater battle such as I had just undergone.

Then, just as I was drawing my sword, preparing to do as much damage as possible before my death, the creatures went right past me, one of them brushing my hip as he passed. Turning, I saw the ripples disappear over the spot where I had just killed their brother of the deep. Soon afterward bits of torn flesh came floating up to the surface, and I realized that they had not come to the aid of their fellow but to feast upon his remains.

Hastening away, I headed once more toward the city, keeping away from any part of the sea surface which was not completely still and placid.

This course of action worked effectively, and I was soon close enough to observe the layout of the city. It seemed to be built primarily about one gigantic palace. In fact, except for a small group of barracks, the palace *was* the city.

There was a large number of soldiers on and about the shore, all wearing the metal of Hin Abtol. I concluded that they must have banded together after the war, although for what purpose I could not even hazard a guess, nor could I see any advantage in locating themselves in this hidden world.

There were piers emanating from the beach, and upon these I beheld many men in plain harnesses and armed with longswords, sitting and fishing. Now and again a warrior would approach them with a command to move elsewhere, or would demand to see what they had so far managed to catch, and I assumed that the fishermen were either slaves or captives.

I knew that were I discovered I could never pass for one of the warriors, and so I removed all my weapons save for my longsword, hoping to pass for a prisoner should I be discovered. I didn't like the idea of shrinking from encounters, but there was Tan Hadron to be considered, and so, with a feeling of regret, I released my shortsword, dagger, and radium pistol and let them sink, one by one, into oblivion.

A strategy was now called for. Should I attempt to gain the island unseen, as had been my original idea? Discovery would mean certain death, and the great number of warriors on the shore pointed toward discovery. If I remained in the water I would be prey to the creatures who haunted the depths of this lost sea, and waiting would serve no purpose, for in this sunless world waiting for nightfall was meaningless; the city would remain as bright as it was, regardless of time. My only alternative was to reach the piers and pose as one of the fishermen until I could gain access to the city. I didn't like the thought of putting myself in their power, but it afforded me the greatest chance of success.

This decided upon, I drew as near the shore as I dared, and then, filling my lungs with air, I dove down and made my way to the piers with long, powerful strokes. When I surfaced I was within twenty feet of them, but just as I was congratulating myself on the ease with which I was accomplishing the first step of my mission, I felt a large, slimy body begin to coil itself about me.

I uttered an involuntary shout of pain and surprise, and all secrecy was lost. Now there was naught to do but defend myself as best I could.

This sea-thing proved far easier to dispatch than the other had. Barely had its snakelike body encircled me than its reptilian head rose above the surface of the water and, eyeing me with a cold, cruel gaze, it opened its mouth, revealing four rows of needlelike fangs, and lunged for my face. Grabbing it just behind the head, I drew my sword with my free hand and quickly severed the thing's neck.

An officer came to the edge of the pier and helped me pull my weary body out of the water, He was a young, frank-looking fellow, and his expression bespoke honor and courage.

"What were you doing?" he asked in a firm manner. "Trying to escape?"

"Credit me with the intelligence to know that there is no escape from Ayathor," I replied.

"Then what were you doing?" he repeated,

"I fell into the sea off yonder pier," I said, indicating a pier which I hoped was out of his jurisdiction, "and had just about reached the shore when that thing attacked me."

"Hardly a likely explanation." commented an evil-looking officer who had just approached.

"Who is the dwar of this pier, Talon Gar?" said the one who had aided me. "You may be the Jeddak's favorite, but when a man is on my pier I will decide what is to be done."

"Bal Daxus, you may yet overstep yourself," snapped Talon Gar. Then he fell silent, eyeing me suspiciously.

"Now, prisoner," said Bal Daxus, turning to me, "what is your name?"

"Dotar Sojat," I replied, giving him my well-worn alias, which I had derived from the surnames of the first two Tharkian chieftans I had killed upon my advent on Barsoom,

"Dotar Sojat, eh?" said Bal Daxus. "The name is unfamiliar."

"Nor have I ever set eyes on Bal Daxus and Talon Gar before just now," I replied blandly.

"We have ways of curing insolent slaves!" said Talon Gar, his hand on the hilt of his sword.

"You may consider yourself free to try and impress your ways on me," I answered with a contemptuous smile.

He whipped out his sword, but Bal Daxus stepped between us. "Any discipline Dotar Sojat receives will not come from Talon Gar," he said, and his tone made the officer sheathe his weapon. "That was a most courageous battle you just waged," he continued, ignoring Talon Gar completely. "Are you badly hurt?"

"No," I replied. "But I am rather tired. Do you suppose I might return to my quarters for a spell?" I saw here the opportunity to gain the city with his permission, and I was careful to avoid any definite mention of time, for how was I to know how time was measured in this hidden world?

"Surely," answered Bal Daxus. Taking a towel from one of his warriors, he handed it to me. As I dried myself off, I thought I saw a look of surprise and cunning on Talon Gar's face, but I wrote it off to imagination and overwrought nerves. I had just handed the towel back to Bal Daxus, wondering what to do next, when he provided me with my answer.

"Come, Dotar Sojat," he said, walking off. "I'll escort you to your quarters myself. I could do no less for such a warrior."

As we approached the great palace, I noticed the designs on the walls. They depicted the race of bearded yellow men carrying out the various functions of their daily lives. The palace, then, must have been built ages ago, long before the yellow race discovered that they could live on the surface of the frozen north by enclosing their cities in plastic domes. They had probably left Ayathor when the domes were perfected, and it had been forgotten for eons, until that day I had broken the dome of Pankor while carrying Llana of Gathol to freedom in my flier. The Panars had probably heard of this legendary world from the Okarians, and when the necessity arose they had sought it out and populated it.

Bal Daxus gave a signal at the gate of the palace, and the massive door swung slowly inward. As we entered, he turned sharply to the right and approached a nearby barracks, stopping when we reached the door. I noticed that Talon Gar was following us at a distance of forty or fifty feet.

"Well?" demanded Bal Daxus. "Have you forgotten the rule?"

"What?" I asked hazily. "Oh, yes . . . the rule." What might it be?

"Don't just stand there, then," he said. "Give me your sword. There aren't any targaths around here."

I liked this not, but there was nothing to do but hand him my one remaining weapon. Evidently some beast called a targath was apt to attack anyone who went outside the palace, which explained why the prisoners were armed. As for returning the swords, that was only logical, for while I could not escape, I was still an enemy.

As soon as I entered I sensed that something was amiss, for there were fully fifty men in the room, and all of them were armed!

"Warriors!" said Bal Daxus sternly. "Do you recognize this man?"

"The Warlord!" screamed fifty voices in unison, and fifty swords were menacing me in an instant.

"Think you, John Carter," sneered Talon Gar, "that you can so easily outwit the forces of Hin Abtol?"

I must have looked my puzzlement, for Bal Daxus produced the towel with which I had dried myself. It was covered with reddish copper stains.

Guessing the truth, I looked down at my body. Not a trace of my red pigment remained!

╪═ IV ═╪
"To the Pits!"

"Now," said Bal Daxus calmly, "you may submit peaceably, or you may prepare to meet your ancestors. It is your choice."

There seemed nothing to do but submit, for dead I could be of no avail to anyone, while alive there was still a chance that I could find some means of escaping and succoring Tan Hadron. Thus it was that John Carter, Prince of Helium, Warlord of Barsoom, surrendered without striking a blow in his defense.

My hands were bound behind my back, and when the job was done, Talon Gar confronted me.

"John Carter," he said, "long have I awaited the day when the Warlord of Barsoom should fall into our hands."

"You had best make the most of your opportunity," I replied, "while Chance so favors you, for when Helium finds out that—"

"Helium?" he interrupted with a sneer. "Helium is doomed!"

"Others have said that before, Talon Gar, and they were all better men than you, yet Helium still stands."

He could scarce restrain his rage; finally a maniacal smile contorted his cruel features and he struck me heavily on the face.

"A most noble gesture," I said. "Bal Daxus, if you will release my bonds that I might engage the courageous Talon Gar, I'll fight him with any weapon of his choosing. I give you my word as a man of honor that I will put myself back into your custody immediately afterward."

"And if you lose?" asked Bal Daxus.

"I shall not lose."

"It seems like a just proposition, for surely no man could tolerate the abuse you have just undergone without demanding satisfaction. What says Talon Gar?"

Talon Gar blanched beneath his copper-red skin. "I would not dignify him by crossing swords with him," he said lamely.

"But you dignify your rank as an officer by striking helpless men?" I asked tauntingly.

He looked as if he would smite me again, but Bal Daxus intervened. "It now remains only to imprison you," he told me, "until the Jeddak desires your presence."

"Yes," put in Talon Gar. "To the Pits!"

With that we set off and were soon in a maze of descending corridors. I began limping, and Bal Daxus immediately noticed the cuts on my leg. "What happened to you?" he asked. "Surely no snake could have done that!"

"No," I said. "It was another creature." I saw no need to tell him any more than that, as I wanted the location of my flier to remain unknown. "They're merely flesh wounds," I added. "They'll heal soon enough."

"You won't be alive to know about it," said Talon Gar.

As we walked on, I asked Bal Daxus what kinds of animals inhabited the sunken world.

"We found nothing but ulsios and targaths when we came here," he replied, "but the Jeddak has since brought in some banths."

The ulsio is the Martian rat, of about the size and ferocity of a cougar, and the banth is the eight-legged lion of Barsoom, but the targath I did not know, and I questioned him further.

"It is rather hard to describe," said Bal Daxus. "Besides, I fear you'll find out soon enough, although I daresay the knowledge will do you little good."

When he heard that, Talon Gar broke into wild laughter which resounded throughout the corridor. I was fast becoming convinced that the man was absolutely mad.

"We shall soon reach the Pits of Ayathor," remarked Bal Daxus. "It does not do justice to your rank and position, but I have my orders."

"I thought the *sea* was called Ayathor," I said, puzzled by his reference to the Pits.

"Both the sea and the city bear the name," replied Bal Daxus, "although the meaning of the word has been lost since the days of antiquity."

The corridor now branched off so often that I gave up trying to remember my way out of it. I had never seen such an intricate maze of catacombs, and I marveled at the skill of those forgotten men who had designed this immense yet detailed palace.

From time to time I heard vague shuffling sounds coming from adjoining passageways, and I noticed that many of my captors had unsheathed their swords. I soon saw the reason for this. At the next turn an ulsio leaped from the shadows and, with a horrid scream, hurled himself at one of the warriors. He was quickly dispatched, and the march recommenced.

"No one seems especially startled," I remarked to Bal Daxus. "Is this a common occurrence?"

"Of course. Why do you think we walk the corridors with drawn swords?"

"Why don't you make a concentrated effort to exterminate them?" I asked, mystified by the apparent lack of concern that these warriors displayed for the savage beasts which might at any moment leap upon them from some nook or shadow.

"Why should we?" he responded. "None of our warriors travels alone or unarmed in the catacombs, and the ulsios are the best sentries we have. You will notice that we occasionally pass a human skeleton. This should serve as a reminder to you, John Carter: men have escaped from their cells and their dungeons, but none has ever escaped from the Pits of Ayathor."

I thought that this remark might tickle Talon Gar's funnybone anew and send him off into another peal of ecstatic laughter, but he merely smiled silently, and so we forged onward.

The air had become heavy and damp, and we began passing heavily barred doors, finally halting in front of the last one in the row. This, then, was where I was to be imprisoned.

"You won't be here too long if I know the Jeddak, for he has a score to settle with you," announced Bal Daxus. "Nonetheless, you will be securely chained and a large guard will be placed by the door."

He signaled the rest of the men to remain at the door, and then, unlocking it, he led me inside. He had me sit upon the moist stone floor, chained my legs to two rings in the wall, and rose to go.

"You have been very decent to me," I said, "I shall remember that when I escape."

He smiled, a bit sadly I thought, and said: "I entreat you to end any foolhardy hopes of escape you might hold, for even if you managed to leave the island of Ayathor, which of course you cannot do, where would you go? No, John Carter, you are doomed, and I, for one, am sorry about it."

He turned and walked out slowly. A moment later the door was closed, and I heard the lock snap into place. Talon Gar gave me a parting look through the barred window of the door.

"We shall meet again, John Carter, and woe betide you when that time comes." He gave me one parting laugh and turned away. Soon I heard his footsteps echoing down the long passageway.

"Cheerful sort of fellow, isn't he?" said a voice at my side.

"Tan Hadron!" I exclaimed.

"Welcome to my luxurious living quarters," he laughed. "It is good to see you again. But tell me what brings you to Ayathor? Has Helium fallen?"

"No," I replied. "We defeated Hin Abtol quite easily, far more rapidly than we had expected to, in fact. I was caught while searching for you."

"And now you have found me."

"I wish I might accomplish all my missions so easily." I smiled. "How came you to this forgotten world, Tan Hadron?"

"Shortly after you were put aground, I locked Fo-nar and myself in the pilot room of the *Dusar* and pulled a few stunts that would have scared our best test pilots half to death. As you know, the ship was an open flier, and fully four-fifths of the mutineers fell overboard. The remaining few proved no match for our swords, which they had left in the pilot's room in typically careless Panar fashion, and we were soon headed toward Helium. When we had covered about half the distance, we were spotted by a number of Hin Abtol's ships, and since I was unable to respond satisfactorily to their signals, they forced us down. Fo-nar was killed immediately, and, though I accounted for a large number of Panars, they eventually overwhelmed me. And here I am," he concluded.

"But why are we here?" I asked. "Who is their Jeddak?"

"Their Jeddak," said Tan Hadron, "is Hin Abtol."

"Hin Abtol!" I exclaimed. "Why, I captured him aboard his own flagship at the beginning of the war, and later he was reported to be dead!"

"Then your reports are false," said Tan Hadron, "for he is very much alive. And it seems that he has not yet given up his insane plan to conquer Barsoom."

"Conquer Barsoom? With what? We destroyed his army and his navy."

"I found out," continued Tan Hadron, "as you must have, that the term 'frozen in,' when applied to Pankor, didn't mean merely surrounded by snow and ice, but referred to the warriors whom Hin Abtol kept alive in blocks of ice, in a state of suspended animation. When they were 'thawed out,' they were willing to fight against their homelands rather than return to Pankor. Hin Abtol has stored almost half a million frozen warriors here, and his philosophy is pretty much the same. Most of the men who have been here as long as I have would gladly kill their mothers just to set foot upon the face of Barsoom again."

"That answers a lot of questions," I said, and then told him all that had transpired since last we parted.

"And Tavia?" he asked. "My mate—is she well?"

"Very," I replied. "When almost all of Helium had given up hope of ever finding you, she had implicit faith in your ability to survive whatever hazards you encountered, and implored me not to give up the search."

We fell silent then, each savouring the memories of his loved ones. I knew that my absence would long since have been discovered, but there was nothing Carthoris or any of the rest could do. Time and again I cursed myself for not going to Helium from Zodanga, for I knew the fears and grief my incomparable princess, Dejah Thoris, must be undergoing, and yet I knew that given the same circumstances I would do the same thing. I have always acted upon impulse where a wiser man than I might have paused for contemplation and reached a more practical decision; but then, I am a fighting man, not a philosopher, and it has ever been my way to act quickly and surely. Many people have called me courageous, but I do not think that my actions constitute bravery, for I have never thought of a single alternative to any of my so-called acts of heroism until the time to enact that alternative has long been passed.

I must have fallen asleep then, and when I awoke I felt well-rested. Tan Hadron was leaning against the wall, looking at me.

"Good morning," he said pleasantly, "if such a thing as morning exists in Ayathor. You have been asleep for a long time."

"I'm sorry," I said, "but I was completely exhausted."

"Don't apologize," he said. "Sleep is one of the rare blessings we have here. Sleep—and the Games."

"The Games."

"Yes. Every city has its games, and Ayathor is no exception. It is good to feel a longsword in my hands now and then, and it breaks the monotony of this dungeon. I have been very successful so far."

"Your presence attests to that," I remarked.

"One could expect no less from a pupil of John Carter," he replied. "Until your arrival, I don't think there was anyone on this island who could defeat me, although I much prefer to do battle with the targaths. The prisoners are my comrades, and although I must kill them lest they kill me, I take no pride or pleasure in so doing."

"I have heard Talon Gar and Bal Daxus mention the targath," I said. "What might it be?"

"A most ferocious beast. It stands about eight feet tall and has a large, muscular body which is covered by tufts of long, gray hair. Like the white ape, it has an intermediary set of limbs which can be used as either arms or legs. The targath's face is perhaps his most awesome feature; it is so matted with hair as to appear shapeless, but it has two easily discernable eyeteeth which protrude well over the lower lip. Once, after I had killed one in the games, I examined its face closely—

and by Issus, the thing has no eyes! It has eyeballs, but evidently it never had any use for them, for this world was steeped in almost total darkness until Hin Abtol took over the city. The eyeballs are in their sockets, but the skin has grown right over them."

"They sound like blind, helpless creatures," I offered.

He laughed. "Hardly. They have a most uncanny sense of perception, and make very formidable opponents on land or in the sea."

"The sea?"

"Yes," he answered. "They became amphibious millions of years ago, when the islands could no longer supply them with food."

"Tell me, Hadron of Hastor: Have they any bones in their hands?"

"Why, no."

"And are their bodies covered with scales beneath the hair?"

"Yes!" he exclaimed. "How did you know that?"

"One of them attacked me while I was swimming here from my flier," I said, indicating my bruised leg.

"You're very fortunate to have escaped with so little injury," he commented.

"So that's what Talon Gar wished upon me."

"What do you think of Hin Abtol's sadistic spy?"

"Spy?"

"Yes. The Jeddak fears for his life, for he is loved no better here than at Pankor, However, he has surrounded himself with a loyal core of bodyguards, and pity the man who is heard to utter any word against Hin Abtol."

Just then a scream of horror and pain came ringing through the corridor.

"What was that?" I asked.

Tan Hadron shrugged. "It is not our lot to question," he replied. "Perhaps an ulsio has caught a warrior unawares, or . . ." He paused.

"Yes? Or what?"

"Or perhaps Talon Gar craved amusement. You will get used to the screams in time. We all do."

I leaned against the wall and did my best to relax as the last echoes of that blood-curdling cry faded into the distance.

╾═ V ═╼
The Pits of Ayathor

During the days that followed, or rather the time, for Ayathor possesses no days or nights, the tedium of my existence became almost unbearable. I am an active man by nature, and confinement of any kind galls me. Had it not been for Tan Hadron's company, I think I should have eventually gone quite mad. I fear I bordered on the brink anyway, for I began looking forward to the occasional screams as a means of breaking my boredom.

Plans of escape were useless, for even if we were to somehow unlock or break our shackles, there was only one exit, an exit which was bolted and heavily guarded at all times.

Bal Daxus brought the first gleam of hope into our breasts. He began visiting us from time to time, and we became good friends, an unusual relationship for captor and captives. He was a frank, honest warrior who was openly displeased with Hin Abtol, but felt morally bound to do the bidding of his Jeddak. This seemed to be the general attitude of Hin Abtol's warriors: they hated and feared him, but obeyed his orders due either to their own integrity or their fear.

"Why has he not sent for me yet?" I asked Bal Daxus during one of his visits. "I had expected to be condemned to death the moment he learned that I was in his power."

"You *are* condemned, John Carter," he replied. "The only reason that your death has not occurred yet is because that arch-fiend Talon Gar convinced Hin Abtol that it would be better to let you rot in the Pits for a while. Talon Gar does not like to see his enemies die too rapidly."

"What, then, is to become of us?" asked Tan Hadron.

"When Hin Abtol tires of keeping you in chains, you will return to the arena to fight in the Games."

"Is there a chance that I might be sent to the Games, too?" I asked, trying to keep the excitement out of my voice. If we two could but reach the arena with swords in our hands, then indeed might we have a chance to put an end to Hin Abtol and his dreams of conquest.

"No. He'd never arm you, John Carter. He is not a man who forgets easily, and when last you were in his power you managed to kill Ul-to, his finest swordsman, and break the dome of Pankor. No, John Carter, he has something else in mind for you."

"And what might that be?" I asked.

"I know not," replied Bal Daxus, "for it is a secret he has guarded well. However, all Ayathor is aware of the fact that he has prepared for the day you would once again fall into his clutches."

"It bodes ill, whatever it may be," said Tan Hadron.

"Nonetheless, I should welcome any chance to get these chains off my legs," I said, "and to breathe fresh air again."

"He is an evil man," said Bal Daxus, "and were I you I would not be so anxious to greet the fate he has prepared." He paused, clenching his fists. "Would that you had killed him when you had the chance!" he added venomously.

"If you hate him so," asked Tan Hadron, "why do you not leave his service?"

"I am bound by birth to fight for the Jeddak of the Panars, regardless of his character," explained Bal Daxus. "It is not he whose honor I defend, but the honor of my people."

"Will you keep us informed of all further developments?" I asked as he arose.

"Of course. I must take leave of you now, for Lirai awaits me."

"Lirai?"

"The girl I am to marry," he replied.

"I didn't know they had women in Ayathor," I said. "I had assumed that they had all remained in Pankor."

"No," said the Panar. "They are in Ayathor. The warriors' wives and families are here, and some others, too. Hin Abtol is shrewd enough to know that most of the men are displeased as it is; take away their women, and they would revolt. So the old devil has prevented an uprising simply by letting us bring our women along." He went to the door. "And now I must go."

After he had left the cell, Tan Hadron turned to me. "Well," he said, "what do you make of it?"

"I believe that Bal Daxus will help us if the chance occurs for him to do so without repercussion. He is a most useful friend to have."

"Yes," responded my companion, "but even he is a prisoner of sorts, for no one can leave Ayathor without Hin Abtol's consent."

"Someone can," I said quietly. He looked inquisitively at me, and I continued: "I still have my flier hidden here."

"I fear it will be of little use to us," he answered. "If ever we made a break for it, we'd have to swim through more than a haad of treacherous sea, and long before we reached the island upon which the flier resides we'd have fallen prey to the targaths or the bullets of Hin Abtol's officers."

"We'll worry about that when we come to it," I said. "The main thing is that the flier is there, and should we manage to extricate ourselves from this dungeon it affords us our sole means of returning to Helium."

"Are you sure that you can find your way to the island?" asked Tan Hadron. "There are no landmarks to direct us."

"I believe so," I said, trying my best to recall its exact location. "At least I can come close. How many islands are there on the Sea of Ayathor?"

"Hundreds," he replied. "Many are only a few ads in diameter, but there are a few almost as large as the one we're on."

"Are any of them populated?" I asked.

"Of that I have no knowledge, but before I was chained here I could sometimes hear weird moaning noises coming from across the sea."

"Might have been the wind," I suggested.

He shook his head. "There is no wind in Ayathor."

"Maybe it was an air current from the shaft," I said.

"Perhaps," he replied dubiously, "but there is a legend in Ayathor about another island at the far end of the sea. It is called the Island of the Dead."

"What is known of it?" I asked.

"Very little," he admitted, "although the Okarian prisoners cringe at the very mention of the name."

"It sounds rather like a burial ground," I said, and then fell silent, my thoughts turning, as they always did, to Dejah Thoris. She must have given me up for dead by now, and the thought of her anguish nearly drove me to distraction. Carthoris, Kantos Kan, Hor Vastus, and all my other officers were probably conducting a worldwide search for me at this very moment, a search that would prove no more successful than the search for Tan Hadron. In fact, my son's flier might even now be passing within twenty haads of the Shaft of Ayathor on its hopeless and futile mission. With such depressing thoughts racing through my mind, I fell into a restless sleep.

I was awakened by the sound of our heavy door swinging open. I sat up quickly, and an instant later Bal Daxus entered, looking very distraught.

"Kaor," I said, in the traditional form of Barsoomian greeting.

"Kaor, John Carter," he said, and hastily closed the door, remaining motionless until he heard the lock snap into place.

"You seem upset," I said. "Is something wrong?"

"Very," he answered. "All my life I have served that calot, Hin Abtol. I have fought unjust wars for him, I have chained the Warlord of Barsoom in his filthy dungeons, I have given up the surface of my planet to live in this sunless hole. All this I did willingly, but now . . ." He stepped, trembling with fury.

"What has happened, Bal Daxus?" I exclaimed.

"Hin Abtol saw Lirai! He demanded that she become his wife—he has nine already—and she refused, saying that she was betrothed. He then imprisoned her in the Tower of Apts and refuses to release her until she reveals the name of the man to whom she is betrothed so that he may slay me and thus clear the path for his marriage."

"Has Lirai revealed your name yet?" asked Tan Hadron.

"No, but it is only a matter of time until Hin Abtol's patience and temper wear thin and he resorts to torture. It is not for myself that I fear, but for Lirai. Issus! To think of her in the hands of that calot! Or at the mercy of Talon Gar!"

"Talon Gar?"

"The Jeddak's loyal servant," he said with a bitter smile. "The great Hin Abtol would never stoop to torturing someone himself; it upsets his digestion."

"I wish there was something we could do to help, Bal Daxus," I said, laying my hand on his shoulder.

"There is," he replied. "That is why I have come. If I release you and Tan Hadron, will you aid me in effecting Lirai's rescue and give us safe entry into Helium should our attempt to escape prove successful?"

"You have my solemn word," I assured him.

"I have the key to your shackles with me," he said, and with that he withdrew the key and knelt down, working on my chains,

At that instant the lock turned, the door opened, and Talon Gar, followed by a detail of warriors, entered the cell.

⊹⇒ VI ⇒⊹
Hin Abtol

"What have we here, Bal Daxus?" demanded Talon Gar.

"I was checking the prisoner's chains," he answered blandly.

Talon Gar stared coldly at the three of us for a few seconds, though it seemed like an eternity. Then he shrugged and ordered one of his men to unchain me.

"The great Hin Abtol," he said, "desires to have an audience with John Carter."

"And I?" asked Tan Hadron of Hastor.

"You, slave," he snapped, "have too long led a life of ease. Tomorrow you return to the Games!"

If he was expecting a show of fear from Tan Hadron, he must have been greatly disappointed, for the Heliumite smiled and said, "I am well pleased. Perhaps I may even cross swords in the arena with Talon Gar, so that his countrymen may see the sadistic monster from whom they cower receive his just deserts."

Turning almost white with rage, Talon Gar, his face contorted in a maniacal grin, kicked Tan Hadron in the groin. Tan Hadron dropped to the floor, but not a murmur of pain escaped his noble lips.

Bal Daxus reached for the hilt of his sword, but I held his arm fast. "Later," I whispered. "He will be avenged, but now is not the time. Think of Lirai." Reluctantly he relaxed his muscles and walked to Tan Hadron's side.

"I should not display such sympathy toward a slave were I you," said Talon Gar, his dark eyes glowing like hot coals.

"A slave is property," replied Bal Daxus. "It must be kept in good condition."

Talon Gar spat on the floor and then, grasping me roughly by the shoulder, led me out of the cell and down the corridor. We took a branch to the left and soon arrived at a massive, delicately carved portal. Talon Gar had taken the precaution of binding my hands behind me, and it was in this condition that I was ushered into the Throne Room of Hin Abtol, Jeddak of Ayathor.

My attention was immediately drawn to the great, diamond-encrusted throne. At the very apex of the golden structure was a large diadem of a color unknown to earthly eyes, and hence a description of it would be useless. Suffice it to say that it was beautiful in the extreme.

However, I had little eye for the beauty of my surroundings, and I looked about the room for Hin Abtol. He wasn't present yet, but almost two hundred soldiers stood in formation along the walls, all of them watching me intently. I noticed that Bal Daxus was among them. Evidently he had followed us from the Pits.

Then the plush red curtains behind the throne parted and Hin Abtol stepped forth regally and seated himself. As I surveyed his face, I could see all the defeat and hatred of the past three years written large upon it.

"Calot!" he hissed, glaring at me. "For years you have persecuted me, warred with me, hindered my glorious plans! Death is far too good for you!"

"If the Jeddak of Ayathor would be so kind as to give me a sword and engage me in combat," I replied, looking him squarely in the eye, "he might thus inflict endless pain and suffering upon me before mercifully sending me to join my ancestors."

A look of sheer terror at the prospect of dueling with me crossed his evil face for a moment, and I observed half-concealed smiles of pleasure on many of the warriors' countenances.

"Insolent calot!" he shrieked. "You shall learn to show respect for the Jeddak of Ayathor!"

"I have a calot in Helium who merits more respect than you, and furthermore, he is far more handsome."

"Silence!" he roared. "John Carter, you have defiled my name for the last time! You shall die the vilest, the most horrible of deaths, a death only John Carter could merit!"

I could do naught but smile at this, for I do not fear death, and it appeared that Hin Abtol was trying to frighten me into the grave.

"So the Warlord finds his fate humorous?" he demanded.

"Not my fate, Hin Abtol," I said calmly, "but my executioner." I paused, and then added: "You are going to do it yourself, aren't you? You wouldn't allow such a feeble-minded madman as Talon Gar to have all the pleasure?"

"Someone bind the prisoner's mouth, that he may no longer debase your Jeddak," commanded Hin Abtol.

Bal Daxus walked over and placed a leather thong about my lips. Before he drew it tight, I whispered, "I don't know what's in store for me, but if you don't hear from me soon, release Tan Hadron and Lirai and escape this place without me."

"I shall never desert you while you live, John Carter," he replied in a low voice, and tightened the gag.

"John Carter," said Hin Abtol, who had recovered his composure, "when last you foiled me I swore that should you ever again fall into my hands you would receive a punishment worthy of your ignominious offense to my person." He was speaking slowly now, enjoying every sinister word. "I have a room waiting for you, John Carter. It has been waiting more than two years for one man, the so-called warlord of Barsoom. You have been a disgrace to your title; Hin Abtol shall teach the people of Helium what it means to be a Warlord. Guards, take him to the Chamber of Madness!"

My last memory of the Throne Room of Ayathor was the sudden swishing sound of a shortsword. Too late I tried to duck, and as the flat of Talon Gar's blade struck the back of my head, I sank to the floor in a senseless heap.

⊱ VII ⊰
The Chamber of Madness

I awoke to a dull throbbing at the base of my skull. Gingerly I put my hand to it; the blood wasn't dry yet, so I evidently had not been unconscious very long.

Beside me was my beloved longsword, a fact which caused me no little amazement. Why had Hin Abtol left it with me, I who was acclaimed far and wide to be the greatest swordsman who ever breathed the thin air of this dying planet? Puzzled as I was, I lost no time in replacing the weapon in its scabbard, which hung at my side.

Looking around, I found myself to be in a circular room. There were a dozen doors spaced evenly about it, each with the carvings typical of the yellow race which had founded the city. The top of the room faded into darkness and shadows some thirty feet above the floor, and there were a few beams of sorapus wood running across the room at a height of about twenty feet.

The room was devoid of furniture, and except for a small circle which was painted in the very center of the floor, there were no decorations save for the smooth and delicately-carved doors.

I systematically tried each door and was not surprised to find that they were all bolted securely from the outside. I then tested every inch of the walls and the floor and ascertained that there were no weak stones or any other flaw which might be the means to escape and freedom.

So this was the much-heralded Chamber of Madness! It was almost a disappointment after the buildup Hin Abtol had given it. Evidently I was to be left alone here to die of hunger and thirst. I smiled as I thought of how infinitely more pleasant this room was than the Pits. Here, at least, I had freedom of movement and had no doubts that, armed as I was with my longsword, I would emerge victorious from any threat to my life which arose.

But nothing arose. It seemed to me that I had been in the room for eons, for I had not seen a single sign of life or movement since I regained consciousness. I hacked at one of the doors with my sword for hours, but to no avail. The doors seem to be petrified, and my efforts succeeded only in removing a few splinters.

Having nothing better to do, I lay down on the floor, hoping that a little sleep would freshen my senses and also my morale, for although the room was not what I had been led to expect, it was still sufficient to keep me entrapped until I should eventually expire from lack of food.

The moment I laid my head upon the floor, a blinding light flashed across my eyes. It was immediately extinguished as I jumped up and drew my sword, and though I again searched every inch of the room, I could find no trace of the light's location.

This happened a number of times. Every time I was about to drift off to sleep that powerful beam of light hit my eyes regardless of the direction I was facing, and always it was gone before I could overcome my temporary blindness.

Finally, in desperation, I took a leather thong from my harness and bound it around my eyes. There was no light this time, but instead an amplified sound of metal grating against metal. It was infuriating. Every time I attempted to sleep, I was brought back to my senses. Seeing at last the utter hopelessness of trying to stave off the light and the noise, I went back to the door and once more began chopping away at it with my sword.

I had been working on the door for what must have been an hour or so when I began sweating profusely. I sat down to relax and cool off a bit, making a mental note not to overtax my strength in the future, as I knew not when I'd need every ounce of it to escape. However, after I had been sitting for a while, I became still warmer.

It was then that I realized that the temperature of the room had increased greatly, and it shortly became so hot that I was forced to shed my harness. My throat was dry and parched and cried out for water, and even as I was wondering how I might lessen my thirst, my eyes fell upon a small bowl of clear liquid which was sitting on the floor directly across from the door I had been working on. Evidently one of my tormentors had quickly opened the door and placed the bowl there while my back was turned.

I walked over to it, and lifted the liquid to my nose. There was no odor, and the container was refreshingly cool. Without further hesitation, I took a long swallow.

Immediately my throat felt as if it were on fire, and I began choking. The liquid tasted something like vinegar, and as I tried to ease my discomfort I heard a hollow laugh ring out.

When I had recovered, I put my fingers in the bowl, the remaining fluid didn't burn or smart, and, as the room was becoming increasingly hotter, I gratefully poured the cool liquid over my body.

Then, of a sudden, the room began to cool with surprising

swiftness. I guessed what was coming and slipped back into my harness. Sure enough, I was able to see my breath in another few minutes, and I huddled my shivering body close to the wall.

This changing of temperatures was kept up for many cycles before the room finally went back to normal. I collapsed on the floor, my strength sapped by the varying conditions my body had been forced to adapt to. Then the light and the grating noise were brought back into play, and, wearily, I walked to a wall and leaned against it, hoping the noise would be lessened if I remained against the side of the room.

I felt my head nodding as I began to fall asleep once more, and, deciding that the noise would, in the long run, prove the lesser of the two evils, I once again strapped the leather thong about my eyes.

This time nothing happened, and I had just drifted off to a sleep of nervous exhaustion when a thin voice spoke out.

"Unbind your eyes, John Carter," it bade me. "You shall not be blinded."

Mad with rage and frustration at being awakened, I untied the strap and found myself facing a huge banth. It was standing not ten feet away, and as its eyes met mine it roared horribly and leapt for me.

There was no time to draw my sword; my only chance was to leap across the room with the aid of my powerful Earthly muscles, which I did not a second too soon. The banth bounded after me, but came to a sudden halt when he was almost halfway across the room. I noticed then that he was chained, and that his iron leash ran back through an open doorway. Here was the chance I had hoped for, for once I slew the banth, there was no man on Barsoom who could keep me from that door.

"Well, Hin Abtol," I muttered under my breath, "I have taken your worst, and you have failed. You should have known better than to think a banth could slay me when I am armed."

Eyeing the beast, my hand dropped confidently to the hilt of my sword, but ere I had drawn it from its sheath another banth charged out from the door behind me.

Sidestepping him, I moved to the center of the room. Neither animal could quite reach me there, and as I was sizing up the two to determine which would be the easier to dispatch, a third banth entered, and then a fourth, until finally I was surrounded by a full dozen of them. The chamber was about eighty feet in diameter, and each banth had a range of a foot less than the radius. In other words, I had barely enough room to turn around while keeping out of their reach.

Looking down at the floor, I noticed that I was standing within the small, painted circle, and I now realized its purpose. It was two feet across, and I was safe only within its confines.

I tried to draw my sword, but a taloned paw reached out viciously and left three red stripes on my arm. Now my fears were confirmed: I had not the room to unsheathe my blade.

For many minutes I remained there, trying to figure a way out of my predicament. I was acutely aware of the hot breath being showered upon my body, and of the hideous roars of hunger and frustration.

Looking upward, I saw once again the crossbeams of sorapus wood, but none were directly overhead. In the lesser gravity of Mars I could reach a height of twenty feet, but the prospect of doing so now was a dim one, for in gathering myself for the leap I would surely extend one or both of my arms outside of my circle of survival.

Yet the thought of jumping intrigued me, and I rapidly pored over its possibilities. The one that seemed to have the most likely chance of success I determined forthwith to apply. Pausing only to place my feet at the absolute center of the circle, I crouched and sprang straight upward. At the top of my leap, which was about twelve feet, I withdrew my sword and, extending my arms over my head, I managed to land within the sphere of safety.

I chose one banth who seemed older and slower than the rest and slashed out at his face. Scarcely had my blade touched him than his neighbor reached out a clawed foot and tore at my arm. It was with great difficulty that I managed to retain my grip on the sword's hilt, so severe was the pain, but manage I did and was quickly out of reach.

So Hin Abtol had figured on everything, even on my succeeding in drawing my sword, and still I was trapped! Nonetheless, I would never admit defeat at the hands of that tyrant, and I soon saw that if I couldn't kill the banths, I could at least make them back away and give me a little more breathing room. I had given up all hope of reaching a doorway, and my aim now was to jump to the relative safety of one of the crossbeams.

Methodically, keeping my arm close to my body and guiding my sword only with my wrist, I began pricking out the beasts' eyes. The plan was far more easily accomplished than I had anticipated, for despite their pain they still strained at their chains. I had blinded nine of them and was working on the tenth when I thought I heard an exclamation of surprise from without the doors.

I worked faster now, excited by the prospect of reaching the beams. Only one banth remained, and I soon put an end to his vision.

Now I had but to drive them back and leap upward. I felt certain that once I reached the safety of the shadows above me, I could discover where the light and noise came from and possibly find some means of escape.

Yelling and whistling, I herded three of the banths into a group. This gave me an extra two feet at one edge of the circle, and I quickly sized up the distance to the nearest beam.

Just then a mocking voice rang out.

"So the Warlord prefers to keep his enemies in darkness, does he? We must by all means oblige him."

Then that unbearable light struck my eyes once more, and, blinded, I stumbled out of the confines of the circle.

⊷ VIII ⊷
The Secret Passage

As I tried to return to the circle, my eyes burning, I waited for the fangs which must momentarily sink into my flesh to strike. None of the banths attacked me, however, and when I regained my vision I saw that the room was empty, the banths evidently having been pulled back behind the doors.

"John Carter!" said the voice. "How do you like our little room?"

"I feel that it justly compliments the courage of Hin Abtol," I replied. "What small intelligence he possesses could only be turned toward such projects as this."

I was hoping to enrage the possessor of the voice enough to keep him talking until I could spot exactly where the voice was coming from. I could easily have jumped to the beams now, but as I was not in immediate danger, there was nothing to be gained from such a move until I could formulate some further plan of action once I had achieved that goal.

"You should speak more kindly of the Jeddak, John Carter, lest he prolong your agony further than he had planned."

"I still live," I replied, "and I shall live to see the death of Hin Abtol."

"We shall see," said the voice, and then all was silent.

I went through another ordeal of the lights and noise, and the extremes of temperature. I estimated that I had not eaten or slept for at least two days, and possibly as many as four.

It was fiendish. Never for an instant was I allowed to achieve bodily comfort, nor was my torment enough to kill me. I felt my hold upon my mind slipping as I went through the perpetual motions of binding and unbinding my eyes, shivering and sweltering, starving and thirsting.

When it seemed that I had reached my physical limit, the room would return to normal until I had regained, not my strength, but my will power. Then I would be forced into the cycles again. The chamber was becoming more and more surely my burial ground, for I no longer thought of escape but only of survival, and then not even that. I ceased to think at all, but merely reacted to my various stimuli, much as an amoeba would do.

I could barely stand up, and my motions were sluggish and ponderous. I fell to jabbering like the idiot I was fast becoming, and always that light, that noise, would drive me about the room.

I realized that I would soon lose hold of my sanity forever and decided to try one last resort. Pretending to go completely berserk (and in truth I was not far from that point), I ranted and raged, screaming curses and banging against the walls. I continued this for as long as I thought it would take to make a convincing display of madness, and then flung myself to the floor and remained motionless.

The light came on then, but I had anticipated this and had fallen with my face buried in my hands. The grating noise came next; I wanted to scream and curse in earnest this time, but I realized that if I did so my fate was irrevocably sealed, and with the greatest of efforts, I remained still. They tried the heat and the cold then, but I had become so accustomed to them that I found it easy to keep my pose.

Then, for what seemed an interminably long time, they made no further attempts to persecute me. I was hoping that they would assume I was dead and carry me out of the room, and once outside I intended to make a break for freedom.

At last I heard a door open, and awaited the sound of metal accoutrements clanking together, but none was forthcoming. Instead, a strange shuffling sound came to my ears.

I made no move until I felt a heavy hand grab my arm, and, opening my eyes slightly, I was greeted by a most horrible sight. I knew at once that I was looking at a targath, for those protruding fangs and that eyeless head could belong only to the creature Tan Hadron had described to me.

I wrenched myself free and backed off from the targath. His movements brought to mind the picture of a giant sloth, but in appearance he was unique. No words can adequately describe that unseeing face, those great patches of long, gray hair, the sheer brute power of his nine-foot frame.

He snarled and lunged at me, but I was too fast for him. Sidestepping quickly, I grabbed one of his massive arms and twisted with all the strength that remained in my weakened body. He spun through the air and landed on his back with a resounding thud.

My sword was out now, and the fighting smile that has ever been my trademark spread across my face. If I was to die, at least it would be in mortal combat with a tangible foe.

He was soon on his feet again, but as he rushed me I jumped to one side and severed one of his boneless hands. With a roar of rage and pain he wheeled and pressed on his attack, but it was only a matter of time now, for he was fighting with the Warlord of Barsoom, not with the pitiful creature who had so recently been teetering on the brink of madness.

I put a deep gash in the targath's breast as he turned to face me, and an instant later his head rolled to the floor.

A quick glance around the room told me that all the doors were locked again, and, without hesitation, I jumped upward to a crossbeam. My act had so surprised my captors that they had turned the light onto the floor of the room before they realized I wasn't there, and for the first time I was able to determine its location. It was set into the wall some fifteen feet above the stone floor in such a way as to be invisible from the ground. As I watched its effect, I learned why I could never escape its rays, turn as I might: the ornamentation on the doors was so highly polished as to act as reflectors, and the blinding light, upon hitting the doors, shot off in all directions.

All this, which has taken so long to relate, happened very rapidly. It couldn't have been more than twenty seconds from the time the targath grabbed me until I discovered the secret of the light. I was now in complete possession of my senses, and knew that I must act with haste if my recent efforts were to avail me at all. To remain on the beam was hopeless; to return to the floor even less than hopeless. I had but one alternative: I must go up.

The sorapus beams were attached to a smooth section of the wall, and I could discern no possible handholds there. Looking above me, I could see naught but shadowy shapes, but it were far better to fall to my death than to remain a prisoner in the Chamber of Madness.

My decision made, I leapt as high as I could. My hand brushed against something hard at the apex of my leap, and I instantly grabbed a firm hold of it. Pulling myself up, I found myself to be on another beam, but this one was broad and thick, unlike the one I had just quit.

As I stood up I was startled to feel a draft of cool air blowing across my face. I walked quickly in the direction from which it had come, and soon came into contact with a panel which gave way when I threw my weight against it. On the other side of the panel was a dimly lit corridor, and, pausing only to replace the panel as best I could, I broke into a run, my footsteps echoing down the winding passage.

I turned into different corridors whenever possible, and after a while I suddenly came to one which had such an accumulation of dust on the floor that I was sure no one had traversed it for many years.

Unlike most of the passages I had seen, this one had no branches, although I passed a multitude of doors. I felt certain that my tormentors would still be trying to find me in the gloomy rafters of the Chamber of Madness, and that it would be some time before they discovered how I had escaped. That, plus the fact that the corridor I was in would probably be among the last to be searched, gave me a feeling of comparative safety.

I had traveled for another half mile before I decided to examine one of the rooms which faced the corridor. Choosing one at random,

I opened the door and entered a long-deserted storeroom. I closed and latched the door behind me and surveyed my surroundings.

There was a finely carved ersite table, a chair of skeel (a Barsoomian hardwood), and several bundles of silks and furs.

A sudden sound from a darkened corner of the room brought me to attention, and I was soon confronting an ulsio. I made short work of the deadly rodent, and then tried to determine how he had made his way into the place. The answer was soon apparent. There was another door on the opposite side of the room, leading into another corridor, and it was partially open.

Crossing the room, I looked into the new passageway. Like the one I had just left, it was dusty and deserted, and was illuminated only by an occasional radium torch, that remarkable invention which can provide light for indefinite periods of time. This door I also locked, and then, turning to the dead ulsio, I neatly skinned it with my sword and cut off its haunches, which I proceeded to eat with relish. I know the thought is repulsive, but if you have never suffered from hunger do not judge me too harshly.

Having eaten, I lay down upon a pile of furs and promptly fell into a long, deep sleep. It was risky, sleeping while an entire city was searching for me, but I was in no condition to proceed.

I must have slept almost an entire day, for I felt as good as ever when I awoke. My arm was still stiff and a bit sore from the banth's talons, but except for that I seemed to have recovered from my ordeal,

I had no knowledge as to where I was, and so, opening the door through which I had entered, I proceeded once more down the long corridor. Far ahead I could hear indistinct noises, but whether they were Hin Abtol's warriors or the ulsios which haunted the catacombs of Ayathor I knew not.

Then, suddenly, the corridor turned abruptly, and I found myself face-to-face with Bal Daxus.

"John Carter!" he exclaimed. "I had given you up for dead, and was on my way to rescue Lirai myself."

"What of Tan Hadron?" I asked.

"Talon Gar became suspicious of me and doubled Tan Hadron's guard. It was impossible to release him."

"You say this corridor leads to Lirai?"

"Yes," he answered. "I came across the maps of Ayathor a short time ago. It seems that the Tower of the Apts, in which Lirai is imprisoned, was once in antiquity the private chamber of a long-dead Jeddak. Fearing insurrection, he had a secret corridor built as a means of escape. Hin Abtol changed the room into a prison, never guessing the secret it held,"

"If we accomplish Lirai's escape," I began, "and I see no reason why we should fail, I must then return to the Pits and try to release Tan Hadron. Will you give me the directions?"

He looked hurt. "Directions? I will lead you there myself!"

"Bal Daxus, you have done enough. There is no need to further endanger Lirai and yourself on our behalf."

For an answer he unbuckled his sword and threw it at my feet. In Earthly terms, this act is the equivalent of his pledging to me his sword, his life, his soul, his honor, and his obedience until death and beyond. It is an oath of allegiance, and from that day on, were I right or wrong, my word would be his only truth. It was a noble and touching gesture, and in accordance with Barsoomian custom, I placed the hilt of the sword to my lips and returned it to him. "And now," I said, "to the task at hand."

"To the death?" It was not intended as a question.

"To the death," I replied, and we advanced grimly along the narrow corridor.

⊹⇒ IX ⇐⊹
Reunion and Pursuit

Far ahead the passage curved again, and Bal Daxus drew to a halt.

"It is here," he said, "that we may begin to run into difficulties. The Tower of the Apts is not far from here, and if anyone else knows of this secret corridor, there will be guards posted."

"That suits me fine," I answered, for after the Chamber of Madness I was ready to wreak my vengeance upon the whole of Ayathor, and there was no better way to begin than by stealing Hin Abtol's newest object of lust and killing a few of his men into the bargain. I drew my sword.

"You do not understand, John Carter," said Bal Daxus. "After we come to the turn in the corridor, it is a straight fifty ads to the door of the Tower."

An ad is about 9.75 Earth feet. This meant that we'd be sitting ducks for the guards, and I had no doubt that they wouldn't hesitate to use their radium pistols on us long before we could close with them.

Slowly and silently we made our way to the turn. Then, cautiously, I looked around the corner and, sure enough, there were four guards stationed by the door.

"What are we to do?" asked Bal Daxus.

"Has Lirai told Hin Abtol that you are her betrothed yet?" I asked.

"No," he answered. "Not to my knowledge."

"Good! Then run out into their vision and tell them that you've seen me in one of the rooms. Since you are still in Hin Abtol's favor, they won't suspect a trick, and if you follow them to the turn, we'll have them trapped between us."

"An excellent idea," he agreed and promptly ran off toward Lirai's cell shouting, "The Warlord! I've found the Warlord!"

The four men immediately ran to meet him. "Where is he?" demanded the one who appeared to be their leader.

Bal Daxus pointed in my direction, and I quickly drew back out of sight. "Go ahead," he said. "I am weary from my efforts and will bring up the rear."

The warriors asked no questions, but hastened toward me. When the sound of their footsteps told me that they were nearing the corner, I stepped out into the middle of the corridor.

"Here he is!" cried the leader, and with that they fell upon me furiously. I stepped back for a moment before this onslaught, but even as I retreated, my blade drank deep of the lifeblood of the nearest of my opponents. He had scarcely fallen ere Bal Daxus was upon them from behind, hewing and slashing before they knew he was there. Soon only one remained, and, sidestepping a wicked thrust, I ran him through. I then proceeded to transfer his shortsword, dagger and radium pistol to my harness.

"Let us hasten," I said, "for we have no idea when their replacements may arrive."

In a matter of minutes we had forced open the door, and shortly thereafter Bal Daxus was holding a beautiful young girl in his arms. This, I knew, must be Lirai.

It was a tender and touching scene, but I had to urge them out, as we were still in immediate danger there. As we left, I closed the door as best I could, hoping that that would afford us another minute of safety from pursuit.

"Now what?" asked Bal Daxus.

"There is a deserted room in which I rested not too long ago," I replied. "Lirai will be safe there while we try to rescue Tan Hadron of Hastor."

This agreed upon, I stopped by another corpse long enough to remove a radium pistol. This I handed to Lirai.

"I don't believe anyone will find you before we return," I told her, "but in case they should, this will offer you ample protection."

She took it and then lifted a dagger from the corpse's harness. Bal Daxus looked questioningly at her, and she met his gaze with a brave expression on her lovely face. "Should you not return," she said.

We soon reached the room which contained the ulsio I had slain. Lirai saw the creature lying on the floor, but never hesitated. I waited in the corridor while Bal Daxus bade her good-bye, and then, following him, I set off for the Pits.

"Once there," I asked him, "how will we free Hadron?" I had been living from one instant to the next, and it now occurred to me that reaching the Pits was just the first step: now we had to figure out how to get into Tan Hadron's cell and unchain him.

"You forget," said Bal Daxus, "that I am Dwar of the Third Utan. I have access to the Pits, and serve guard duty there daily."

"How will you explain my presence away?" I asked.

"If you have any red pigment left, we can go back and rob one of the men we just killed of his harness; then you could easily pass for one of my warriors."

I shook my head, explaining that the pigment was still aboard my flier.

"I must admit that I am now at a loss," he said.

Then a plan struck my mind, and I immediately proposed it to him.

"How is time measured here?" I asked. "I remember you said that you served guard duty 'daily.'"

"There is a large clock in the Throne Room."

"And the guards have no way of knowing the time until they are relieved?"

He gave me a smile of comprehension. "Of course!" he exclaimed. "I could relieve the dwar on duty and never be challenged."

"Once you are in charge," I continued, "it should be an easy matter to unlock Tan Hadron. Should anyone ask you, reply that you are taking him to the Games."

"An excellent plan!" he exclaimed. "So simple, and yet that simplicity is the beauty of it! Come, and I will show you where you may wait until we return."

He led me to a point where the corridor came to its last fork before reaching the Pits.

"In this direction," he said, "lie half a million frozen warriors. Unless we are attacked and have immediate need of them, you will be safe here, for only one man is needed to guard Hin Abtol's frozen army. Should anyone chance upon this corridor before I return, I think you will know what to do."

Without another word, I slipped into the dark passageway while Bal Daxus continued along the main corridor. So this was the location of Hin Abtol's army! I fixed it in my mind, for it might soon prove very useful indeed.

I wondered how our ruse would fare, nor did I have long to wait for my answer, for soon Bal Daxus returned, and at his side was Tan Hadron of Hastor.

"It went very smoothly," said Bal Daxus. "but we have no time to lose. The dwar I replaced will discover our plot shortly, and we had best put as much distance as possible between the Pits and ourselves."

We hastened to Lirai's room and were dismayed to discover that she was gone. The pistol and dagger were on the floor, and the room showed signs of a struggle.

"The other door is open!" cried Bal Daxus, and raced into the adjoining corridor.

"Finding her will be child's play," I said, as Tan Hadron and I followed him out of the room.

"What do you mean?" he asked.

"Observe the floor of the corridor," I said. "There are two sets of prints in the dust, one much larger than the other. Some man evidently followed our own prints in the other corridor, entered the room, and abducted Lirai."

The dank, dust-filled corridor was unfamiliar to Bal Daxus, and, as it became lighter, we slowed our pace and proceeded with more care. There were no forks or branches, and we had no trouble following the trail Lirai and her abductor had left. Then the corridor took a sudden dip, and we descended until it seemed certain that we must soon rise again or suffocate from the lack of fresh air. Yet two people before us had followed this path, and we would do it, too. So, never faltering, we hurried onward.

At last we came to a large wooden door, which marked the corridor's end, and, opening it, we found ourselves on the shore of the Sea of Ayathor.

Some half a mile away, lying trussed upon a raft, was Lirai. Her captor was paddling furiously, and I recognized him at once, despite the distance and the darkness; it was Talon Gar.

"Evidently he learned where Lirai was hidden," said Tan Hadron, "and made off with her before Hin Abtol could stop him. Probably no one is yet aware of his absence."

"Where is he going?" I asked. "I believe the shaft lies in the opposite direction."

"It would be useless for him to try and escape through the shaft without a flier," answered Bal Daxus, "and Hin Abtol controls all the fliers. No, John Carter, he is not headed for the shaft."

"What, then, is his destination?" I asked, mystified.

"There is only one place he could land in the direction he is heading: the Island of the Dead."

"What are we to do, then?" asked Tan Hadron. "We cannot follow him without some craft."

We fell to searching the shore, but there were no more rafts. Then a wild idea occurred to me. It seemed absurd, but there was no alternative if we were to save Lirai from that sadistic maniac.

"The door!" I said, "We'll make a raft out of the door!"

They looked skeptical, but fell to work immediately. The door was about twelve feet in height, and better than five feet across. The three of us tore it off its hinges and, hoping against hope, set it in the water.

It floated, and, pausing only long enough to hack off part of the frame to serve as crude paddles, we soon were in full pursuit of Talon Gar, the moaning sounds from the Island of the Dead ringing louder and ever louder in our ears.

X
The Island of the Dead

The sea was still and placid, and only that fact kept our makeshift craft from capsizing; Talon Gar and Lirai were out of sight now, but Bal Daxus directed us accurately along our course, and soon the island loomed large before us.

We saw Talon Gar's raft lying on the shore and landed next to it. Then, walking ashore, we again picked up his trail.

We walked by a group of deserted huts, and I was reminded of an African village, so closely did the layout resemble various native bombas I had seen during my travels on Earth. There was no sign of life, however, and we did not stop to investigate the dwellings.

"Why is this called the Island of the Dead?" I asked Bal Daxus. "I have seen no sign of anything either living or dead."

"I know not, John Carter," he replied. "It is a legend, and for all anyone knows it may be only a legend."

"Look!" said Tan Hadron suddenly.

We all looked in the direction that he indicated, and there, advancing slowly toward us, was a group of small, gnarled, dwarflike men. They wore only ragged loincloths, and none of them was armed. The tallest of them stood less than five feet, and his posture, like that of his fellows, resembled the carriage of an ape. Filthy, toothless, markedly aged, and grinning, they came toward us in a pack.

"Peace!" I said, raising my hand. "We come not as enemies, but in pursuit of two of our own people."

"We know you are not an enemy," said one of the grinning dwarfs. "We have no enemies."

"Have you seen the two people we seek?" I asked.

"Come feast with us in the village of I-Pak, and we shall talk," said another.

Bal Daxus was anxious to continue our pursuit, but I convinced him that we might be able to enlist I-Pak's help if we played our cards right. It was a large island, the Island of the Dead, and we three could spend days searching for our quarry.

The gnarled little men led us hither and thither about rocks and other natural hazards until we came to a larger group of huts: this, then, was the village of I-Pak.

The women ran out to greet us, and I saw that their physical appearances differed but little from the men's. They surrounded us with happy, smiling faces and made us feel genuinely welcome. We were taken to a large clearing in the midst of the huts, and here we sat down amongst our hosts and prepared to eat.

I-Pak, a shriveled little man, approached and officially welcomed us to his land, telling us how honored and privileged he felt by our visit. When we questioned him about Talon Gar and Lirai, he insisted that we quell our hunger and thirst first, and then he would aid us as best he could.

"Have you had any contact with the outside world?" I asked I-Pak during the meal.

"Outside world?" he repeated incredulously. "Why, there is no other world save this one. We float upon an ocean, and the top of the Universe is directly overhead."

I tried to explain to him that Ayathor was merely a hidden and forgotten sea, and that somewhere above him was a brightly lit world many times larger, but he only smiled condescendingly at me.

"Swim as far as you can," he said, "and you will reach the end of the Universe, beyond which you cannot go."

"There is an opening through which you can go to the outer world," I said.

He laughed at that, and I really couldn't blame him. How would *you* feel if a complete stranger told you there was a hole in the sky?

"How do you account for the race of men we belong to?" asked Tan Hadron. "We have only recently discovered your world."

"Nonsense," said I-Pak. "You were placed here by Zar for his amusement."

"Who is Zar?" I asked.

Immediately the group of natives fell silent and stared at me in disbelief! I-Pak looked absolutely shocked.

"Why, Zar is Zar," said the Jed at last, as if speaking to a small child. "How else may one describe him?"

"Is he your god?" asked Tan Hadron of Hastor.

"He is everyone's god," replied I-Pak. "We all exist only in his mind. Even our great treasure exists nowhere but in the infinite mind of Zar."

"Your treasure?" I asked, wondering what kind of treasure could be possessed by these isolated people.

"Yes," said I-Pak. "When you finish with your repast, you may see it."

"How about Lirai and Talon Gar?" demanded Bal Daxus.

"Of course," said I-Pak. "I have not forgotten."

Then the Jed returned to his meal, and Tan Hadron leaned over to me.

"Have you noticed their age?" he asked. "There is not a young one among them."

This was indeed unusual, for on Barsoom the life span is about a thousand years (although few survive the constant warring that long), and the body does not commence to show any signs of age until shortly before death.

"Living in a sunless world," I answered, "their eggs would be unable to hatch. And even the oldest of them evidently has no memory of any home other than this island. They seem amiable enough, though," I added.

"They're a little too friendly, if you ask me," said my companion.

The meal was soon concluded, and I-Pak arose and faced me. "Come," he said, smiling curiously. "You must now see our treasure."

Surrounded by the apelike dwarfs of I-Pak, we followed the old Jed down a winding pathway. We shortly arrived at the base of a gigantic rock, which must have stood nearly three hundred feet high. I-Pak walked directly to a large patch of moss which grew on the rock, carefully brushed it aside, and a rudely carved tunnel was revealed. Through this we went, and I noticed a strange odor filling my nostrils.

When we emerged from the tunnel, we found ourselves in a small crater. Nowhere were the walls less than eighty feet in height, and the moaning noise was almost deafening now.

"There!" said I-Pak, pointing. "What do you think of our treasure?"

We looked in the direction he had indicated, There, in various poses, were lifelike figures of the yellow men of the Okarian race. Some sat astride their thoats, some were engaged in swordplay, and a few were standing at attention.

It was an impressive spectacle, a tableau of unexcelled artistry, and I turned to I-Pak.

"This is an exquisite work of craftsmanship," I said admiringly. "Who is your sculptor?"

"Sculptor?" he repeated. "What is a sculptor?"

"Why, your artist. The man who carved and painted these statues. The fellow is a genius at realism."

"We have no artists among our people," he answered. "Study them more closely."

We stepped forward and examined the figures.

"They're men!" exclaimed Tan Hadron in amazement. "They've been preserved in a waxlike substance."

And indeed they *were* men. I saw now that there was little likelihood that even the most skilled of artists could reproduce so perfectly the detailed structures and coloring of the figures before us.

The warriors of I-Pak were pushing us forward in their enthusiasm to observe their precious "treasure" more closely, and I concluded that they saw it rather infrequently.

"This must have been a religious practice of the founders of Ayathor," I remarked to Tan Hadron, and he nodded in assent.

We walked about the display, always in the midst of the little men, examining the pieces. I was just reading the inscription on the harness of one of the Okarians when Tan Hadron grabbed my arm.

"Look, John Carter!" he exclaimed, and pointed to the figure of a red warrior wearing the insignia of Hin Abtol.

At the same instant, a woman's voice rang out above the moaning noise. "Flee, Bal Daxus!" it cried. "Flee for your life!"

Bal Daxus turned in the direction of the voice. "Lirai!" he shouted, and now we saw her in a wooden cage which was almost hidden within the shadows of the wall.

I tried to run to her, but I discovered that the little men had crowded about me so closely that I couldn't move. Looking around, I saw that Bal Daxus and Tan Hadron were in the same predicament. I was in such tight quarters that I couldn't even draw my sword, and then, at a signal from I-Pak, the three of us were overpowered, disarmed, and bound. Then we were taken to a cage that adjoined Lirai's, and we saw that Talon Gar was enclosed in a similar cage a short distance away.

"What is this?" I demanded. "We are not your enemies!"

"As you were told before," said I-Pak, his hands resting triumphantly on his shriveled hips, "we have no enemies. You are to be sacrificed to Zar, and should consider it a great honor."

"You mean we are to be added to your art gallery?"

"It is not ours, but belongs, as does all else, to Zar. He created it; we merely discovered it long ago. In answer to your question, the girl will be given immortality by becoming a part of our sacred treasure, and her beauty will be admired forever."

"And what of us?" demanded Bal Daxus.

"Zar would not benefit from an inferior sacrifice," said I-Pak. "Only one of you will be so honored. As women are judged by their beauty, so are warriors judged by their fighting ability. Two of you will duel to the death; the victor will face the third, and the victor of that the fourth. The one who emerges victorious from this combat will have proved by virtue of his courage and his skill that he is worthy of Zar."

He signaled one of his men to unlock Talon Gar's cage, and the Panar was dragged out into the open.

"Release the white-skinned one," commanded I-Pak. I was led into the circle his men had formed, and faced Talon Gar, who was eyeing me hatefully.

"You have doubtless wondered what the noise coming to your ears is," I-Pak said presently. "You should have an explanation before your deaths. Far beneath the ground is a foul-smelling liquid which has been boiling ever since our oldest man can remember. The steam escapes through the top of the tunneled rock we passed through, creating the sound you hear. Our people entrap vast amounts of the vapor, and as it cools we add ingredients which will form the final mixture which the victor will be coated with. It sounds painful, I know, but surely the pain is negated by the knowledge of the magnificent honor in store for you."

When he ceased speaking, our bonds were cut and we were given our longswords.

"You may salute each other and commence," said I-Pak, and his dwarfed men leaned forward in keen anticipation.

I complied with his request, and as I did so Talon Gar lunged forward and pricked my wrist. He came at me again, but I parried his blow and drew blood from his cheek.

"You shall regret that, Talon Gar," I said, pricking his other cheek. "It is a shame that you will not live long enough to learn to properly acknowledge your superiors."

I commenced to take Talon Gar to pieces. Always he was the aggressor, and always I would inflict wound after wound upon him while stepping nimbly out of his reach. He was a good swordsman, but he had not mastered the one essential of his art: a cool head. With death staring me in the face, I would never have followed Talon Gar's rushing tactics, but would have retreated and waited for an opening; but the Panar, blood streaming down his body from a hundred cuts and slashes, kept trying to reach me, all the while cursing and grinning like the madman he was. I disarmed him and sent his sword flying some fifty feet away.

"Give him another sword, I-Pak," I said, putting the point of my blade to the ground. "John Carter does not murder defenseless men, no matter how much they may deserve it."

"We have no weapons here," replied the Jed patiently, "for as you have been told repeatedly, we have no enemies. You must wait while he retrieves his sword."

This put an entirely different complexion on our situation; if they had no weapons, they had no means of defense!

I had little time to mull over the possibilities that I-Pak's revelation had presented, for Talon Gar was soon upon me again, attacking with renewed fury. My blade moved with the swiftness of light, weaving a web of steel about me and taking its toll upon Talon Gar's tattered flesh. I wondered why he had not grasped the opportunity to turn on I-Pak's unarmed men, but one look at his face and I knew the answer:

he had the same mad grin I had seen when he had kicked Tan Hadron in the dungeon. He cared nothing for escape; only blood would satisfy him.

As I sidestepped his next thrust, I lopped off one of his ears, yet he seemed as oblivious to pain as a hormad, and, realizing that I could punish him no further, I moved in for the kill. It came quickly, for I bound his blade up when next he lunged and slid my point along it until I had pierced his heart.

I was greeted with cheers and applause from the warriors, and Tan Hadron was led into the circle. He, too, had understood the import behind I-Pak's words, and the instant he was given Talon Gar's sword he turned on the Jed, and I quickly leaped to his aide.

"What!" shrieked I-Pak, infuriated. "You would attack the chosen one of Zar? For this you shall both die!"

"By whose hand, I-Pak?" I demanded. "You have already admitted you have no weapons."

"My warriors will slay you with their bare hands!" he screamed, his eyes burning with a fanatical light. "We are the Chosen People and can do no wrong!"

"Who among you," said Hadron to the stunned warriors, "will be the first to face the sword of John Carter, Prince of Helium and Warlord of Barsoom?"

Not one of them moved, although I-Pak ran among them, alternately demanding and pleading for a hero.

"Zar!" he screamed at last. "Zar, descend from the roof of the Universe and strike down the infidels who threaten your chosen son!"

I grabbed the little Jed and held him firmly.

"Listen to me," I said sharply. "Your men will not attack us, and your god, like most gods, favors the side with the best weapons. If you attempt to keep us here, we will kill anyone who stands in our way. We would go now: What is your answer?"

Sullenly, with the air of a spoiled child, he directed his men to release Lirai and Bal Daxus and escort us back to the village. From there we had no trouble finding our way back to the rafts. We took the one Talon Gar had used and set the door adrift, just in case I-Pak had a change of heart.

"Where to now?" asked Tan Hadron.

"The flier," I said, "and then on to Helium, where I'll gather our forces and lead them against Ayathor."

"It could be a disastrous war, John Carter," said Bal Daxus, "for one ship may guard the bottom of the shaft from which you must emerge and hold off an entire navy indefinitely."

"We could guard the outer end of the shaft," suggested Tan Hadron, "and starve them out."

"No," said Bal Daxus. "The fish are plentiful here. The Panars can thrive for years without leaving Ayathor."

"True," I mused. "We'll have to map out our strategy once we are safely within my palace. At present, getting there is our main concern."

When at last we came to the island where I had hidden the flier, we found that it had been discovered and destroyed. The tanks containing the ray of repulsion were punctured, and the control panel and compass were damaged beyond repair.

Dejected, I looked into the distance and saw the dark outline of the great, yawning mouth of the shaft beckoning to me. So I was to be frustrated in my escape after all! I had lived through the Pits. the Chamber of Madness, and the Island of the Dead, and yet I was no closer to freedom than I had been at any moment since I had arrived in this forgotten world.

I kicked the hull of the ship in disgust, and Tan Hadron laid an understanding hand upon my shoulder. I looked up at him, and though he tried to smile confidently at me, I could see defeat written large across his countenance.

⊹⇌ XI ⇌⊹
The Frozen Army

"What next shall we try?" asked Bal Daxus presently. "We cannot long remain here, for we would soon be spotted by the next flier that comes to or leaves the city."

"If only Carthoris knew of our whereabouts," I said. "If he could but gain the city . . ."

"It would do no good," said Bal Daxus, "for even if he managed to traverse the shaft, he would be met by almost half a million warriors at the city's gates."

It seemed pointless to argue with that, and I fell into silence. Not so Tan Hadron, however.

"Impossible," he said. "I was told by the crew of the *Dusar*, all Panars or men who had been to Pankor, that it takes hours to bring one of the frozen warriors back, and it takes two or three men to hold each of them until their senses return."

"That is no longer so," corrected Bal Daxus. "Hin Abtol believes that the reason he lost so badly to Helium and Gathol was because he formulated his frozen army so slowly. For many months thereafter he and his greatest scientists labored over a new method of revival, and in the end they discovered an entirely new concept, one which has proved effective in small trials. In theory, Hin Abtol can now revive, arm, and mobilize his army in less than a zode."

"Where are they kept?" asked Tan Hadron. "I have seen naught of them since I have been here."

"They are in a single immense chamber," replied Bal Daxus. "It is not far from where John Carter met us after I released you from the Pits."

"Do you know how to revive them?" I demanded.

"Yes," he answered. "I helped install the apparatus."

"Then we shall return to the city at once!" I exclaimed, and hastened toward the raft.

"What for?" asked the Panar. "Surely you don't intend to revive Hin Abtol's army for him!"

"That, Bal Daxus, is precisely what I intend to do," I told him.

"They will fall upon us and kill us!" he said.

"I think not," I replied. "Have some faith in the man at whose feet you placed your sword."

"I shall willingly follow you to my grave," he replied with a smile, "but only if I can't convince you not to lead me there."

"It is the only way by which we may ever overthrow Hin Abtol. Are you with me?"

He nodded.

"And you, Hadron of Hastor?"

"The Warlord should know better than to ask," he replied.

"Lirai," I said, turning to the girl, "I am afraid you must return with us to the city. We shall see to it that you are well-protected."

"Where Bal Daxus leads, I shall follow," she said simply.

We pushed off and approached the city from the rear. When I thought we were comparatively free from detection, I drew near the shoreline, where it was an easy matter to find the doorway we had passed through when we set out for the Island of the Dead.

We carried the raft inside with us and leaned it against a wall. Then, with drawn swords, we advanced up the inclining corridor, Tan Hadron and I in front and Bal Daxus in the rear, thus protecting Lirai from any ulsios that might be lurking in the shadows.

"It appears that no one has yet discovered how we left," remarked Tan Hadron, "for there are no new footprints in the dust."

"That means that only Talon Gar knew of the secret passage," I said, "and with him dead, Lirai should be quite safe in the same room."

We heard voices in the adjoining passage and ceased speaking then. In a few moments we were once again in the room that contained the rotting carcass of the ulsio.

"Lirai," I said, turning to the girl, "from either corridor this room appears the same as any other of the multitude of rooms, but to us it has a greater meaning and will be easy to find. I know that you may have your doubts as to its safety, but are you willing to wait here again?"

She nodded in assent, and, crossing the room, I stepped out into the corridor which led to the Pits, the Throne Room, and, most important, the chamber that held Hin Abtol's frozen army. We cautiously proceeded to the spot where it forked and followed it to a heavy metal portal.

"Halt!" commanded a lone warrior. "Who goes there?"

" 'Tis I, Bal Daxus, Dwar of the Third Utan."

"Bal Daxus!" exclaimed the guard. "The whole palace has been searching for you, traitor!"

With that he hurled himself at us. Tan Hadron was in the vanguard of our trio and quickly engaged him in combat. The guard was good, let there be no denying it, but Tan Hadron of Hastor is superb, and scarcely had they crossed blades ere Hadron was stepping over the dead body of his foe and advancing toward the portal.

"How may we pass?" he asked. "I see no latches."

Bal Daxus approached the metal door and turned to the wall beside it, pushing a neatly concealed button. Slowly the massive panel rose, until there was room for us to step through. We found ourselves on a balcony overlooking row upon row of blocks of ice, and inside each block was a warrior. These warriors represented every race on Barsoom: red men, yellow men, green men, Black Pirates, even an occasional thern and Orovar.

"Half a million souls," commented Tan Hadron, "awaiting their resurrection."

"Once we release them from their icy prisons, what will we do?" asked Bal Daxus. "We'll be caught between them and Hin Abtol's palace warriors."

"I think not," I said. "I plan to enlist their aid."

"I had guessed as much," said Tan Hadron. "How do we revive them, Bal Daxus?"

The Panar led us up a ramp which brought us to a large machine that contained many lights and dials, and promptly began pressing buttons and turning knobs. It made no sense to me, but it was clear that he knew precisely what he was doing.

"Their blocks of ice will soon melt, John Carter," he said at last. "Here is an amplifier through which you may speak to them from this balcony."

I took the microphone and watched the unfolding panorama below me. Here and there the ice had already turned to water, and a fine chemical spray was showered down upon the warriors. This done, their ersite tables began vibrating, and soon the bodies were stirring, life returning to their long-frozen limbs.

It was an awesome sight, seeing those half-million men return to the world of the living, but I had no time to appreciate it. Putting the microphone to my lips, I waited until I thought they could comprehend what had happened to them, and then I spoke.

"Warriors!" I said. "This is John Carter, Warlord of Barsoom. I have just liberated you from your prisons; for this each and every one of you owes me his attention. Some of you are unaware of your surroundings. You are in Ayathor, a sunken world beneath the surface of Pankor. Hin Abtol brought you here when he was defeated in his war with Helium and Gathol. He intends to use you in his mad scheme of world conquest, and only by acceding to his demands can you ever see the sun again."

A loud groan arose from half a million throats.

"There is but one way by which you can avoid the fate Hin Abtol has planned for you," I continued. "Most of you have been taken prisoner by him; those few among you who are Panars owe him no allegiance. I have revived you for a purpose. Should you fail to agree to it, you will once again be encased in ice." I doubted that this could be done, but they had no more knowledge of the new process than I did, and it made the proper impression. "Warriors, give me your pledge that you will aid me in overthrowing Hin Abtol, and if we succeed, you will all be granted your freedom!"

They were silent for a moment, and then one man, whom I recognized to be a long-lost Heliumite, gave a loud yell: "Down with Hin Abtol!"

More and more of them took up the chant until the din was deafening.

"Listen!" I shouted over the roar. "We have no weapons for you. However, Hin Abtol has no more than thirty thousand men at most, and many of them will join our cause. Kill no one unless they resist. You see beside me Tan Hadron of Hastor and Bal Daxus of Pankor; we three will be your leaders. When you are released, you will follow us to the branch in the corridors. From there I shall proceed to the Throne Room, Tan Hadron will go to the Pits to release the other prisoners, and Bal Daxus will lead you to the soldiers' quarters. You are free to follow whomever you choose."

I turned to Bal Daxus and nodded to him to open the portal all the way.

I was soon approaching the Throne Room with almost two hundred thousand men at my heels. Hin Abtol must have heard us from afar, for when I burst into the room I was greeted by a blast of fire from twenty radium rifles.

I dove to a side, but the vanguard of my forces was mowed down like sitting ducks. Hewing my way through a wall of the Jeddak's loyal officers, I drove onward to the throne, where Hin Abtol sat ashen-faced, screaming unheeded commands.

Countless times my blade paused to still a Panar heart forever or quench its thirst in the throat of a new foe. I ceaselessly shouted taunts at my enemies, as is my wont in the heat of battle, and must have accounted for two dozen men before I had time for a quick glance at the door.

To my dismay, I saw that the pile of corpses was so high that none of my men could get past them. The dead were stacked literally from floor to ceiling.

I turned back at the throne: Hin Abtol was gone! My eyes fell on the red curtain behind the throne, and I knew that he could have retreated to no other place in so short a time. There was only one man standing in my way, and I recognized him immediately: it was Rab-zov.

With a single bound I was upon him. He had barely raised his sword to defend himself before his head rolled to the floor and I ran through the curtains.

There was a door, and this I opened and raced through. It led to another part of the catacombs, and far ahead I could see the figure of the cowardly Jeddak as he ran for his life.

✥ XII ✥
Adventure's End

I pursued Hin Abtol with great leaps and bounds that quickly lessened the distance between us. When the tyrant saw that escape was impossible, he drew his sword and turned to face me.

"Let us see," I said, engaging him, "if you are as excellent a swordsman as you told your people you were when you returned from Horz with my stolen flier four years ago, and if you are brave enough to face me when my hands are not bound."

He said nothing, but began fighting like a cornered ulsio. His terror increased his proficiency, and though I touched him a hundred times I could not deliver the fatal blow.

Suddenly there came to our ears a great cheer from the Throne Room.

"Did you hear that, Hin Abtol?" I said. "Your warriors have capitulated to your frozen army. Your empire is lost."

My words struck home, and the arrogant tyrant's mind snapped. He began chattering and gibbering like a lunatic, and tears rolled down his face even as he pressed on with his attack. He was a sorry figure, but I could feel no pity for a man who had destroyed so many innocent lives, and shortly I ran my sword through his putrid heart.

I returned to a scene of triumph and elation in the Throne Room. It was jammed with my men, and they gave me a rousing welcome. Tan Hadron soon appeared, and not long after that Bal Daxus returned. Both had been completely successful in their missions. Bal Daxus was weary and bloodied by a heroic charge that had saved the lives of a thousand of his men.

"Long live John Carter!" cried one of the warriors. "Long live John Carter, Jeddak of Ayathor!"

I raised my hand to still the cheering voices.

"Thank you, my comrades," I said, "but the Jeddak of Ayathor should be one of your countrymen, and, as you may know, Pankor has had no Jeddak since the defeat of Hin Abtol three years ago. It, too, needs a firm and noble ruler. "Warriors!" I continued. "How sounds Bal Daxus, Jeddak of Pankor and Ayathor?"

The men who fought beside him quickly raised their swords, and soon every sword in the room was raised in boisterous approval. With that act the dwar who had chosen his honor ahead of his country became the Jeddak of the latter.

There was a wild victory celebration throughout Ayathor while the fliers were being made ready to transport those who wished to leave for the surface of the planet, and before I departed for Helium with Tan Hadron, I had the pleasure of attending the ceremony which forever united the new Jeddak with Lirai, who we had found greatly worried but quite safe in the room where we had left her.

Our homecoming to Helium was celebrated by a great festival at which Tan Hadron and I were the guests of honor. The entire world had given me up for dead, and the news of my return brought greetings and visits from jeds and jeddaks the world over.

Tars Tarkas, Jeddak of Thark and my greatest friend, was there to greet me, and there were tears of joy in the fierce green warrior's eyes. Carthoris, Thuvan Dihn, Jeddak of Ptarth, Kulan Tith, Jeddak of Kaol, Talu, Xodar, Kantos Kan, Hor Vastus, and all my other comrades of peace and war were present, too, but I fear that I took little notice of them, for I was too busy enjoying the only honor I ever cared for: that of once again putting my arms around my incomparable Dejah Thoris.

⊷⇒ Epilogue ⇐⊶

His narrative ended, John Carter stood up and stretched his powerful frame.

"Did you enjoy my story?" he asked pleasantly.

"Oh, yes!" I exclaimed. "How long were you in Ayathor?"

"Unbelievable as it seemed to me, almost a year. I suppose most of it was spent in the Pits."

"This must have happened many years ago," I said. "What has taken place since then?"

"Many strange intrigues and adventures," he replied. "Adventure and I seem to attract one another."

"Could you tell me some more of your experiences?" I asked.

He looked out the window, across the silent Arizona desert.

"The sun will soon be rising over the hills," he said at last, "and I must be gone."

"Can't you stay a little longer?" I pleaded.

He shook his head. "The woman I love and the planet that gave her to me are beckoning. I must return to them."

"Will you come back someday?" I asked hopefully.

"Perhaps," he half promised, the trace of a smile flickering about his lips. "Perhaps I will."

And with that, he was gone.

⊷⇒ END ⇐⊶

Shoz-Dijiji encompasses the best of two worlds—a white man who was raised as an Apache. Burroughs knew this milieu, and one of us (Mike) thinks The War Chief *is the best of ERB's many novels. Ralph Roberts, publisher, editor, and author of more than 100 books and 4 screenplays, revisits Shoz-Dijiji and his lady love, Wichita Billings.*

—Mike

Apache Lawman

Ralph Roberts

I
Geronimo Is Off the Reservation Again

Shoz-Dijiji, whose name meant "Black Bear" war chief of the *Be-don-ko-he* Apaches, son of Geronimo, fiercest of his fellow savage warriors, known as the dread Apache Devil, once implacable enemy of the white-eyes—the hated *pindah lickoyee*—labored mightily in pushing the errant calf up the side of the arroyo. The young calf had blundered into the depression and found it had not the ability to get out again. At the top of the bank, the mother cow watched anxiously.

With a last heave to its hindquarters, the panicked calf scrambled over the arroyo's lip. Shooed away from danger by the mother cow, the little animal was receiving a welcoming licking from its parent as Shoz-Dijiji pulled himself back to level ground and stood.

Shoz-Dijiji, yet a young man, now looked nothing like the fierce warrior he had been until recently. He wore the garb of a cowboy—faded denim pants with chaps to ward against the thorns, an equally faded checked shirt, an old hat on his straight black hair, above a dark face with high cheekbones. From his belt hung a six-shooter and the hilt of a knife peeked from his right boot, a boot—like its brother to the left—unpolished and well-worn with dulled spurs attached. Even for an 1880s cowboy, he did not appear especially prosperous. For he was not. He had the clothes on his back, his weapons—for a warrior must always have weapons—and little more than that.

A smile of satisfaction came to his face as he watched the reunion of mother and daughter before him while lifting his hat and wiping sweat from his brow. There were small rewards to this new life of his. He had fallen for the white goddess Wichita Billings, his beloved Chita. Feeling that Usen, god of the Apache, had forsaken the Apache and their way of life, he had left them and accepted the offer of Chita to become foreman of the small ranch she inherited from her father.

Because of the slight sound of a horse approaching, Shoz-Dijiji whirled, ready for action. On a horse saddled only with a blanket sat an old Apache, scrawny, tired-looking, in need of a good meal, but dressed only in a single loincloth and headband, and clutching a small sack. Armed with a bow and flint-tipped arrows, he was Go-yat-thlay, called 'Geronimo' by the white-eyes. The old man looked little like the war chief of all the Apaches. He who had led the army of the Great White Father on a futile chase for years over an area of the Southwest the size of Europe. He who had finally concluded Usen, the Apache god, had deserted them and gave up, surrendering to those who could not catch him.

"Hello, Father," Shoz-Dijiji said in their language. "Have you escaped the reservation again?"

The old man shrugged. "Geronimo return soon, must talk to son first." He looked to where Shoz-Dijiji's horse grazed. "You grow careless now that war is over. I could have stolen horse."

Shoz-Dijiji smiled. "And I could have tracked you to Mexico and taken the horse back one dark night."

Geronimo nodded, pleased. "You learned well, war chief of the *Be-don-ko-he*. Geronimo proud. Now, we must talk and I must honor word to return to reservation."

Shoz-Dijiji whistled for his horse, which came promptly. He climbed into the saddle and pointed westward. "I know a hidden spring where we can talk unobserved."

Geronimo grunted. "Me drink from that spring little while ago."

At the spring, secluded in a small canyon, his father watched as Shoz-Dijiji retrieved items from his saddle bags, pulled together some dried mesquite brush, made a small fire, put a small coffee pot of water near it to heat, and threw in a handful of coffee beans. From a cloth, he unwrapped two sandwiches, giving one to Geronimo.

Geronimo lifted one slice of bread and looked at the filling suspiciously. "What is?"

"Refried beans, Father."

Geronimo grunted. "Why not kill cow? Have beef. Beef better than beans."

"Times are hard. The cows are our only chance to make money. They are too few and precious for us to eat."

Geronimo shook his head but wolfed down the sandwich. Shoz-Dijiji watched until he finished, then handed over his own sandwich. It, too, disappeared rapidly. Geronimo accepted a tin cup of the cowboy coffee from the pot and relaxed.

"Shoz-Dijiji is happy with his white woman?"

"Yes," Shoz-Dijiji answered simply. Then, after a moment, added, "It great shock when Geronimo told me I was white, taken as a baby. A greater shock when Geronimo urged me leave the Apache way."

"Usen has turned his back. The Apache way is dead. You must accept your white side and live as one. Shoz-Dijiji must join strengths of both Apache and white-eyes to become as great in his new world as he was in the Apache world."

"And how do I do that, Father?"

The old man shrugged. "Not know. Your problem. Geronimo has spoken." He reached for the small sack that he had brought from his horse. "Now Geronimo give Shoz-Dijiji two things, hidden for years."

A small gold locket was first. Geronimo opened it and passed it over. "Your real father. Locket was around your mother's neck."

Next, Geronimo removed a leatherbound book, a family Bible. "Their book of great magic." Geronimo opened it to the first page and showed where there was a handwritten list. "Important things," he said.

"What are they?" Shoz-Dijiji asked.

Geronimo shrugged. "I cannot read this. You are the white-eyes now." But he smiled and patted Shoz-Dijiji's leg. "Ask your beautiful white woman. Now Geronimo has spoken his last and will go back to reservation."

Geronimo stood and moved toward his horse.

"You will always be my father," Shoz-Dijiji said.

Geronimo paused without turning. "I know, my son. Geronimo knows and is pleased. He is glad he kept Juh from killing you."

The old man then mounted and rode away. Shoz-Dijiji watched until he was out of sight. Then he reverently returned the two gifts to the sack, set aside the coffee pot to cool, put out the fire, and erased the signs that the area had been used. Old habits but good ones, he thought. Down deep, he was still an Apache warrior despite his cowboy hat and the spurs on his boots.

Riding back to the ranch headquarters, Shoz-Dijiji allowed himself a small glimmer of hope. His courtship of the beautiful Wichita, his dear Chita, had slowed. Both waited to see if she could truly love an Indian—worse than just any Indian, an Apache devil, as the white-eyes called them. And he was *the* Apache Devil, now off the war trail forever.

Shoz-Dijiji knew Chita had accepted that she truly loved this Indian warrior. So he had decided to tell her finally and had been trying for the last few days to find a way of revealing his white parentage. Geronimo had given him the perfect way to tell her. He touched the sack holding the family Bible and locket tied to his saddle horn. Now he had proof of being white. Could this make the difference, for him most of all? Or was he lost between these two worlds—that of the Apache and of the whites—and must still find his way to her?

❧ II ❧
Beans For Supper Again

The headquarters of the Billings ranch had little enough to recommend it. Under three bedraggled cottonwood trees was a small ranch house that had not seen paint in many long years of being abraded by sandstorms rolling in off the high desert. A ramshackle barn and attached corral with a few weary-with-life horses, and a seriously Spartan bunkhouse concluded the facilities, other than an outhouse behind the bunkhouse. Smoke was coming from the bunkhouse's tin stovepipe as Shoz-Dijiji—carrying the sack of treasured items given to him by Geronimo—walked over from unsaddling his horse at the barn. He had finished checking the fences, his chore for the day, and it was coming on to evening.

The bunkhouse had only two rooms. The larger had frames for several bunks—only three of which were now used—in an area where additional men had slept in more prosperous times, when Wichita's father had been alive. Shoz-Dijiji slept in one of these, the other two cowboys still at the ranch in the other two.

It was into the second room that he entered—the combination kitchen and dining room, where the rest of the ranch's inhabitants were sitting down to supper. The room had few furnishings. A stove was near one wall, the tin stovepipe disappearing up into the ceiling. Shelves near it held their few supplies—a little salt, some flour, and a few empty bottles and cans from better days. There was not much else except several large bags of beans leaning against the wall beneath the shelves. Beans were the staple of their diet during these times of hardship. Chung's narrow cot stood in one corner—a shelf of his treasured cookbooks above it—and most of the remaining floor space was occupied by the large, rough-built table where they ate. Like the bunkroom built for a larger crew than now worked the Billings ranch, there was lots of extra room.

He solemnly greeted each person in turn—still not sure of how white-eyes interacted, usually being cautiously overly formal. There was his beautiful Wichita Billings, owner of the ranch but who ate with the hands because there was little enough food as it was. She was as strikingly wonderful to look at as when he first saved her life. He gave one of his rare smiles to her, recalling the look on her face when she had first seen a painted, all-but-naked warrior leaping down the steep canyon side toward her.

"Sit down, Shoz-Dijiji," she said, returning his smile. "We are having Italian food tonight. Spaghetti!" She gestured to the remaining empty chair, next to her and saved for him.

Shoz-Dijiji had no idea what she was talking about. All he saw on the stove was the usual pot of beans. Beans were cheap, filling, and a survival food. It was all they had anymore except for a bit of bread now and then, but he knew they were running out of flour, and coffee, and just about anything else you could think of.

Before sitting, he greeted Luke Jensen, a short, young cowpuncher whose life he had saved also. For a bloodthirsty savage, he had certainly saved a lot of people, Shoz-Dijiji reflected. Now he was glad. Luke wore their uniform of faded denim and checked shirt, as did also Luis Mariel, once of Mexico and yet another saved by the savage Apache who was now their fellow cowboy or *vaquero* as Luis insisted they all were. Luis was also short, dark, and sported hair on his upper lip that hung down on each side of his mouth—he called it a *bandito* mustache. Everyone here was shorter than Shoz-Dijiji, he towered over them all. He sat down and looked to the remaining member of the ranch's crew; Chung, the Chinese cook.

Chung was the oldest and smallest of them all, shorter even than Chita. Chung's wrinkled face was always smiling, and the old cook loved jokes. His English was good, and he could actually read, devouring the cookbooks that old Mr. Billings' wife, Chita's mother, had brought to the ranch from the east many years ago. Chung placed a tin plate in front of Shoz-Dijiji, heaped with beans from the pot on the stove. He added a tin cup of black coffee.

Shoz-Dijiji looked at the beans. "You have to help Shoz-Dijiji," he said, a twinkle in his eye. "What is this amazing foreign food you serve?"

Chung straightened himself proudly. "It is *spaghetti*. Italian noodles in a special sauce. My people, of course, invented noodles long before the Italians learned to cook."

Shoz-Dijiji took a bite, savored it, and nodded. Chung could certainly make good beans. "I have not had this type of food before. Thank you."

Wichita cleared her throat, her face serious. "Now that we are all here together, I must again discuss our situation. I had another letter from the bank today. Banker Adams says we must soon pay the loans my father took out. We are almost out of money. No one's buying cows right now." She suddenly looked about ready to cry.

Shoz-Dijiji put his hand on her shoulder in concern. She sniffed and patted his hand, then continued bravely.

"Well, I just wanted to say that I'll do everything possible to keep us going."

The others nodded. Shoz-Dijiji, too, but his face was impassive. Yet, inside, he was sad and a little scared. He vowed to himself that

Chita would not lose her ranch nor his friends their home. No matter what *he* had to do to save them.

Wichita did not finish her supper but went back to the ranch house. Shoz-Dijiji helped Chung and the others clean the dishes. Then he left, picking up the sack he had left by the door.

⊶⇒ III ⇐⊷
My Name Is Andrew

Walking across the ranch house's small porch, Shoz-Dijiji knocked softly on its front door. Wichita opened the door and stood aside for him to enter. He could see that she had been crying. He embraced her and she laid her head on his chest, taking what little comfort she could get.

"Chita," he said quietly. She hugged him tighter.

Theirs was indeed a complicated relationship. They had agreed to wait and see how things worked out. To test how their very different backgrounds meshed. To find if she could love an Apache warrior. He did not worry about that now. While he ached in every bone of his body for her, that did not matter. He would protect her no matter what the cost to him.

Shoz-Dijiji reluctantly released her and held up the small sack. "Shoz-Dijiji needs your help on a very important thing."

She dried her eyes. "Yes, of course," and she led him into the parlor where a lamp—trimmed to preserve precious kerosene—cast a dim light. They sat together on the horsehide settee. Shoz-Dijiji placed the sack on the floor between his feet and looked at her. He could not help smiling at how beautiful she looked in the flickering light.

"Chita," he began, "You know Shoz-Dijiji loves you more than *Klego-na-ay*, the moon. More than the sun. More than . . ." He struggled for more English words.

Wichita smiled softly, placing one hand on his well-muscled arm and patting his sun-bronzed face with the other. "This I know,

Shoz-Dijiji. But thank you for mentioning it again. That message is always welcome, for I love you just as much."

Shoz-Dijiji was almost overcome with emotion but forced himself to continue, now nervous.

"Shoz-Dijiji know we have waited to see if Chita could love Apache warrior."

Chita patted his face again. "*You* have waited. I already am sure."

Shoz-Dijiji swallowed. "Yes . . . Moons ago I promised Chita, when I accepted the offer to become her foreman, that I had a surprise for her."

"Gifts are not necessary," she answered.

"This one is, Chita. For me to give."

Shoz-Dijiji placed the sack on the settee between them and first withdrew the locket.

"Geronimo come to Shoz-Dijiji today. Bring him these things."

Wichita gasped.

Shoz-Dijiji grinned. "Not worry. Old man go back to reservation. He done with war. Geronimo say so."

He carefully opened the locket and gave it to her. "My real father."

Wichita turned it in the sparse light to see the face there better. "A white man? What's his name?"

"Not know," he said and took the family Bible out of the sack. "Maybeso in here? Reading you teach me not good enough for this yet." He showed her the page with writing.

Wichita positioned the Bible and read the list of family births and deaths laboriously scrawled with a shaky hand in black ink.

"Yes," she said, a little breathlessly from the impact. "Your father's name was Jerry MacDuff. Your mother's, Annie. And . . ." She paused and looked him in the eyes. "You are Andrew Seamus MacDuff."

Shoz-Dijiji breathed deep and savored the name, committing it to memory. "Andrew Seamus MacDuff," he repeated.

"Your mother added a note. They called you Andy," she said.

Shoz-Dijiji scowled, then smiled. "That secret name. You call me Andy when we alone. Other people must call me Andrew. It more dignified."

Wichita smiled in pleasure. "Glad to meet you, Andrew."

He grabbed her hand and shook. "The pleasure mine."

Andrew shook his head in wonderment. "Now Andrew must learn to think of himself as Andrew."

"And maybe say 'I' instead of talking in the third person," she said, playfully punching his shoulder. "Andy."

He smiled. "You keep Bible and locket here for me, please Chita." He paused, then asked, "You love Andy as much as Shoz-Dijiji?"

"Hard to say," Wichita answered. "I've only just met him, but he seems very nice. Reminds me of a certain Apache warrior."

They grinned at each other.

She put the items on a side table, they kissed good night, and he returned to the bunkhouse.

The next evening, all chores completed, they sat eating beans once more. Just like for breakfast and lunch.

"This French food tonight," Chung said. "Wee, wee."

Luis pointed out the back window to the outhouse. "Go there, if you must, *amigo*."

Wichita laughed. "No, I believe Chung is speaking French. And what is the name of this delicious dish, Chung?"

Chung screwed up his wrinkled face even more, trying to recall. "Soufflé," he said. "It is bean soufflé. Served in all the best restaurants all over France. I season mine with secret spices. Salt and pepper."

"Might I have some more please?" Luke asked, holding up his plate.

As more beans were ladled out, Wichita pulled a handwritten list and a small amount of money from her pocket. "Luke, take the wagon tomorrow and go into Sunrise. Get salt, sugar, a big bag of beans. That's the last of my money, but we have to have the supplies."

Luke nodded around a mouthful of beans and reached over the table to accept the list and money.

Andrew tapped his spoon on the table. "I have announcement." He waited for them to look at him expectantly. "I now have white name. Call me Andrew."

They smiled at him while Chita explained about him being stolen as a baby and raised by the Apaches.

Luke offered his hand. "Welcome back, Andy."

Shoz-Dijiji, now Andrew, pulled out his knife with one hand and shook Luke's with the other. "No call Andrew Andy." But he smiled. Luke eyed the knife and nodded.

"*Hola*, Señor Andrew," Luis said.

"More soufflé, Andrew?" Chung asked, indicating the pot of beans.

Andrew shrugged with a smile and pushed his tin plate over for more. Now that he was white, he supposed he could learn to enjoy French food.

⊰⊱ IV ⊰⊱
The Fast Arm of the Law

The next day Andrew returned from checking the cattle. When he walked into the kitchen, he found Luke helping Chung stow the supplies from town. Andrew patted a large bag of beans and smiled. "More French food, hah?"

Chung nodded enthusiastically. "Yes, but tonight I make Hungarian goulash. I have recipe. First add beans. Next, more beans."

Luke rubbed his face, looking worried. "Andrew, there was a U.S. Marshal in town, asking if anyone knowed about an Apache cowboy hereabouts. I didn't tell him nothing."

Andrew grunted, thinking. "A man of the law?"

Luke nodded. "A lawman, yeah. But there's others in town who knows you're here. Hard keeping a secret like that, an Apache who's now a ranch foreman."

Chung said, "Not as unusual as a Chinese cook who makes Hungarian goulash."

They heard a horse entering the ranch yard. A deep voice called "Hello the house?"

Luke groaned. "Guess that'll be him. Be careful, he's known as the gunfighter marshal. No outlaw's ever won against him. That's one dangerous old lawdog. They call him Fast Sam."

Andrew shrugged and left the bunkhouse, followed by Chung and Luke. Chita came out from the ranch house. U.S. Marshal Samuel Dawson was a grizzled but tough-looking man in his sixties. He wore a dark suit and a big white hat. Two pistols hung from his gunbelt, the loops of which were full of cartridges, and a marshal's badge reflected sunlight from his chest. A rifle was in the boot of his saddle.

"I have come to see the son of Geronimo," he said, looking straight at Andrew.

Inside the seldom-used parlor of the ranch house, Dawson smiled at Andrew while Chita ran over to the bunkhouse kitchen to get some coffee for them.

"Lieutenant King told me about you. Claims you saved his life," the marshal said. "Also told me you are not only a brave Apache warrior but also a very moral one."

Andrew agreed. "But I no longer Apache."

Chita had come back in during that exchange with three cups of coffee on a small tray. "That's right, Marshal. He was captured as a baby and raised by the Apaches. His real name is Andrew Seamus MacDuff."

Dawson smiled. "That's mighty fine, a good Scotch-Irish name, but it's his Apache talents I need."

Andrew carefully sipped his coffee. The last thing he wanted to do was to spill something on the furniture in Chita's parlor. In his Apache days of living in dirt-floored hogans, one did not have to worry about such.

"Yes, I will listen," he told the marshal.

"There is," Marshal Dawson said, "an Apache called Death Bringer. He's now war chief of the *Chi-e-a-hen* Apaches—but he was captured years ago as a young teenager by the army and sent back east to school. Educated, he returned to the *Chi-e-a-hen* and engaged in ruthless but very cunning slaughter of every white he could find."

Andrew grunted, leaning forward in interest.

"Do you know him?" Dawson asked.

"Yes. Met once before he was captured. Older than me. Killed his father." He looked at Chita. "You were there in your friend's ranch house."

She smiled. "He's saved me several times."

The marshal continued. "Death Bringer is using his education to infiltrate and subvert the territorial government. The cavalry is very good at chasing Geronimo over an area the size of Europe but useless when a band of Apaches hides in the general population."

"Cavalry learn lot from Apache, get much experience in being sneaky," Andrew said proudly. "My friend Lieutenant King is very smart, much experienced. But how Death Bringer and warriors hide among white-eyes? Apaches dark savages."

"They masquerade as Mexicans, Italian immigrants, or just well-tanned white men," the marshal answered. "No one expects Indians in their midst. They are invisible."

Andrew nodded. "So you want me to be scout, seek out and find these Indians hiding in plain sight?"

Dawson set down his cup. "Mighty fine coffee, ma'am." He looked at Andrew. "No, son. I want to offer you a career as a Deputy U.S. Marshal. I need someone like you for a long time to come."

Andrew glanced at Chita. "What it pay?" he asked.

"Hundred a month, and you get an allowance for travel, lodging, and ammunition."

Andrew looked at Chita again. "That enough to save ranch?"

She sadly shook her head. "But you do it, Andrew. It's a lot more than a cowboy makes. I don't think we'll be able to stay here much longer. The bank is getting really insistent."

Andrew frowned, worried about the threat of foreclosure.

Dawson quickly interceded. "Did I mention President Cleveland has personally authorized a $20,000 reward?"

Andrew turned to Chita. This time she nodded.

"Andrew think about it," he said.

Dawson nodded, pleased, and stood up.

"Okay if I come back about this time tomorrow?"

Andrew and Wichita indicated agreement.

After Dawson rode out, Chita and Andrew discussed the offer.

"Being a marshal," Wichita said, "is too dangerous."

"I was Apache warrior. Compared to that, not so dangerous. But no want to leave *you* unprotected."

They called in Luke, Luis, and Chung.

Wichita explained. "The marshal wants Andrew to become a deputy. There is regular pay plus the chance of reward money that would save the ranch. I don't want him to do it. Way too much chance he'll get hurt."

Luke spoke up first. "Well, maybe it's a good idea so far as the money goes. But it is mighty risky, and Andrew would be gone from here a lot."

"I think we could make up for the work," Luis said. "For my *amigos*, I am willing to do more. We can sleep when we are dead, *sí*? But not at the cost of losing our Andrew."

Chung nodded. "We need Andrew here. He likes my cooking. He would not eat well on the trail of outlaws."

Andrew stood up and raised his hand to quiet them. "I have decided. It is the only way to save ranch. I will take chance."

They all began to object. Andrew held up his hand again.

"I will take chance if all of you help me. Wichita and ranch must always been protected. I am Apache learning ways of the white race. I will need lots of help from you so that I do not make fool of self."

Discussion continued, but finally consensus was reached. They decided they would support Andrew and each other.

"Good," Andrew said. "We now tribe. Can I be war chief?"

Chita punched him on the shoulder with a smile. "I was hoping for Chung but you'll do."

Chung grinned. "Is okay. Tonight we celebrate with *Chinese* food."

Luis groaned. "*Sí*. Chinese beans. Bet they taste just like Hungarian goulash."

"No, have little more pepper," Chung said.

⊹⊱ VI ⊰⊹
Deputy Marshal, Arizona Territory

The next day, Marshal Fast Sam Dawson returned, riding into the ranch yard whistling. After he dismounted, Luis led his horse away and Wichita invited the marshal into the parlor. Andrew, Luke, and Chung also came in, finding themselves seats as Wichita fussed around making the marshal comfortable in the place of honor, her father's old chair.

"I suppose we can talk about the weather or something until Luis gets here," she said, sitting.

The marshal nodded. "Fine by me. Don't reckon it's rained in the last three months. Don't reckon it'll rain for the next three."

"We live in the desert," Luke said in agreement.

"Stay for lunch, Marshal," Chung said. "We having recipe from Alaska. Roasted whale blubber. It will cool you off."

The marshal looked at Luke. "Beans again, huh?"

Luke grinned. "For the next three months."

At that moment, Luis came in from having taken care of the marshal's horse.

"Marshal, your horse is watered and fed," he said.

"Thank you, Luis. I appreciate it," replied the marshal, who then turned slightly to look at Andrew.

"Andrew say yes," Andrew said.

Marshal Dawson reached into his shirt pocket, retrieved a paper, unfolded it, and handed the paper to Andrew.

"This here, Andrew, is a contract that guarantees your terms of service. Look it over and, when you're happy with it, sign, and we'll swear you in."

He looked at the contract and passed it to Chita. "Learning to read but not up to this yet," Andrew said. "Besides, my word better than any paper."

Chita returned the contract to Andrew, "Looks okay. Pretty simple. I will explain it to you later. You can sign it after that."

"No, I will sign it now if marshal explain," Andrew said.

"Simple, I reckon," Dawson said. "You get hundred a month and expenses. For that, you get to enforce the law of the United States on people who mostly are shooting at you at the time. I get paid a bit more, but then I'm a bigger target." He patted his stomach.

Andrew grinned. "Sounds good. Better to hide behind. I sign now."

Wichita got up and opened a table drawer, taking out a pen and bottle of ink. Andrew took the pen, dipped it in the ink, and casually signed "Andrew MacDuff."

"He's been practicing that all morning," Wichita said proudly.

The marshal smiled and stood up, motioning for Andrew to stand in front of him. He then pinned a badge on Andrew's shirt.

"Ma'am, would you have a Bible here?"

Wichita handed him Andrew's family Bible. Andrew said, "My real mother and father's Bible. Oath sworn on that stick tighter than any paper. Big magic."

Dawson looked him in the eye. "Reckon it would, Son. Reckon it would." He then swore in Deputy U.S. Marshal Andrew Seamus MacDuff, former Apache Devil and war chief of the Billings ranch.

"Now," the marshal said, having waited for everyone to congratulate the new deputy marshal and shake his hand, "let's talk about a little training. I want to take a few days and make sure Andrew can handle a gun. Give him some general tips. Smooth out some of the roughness so that he can pass okay among other white folk." The old marshal smiled at Wichita. "I think you might have gotten a bit of a start on that part, ma'am."

"I've heard," Andrew said, "that the marshal is well-known as a gunfighter. It would be good if all tribe could take the training so that they would be safe when deputy marshal away."

The marshal looked around. "This the whole tribe?"

Andrew nodded. "Cows and horses do not count. They lousy with guns."

"Reckon that might be a good idea," the marshal said in agreement. "In the case of Death Bringer, I reckon he might take Andrew's killing of his father a mite personal."

"All of the *Chi-e-a-hen* take it personally," Andrew said. "But was not me. It Shoz-Dijiji who killed him." He grinned. "I think that not big difference to them."

"To kill Shoz-Dijiji and a white man with one bullet, that would appeal to them," the marshal said. "That's why you need a little training. We want to keep both of you alive."

⊷ VI ⊶
A Little Training

The marshal, having allowed as how he had a few days to spare, had a bunk fixed for him and ate supper at the table with the others. Tonight Chung—in honor of the guest—prepared Delmonico steaks, baked potatoes, and a Greek salad, all served with a fine red wine from Spain at the suggestion of Luis. The steaks were as tender as twice-baked beans, but the wine had a strong aftertaste of weak coffee.

The marshal eyed the sacks of beans leaning against the wall. "You folks eat this good all of the time, do you?"

Luke looked up from his plate of beans. "Not all the time. We got company. More beans than usual."

The marshal sighed and waved away Chung's offer of seconds.

"Andrew's and our training takes priority," Wichita said. "Marshal, we'll work our chores around your training schedule."

"I can help with them chores some. Done more than a little ranching in my time. After what chores need doing in the morning, we'll get started," he answered.

The next morning, in the bright sunlight but before it got really hot, they gathered out at the fence line. No cows were in sight. The marshal had borrowed a few old empty glass bottles from Chung—who saved such for no good reason—and placed a couple bottles on the top of fence posts.

They backed off about twenty feet. "Okay, son, let me see your wheelgun, there."

Andrew pulled his six-shooter from its holster and handed it over.

The marshal examined it, then emptied the cartridges from it, handing them to Andrew, who put them in his pocket.

"Mighty nice revolver. Colt 1878 Frontier in .45 caliber, double-action. Factory engraving but custom-carved walnut grips. Looks almost new. Not cheap. How'd an Indian get hold of something this modern?"

"Store," Andrew said.

"Which store?" Luke asked, perplexed that a savage could walk in and buy weapons.

"Big store. All over place. Apache shop there plenty."

Luke started to ask another question, but the marshal held up his hand. "Best we not go there, Luke. I'm familiar with that kind of shopping. Did a mite bit of it myself back in the war."

He handed the empty gun back to Andrew. "Put it in your holster there." And then the marshal took out his right-side Colt, emptied it, and holstered it again. "I prefer the older single-action, but it's just because I've used that for decades and it fits me like an old glove. The rest of you, empty your guns also."

The marshal backed up about ten feet. "Now, here's a little close for gunfighting, but let's see how fast you are. Luke, you give the word now."

Andrew readied himself, hand hovering over the grip of his gun. Luke yelled, "Draw!"

In a blur, Andrew's revolver came up and clicked twice before the marshal's clicked once. Fast Sam dropped his hand to his side, looking a little astonished.

"Reckon that's a good lesson for the both of us," he said. "There's always the chance of someone out there faster than you are. Gunfighting should be the last resort of a lawman. Outsmart the bastards is your best course."

He then tried the others in turn. The old Chinese cook, Chung, was surprisingly fast, showed he had gotten some experience somewhere, but nothing compared to Fast Sam. Luke, Luis, and Wichita were nowhere close, either, but had serviceable draws.

"Can't teach nothing to Andrew about drawing. He's a natural. But I'll work some with the rest of you. Show you a few tricks that will speed up getting your gun into play." The marshal smiled. "Now, Andrew, load up your gun, and we gonna draw on them two hombres up there on the fence posts. Speed's nice, but accuracy saves yore life."

The marshal and Andrew stood side by side. "Luis," the marshal said.

Luis waited a moment, then, "Draw!"

Two shots rang out, Andrew's a split second before Fast Sam's. Both bottles flew from the posts, both shattered.

"Hellfire, son, you got both speed and accuracy," the marshal said as they put away their Colts. "Nothing much I can learn you about that. But reckon I can teach you about when to *not* shoot and how our laws work." He gave Andrew a quick pat on the back. "Now you go off and do a chore or two, and I'll work for a while with the rest of yore tribe here."

Andrew went over to the barn, grabbed a shovel, and started cleaning out the corral, pushing the horses aside as needed. This was sure one ranch job he'd not miss. Some of the rest, like riding the range checking the cattle, evenings sitting on the ranch-house porch talking with Chita, and interaction with his other friends here—yes, he would miss that. A lot.

Shots rang out from time to time, and he could occasionally hear the marshal's voice rise in momentary frustration as one or the other of his friends made a boneheaded, or at least inexperienced, mistake interpreting the lawman's instructions. He grinned and kept adding to the pile just over the corral's back fence. Chung had told him he wanted some to fertilize a small garden if they ever got a little rain again.

They fell into a routine. Mornings were for the physical stuff. How to subdue a prisoner and tie his hands (the marshal showed Andrew how to carry short pieces of small diameter rope for that purpose). They practiced the best way to approach a cabin or other building when you were not sure who was there and when you were. What to look for when checking the brand on horses or cattle, and much more about a lawman's routine duties.

Afternoons and evenings, they sat around the bunkhouse table or on the ranch-house porch and discussed laws and the other things Andrew needed to know. This latter included how to interact with people, table manners, and all sorts of, to Andrew, arcane knowledge, the lore of the white-eyes. He found it, to his surprise, fascinating. And having Chita telling and showing him a lot of it made the ordeal a good deal less onerous. Being schooled in how to read was fun also, and he promised himself he would keep practicing that.

By the third day of beans for breakfast, lunch, and supper, the marshal counted out some money from his "eating expenses." He gave it to Luke along with a shopping list for the general store in Sunrise. Luke rode out in the wagon, and, after he returned, they ate well for the rest of the training period. Chung was in heaven—he really did know how to cook, and now he had rows of cans on the shelves, a selection of spices, and other good stuff, including some fresh beef, as the marshal had bought a cow from Wichita for that purpose. By general consensus, beans were *not* served as a side dish.

The training took ten days. Everyone worked hard. But at last the marshal expressed his satisfaction that Andrew was ready to go out with him, that the others could protect themselves and the ranch, *and* serve as backup to Andrew when he would be on his own.

"Right now," the marshal said, "counting Andrew here, I have three deputy marshals to help me cover all of the Arizona Territory and the western part of New Mexico Territory. After we take care of the Death Bringer problem, Andrew, you will be policing most of southern Arizona. A place you know well. You can operate out of here."

Andrew nodded. The others smiled at that news.

"Reckon it's time we got to work, then. Andrew, we ride out at first light." The marshal removed his wallet and counted out a hundred dollars. "Your first month's pay. I'll do the paperwork later."

Andrew took the money, looked at it, and passed it all to Wichita.

The marshal shook his head, and Wichita was already handing half of it back to him. The marshal smiled. "That's about right. You need to have some money on you, son, to buy food, lodging, and the like. I'll show you how to do an expense account as we go along."

╌╌ VII ╌╌
The Marshal Business

The next morning, early, Marshal Dawson and Andrew rode away from the ranch, their bedrolls tied behind their saddles.

"Where we going, boss?" Andrew asked.

The Marshal grinned as their horses plodded along the dusty road. "Now you're sounding more like a deputy marshal, but call me Sam or even Fast Sam. Does me good to foster that legend, gets the bad yeggs thinking of surrender instead of gunsmoke. May I call you Andy?"

Andrew looked at Sam. "No. Name is Andrew." The marshal shrugged good-naturedly.

Andrew relented. "Yes, you can call me Andy. But only when we alone."

They both laughed. "Now," said Fast Sam Dawson, "I've got a few chores that will give you some practical law-enforcement experience. And, as we ride, I'm gonna talk some more to you about how to be a U.S. marshal and what it means."

"That good ... ah, I mean, that *is* good," Andrew said. This way of talking took some extra effort. "Do you really know Great White Father?"

The marshal laughed again. "I've seen him only once. It was in Kansas City. He had come there on political business and called my boss and me in to a private meeting. Both of them made it clear I had been summoned because of the seriousness of Death Bringer's threat and that it was up to me to find and stop him. The army did not have the first idea in this kinda situation. President seemed nice enough. Has a lot of problems in a lot of places, though."

"And Great White Father suggested you find an Indian to help you?"

"No, Andy. I done thought of that myself out of pure desperation."

"You'll not be sorry," Andrew said.

"I know, Andy. Marshals learn to see men as good or bad. You're good."

"Then I get raise?" Andrew asked, grinning.

"Don't push it, son. I already blew a good part of my expense budget on buying food to replace them beans."

"For which everyone at the Billings ranch is eternally grateful, Sam."

The next day, they stopped at a town on the new railroad, where the marshal, with Andrew in tow, visited the telegraph operator's small nook in the train station. "This here," the marshal said, "is Willy Swartz. Willy, my new deputy, Andrew MacDuff."

Willy shook hands with Andrew. "You the Apache lawman, huh? Sure don't look like no Scot." He grinned good-naturedly.

Andrew returned the grin. "Scotch-Irish actually, by way of the *Be-don-ko-he*."

"Here's one of my big secrets, Andrew," the marshal said. "I'm the only U.S. Marshal right now in all of the Arizona Territory. I got just three deputies to cover this whole dang area, and one of them is plumb worthless so far."

Andrew's face went Apache-impassive. Sam patted him on the shoulder. "No, not you."

"He's talking about Billy Windom," Willy said. "That boy couldn't find his way outside if all the doors and windows were wide open. Dumber than a cow in the middle of the road."

"So here's the thing, Andrew," the marshal continued. "I've made friends with all the telegraphers up and down the railroad. People ignore these men, but they see and hear everything, and they got the means of communicating all over the territory. Gotta adapt modern technology to get this here nigh-impossible job done."

Willy tapped out something on the key, and the marble-based telegraph sounder quickly replied at length. Willy wrote down the message and handed it to the marshal.

Sam scanned it. "Hmmm. When's the next northbound train, Willy?"

Willy cupped his ear and listened out the open window. They heard a not-so-distant steam train whistle. "I'd say 'bout a minute or so, Marshal."

Sam passed a bit of money to Willy. "Thanks, Willy. C'mon, Andrew. Time for your first train ride. Go get the horses and we'll get them loaded on the stock car."

Andrew intently watched the scenery flash by. Sam, sitting next to him, was amused. "How you like your first train ride, Andy?"

Face blank, Andrew turned and looked at the marshal. "Him like iron horse. Run fast as wind."

The marshal let out his breath. "Son, sometimes I'm just not sure how to take you."

Andrew suddenly grinned. "Good trait for a lawman, huh?"

The marshal laughed. "Reckon so, Andy. You scare me how quick you're learning stuff sometimes."

"Like how to use the telegraph network for information and trains as fast transport to reach problems, thereby magnifying our efforts?"

The marshal grunted, pleased. "Yep. Now, here's another valuable lesson." He settled in the seat and pulled his hat down over his eyes. "Sleep whenever you can. Be fresh and ready for emergencies."

On his own, Andrew, his badge in his pocket, pushed aside the swinging doors of a saloon. It was mid-afternoon and the place was not very crowded. He walked across the sawdust floor and passed a couple of mean-looking cowpokes leaning on the bar and flipping a coin to see who would buy the next round. He bellied up to the bar beyond them.

The bartender, wiping his hands on a dirty towel, wandered over to see what he wanted. Andrew missed the barkeep's arrival at first, staring open-mouthed at the painting of a mostly naked lady hung behind the bar.

"You an art critic or you here for something?" the bartender asked.

Andrew shut his mouth. The two cowpokes glanced back, then dismissed him. No one—a little to his surprise—was yelling *redskin* or anything like that. He placed a quarter on the counter. "Cold beer."

The bartender snorted. "Funny, this here's Arizona in summer." But he took the two-bit piece and went to draw the beer.

Andrew was hoping not to have to drink the beer, when Marshal Dawson came through the door, hands close to the butts of his two revolvers.

"Oh, hell," said one of the cowpokes. "It's Fast Sam!"

Still ignoring Andrew, they both lined up facing Sam, their hands close to their six-shooters.

Andrew took a couple of quiet steps to close on them and jerked both their guns from the holsters and stepped back. They whirled to find what they had assumed was a harmless cowboy covering them with their own dang guns.

Sam came up. "Say the words, Andrew."

"Butch Martin and Ike Clavers," Andrew said with a formal intonation, "We are U.S. Marshals, and you are under arrest for murder on the Navaho Indian Reservation."

"He was just an Injun," Clavers said.

Andrew's hands trembled slightly, but he did not shoot them. The marshal nodded his approval.

"Let's go, boys," Sam said. "The sheriff here is gonna give you room and board until the circuit judge gets up this way."

On the way out, Andrew saw the bartender pouring his beer back into the barrel. He walked over and held out his hand. In disgust, the man returned his quarter.

After they had deposited the prisoners, Sam treated Andrew to a steak at what passed for a cafe in this one-horse, one-train town.

"Very handy getting information by letter and telegram. Coulda used something like in my old job."

The marshal cut and speared a piece of steak. "Got a network of law-enforcement officers and others all through this here territory. But you had smoke signals, didn't you?"

"Smoke signals low word count. Not much information. Can't carry around to read later."

Sam laughed, then grew serious. "And what did you learn from today?"

Andrew waved a fork of steak. "Trickery better than gunfight. This Apache concept also."

Sam nodded. Pleased.

A few days afterwards, late one evening, Homer McClusky and his pard Texas Slim Smith were moseying their trade wagon, pulled by two mules, along a trail toward a nearby Indian reservation. They were licensed by the federal government to trade foodstuffs, geegaws, and whatever else the savages would accept in return for skins. Back in civilization, McClusky and Smith got good money for the skins. It was a high-profit occupation, but they had devised ways to make it even more profitable.

As they rounded a bend, they found an Indian setting on a horse saddled only with a blanket. He was naked except for a loincloth, bronzed and muscled. He held up his hand, but they had already stopped.

"What you want?" Homer asked, a bit nervously.

"Want trade."

"Wal, we'll be set up near the chief's hogan tomorrow. Come on by then," Texas Slim said.

"Want trade for something no can on reservation."

Homer glanced at Texas Slim, avarice in both their eyes.

"Want some firewater, d'ye?" Homer asked.

The Indian shook his head and waited, staring at them.

"Ah, what do you have to trade?"

The Indian reached in his loincloth and pulled out a roll of greenbacks.

"Now, where would a heathen Indian get real money?" Texas Slim asked.

The Indian just stared at them.

"Ah, right, none of our business, now, is it?"

"Reckon not," Texas Slim said. "You wanting a rifle or pistol? We got both for sale."

"Rifle," the Indian said.

"That'll be $50 for a good Winchester," Homer said while Texas Slim bit his lip to keep from laughing. The junk weapons they had were about as far from Winchester as you could get. As liable to blow up in your face as roll a bullet out from the rusted barrel's business end.

The Indian looked at his roll of bills in confusion.

Homer was quick on the uptake. "Reckon you might be a little short, but we'll take what you got for one rifle."

The Indian nodded. "Where rifle?"

The two men got off the wagon, moved some trade stock, and pried up some false floorboards. They never heard Marshal Dawson come up behind them until he cocked both his weapons, which sounded mighty loud in the cool, quiet evening. The Indian had pulled a big revolver from under his saddle blanket and had them covered as well.

"U.S. Marshals," Andrew said. "You are under arrest for gunrunning. That's a federal crime."

Homer and Texas Slim resignedly raised their hands while Sam disarmed them.

"You purely make a convincing Indian, Marshal," Homer said.

"I do, don't I," Andrew said in agreement.

⊰⇒ VIII ⇐⊱
Gunfight at the Not So OK Corral

Two days later, near noon, the marshal and Andrew were back on horseback. The marshal had gotten a telegram about trouble in the small town of Red Rock but didn't want to arrive so obviously as getting off the train in sight of anyone who might be watching for someone like them. They had gotten off the train one town earlier.

"So when do we start looking for Death Bringer?" Andrew asked.

"After we take care of this gang that killed the sheriff and postmaster and took over Red Rock. Federal crime killing a mailman." Sam removed his hat, wiped sweat from his forehead, and replaced it.

"Andy, to be honest, I ain't got much idea how to find him. I've heard rumor he's in Tucson, the territorial capital. Reckon we'll just have to go down there and let you see if you detect any Apaches masquerading as white men."

"Like me, Sam?"

Sam looked at him. "No, not like you. These are bad men. Very bad men."

They rode on for a bit, and the buildings of Red Rock came into view.

"The Billings ranch is on our way back down south. We can stop in for a visit."

Andrew nodded in enthusiasm. He was sure missing Chita. Luke, Luis, and Chung also.

"Hope they got the last bit of money I mailed," he said. "I'm not hankering to eat beans again."

"You and me both," Sam said as they reached the edge of town, dismounted, and tied their horses to a rail. "Check your gun, Andy."

"And the lesson here?" Andy said, spinning his Colt's cylinder to make sure it was fully loaded, then adding a round to the empty chamber so he'd have a full six shots.

"Sometimes there ain't nothing for it but to shoot their damn ears off," Sam answered. "You carry the rifle. We might have need of it."

Andrew worked the rifle's lever to jack a shell into the firing chamber.

They walked up the dirt street, hard packed by the hooves of many horses over the dry, hot summer. Their approach was not unobserved. Six gunslingers came out of the saloon and spread out across the street. It was obvious they were not interested in talking.

Shoz-Dijiji—savage war chief of the *Be-don-ko-he* Apaches— walked the battleground now. Andrew was pushed to the back of his mind. They were at the sagging fence of the corral attached to the town's livery stable.

"Two on roofs with rifles," Shoz-Dijiji said.

"You take them. I'll plug as many of the six on the ground as I can, but you help me quick like."

Shoz-Diji grunted. "No need give chance." He whipped the rifle to his shoulder and quick-fired left then right. Two bodies plummeted from buildings opposite each other. That started the six gunslingers on the street firing from farther away than they had meant to. Fast Sam's two sixguns were blazing before any of them had finished their draws.

Andrew dropped his rifle, drew his Colt like lightning, and rapidly fired at the two gunmen still standing. They dropped.

"You are Fast Sam, you got four," he said, turning to look at Sam, only to find him lying there, clutching his side and groaning as blood soaked into the hungry dust. Andrew, returned again now that battle was ended, dropped to his knees and tried to staunch the bleeding.

Across from the corral was the doctor's office, its waiting room a few chairs on the small front porch, but a handy place right now for a doctor's office to be. The doctor, seeing the action was over, rushed out with his bag and knelt in the street next to Andrew. He checked the wound then called over some of the townsfolk who were now coming out of hiding. He pointed to a couple of the stronger-looking men. "Get this man inside and on the table so I can try and save his life. And be gentle with him. These two heroes here just saved your worthless hides."

Andrew followed them inside, but the sawbones shooed him out and went to working desperately to save the marshal. Andrew, for something to do—and to put out of his mind how pale and helpless the unconscious Sam looked—went over to the depot and found the tiny telegraph office. He showed the operator his badge.

"Name's Boyles, Jake Boyles," the man said. "Heard the shooting. Glad Sam got my message about the gang here. Sam okay?"

"No, he's hit bad," Andrew informed him. "Your doc's working on him. I need something to occupy my mind. Any messages?"

"Oh, God," Jake said but tapped on his key and soon was copying down a telegram as the Morse code characters clicked the sounder. Finished, he handed Andrew the message.

Andrew started trying to puzzle out the message, having to silently move his mouth in sounding out unfamiliar words. Seeing this, Jake took the paper from him and read the message aloud.

The telegram said the Death Bringer's move against the territorial government had been moved up to September 10, less than two weeks away. The marshal's intelligence network was reaching out and pulling in information. He thanked Jake and returned to the doctor's office and was told to wait on the porch by the doctor, who was still working to extract the bullet.

* * *

Finally the doctor came out and collapsed wearily into the rocker next to Andrew. "He will live, I think," the doctor said, "but he will be laid up for weeks at least. He's awake for the moment. Wants to see you."

Andrew went inside. Sam was still deathly pale, obviously in pain, and barely awake. He grabbed Andrew's hand. "It's all up to you now, Andy. Take all my papers, talk to the telegraphers, and stop that monster."

Andrew nodded. "Already been down to see Jake here. Got some information about Death Bringer that can't wait. I'll take care of it."

Sam sighed. "You do the best you can, son. I sure made the right decision taking you on as a deputy. You be careful, though!"

"Shoz-Dijiji will. He has spoken."

But Sam was now asleep. Andrew found the marshal's wallet, took out the folded papers, and put what little money he had with Sam's.

"I'll take good care of him," the doctor said in assurance. "Known him for years. I'm Doc Finch, by the way."

They shook hands, and Andrew left after telling the doctor to take what money he needed. "I'll be back as quick as possible."

⊰ IX ⊱
Losing the Ranch

Andrew rode to the Billings ranch, only to find things dire there as well. Wichita—very glad to see him but almost distraught, certainly worn to a frazzle—told him the bank had sent a foreclosure letter. They had two weeks to repay the outstanding loans or forfeit the land and cattle.

In the bunkhouse, Andrew sat down at the kitchen table with Wichita, Luke, and Luis. Chung was bustling about, getting supper ready. On the stove a huge pot of noodles—handmade by Chung— bubbled, as did a saucepan of his special topping. "Only got real spaghetti tonight, Andrew. But you can pretend it beans if you like."

Andrew shook his head, pleased to be back. He turned to Wichita as they continued their hastily convened council of war.

Wichita was paging through the marshal's papers and re-reading the telegram Andrew had gotten from Jake. "This information," she said, "it comes from lawmen and others like the telegraph operators talking to people?" Andrew nodded. "Andrew, such secrets are often a two-way street. Word of the law's interest might already have gotten back to the conspirators. They will act fast to protect their conspiracy."

Andrew watched as Chung heaped a tin plate with noodles, poured sauce on it, and placed it in front of him. Picking up his fork, he said, "I agree, Chita, but I got no idea right now how to find Death Bringer, much less stop him. Things could not get worse."

"Beans," Luke said. "We could still be eating beans."

Meanwhile, in town at the Bank of Sunrise, banker Sheridan Adams was hosting a visit from the newly elected Mayor William F. Foster of Tucson, capital of the Territory of Arizona. Flattered for such an important, up-and-coming political personage to be visiting his small bank, Adams was withholding nothing. He mentioned the news that Marshal Fast Sam Dawson was shot and that their own local man, Andrew MacDuff, was now acting U.S. Marshal of Arizona Territory. The mayor turned to his assistant, dark-looking like the mayor, who said he was from Boston originally—and who actually had gone to boarding school there like his boss—and smiled. The marshal had been a bit worrisome, but now it seemed he was out of the picture.

Adams offered his visitors cigars, and they lit up. "He's an Apache, you know," Adams said.

Foster dropped his cigar but quickly picked it up, his face betraying nothing. "Is that so?" he asked.

Adams continued blabbering. "And we're foreclosing on the ranch he's foreman at."

Foster blew smoke in thought. "By the way, I'm looking for a few investments in this area. Sounds like that might be a good one."

"Comes with the cattle," Adams said eagerly, going into selling mode—anything to get rid of these worthless loans. "We got a lien on them, too." They dickered a bit and Foster bought all the paper on the Billings ranch for a song.

✳ ✳ ✳

In his hotel room a few minutes later, Foster talked with his "assistant" and two more of his fellow *Chi-e-a-hen* Apaches, both masquerading as Mexicans.

"The interfering marshal is shot and perhaps dying. He is no longer of concern, and white-eye outlaws have done our work for us. The only one left is his deputy." He looked at each of them sternly. "This man is an Apache. He might expose us before our plans go into effect. We kill him tonight and return to Tucson."

"But where is this Apache? Who is he?"

Death Bringer shrugged. "It does not matter. He will soon be dead. He is at a nearby ranch, which we now own. There's still daylight. Let us go evict the owner. Her Apache foreman will die resisting our legitimate serving of foreclosure papers."

After supper, Andrew, who had been to the outhouse back of the bunkhouse—for even former Apaches and Scotch-Irish people have to go sometimes—was returning around the corner when he heard horses come into the yard. Except for the knife in his boot, he was unarmed.

When he could see the yard, Wichita, Chung, Luis, and Luke were already facing the newcomers, most of whom pointed drawn guns. Their leader was a swarthy man but very distinguished looking in an expensive suit. The others looked like Mexican *vaqueros*. The distinguished man had a sheaf of papers in his hand.

"Miss Billings?" Wichita warily nodded. "My name is Mayor William F. Foster of Tucson. I now hold the papers on this ranch. We are foreclosing immediately. These gentlemen with me will assist you to pack personal items only." He gestured at them with the papers. "Disarm them."

Several of the men slid to the ground to do so. But Andrew had recognized Foster for who he was.

"Death Bringer!" he called. Foster turned in his saddle and looked at Andrew. Recognition was immediate.

"Shoz-Dijiji," he said in disbelief. Then, "Kill him now," to his men.

Andrew did the only thing he could. He ran behind the bunkhouse, rolled under the fence, and sprinted out into the desert range, melting into the terrain as only an Apache could. But those now chasing him on horseback were Apache also. "Death Bringer will kill your woman if you do not come back," one of them yelled.

━✦━ **X** ━✦━
Dark Night of Defeat

Andrew huddled in dejection at the secret spring where he and Geronimo had conversed not so many weeks past. He had lost everything. The woman he loved was in danger, if not already killed, as were his friends. The ranch that had become his home was in the hands of others. He could not even return to the *Be-don-ko-he* band of Apaches. They were all dead or surrendered like his father and on a reservation. He had gone from hope to *nothing*.

For a time he sat still. Then he looked up at *Klego-na-ay*, the full moon. Well, he had himself, and that had to be enough. He moved to a nearby boulder and started feverishly digging under its edge. Soon there came to sight a bundle. From it he removed a bow, then flint-tipped arrows, then several other items.

He quickly stripped and dressed in the G-string, rough sandals, and buffalo headdress of an Apache warrior on the war trail. He hung a small medicine bag around his neck. Squatting, he opened small jars and dabbed the colorful war paint on his face. Shoz-Dijiji was *back* and *this time* it was *personal*.

He rose and paused, looking at the discarded clothes of his white persona. Kneeling, he retrieved his deputy marshal's badge. Having no place to pin it, he put it in his medicine bag.

If he could no longer be either an Apache or a white man, he would become *both*. And win!

Back through the desert ran Shoz-Dijiji, the Black Bear, the Apache Devil, the Deputy Marshal of the Arizona Territory. If they had harmed his Chita they would not die, not for a while. He would stake them out on ant hills and dance around them while they lay in agony in the hot sun.

Thus did Shoz-Dijiji vow!

Near the ranch he slowed and crept close in Apache stealthiness. Most of Death Bringer's men were gone, as it seemed was Foster. After all, they had a territory to take over. Only three were left, judging by the three horses still tied to the hitching rail.

Two men walked through the ranch yard, smoking and laughing. Through the window of the lamp-lit parlor, to his joy, Deputy Shoz-Dijiji could see his beloved Wichita and friends still lived, guarded by the other man, who appeared to be fighting off sleep.

Shoz-Dijiji allowed himself a grim grin, waited a moment until the men were turned slightly from each other, then rose silently and put an arrow through the throat of one.

As the other turned to see what the small noise was, he too received an arrow.

In a flash, Shoz-Dijiji, still moving silently, was on the porch and through the open door. As he came into the parlor, arrow drawn back to his ear, Luke had grabbed the remaining fake Mexican's gun and had him covered.

Luis pointed to the painted, almost naked Shoz-Dijiji and said, "Chung, you see what your spaghetti does to people, *amigo*?"

Shoz-Dijiji and his beloved Chita embraced and kissed. Luis whistled.

Luke looked at Shoz-Dijiji as he turned to them. "You ain't leaving a lot to the imagination, Andrew."

Shoz-Dijiji looked down at his painted body and grinned. He pointed to Wichita, who now had war paint on her face and dress. Then he turned serious. "We have to move. Death Bringer will be acting faster now that he thinks no one is on to him. Luis and Chung will stay to protect the ranch. Wichita and Luke will come to help me."

"You have a plan?" Wichita asked.

"Of course Shoz-Dijiji have plan. He Apache." Andrew shook himself like a dog shedding water. "I mean, yes, ma'am, Deputy Marshal Andrew S. MacDuff, Acting U.S. Marshal of the whole dang territory, has a plan. Yes, ma'am."

They all laughed.

"We'll sleep two or three hours, then ride to catch the train to Tucson and give His Honor the Mayor a little surprise, Apache and Scotch-Irish style." He grinned again. "As soon as I retrieve my clothes, anyway."

Wichita nodded. "Guess it's up to us now to save the territory."

"Pretty much," Shoz-Dijiji said as moved to the door. He jumped on one of the fake Mexican's horses and rode out to get his clothes and turn back into Andrew.

When he returned, he halted their preparations long enough to deputize them all, using his family Bible for the swearing in.

"What do we get paid?" Luke asked.

"Beats me," Andrew said. "You better hope Sam recovers, 'cause he didn't get around to showing me how to do payroll." Andrew stopped for a moment, embarrassed. "Speaking of money, I need all you guys have so we can buy train tickets to Tucson."

⊹⇒ XI ⇐⊹
The Train to Tucson

The sun was up in the railroad town when they rode in. They had a couple of hours to kill, part of which Andrew and Wichita spent with Willy Swartz composing and sending two telegrams.

"You really sending a telegram to *him*?" Willy asked.

Andrew nodded.

Willy shrugged and sent it and the other, both of which Wichita had helped Andrew compose.

"Hey," Willy said. "Jake telegraphed me last night that Marshal Sam is able to get up and about a little. Needs a lot of recovery, though."

"Billings ranch," Andrew and Wichita said simultaneously.

Willy thought that was a great idea also. "I'll tell Jake to pass it to him," he promised.

That evening, the train pulled into Tucson on time. Andrew, Wichita, and Luke stepped off, crossed the platform, and onto the street. Three people to stop an entire revolution. A novice deputy marshal on his own, a beautiful cowgirl who no longer legally owned her ranch, and a determined Luke Jensen, who owed Andrew his life and would follow him anywhere. Show time!

⊰≒ XII ≒⊱
The Battle For Arizona Territory

As they walked up the street, Luke asked, "What's your plan, Andrew?"

Andrew grinned. "Combination Apache and white-eyes. Move fast, shoot them a lot."

"Which part of that is which?" Luke wanted to know.

Andrew shrugged. "Beats me these days." He clapped Luke on the shoulder as they walked. "Don't worry, Luke. I do have a bit of a plan going."

Andrew asked a passerby where the mayor's office was. As they walked there, a Tucson city policeman barred their way with drawn gun. "No weapons in town, mayor's orders," he said.

Andrew pointed to the badge on his shirt. "Acting U.S. Marshal, Arizona Territory. Official business. Come with us." The police officer joined them.

Andrew winked at Wichita. "Who said being a white guy isn't fun?"

As they passed a large, lighted building, Luke asked the policeman, "What's that?"

The policeman was puffing from trying to keep up with them, but answered proudly. "Oh, that's the headquarters for the mayor's new militia. He says we need our own troops in case the Apaches attack us and the army's not around."

"Got many, does he?" Luke asked in apprehension.

"Not so many at first, but they been pouring in like crazy today and joining up. Some of them boys look right experienced, too."

Ahead of them was the Tucson City Hall, with a freshly painted sign on the front reading: "Tucson, Arizona Territory—Mayor William F. Foster."

Suddenly troopers appeared out of alleys and doorways, aiming their rifles at Andrew and his companions. From behind them strode Mayor William Foster.

"Get away from those criminals, Clancy, you idiot," he said.

The policeman sidled away in embarrassment.

"Disarm them," Foster ordered. The militiamen quickly took their weapons, missing the knife in Andrew's boot. Foster nodded in satisfaction. He turned to the officer commanding the troops, he was dark-skinned with high cheekbones. "Captain Antonelli, these prisoners are trying to escape. Shoot them."

A grizzled old militia sergeant in the back of the troops suddenly fired a flare into the air. The majority of the militia had fallen back a bit and now had their weapons pointed at the front ranks. The original members of the militia wisely dropped their weapons and raised their hands.

Then they all heard the rattle of harness, the clomp of war horses, and the disciplined, quiet voices passing orders of U.S. Army Cavalry soldiers. At their head, as they arrived in front of city hall—saber out and raised—was Lieutenant Samuel Adams King, another who owed his life to Shoz-Dijiji.

"Glad you got my telegram in time. I am declaring martial law," Andrew told Lieutenant King.

"Yes, sir," King said and reached down to shake Wichita's hand. "I got your telegram and would have acted on it, but the one from President Cleveland really got my commanding officer's attention. How do you know *him*?"

"Apache get around," Andrew said. "Now, if you would be so kind as to secure the town, we'll stop this revolution before it happens. And arrest—" But he turned to find that Death Bringer was gone. The sound of galloping hooves echoed down the alley.

"Need a horse," Andrew said. Lieutenant King slid off and handed the reins to Andrew, who vaulted onto the horse and galloped away.

The going was slow in the dark, but Apaches can track, and Shoz-Dijiji was better than most. In the full moon's light he could catch enough telltales to know his quarry was still ahead of him. In his haste, he had not thought to get a gun, but what did an Apache warrior need with a gun? He had his knife and his wiles. That would be enough.

As the sun came up, Death Bringer came into sight not all that far ahead. He was flogging his horse, but the animal had tired from the night of carrying its burden and was not responding. In desperation, Death Bringer turned and emptied his pistol at Andrew. All of which shots missed at that distance.

"White man's education," Andrew yelled, "does not include shooting accurately from horseback."

The chase continued for a little while until Death Bringer's horse just stopped, refusing to go farther.

Death Bringer sprang from its back and pulled a knife. "Now I will gut you like you did my father. I have killed many. I will kill you."

Andrew dismounted and closed, his knife now out and ready. "Years at school in the east," Andrew said, "do not do much for knife-fighting skills, either. I am a deputy U.S. marshal. Are you resisting arrest?"

He sucked his stomach back out of the way as Death Bringer's knife flashed by. "Guess so," Shoz-Dijiji said—for he had taken over the fight from Andrew. He parried Death Bringer's next wild swing and pushed his knife into his enemy's heart.

Searching the body, Andrew emptied all the pockets. He found a small box of cigars, a pack of wooden matches, and the ownership papers to Wichita's ranch. Smiling, he tossed away the cigars and used one of the matches to light the papers, dropping them on the sand and watching until they were ashes. Accidents will happen.

Deputy U.S. Marshal Andrew Seamus MacDuff—known, when in the course of his duties, the occasion demanded it, as Shoz-Dijiji, the Apache Devil, rode—wearily into the ranch yard of the Billings ranch. Luke was there to take his horse and lead it away to water and feed. Chung leaned out of the bunkhouse kitchen. "Mr. Andrew. Beef tonight. With side of beans."

Andrew grinned and nodded. He entered the ranch house to find Wichita and a still wan-looking Marshal Fast Sam Dawson sitting in the parlor.

"Looking better there, Sam," Andrew said. "I caught them bank robbers up near Black Mesa. They're the guests of Sheriff Ames now."

He turned to Wichita, and the fierce Apache warrior was suddenly shy.

Sam tried to rise. "You folks need some privacy."

Andrew held up his hand. "No, what I need is a witness so I won't back out of this." He gazed deep into the eyes of Wichita Billings. "Chita, you know I love you. Will you marry me?"

Wichita looked at him. "And will I be getting Andrew MacDuff or Shoz-Dijiji the war chief?" Before he could answer, she was in his arms. "Yes, of course. I'll take you both."

"Reckon I'll have to give one of them a raise," Sam said.

 END

The Moon Maid *is ERB's multi-generational SF saga, and tells of the years-long struggle between the Moon's Kalkars and humanity. With the help of the human traitor Orthis, the genocidal Kalkars first take over the Moon and then Earth. The history of this war is related by "Julian," a man reincarnated through generations of his descendents. Bestselling author Peter David tells the tale of the survivors of the doomed battle for the Moon,* The Moon Maid, *Nah-ee-lah, Princess of Laythe, and Julian 5th, after they fled to Earth.*

—Bob

Moon Maid Over Manhattan

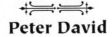

Peter David

It is called the Blue Room, an extremely pleasant place, where the end of the fifty years' war is being celebrated.

I stroll across the room, attired in a dress that is an even darker blue than the room itself. I am puffing on a cigarette that extends from the far end of the holder, inhaling and exhaling and enjoying myself. The war is finally over and there is nothing to serve as a problem for the future. We no longer need concern ourselves about villains trying to destroy us. Instead our attentions are turning outward, focusing on other worlds, other lands that seem interested in communicating with us. Barsoom calls to us, and we will find an answer somehow.

Suddenly I become aware of the fact that someone is watching me. Having no desire to make too much of a deal about it, I stop where I am and take a slow drag on the cigarette as I allow my eyes to encompass the room. Take it slow, take it casual. Do not do anything to attract attention.

My eyes rest upon a man who is, in turn, watching me. There is another man with him, shorter and slimmer and clearly somewhat puzzled by the fact that his companion is focused upon me. The first man, the one watching me, does so with easy confidence. His hair is a shock of black. He is neatly attired and clearly in his element. As

165

opposed to his mustached companion, the man watching me is clean-shaven, although he pulls vaguely at his chin as if trying to reconnect with something that is long gone. He chuckles softly, perhaps amused at some joke that he is reminded of, or that I remind him of. Who is he? What does he want? The questions come to me clearly enough; the answers continue to mystify me.

And then, just like that, he looks away from me, as if he has sought all the answers from me, received none, and is now set upon the deliberate endeavor to trade answers with his mustached friend. I am no longer of any concern to him whatsoever.

I should like to determine just precisely how rude he is, but cannot find it within myself to do so.

So instead, with a clearly pronounced "harruuumph," I continue upon my business. I only give a few moments passing thought to the idea that following him about might well make more sense than anything else, but I choose not to pursue the notion. He can go about his business, and I about mine. Never shall the twain meet.

And yet why did he seem so familiar?

Why does it seem that time is so meaningless?

✦⇒ I ⇐✦

The photographs are relentless, so much so that I literally have no idea which way to look first. Everywhere I turn, every direction in which I could look, there are photographers with flashbulbs that explode in my face.

Julian 5th is next to me. He is the only thing that has any reality to me at that moment in time, and even he is almost lost to me in a sea of photographs and shouts toward me. "*Nah-ee-lah!*" they shout. "Over here!" they shout. "Nah-ee-lah, *this way!* Over here! *Just one more!*" But for every photograph that is aimed, it seems that a thousand are taken.

I have no idea what to do or where to look. There is simply too much photographing for any human, much less a nonhuman, to absorb. I turn away, and the only sound I can think of to produce is a sort of frightened, disgusted whisper. "Julian, please—" I manage to say, and that is all the words that I can produce.

Fortunately it is all that is required.

Julian 5th has endured all that he is going to take on my behalf. When he speaks, his voice is loud and vibrant. "All right, that's enough!" And a moment later, "*That is enough!*" His voice is loud and proud, and the reporters are actually taken aback by the stridency of his declarations. It is not much but, as it turns out, it is more than sufficient.

There are oh-so-many reporters and photographers jammed into the hallway between his hotel room and the elevator from which we are endeavoring to emerge, and for a few moments that had seemed far more than enough. But then Julian 5th had made it clear that he would endure their blockage no more. He began shoving through, and the reporters did nothing to prevent him save for shouting out more questions and endeavoring to stop us with their bark but not their bite. Consequently Julian 5th managed to push both of us past the gathering, and moments later we were inside the simple hotel room. Julian slammed the door behind us and slumped against it, letting out a loud "*Whewww*" that seemed to take up all the air in the room.

I looked around, still stunned at what we had endured but quickly adapting to the new situation as it presented itself. There were flowers everywhere, from everyone. The president, the governor, the mayor, and many other gentlemen who fancied themselves to be of the slightest interest to me had sent flowers and such as extensions of their curiosity.

I supposed that I could not blame them. They had not, after all, ever had a woman from another world walking among them.

"A goodly number of flowers," I said after I was done assessing them. "Quite a few."

"I cannot say I'm surprised," said Julian 5th. "Your presence is nothing short of astounding to the people."

"Is it really?" I gave that some consideration but could not fathom it. "I admit," I said slowly, "that I can imagine some manner of confusion or bewilderment. But not to such a degree. It is, after all, just me."

"Just you!" Julian laughed loudly, at that and after a few moments I found myself having to agree.

I was, after all, Nah-ee-lah. I was a princess of the Moon or, more specifically, a U-ga, from the city called Laythe, and daughter of the man known as the Jemadar. For a time it seemed that I would inherit the land when my father passed away, but all that has ended. Instead others now fight for dominance while I have taken refuge here in the world whence my Julian 5th has originated.

Earth. It is called Earth. Not a particularly inspiring title, I have to say. It is hardly one that inspires a great deal of well, anything, really. Just Earth. Yet the people seem content with it, nor do they expect much from it, and so I follow in their path and remain satisfied with it.

After spending ten years upon my own home world with Julian, we traveled via their spaceship to here. Lieutenants West and, Jay, and Ensign Norton, Julian's other companions from the Earth, were nothing but respectful to me. West and Jay even suggested that rather than taking leave of the world, we instead return to my underground stronghold and endeavor to recapture it. But I would have none of it. My father had died in the struggles just before I departed, and there was quite literally nothing there for me anymore. Consequently, I decided to push my fortunes with the people of Earth rather than continue cultivating the world of the Moon any longer.

My arrival upon the world from which Julian 5th hailed was astounding. The landing itself was nothing short of remarkable, but when their local news service, their "press," as they termed it, discovered the existence of a true moon maid, they were delighted about it. They were practically falling over each other to have the first, detailed interview with a being from another world.

My inclination was to stay as far from them as possible, and for a time Julian backed up my uncertainty. That, however, did little to serve us, and eventually I agreed to do a single, one-on-one interview with a feature writer from something called the *New York Times*. I was wholly unfamiliar with it, of course, and so Julian agreed to remain with us and help shepherd us through the discussion.

The *Times* reporter was a gracious young woman, aged somewhere between her forties and death, I suppose. Her name was Miranda Kittain, with a tightly knit suit and wiry glasses that she would peer over from time to time as she asked me about all manner of personal things. I became increasingly irritated as we spoke, but Julian kept a patient hand on my wrist, which helped me weather the various intimate questions.

"And how do you see Earth now?" inquired Kittain at one point. "You are, after all, royalty of the Moon. Do you feel that they now owe you homage and deep fealty here on Earth?"

"I ask no one to owe me anything," I said, and wrapped my fingers around Julian's wrists. "All I request, really, is to be left alone and accorded the benefits that any pleasant outworlder be allowed to accrue here on your . . ." I paused and mentally sought for the correct word. "Your generous planet," I finally finished.

Apparently that was the exactly correct thing to say. "Our Generous Planet" was the headline in the very next edition, and from that point onward matters were much more beneficial.

Still, it was something of a challenge whenever we tried to do something as simple as go into and out of our apartment. There were always reporters asking us about our opinions of the day, no matter how utterly trivial that day's events might be. I couldn't quite fathom the reasoning behind the thinking. Why did it matter to them what we thought of anything, really? We had landed on Earth with Julian for the first time in ten years and me for the first time ever. What possible difference did our ill-informed opinions make?

A great deal, as it turned out. Eventually I decided not to put any serious thinking behind it. We were, to them, mere oddities in the world. They accorded our opinions far more worth than any of them were truly entitled to, and if that was to their benefit, then so might it be. It was of no consequence to me.

I flopped down into the couch in our sizable living room. It was nothing especially elaborate: living room, kitchen, bedroom, bathroom. Though the shower was particularly amazing to me, and I would spend half an hour at a time simply standing there and allowing the water to cascade all over my naked body. Every so often Julian would stick his head in to make certain that I had not gotten myself into any manner of trouble, and he would laugh as I assured him that there was nothing to be concerned about. I was fine, he was fine, all was fine.

Now, though, I was not considering all to be fine. I had been on this world for several weeks and was still feeling as if I were some manner of strange device rather than a contributor to the world around me. I lay slumped upon the couch and stared off into nothingness until my Julian finally asked after my concerns. "I am bored," I informed him.

"Bored?" His voice echoed the sentiment, sounding more puzzled than anything else. "Why bored, my sweet?"

"Because I have naught to do." I picked idly at the clothing that attired me. "Moon clothing," I said with an air of frustration. "Moon shoes. Moon hair. Everything about me fairly screams of the world from which I came. What is the point in pretending to be that which I am not?"

"Well!" Julian sounded a bit aghast, but not by much. "I can see where one such as you might well be bored. We shall have to attend to that immediately."

A half hour later, a lovely young woman was at the door. Taller than I was by a full head, her name was Mimosa (devoid of last name), and her skin was so distinctly red that one would have thought her to be a native of Barsoom (the likes of which we were only hearing from over radio phones via the colony founded by the esteemed John Carter of Virginia). Tall and elegant, Mimosa looked me up, down, and then up again before finally shaking her head, sighing heavily exactly once, and declared, "This simply will not do. Make no mistake, princess of the Moon." She added as an afterthought, "You are charming in your own right. You are petite and well-balanced, and clearly also possess some native strength. But those who see you, once they have managed to leave aside the curiosity of your gait, will perceive you as hopelessly postmodern. Do you understand?"

I shook my head "no."

She brushed away my response as if it meant nothing. "Worry not. There are matters of far greater consequence than whether you simply understand what I'm talking about."

"Oh," was all I could manage to say.

Whereupon I was quickly, and without any further loafing, gathered up and shunted off to various stores throughout Manhattan. We moved so rapidly that much of what I encountered could readily be referred to as a blur. It was clear that my concerns and speculations were of little to no relevance: Mimosa knew precisely what she wanted, and my thoughts on the subject, to say nothing of Julian's, were quite simply beside the point. Indeed, I discovered halfway into the journey that Julian 5th had been left behind somewhere. Doubtless he was wandering around helplessly in one of the stores that we had long ago left behind. Upon being informed of this predicament, Mimosa merely shrugged and waved it away as if Julian's presence was of little to no consequence.

Clothes, shoes, furs, hats, purses, makeup. All that and more was piled onto me while Julian's assorted charge cards were utilized with wonder and splendor. Whenever one was filled up, another was merely brought out in its place. This was fine with me. As long as he had enough whatever-it-was to deal with the expenditures, I was more than happy to allow them to be made.

We were not done until well into the night, having stopped briefly to enjoy a fine meal consisting of who-knew-what which was subsequently washed down by even more of who-knew-how-much. Consequently, when we finally returned home, we were barely standing. I have to admit, it had been quite some time since I felt that good. So much so, in fact, that when I returned to Julian's apartment (to which he had returned at some point, obviously), his stern expression was so high-handed that all I could do was giggle. Julian 5th continued to stare at me as I sank into the nearest chair, several large bags slipping out of my hands.

"Would you mind telling me," he said with measured stiffness, "where you were the rest of the afternoon? I lost track of you somewhere around the Middle Squares."

"Well, that's a very fortunate circumstance, because I'm not quite sure how you would have been able to keep track with us." That was Mimosa's take on the subject, and then she was no longer able to withhold herself and she began to cackle dementedly. I, having flopped down onto the chair, continued laughing.

"I think that will be quite enough, Mimosa," said Julian. There was nothing but seriousness in his voice and he was clearly already quite annoyed. "I called you here to help Nah-ee-lah get herself focused. Not get herself drunk."

I pointed an accusing finger to him and declared loudly, "You would speak in such a way to the daughter of the husband of—" Then my voice trailed off as finally I said blankly, "What was I saying?" Then I started laughing once more and continued to laugh. I was vaguely able to hear Julian's annoyed protests over my condition, but eventually I was able to do nothing else save to fall asleep.

When I awoke it was close to five in the morning. Julian had left me on the couch. Slowly I extracted my legs and moaned with pained softness in acknowledgment of the dire straits in which he'd left me. I carefully made my way through the darkened room, stepping carefully over the pieces of clothing that lay scattered around. Within minutes I had denuded myself of my clothing and entered the room, sliding across the bed and draping an arm around his steadily snoring body.

"Oh," said Julian. His voice was very controlled; if anything, there seemed to be largely a vague sense of disappointment. "How nice of you to join me."

I moaned softly, feeling the first surges of energy thumping against my head. I swallowed the rest of the noise and found myself speaking in a most offhand manner, as if I had just awoken seconds earlier and was about to be humiliated by the captain of the guard. "Are you okay?" I said cautiously.

"Me? Oh, yes. I had something to eat hours earlier," he assured me.

"And Mimosa?"

"That's who I ate."

Another moan in response, but it was about all I could manage. "I don't feel too well."

"That's to be expected."

"What happened?"

"I'm reasonably sure you got drunk." There was passiveness to his voice. "Pretty badly drunk, if I'm not mistaken. I stuck Mimosa in a cab and sent her home. And I left you where you were."

"Oh, Julian." I began to sit up, and suddenly dizziness swept over me. All I could manage was to fall backwards. "I'm so sorry."

"What are you apologizing for? You are a moon maid. You may do whatever you want with whomever you want. Don't let it trouble you."

"Of course it troubles me. I don't feel well, and it's dark, and I'm reasonably sure I completely screwed up everything. How can you love me?"

"Because that is what is supposed to happen," he assured me. He nudged me around and slid his arm under my head. "I mean, granted, not every day. But there will come the occasional time where you do things you can't do or shouldn't do. When you have imbibed yourself into a corner and no longer feel any sort of—"

I placed my hand atop his mouth and silenced him. "You need to stop talking," I finally told him. I pushed myself up on my elbow and brought my mouth down upon his. At first he tried to voice some manner of protest, but it was thin and not especially convincing. The kissing grew in intensity and conviction, and in short order all manner of discussion had been set aside. Only the physical aspects of what we were encountering were left to be felt, and I can assure you that every morsel of it was there for us.

I fell asleep shortly after that and did not awaken until one in the afternoon. Blinking away the lights, I hauled myself out of bed and pulled on a short robe. Moments later I had staggered out into the afternoon light and saw my amused lover waiting for me in the living room. "Good morning. Or should I say good afternoon. There is much we need to discuss."

"Yes, I'm sure there is."

"Understand," he began, "that I have much money saved up. Ten years' worth, to be precise. And yet there are certain necessities that have to be attended to, such as—"

"I'm pregnant," I informed him before he could utter another word.

He drew back his head, looking astounded. "Wh—when did that happen?"

"Last night." I went to the coffee machine and found that there was still some in the receptacle. I removed the pitcher and began pouring some into a mug despite the lateness of the hour.

"But how could you—?"

"Know?" I shrugged. "I just know."

"Are you sure?"

"Of course I'm sure." I set the coffee pot down, strolled over to Julian 5th with the filled mug, and ruffled the top of his head. He was still sitting there with a stunned expression; it gave me a warm feeling. "It's going to be Julian 6th."

"You can tell?"

"I can tell. So, now, what would you suggest?"

"Well—" He shrugged helplessly as he grinned. "I suppose now we get married."

"As you wish," was all I said.

The wedding was held not too long after that. The soldiers who had been waiting for us on the space vessel were there, and a number of others as well: politicians, scientists. The President of the United States was there, mostly because he seemed to feel that that was where he should be rather than as a result of any asking on my part. There was no hurry; humans may be able to churn out children within nine months, but the process requires seven months for me, a fact that I did not happen to mention to him until the sixth month.

And so it was that after precisely seven months of pregnancy, Julian 6th was born into the land. By that point the excitement over my presence on Earth had diminished somewhat, nor were people impressed when Julian 6th was nothing more than a purely average-looking youngster. Furthermore, since the birth of the child meant that we could no longer attend to outside activities, Julian 5th and his beauteous wife (that is what they called me, rather than my referring to myself in that manner) became mostly creatures of the indoors.

The child grew up quickly, and, even though he was not really supposed to (thanks to laws that dictated only the shortest of swords were permitted) no one hyped matters up too much when Julian began training his like-named son in the fine art of swordsmanship. "It is for the benefit of his maturity," Julian 5th said in such a way that guaranteed that only he, Julian 5th, would conduct the teaching, and only he, Julian 6th, would benefit.

And who was I to say no? My every day with Julian 5th was a delight. I could say nothing to this wonderful man who had saved me from a deterioration that would have led to depression and death. "As you wish, my love," was the entirety of my sentiments to him. How could they not be? He was my everything. We would be happy and free forever.

Yet there were times when my attention was drawn back to the land of the Moon. There would be periods where I would scan the skies, watch the waxing and waning of that endless vehicle that always circled the Earth, and wonder what was going on there exactly. We had left at a time of confusion, when the Moon was in great chaos and different groups were fighting zealously for control. What had happened with them? What had transpired with Orthis, the monstrous human who had long craved me and settled for endeavoring to drag the whole of my world down to his level?

Ultimately I decided that there was no use in worrying about him anymore. The chances were that he would never be seen again, that the forces of the Moon had disposed of him and were back to fighting their internal wars.

We had no need to worry about them.

I am the moon maid, and my world is set.

Time has no meaning. That is what Julian would say to me. He would tell me that time has no meaning. That everything is happening at once.

The first time he actually said that to me, we had been together five years on Earth. He had simply sat there at breakfast, in our kitchen in our remote cabin, and he smiled. "Time has no meaning," he had said. "I've come to that realization, and I simply thought I owed it to you to tell you that."

"Thank you." I had no idea what to say to that.

He saw my puzzlement and felt the need to explain a bit further. "We will always be together. We will always be two as one. This life— next life—previous life. Sometimes you'll understand and sometimes you won't. It will be fine. It will all be fine."

He went back to his breakfast and did not speak of it again.

It is madness. Madness everywhere.

They were not supposed to have come here, and yet they have.

The Kalkars. The people of the Moon, vicious and furious and unable to be stopped. The Kalkars, creatures of violence and anger, who battled everyone and everything, including each other. Shorter, broader, more vicious than humans, and far nastier than anything anyone has to throw at them.

The Kalkars who had finally become united under the sword of the man who had dominated them.

Orthis. Orthis the untamed, Orthis the terrible. Orthis, the man who had now returned and had brought tens of thousands upon thousands of Moon Men with him.

Earth was a world ripe for conquest, and the citizens didn't even realize it. For five decades in the previous century, Earth had waged nothing but constant war. Now that endless battle was over; the Earth had done everything it could to undo what it had become. All guns save for the most minimal ones in existence had been disposed of. No blades, save for the swords that Julius 5th and 6th handled, were allowed to be wielded.

Earth was tired of war. It had become a harrowing point for everyone and once it had been finished, *it was finished.*

Except not anymore.

The ships came hurtling down, and they were utterly destructive, bearing with them a full one hundred thousand of the Moon's deadliest enemies. At the head of the assault: Orthis, who had been relentless in his endless battles that had finally resulted in what had been, for him, the only possible outcome.

It was unknown to any on the Earth how long it had required Orthis to carve out his plan of attack. All anyone on our world knew was that beings from another world were coming to visit.

Only Julian 5th knew of a certainty. At this point, fourteen years had passed since he had returned. He had worked his way up to leader of the International Peace Treaty, but for all the suggested strength of the title, he had in fact little to no power accompanying it. War was descending upon an Earth that had only a quarter of the number of defenders to respond to the assault that the men from the Moon had planned.

And they laughed.

At the one man who could have saved them.

They laughed. At him.

Once Orthis and his men reached Earth, the laughter quickly ceased, unless one counted the boundless laughter that emerged from Orthis's lips. With his many vessels and fearsome weaponry, they rolled over both Washington, D.C. and London almost simultaneously. On the flagship, off which Orthis operated, there was a devastating weapon that was known broadly as an electronic rifle. It was the single most devastating firearm of its kind, and that was accounting for the fact that no one quite knew what its kind was.

Julian 5th, of course, figured it out almost immediately.

To test his theory, Julian withdrew his ships to a remote part of the world—the forested place to the north called Alyeska—and there he hid and planned. He had brought me, along with our then-fourteen-year-old son, and kept us secured, for he worried about our safety more than anyone else's.

Orthis searched long and hard for him, and finally, upon the close of the year 2050, the two fleets met once again. I was on the ground, still furious that Julian had not brought us along. "You," he said firmly, "have a far more important mission ahead than I. Only you can raise our son properly so that he can take his place in the order of our family." I considered this admonition to be less than sterling; it was my intent to be by Julian's side. But he would not have it, and so it was that, despite my desire to be elsewhere, instead the ship of Julian sailed into battle against his archenemy while I watched from below.

The ship of Orthis led the charge, and while Orthis cried out his certain triumph, Julian 5th simply tapped a button on a device that he had crafted over the lengthy period of their separation. Within seconds the electric ray device simply vanished and, simultaneously, the two ships collided with each other. Even though I was thousands of feet below, I could practically feel the impact from where I was standing.

The two vessels were pinned against each other, and I saw Julian, my beautiful Julian, leap from one vessel to the other. He had a sword in his hand, unlike all of the other men, who were toting rifles.

Crisp rifle shots reached my ears, and I clasped my hands to my bosom, convinced that this was all but over. And it was . . . but not the way I had thought.

Because suddenly there was an ear-splitting, thunderous explosion of noise. I stared up, shielding my eyes, squinting against the light, and then gasped in horror. Detonations ripped through the one ship and instantaneously leaped into Julian's as well. I had only the briefest flash of light that for half a heartbeat illuminated Julian 5th. It was an image that would stay with me forever, and then it was gone. *He* was gone. The entire ship was ripped to pieces, and the last sight I had of my Julian was his looking more surprised than anything else. Then the entire area exploded around him. Within seconds there was nothing left save for large bits of debris that were being torn apart in the violent thrust of the ship's detonation.

My heart stopped. Literally, it stopped. I clutched at my chest and felt nothing happening there for what seemed ages. Then, seemingly hours later when it must have instead been seconds, I felt the organ pounding away in my chest once more.

Desperately I tried running the images I had just witnessed through my mind. I endeavored to pull out of it some sort of quickly garnered lesson that would drive home for me the certainty that, yes, my husband had survived. Yet I knew that was not remotely possible. One moment he had been there, and the next he was gone. Orthis, who had envied my Julian for years, had finally gotten the better of him, even though the cost was his own life.

I heard a distant and frustrated screaming near me and realized it was my own son, Julian 6th. I clutched him tightly as he continued to shout, "*No! No, it can't be! It can't!*"

"It is," was all I said. It was a tight, sharp whisper, but it was enough to pull him away from his youthful frustration. "It is. Your father is dead, and unless we do something right now, we're going to follow him."

"But—"

I had no time to allow for his retrieving his wits. There were still many of Julian's men here, ready to battle, but I knew they had no chance. Julian's men were many, but the Kalkars were many more, and there was no question that they would triumph over the ridge in a matter of minutes. "Get your bag," I warned him. "One bag, right now. I will meet you at the door of our home, and we will get going. Immediately." When he paused, looking concerned, I slapped him briskly on the shoulder to reconnect his eyes with his head. "*Now!*" I insisted. "Not later! Now!"

He managed a nod and did as he was told. By the time I reached our cabin, he had already gathered the small amounts that I had instructed him to. My own material was already in a bag and ready to go.

There, in the section of the country known as Alyeska, we fled. There was no time to mourn the loss of my husband. There was no time to dwell upon having him torn away from me. All I had time to think about was putting as much distance between myself and those who would have torn us apart. We had to flee.

We traveled as quickly and expeditiously as we could. The sounds of the land behind us dissolved into shouts and battles as the troops of the Moon rolled in to do combat with those who remained behind us. They did not do so out of any great compulsion or sensitivity for what happened to us. I daresay most of them were unaware that we had even fled. No, at that point they were obsessed with one thing and one thing only: visiting whatever damage they could upon those who had assaulted us.

Their shouts of fury and bursts of gunshots were quickly destroyed by the sounds of blasts coming from the invading Moon Men. Men who had, once upon a time, been people who were not dissimilar to me. Moon Men who had, not all that long ago, thought of marrying me (or at least some of them had). Now all they wanted was to get their hands on me and try me or destroy me or try me and then destroy me. No matter which path was chosen, it was not one upon which I desired to tread.

And so we left.

Several days passed as we made our way down the mountain ridges toward the south. We continued to be hammered by the steady winds that almost seemed to be ready to blow us down the Canadian border. From time to time I wanted to do nothing save for flopping down and dying, or at least pulling into a complete sense of frustration due to my seeming helplessness. What point was there in moving on, really? My husband was dead; of that there was no question. Now I was being asked to do even more. I had to go on without him. And I just didn't think that was going to be possible.

I lost count of the days that went by as we traveled through Canada. With each passing day, the small amount of food we had with us dwindled, until it reached the point where I was left with virtually nothing. Nor was Julian 6th much better off, even though I had made sure to leave food over for him.

Finally one morning, when we had taken residence inside an otherwise empty cave, I woke up to find that I was incapable of sitting up. I simply lay there upon the ground, staring up at the ceiling, and when Julian prodded at me, at first I made no reply. Finally, when he kept saying my name and spoke with greater urgency, I said softly, "Leave me here, Julian. There is an entire world out there for you to explore. I wouldn't advise leaving it to me."

"Absolutely not," he said firmly, with an air of determination that reminded me of his father. It was almost enough to bring tears to my eyes, but I kept them suppressed. "I will find you whatever you need to build back up your strength."

I have naught to build it up for, was what I wanted to say. I felt as if my continued presence in his life was simply unnecessary. But he wanted me there, and so I saw no way but to do all that I could to remain. I managed a nod. "Very well," I said. "Do as you will."

He nodded and headed off. I lay there, listening as closely as I could until the sounds of his footsteps faded.

There I remained, doing nothing. Much of the day passed and well into the night and still there was no sign of his return.

I had no idea when I fell asleep. It was well into the night, I knew that much. Other than that, however, I was unsure of what time I actually drifted off. The following morning, however, the circumstances were made far more explicit to me, because I awoke, not to silence, but a good deal of noise.

There were Kalkars at the front of the cave. Half a dozen or more, and they were gazing at me with large, rapacious eyes, grinning wildly.

Energy surged into me when there had been none before. With a yelp, I staggered to my feet and began shoving my way back up into the limited shelter that the cave provided. The Kalkars created a temporary jam-up when they all tried to come in after me simultaneously. It took them a few moments to get themselves sorted out, right up until the largest of the group pushed the others aside and came in after me. I tried to keep him back, kicking as furiously as I could. But I was tired and less focused than I should have been, and it took him almost no time to get a firm hand on me. He yanked hard, and I was hauled forward and down toward the entrance. I fought as valiantly as I could, but it did no good. Moments later I was pinioned by the legs and arms and held down outside the cave. I struggled valiantly, but my strength was as nothing compared to theirs.

Nevertheless I fought back as bravely as the spirit of the moment allowed. I kicked out, lashed at them with my feet, sank my teeth solidly into their forearms. Even that was simply serving as best as my ravaged body would allow, and then I heard a sardonic voice announce, "Hold it. I believe this to be her."

It was, much to my surprise, a female voice. A woman stepped forward, looking mightily like a Kalkar, but taller and more powerfully built. Her hair was thick, dark brown, and equally darkish eyes were resting upon me. There was a grim smile in her face.

"Nah-ee-lah?" There was no real doubt in her voice; merely curiosity. "You would be . . . Nah-ee-lah?"

I wanted to tell her to go to hell. To tell her that under no circumstance would I give up my true name to her. Yet somehow I was fascinated by her, this woman who was not much taller than I myself was. "Yes," said I to her. "I am Nah-ee-lah. And you are . . . ?"

The Kalkar woman actually laughed at that, as if speaking her own name aloud amused her. Finally, when she had managed to adjust herself, she said softly, "I am Kel-ee-kni."

"Hello." I wasn't entirely sure of what else to say.

Her eyes narrowed; there was a directly sinister look to them. Her mouth twitched in clearly growing anger and I had no idea why. "You have no idea what you have done, do you."

"I admit I do not."

Suddenly, quick as a snake, she grabbed me by the back of my hair and yanked me forward. "I am Kel-ee-kni, and I am—I was—the beloved of Orthis. For fourteen years I benefited him. For fourteen years I loved him, cared for him, and raised his son. And that is over *because of your damned husband.*"

Well, now I knew.

I did not, however, care overmuch. "Our husbands killed each other," I said with as much indifference as I could muster. "As of this moment, it is now, by my count, five against one . . ." One of them off to the side raised his hand, and I nodded in acknowledgment. "Sorry. Six against one. There is little to nothing I can do about that. If you wish to kill me, then do so. If you wish to let me go, then you can do that as well."

"Let you go?" She sounded appalled at the notion. "Why would we do that when we can even the score right here, right now?"

I was still being held down, pinned at the shoulders and knees. Helpless as I was, I was still moved to snort in derision. "Is that what you think is going to happen? That some manner of evenhandedness is going to be meted out here? You are very sadly mistaken, if that is what you assume will transpire."

"Kill her," mumbled several of the Kalkars, muttering that they were growing tired of having to endure my speeches. "*Kill her.*" "*Eat her.*" That was another popular one with the Kalkars, demanding that I be consumed. It was certainly a tradition with their kind, and I was not expecting them to pass up on that philosophy now.

But Kel-ee-kni was not allowing matters to spiral out of control. Instead, maintaining her calm, she said tightly, "I think that allowing my men here to consume you is perfectly justified. How do you think it will not be?"

"Because you will simply have taken the first step to your own demise."

Several of the Kalkars still made noises over how they desired to spread my flesh thin and devour it as quickly as they could. Yet my firm words took up a stance in Kel-ee-kni's mind that would not banish itself quite so quickly. "How do you figure that?" she asked challengingly.

I did not answer immediately. Instead, I simply sighed aloud and looked off in no particular direction. I was allowing my mind to drift in the vague hope that maybe I might simply fall unconscious and perhaps even fade away before she could do anything about it. But then Kel-ee-kni shook me violently, snapping me back to the present. "How," she demanded again with the tone of voice of one who would brook no challenges, "do you figure that?"

Notching up the defiance in my voice, I said, "Because my son is out there right now. The son of Julian 5th. He stalks these woods and he will hunt you down and finish you. That is something you will have to face. Maybe not today or tomorrow, but soon. So rest while you can and smile to yourself about how clever you are, because time is abandoning you even as we speak."

Kel-ee-kni heard that and laughed, but there was something beneath her voice that spoke to the pure terror of contemplating such an end for herself. Once she had ceased quaking with amusement, her considerations appeared to slip into the zombie breach. The unsettled urgings of the Kalkars, who seemed to be equally split between letting me go and devouring me immediately, seemed rather testing on the subject.

Finally she could stand it no longer. "Fine," she said, and extended her hand. Without having to reinforce it by so much as a word, a broad-handled axe was slid into her hand. "I shall attend to this myself, if you're all going to be debating about it."

I closed my eyes and waiting for the inevitable end.

"You don't wish to see it coming?" said Kel-ee-kni, and she cut loose with a careless cackle. "Very well then! Such do I grant you!"

Against the soundlessness of the night, I heard an axe come swinging around, slicing through the air.

And then there was a sharp *clang* and it jolted my eyes to wideness. I looked around just in time to see that my son, the accomplished Julian 6th, standing just behind me and smacking Kel-ee-kni of the Kalkars into a more charitable formation.

Julian lashed out with his right foot. Even though he was only fourteen, he was already a bear prowling the mountains amongst shorn-down sheep. He had grabbed up Kel-ee-kni with the same bravado that would have been required for simply standing there empty-handed and then, with only a sample of his assault level, knocked aside the nearest Kalkars.

"No, you can't!" screamed one of the Kalkars, but there was nothing around to prove that he could possibly do otherwise.

Tearing, snarling, ripping through his opponents, Julian set to work on them. He had a sword and a gun, but wasn't even bothering to touch the latter. Instead, he carved through the Kalkars with nothing but sheer determined gusto. By the time he had gutted the fifth one, the first was still sinking to the ground with a look of great surprise upon his face. In all, it couldn't have been more than ten seconds for Julian 6th to carve our assailants to pieces.

He whirled and saw Kel-ee-kni back up, her hands in the air, her eyes wide with fear. At the same time, though, there was still determination. "My . . . my son, Orthis, will destroy you!" she cried out. "No matter what you do to me! No matter how determined you are to battle me! No matter how—!"

"Oh my God," muttered Julian, who had clearly had enough. He took two quick steps and swung his left fist around. He struck her squarely in the jaw, and she went down, hitting the side of her head on the rock as she fell. She lay there, arms and legs splayed to either side, and he stood over her with his sword pointed squarely at her throat. "Shall I dispose of her, Mother?" he asked. The tone of his voice was utterly bland: I could have ordered her spared or gutted and it would have made not the slightest difference to him.

That awareness was too much for me to bear. "Let her be," I said finally.

"Are you sure?"

"Yes. With any luck, this will be the last we see of her."

He shrugged and returned the sword to its scabbard. Then he unslung a bag from his shoulder and opened it for me to inspect. There was much fresh meat within; my son had been busy.

I should have seen it as nothing more than a collection of food to be added to our larder. Instead, I took one look at it and began to sob. Immediately, obviously concerned that he had committed some great wrong, Julian moved to comfort me. I pushed him away even as I pulled myself together. "You've done nothing wrong. It's me. I'm just thinking of how proud your father would be of you. And I . . ." The tears began rolling down my face.

Julian 6th reached over and rubbed away the tears, smiling at me gently. "Let's go," was all he said.

We went.

⁑ III ⁑

I do not know why I feel the way that I do.

There is a dull ache in my side, one that had not been there before. I have felt it more than once in recent days, and I simply cannot understand why it keeps turning up.

It haunts me in my dreams, and I am even aware of it when I am awake. I scratch at it and there is nothing there, yet it continues to pursue me.

And through it all, there is my Julian 5th. I see him standing not far away, gazing upon me, reaching out to me. Curiously his face keeps changing, and sometimes he is Julian 5th, and other times the Ninth, and still other times the Third. He smiles to me, and I smile back, never knowing or understanding his reasons for being in the vicinity.

Why is he here? Why has he come?

No answers. Only more questions.

✳ ✳ ✳

The cabin is quite small, and yet it has served us well over the years.

We have traveled from one end of the country to the other and have taken up residence at the New York/Ontario border. Not that it makes much difference anymore which side of the lakes we're on. We are all of us, all of us, Kalkars.

And we feel good about that.

We have to. Because otherwise we are dead.

Not that any of *us* are feeling good about it, you understand. There are those of us, a precious few, who remain opposed to the situation in front of us. The Kalkars, our assailants from the Moon, have continued to rain down upon us, more and more showing up every year. Millions in all, leaving all of us to wonder where in the hell can they be coming from? I cannot fathom it. No one can. In the end, it is not ours to fathom, but merely to live with.

As for us, we endeavor to live as far from it as possible.

The woods around Niagara Falls remain relatively indifferent to those of us choosing to live around there. We had discovered our particular haven about a year or so after we avoided capture in the lower west end of Canada and instead made our way to the far east. Day after day after day we had lived outside or in caves or in small homes whose owners would, however temporarily, allow us to stay with them before insisting we moved on. How could we do otherwise, especially when Julian would start talking about overcoming the enemy and reestablishing a world for humanity? No one wanted to hear such talk. It made them nervous. And each time we would excuse ourselves and thank the people for whatever small amenities they could provide us, and each time Julian would subsequently apologize to me for talking us out of yet another home.

Yet I could never blame him. He was far too much like his father. I swore I could see the changes in his muscled body with every passing day. Within that first year of our journeying across the southern border of Canada, I watched him mature until he was within an inch or so of his father's growth. The following year he continued to grow and kept doing so. By the time he reached sixteen years of age, he had reached his full height of six and a half feet tall: taller and broader than his father by a good few inches.

Look at him, the ghost of Julian would remark to me. As each year continued to pass and Julian 6th grew stronger and more powerful, filling out his body, his father, Julian 5th would remark to me about it. *Look how strong and powerful he is. His time is going to be ready before you know it.*

And I would do the same thing I always did. I would sit there and shake my head and respond with determination, "No. He will not be you, Julian. The battle is done and the fight lost. He will live out his life and that will be that."

You know it will never be that, replied Julian's ghost, who seemed to have an inordinate amount of interest in him.

We had taken up residence in the small cabin after the first year of our journey on foot. The first couple of times the Kalkar reavers had pursued us, but by the third month of our drive, they seemed to have given up on us. Their concerns were with weightier matters, like keeping an eye on the world around them. Still, when we found the empty house up in the Canadian forest, some distance away from Niagara, we were initially unsettled by it. Who knew to whom it belonged?

As it turned out, it belonged to us. The day we found it, or more accurately the evening we found it, we tapped gently on the door and awaited a response. When none was forthcoming, we entered the room slowly, glancing around to see what we could see. The place was well stocked and there were gun bits and such that would enable continued hunting for food as needed. We glanced at each other and wondered aloud where the owner of the shack might be.

Turns out we found him easily enough when we wandered into the bedroom. There was Mister Whomever-Had-Been-There, and now would not be anymore. The good lord had called him home, and we had no idea what the reason for it might have been. All we knew was that it hadn't been all that long ago, and that was to our advantage. We removed him from his previous place of residence and buried him not all that far away, but with enough depth to hide any perceptions of him.

And that had been that. No one had come around for another six months after that, and when they did, all they found was some harmless older woman and her son, who was, at the time, growing like a weed.

We presented a united front. We gave food where we could. We sent people on their way.

If they refused to go, we would kill them. Chop them to bits and bury them a distance from the cabin.

That was our lives.

Year passed into year and we were content with that, or at least I was. The voice of Julian 5th would continue to seek me out on occasion, but I would turn away from it. I had no desire to leap into battle. Julian 6th, he certainly did, but he would not take the step unless I approved it. Which is not to say that we did not discuss it. "Mother!" he would say to me in mounting exasperation, "how can we do this? How can we simply sit by and allow the bastards to take over our world?" And we would talk about it back and forth, but every time it came down to the exact same observation from me: "It's already done. Now we simply ride it out."

And it was true. No one, not even Julian 6th, could deny it. The hundreds upon thousands of aggressive Moon Men had seen to it. Had we been up and running at the beginning, we might have been able to thwart it. As it was now, all we could do was ride matters out and wait for . . .

For what?

I had no clue.

And then one day . . .

. . . things changed.

A number of years had passed. Julian was well into his twenties, and he was as big and strong as I had ever seen him. He continued to work with his sword, every single day, two solid hours. He could whip the blade around so quickly that I almost never saw it. He kept a gun at his hip and would occasionally practice his marksmanship with it, although that wasn't quite as necessary, since his aim was so redoubtable. By this point in time he almost never spoke of taking up the banner against the Kalkars, because he knew I would never approve of it. Several times over the years he had spoken of simply leaving me to my own devices while he went off to do what had to be done. In those instances, I would simply shrug and tell him to follow his instincts. Yet every time he would reconsider his options and remain with me.

I was grateful for having that elevated position in his opinion.

The day when things changed, however, happened when I was sitting in our cabin, making brownies. An utterly routine thing to be undertaking, I know. But who could have been aware of the changes that were about to befall us?

There was a sharp knock at the door. Immediately I took a gun in my hand, something small but accurate. I then went to the door and stood to one side, casting my voice so that if someone shot through, they'd have nothing but emptiness to greet them and a .45 to spit back into their faces. "Who is it?" I called, my voice wavering falsely.

"Help me," came the whispered response. "Help me . . . please . . ." and that was followed by a most audible thud.

I knew I was taking a chance, but I didn't see as to how I had any choice. Sliding the gun into my back pocket, I hauled open the door and looked down. There was a young man there, roughly Julian's age, and he seemed badly injured. He was clutching at his shoulder and grimacing. "I'm sorry . . . I'm so sorry," he managed to say, and then his eyes rolled up and he sank quickly into unconsciousness.

By the time Julian 6th came home from hunting, he was astounded to see the young man seated upon the living room couch. The young man's eyes widened when he saw Julian studying him. I had helped him to sit up, and he was dabbing at some blood that had dried upon his forehead. His shoulder was already bandaged up. "Are you . . . ?" he began to ask, but then couldn't bring himself to finish the sentence.

"Am I who?" said Julian.

"Are you . . ." He took a deep breath and then let it out. "Are you Julian 6th?" Quickly he added, before Julian could respond, "Please don't consider me forward for asking such an obvious question. I know that it couldn't be you. There is no way that—"

God bless my son for his inability to lie. A wise young man would have known enough to say, "Get out before I throw you out." But not my Julian, no. Instead, with a look of deepest surprise, he said, "Yes! Why, yes, I am Julian 6th."

The young man who had come to us out of nowhere grasped at his heart as if the fondest stroke of luck had been granted. "I don't believe it. Is it true—?"

"Yes, it's true, and this is my mother, Nah-ee-lah. Which leaves us the question of—?"

"Oh, of course!" The new arrival appeared mortified. "I am Stubs."

"You don't look like a Stubs."

Stubs merely shrugged. "We are what we are. I was given the name over twenty years ago. I suppose my parents believed it fit me back then. But now . . . Gods, I still cannot believe it."

"Believe it and speak quickly, Stubs, because there are none who know that my mother and I reside here." There was an edge of severity to his voice. "We live in peace . . ."

"Then you live in a fool's paradise!" said Stubs urgently. "I tell you right now that there are people who continue to search for you. They remember who you are and what you are capable of. And more to the point, they will be more than happy to dispose of you once and for all. This you cannot allow."

"What are you saying?" Justin seemed utterly bewildered at what Stubs was telling him.

"Do you see these?" He pointed to the injuries on his body. "These are from people who attempted to avail themselves upon me. These are from people who tried to injure me once they found out about my mission! The world *needs* you, Julian! And you as well, ma'am," he added in quick acknowledgment of my presence.

"Kind of you to say," I told him cautiously. I rose up then, studying Stubs carefully. "And you found out all about my boy and came here . . . out of coincidence?"

"Not coincidence," said Stubs proudly. "Destiny."

"I see," I said to him.

There were so many other things I could have said as well, but instead I restrained them. I rose to my feet and said with studied indifference, "Son, I believe these are matters better left to you. I leave you to discuss them."

"Mother?" Julian was surprised to hear me speak so. In the past, others had attempted to intercede themselves in our affairs. This time, however, this day, I was inclined to let matters run their course.

So instead I simply reached out, took one of his hands in the two of mine, and squeezed it tight. "Do what you must," I said and then headed out of the house.

Once I had emerged, I immediately sought hiding under the darkening shadows. Even if someone had been watching me upon my first exit from the building, they would not have been able to maintain their sight of me. I circled around, keeping low and tight.

I was moving so quietly that none could have heard me. Minutes later, though, I heard them. A single, gentle snapping of a twig in the still of the night was all that was required.

I froze exactly where I was and waited.

A long pause and then another movement.

There she was: Kel-ee-kni. Older than when I'd last seen her, certainly, and better armed. She had a blaster tucked beneath her arm and she was trying as best she could to see the cabin. She was attempting to target the young man who had arrived at our house.

Except I knew that was not the case.

I had my gun up and leveled at her before she knew what was happening. "Don't move," came my soft voice purring in the darkness.

She moved, swinging her blaster toward me.

I only had to fire once to shoot the gun out of her hand. She cried out as it went flying, and she clutched at her hand, shoving it under her arm to help assuage her pain. A fairly steady stream of profanity emerged from her lips until I ordered her to be silent. She did so immediately. From nearby I could hear the river continuing to run steadily. Anyone falling into it would be pulled toward a fairly large waterfall that would provide a one-way exit from the area.

Slowly I advanced upon her. She saw me emerging from the darkness for the first time and instead of moaning actually grinned. "So it comes to this," she said.

I nodded ever so slightly. "It certainly took you enough years. That," and I gestured with my head toward the cabin, "is young Orthis, I take it?"

"You knew?"

"I suspected. Now I know."

She sneered at me. "My Orthis is going to kill your Julian."

"Perhaps," I said. "Or else it may well be the other way around. Or perhaps the both of them will get loose this time and the final resolution will occur at some point in the future, when neither of us is there."

"That will not happen," said Kel-ee-kni. "We did not spend so many years tracking you down so that matters conclude on an uncertain note. One way or the other, it ends tonight."

"Then you'd best hope it ends well for your man," and I leveled the gun at her. "Because for you, this is the last ni—"

An explosion hit my shoulder. I never even saw it coming. One moment I was there, on my feet, my gun leveled, and then the next something had exploded against me.

The gun went flying out of my hand as I stumbled backwards, slamming into a tree. Even as I tried to pull myself together, Kel-ee-kni advanced upon me. She had pulled a second gun out of nowhere, and she was drawing closer, firing again and again. Desperate, I threw myself behind a tree that provided me minimal blocking. Pieces of bark were blown away, and the tree remained solid, but not for long.

"Never again!" shouted Kel-ee-kni as she advanced upon my position.

The door of the small cabin banged open and I heard my son's voice call out to me, demanding to know what the hell had just happened. Suddenly he seemed to realize that all was not as he was supposed to believe, and he threw himself to one side just as a blast erupted past his head.

Kel-ee-kni spun and saw him and shouted an angry imprecation at her son. "Can you not do anything right!" she bellowed and swung her gun around to take aim at Julian.

Grabbing the only opportunity I could, I scooped up a rock and flung it at her.

The small missile sailed straight and true and ricocheted off her head. Down she went and immediately I sprinted across the divide between us. The water was continuing to rush past us as I came at her, trying to dodge right and left in order to make myself harder to hit.

Not hard enough.

Two feet away from her, and that was when she turned and shot me.

No screech. No screech for her. I provided her nothing save for a gasp as the blast ripped through my upper chest. By all means, I should have been dead right then. As it was, I staggered and then fell straight forward onto her. She was half standing when I struck her, and she laughed as my body crashed into her. It was all I could do not to lapse into unconsciousness that would take me to my final rest.

She tried to angle the gun around to get another shot off, looking surprised that I was still alive. Her surprise grew when she realized that she couldn't aim the gun at me. As if my mind had mentally disconnected, I kept the gun faced away from me. My legs went out from under me as I fell backwards, and still my hands kept locked around her wrists as if in a death grip.

She went down under me and we rolled along the sloped hill, banging, jostling against each other. Not once did Kel-ee-kni give up trying to shoot me. Instead she wrestled desperately, her frustration growing as she proved unable to dislodge the gun from my iron grasp.

"*You can't win this!*" she shrieked.

"I don't care about winning," and it was only then that I realized how little energy I had left. "I just have to make sure you lose."

At that moment she ripped the gun from my hand as we tumbled down the hill, and for half a moment there was a look of triumph on her face. But the joyous expression instantly morphed into horror as abruptly the ground went out from under her and we hit the water.

And I landed on top of her.

With the last amount of strength I had within me, I kept her under the water. As we plowed down the river, moving faster and faster, I felt her struggling. Her hands were trying to pummel me aside, to shove me off to one side or other of the bank so that she could manage to keep herself in the fray.

"No chance," I whispered. "No chance."

She fought and fought and came that close, so very, very close, to pushing me aside. She might very well have made it if she hadn't run out of water.

We sailed over the edge, and there was nothing but a vast drop beneath us. For half a second she emerged and then looked down and screamed.

I found that satisfying.

And then I fell . . .

And a hand touches my shoulder.

I look around and find myself in the Blue Room again. It is much as I remembered it before.

Why am I here?

Then there is a gentle touch upon my shoulder. I turn around and there is Julian 5th. He is smiling down at me, and he touches my chin, causing my head to look up at him.

"Do you remember now?" he asks.

I do. Suddenly I do. It all flashes back to me: the things I did do, haven't done, am going to do yet. "We haven't met yet," I say to him. "You're Julian 3rd."

"I am. And you are someone else, and we will be together and separate and lose each other and find each other. And so it will go."

I let out a breath. "It sounds exhausting. What of Julian 6th?"

"Our son? He will have his own adventures, find another you . . . it will all be okay, because it always is."

"Are you sure?"

"I am always sure."

He puts out his hands to me, and I slide into his arms. I have never felt so free. "Am I always going to remember this?"

"Who knows about 'always?' Be happy for what it is."

In the back of my mind, I see Kel-ee-kni is floating away, facedown, no sign of life within her. From somewhere above, I can see myself drifted up against the edges of the water. There is a faint smile upon my face.

"Yes," I say. "I will always be happy for what it is." I embrace him tightly, and we dance away into our eternal night.

 END

Everyone knows that Edgar Rice Burroughs invented Barsoom (Mars), just as he invented Tarzan. He never put the two together, and though there was an attempt by a second-rate science fiction magazine to publish Tarzan on Mars *by an anonymous writer back in the early 1950s, nothing ever came of it.*

But bestseller Kevin J. Anderson and prolific author and anthologist Sarah J. Hoyt have taken a totally different tack here. Yes, Tarzan meets Martians—but they are not from ERB's Barsoom, but from a Mars of Anderson's and Hoyt's devising. Vive la différence!

—*Mike*

Tarzan and the Martian Invaders

By Kevin J. Anderson and Sarah A. Hoyt

John Clayton, viscount of Greystoke, sat in a red leather chair in the study that had belonged to his ancestor. The setting would have seemed perfect to any civilized man, yet Lord Greystoke was uneasy.

In informal attire of shirt, trousers, and waistcoat, he was more deeply tanned than one might expect, and his powerful shoulders seemed ill-confined by stylish garments. As he turned the page of the book resting casually on his knee, his movements gave an impression of grace and power not normally seen in his class. The Greystokes had always been exceptionally well built and powerful, however; the portrait gallery above gave ample evidence of a long line of strong-featured, muscular, gray-eyed men.

Yet in this comfortable, relaxing setting, the man flung himself from the chair, closed the book he'd been trying to read, and slapped it on the polished mahogany desk before pacing from heavy-curtained window to blazing fireplace. His steps were those of a beast uneasily confined in a human space and bound by human conventions.

As Lord Greystoke twitched the curtain aside and looked at the

English night washed in a cold late-autumn rain, in his mind's eye he saw quite another landscape: the lush and untamed jungle of equatorial Africa.

Though he tried his best to look after his estates, speak to acquaintances at his club, or weigh in on issues in the House of Lords, he always felt apart from other humans. After his parents, Lord and Lady Clayton, had met untimely deaths in Africa, the infant John Clayton had been raised by Kala, from a tribe of anthropoid apes. The young boy's ape-mother had called him Tarzan, meaning "white-skin" in ape language. He hadn't seen another human until the age of fifteen and not seen a white man until he was twenty, the age at which he had first worn human clothing . . . and then everything had changed.

How odd it was to wear shirt and trousers, waistcoat and coat. How odd it felt to have a valet cater to his needs now. *Were it not for Jane*—Lord Greystoke thought, not for the first time, as he paced from the window to the fireplace. He paused to glare at the fire, that thing he'd once thought a living creature, the spawn of storm and lightning. The flames now sat confined in a stone-cased fireplace, just as Tarzan himself was held within this stone house, within his tailored suit, within the straining bonds of civilization and manners. Flaring his nostrils, he closed his eyes and imagined himself in his jungle again, swinging free from branch to branch, spending time with his friend the elephant Tantor, or Sheeta the panther, or even hunting with the Waziri warriors of whom he had become king. Now, in the stuffy, clammy manor house, his skin longed to feel the warm breezes of Africa, and his feet wanted to be freed from the confinement of shoes. He could stand it no longer!

Overcoming his feigned Greystoke dignity, Tarzan had succeeded in divesting himself of shoes and socks and dug his calloused toes into the soft pile of the oriental carpet, when a soft knock sounded upon the door.

Tarzan looked up guiltily. "Yes?" He half expected the opening door would reveal his stern, uncomprehending valet, but instead, he saw the delicate features of his wife, Jane Clayton, Lady Greystoke— the daughter of an American scientist who had come to Africa and there found Tarzan in his solitude. Had it not been for Jane . . . Jane's face . . . Jane's sweetness . . . and the hold she had over his heart, Tarzan would never have come to England. He would rather have let the lands, fortune, and accolades fall to some relative, while he claimed his true jungle kingdom and the mastery of his anthropoid apes.

Jane's face creased in a smile, and a gleam of amusement danced in her eyes. "May I come in? Would I be quite safe entering the domain of the king of the jungle?"

Although normal expressions still did not come naturally to him, Tarzan gave her the best smile he could command. He extended his arm to her. "You are quite safe with me, Jane. Human or ape, I am always your husband."

She came swiftly to be enfolded in his embrace. "Don't I know that? Have I not seen you when you still didn't know how to form human words? And yet . . ." Her hand caressed his powerful arm, feeling the muscles beneath the shirt. "You've always been human to me, the best of men."

His smile was now genuine. At that moment, he considered the freedom of his jungle well-lost for the sake of this.

Jane knew him all too well, however. "But you were dreaming of the jungle, weren't you?"

"Only a little," he admitted, and his hand gesture dismissed the surrounding countryside, tamed by sheep, covered in sheared grass, washed by rain. "I never liked the rain and cold, even when I was a little ap—*boy*, watched over by my faithful Kala." He kissed her forehead reassuringly. "Go to bed, and I'll be there presently. I'm only blue deviled by the rain. I shall find a book to read, and I'll use it to lull myself to sleep."

She wished him good night and left the study, closing the door softly behind her. As Jane was well aware, Tarzan was often unable to sleep inside the house upon the too-soft bed, so he spent many nights beneath the boughs of a tree on his estate. For her sake, he always made sure to return to the house, dress in his night clothes, and be by his wife's side come morning.

Left alone in his study, Tarzan resumed his pacing, resisting the urge to head out into the rain-washed night. It was true he'd never liked rain, but sometimes he liked the inside of houses even less. His restless hands fidgeted with the numerous books on the shelves, and behind a row of dusty tomes, in a space he'd never before explored, he found a thin book. Out of curiosity, and remembering the many years he'd spent reading every book his late parents had left behind in the treetop jungle cabin, Tarzan brought out the small volume. It was a diary, much like the diary his father had kept. This volume purported to be the diary of . . . John Clayton, Viscount Greystoke. Another John Clayton? He carried the volume with him back to the red leather chair.

A quick perusal revealed that the diary belonged to a long-forgotten ancestor from the days of Queen Elizabeth I. After studying the unfamiliar spelling and wording, Tarzan realized that his forgotten ancestor, that other John Clayton, had been a privateer in the Drake mold who sailed all over the world, even to Tarzan's beloved Africa.

Reliving his ancestor's adventures, Tarzan forgot that Jane was waiting for him to come to bed; he even forgot the walls around him, and the sound of beating rain outside. Instead, he revisited the lush jungles, survived onboard mutinies, and imagined the bright pattern of the Southern Cross above.

Suddenly, however, his mood changed. His eyes narrowed as he read an ordeal his ancestor had endured, one that was more peculiar than even the many perils Tarzan himself had faced. With a furrowed brow, he read through the book. His toes unconsciously clenched the thick pile of the carpet. He turned the page to find a series of drawings, and stopped.

He took the small telescope from the mantel, but though he looked out the window, the overcast sky revealed no stars. Then Tarzan recalled his father's mechanical celestial sphere, a wedding gift to the elder John Clayton on the occasion of his union with the ill-fated Lady Alice. He displayed the precious artifact on its special table in the study, and servants kept it scrupulously clean and oiled, even without being instructed to do so.

Tarzan went to the celestial sphere and referred to the crude drawing in his ancestor's diary, comparing the notations. He felt a chill, and the deep tan of his skin became visibly paler.

His hand clenched into a closed fist. "It will not be allowed!" His tone would have frightened anyone who listened, but in the silent chamber there was only the sound of the rain against the window glass.

The butler was astonished at his enigmatic master's request so late at night. "Milord? But—"

"See the car brought around, Jones. I must go to London. At once."

"In a night like this, Milord? You'll not have enough light to see by, and you—" The man was more worried than rebellious, but Tarzan couldn't afford any delay. His eyes had first learned to see with no artificial illumination, and he had found his way through the jungle so thick that no glimmer of light penetrated to the lower levels. He would not be deterred by a rainy night in the English countryside. Pulling on his driving gloves and hat, he said, "Don't worry, Jones. I shall be well." He suspected the only peril ahead of him was a very boring drive at the end of which, with luck, he would secure passage to Africa.

As he got behind the wheel of his latest-model automobile, a single doubt assailed him. He ought, perhaps, to have told Jane where he was going. She would worry.

But if he revealed his plans, she might insist on joining him, and he could not put her at risk against such unearthly dangers. Tarzan, ape-man, Lord of the Jungle, would have to face this threat for all mankind. And win. He would not let Jane or their son, Jack, become victims of such a terrible menace.

Next morning, Jane realized that Tarzan must have spent the night sleeping out in the rain, for he had never come to bed.

She was aware that in forcing civilization upon her wild husband, she had in some unknown way injured him. Other people thought that she'd redeemed a poor savage and bestowed the great boon of culture upon him. But Jane wasn't so sure. She remembered the sparkle in his eyes when he was in the jungle, and she wasn't sure that bringing him to refined, and confined, England was a good thing.

At the back of her mind she held the idea that once Jack grew a little older, they'd acquire a plantation in Africa and Tarzan would be able to disappear into the jungles he loved, now and then, while she would still enjoy the comforts of civilization. Someday.

But for now Lady Greystoke had to go through the morning rituals without letting on to the household that anything might be wrong between them, or that she was worried that her very peculiar beloved hadn't managed to slip quietly back inside before dawn, as he always did.

She allowed herself to be helped into her clothes, and she approved the menus for the day with barely more than a glance. She visited Jack in the nursery and discussed with nurse how to break the young master's bad habit of sucking his thumb. She preoccupied herself, but Tarzan's continued absence was very odd. It wasn't like him to remain away from her for so long.

A few discreet questions revealed that no one had seen Lord Greystoke that day. Wondering if some accident could have befallen him in the seemingly safe environs of the manor, she hastened to his study to find a letter propped against the ornate celestial sphere. In her husband's handwriting, the envelope said only "Jane." She tore it open and found a single sheet of paper embossed with the Greystoke seal.

> *My very dear Jane, believe that I would not leave you like this if I had any other alternative. In an old diary I've found credible evidence that our world will shortly be invaded by a species more ruthless and determined than even our own—and I recognize all too well the place where they are supposed to land. My only chance is to go back to Africa and fight them there, before they reach the world of civilized men.*
>
> *Doubt not that I will win this battle, my dear Jane—for I am Tarzan, Lord of Apes and Lord of the Jungle. I shall defeat these monsters who would use the creatures of Earth as fodder and slaves. And then I will come back to you.*
>
> *Yours ever, Tarzan.*

Beneath it, as an afterthought, he'd scribbled, *John C., Lord Greystoke.*

Jane stared in disbelief at the letter in her hands. What did he mean by the whole world being invaded? Countries got invaded, not worlds. She looked towards the mechanical celestial sphere, thinking of all those other worlds out there, and a doubtful frown formed on her delicate face. What if something came from those other globes to Earth? She shivered.

She noticed that Tarzan had left the paper askew on the desk, and his pen lying beside it, uncapped. Mechanically, she capped it.

Tarzan would have a head start of a night and a day, but it was clear where he was headed, one of the places familiar to him from his childhood. Which meant she knew where to find him. And she would. It was no part of Lady Greystoke's intentions to let her husband face a cruel invader alone.

"Jones," she called. "Bring our other car around."

Days later, Tarzan was let out of a small rowboat on the coast of Africa, and he climbed onto the familiar shore, setting foot again on the land of his birth. Just breathing the air exhilarated him! He waved good-bye as the sailors rowed back to the steamer that had carried him here. He marveled that for once he had not met with mutiny or assassination attempts or other villains intent on eliminating him. Perhaps the very fact that he was here to save humanity from a terrible fate meant there was some protection from God or Fate.

Tarzan wasn't sure in which he believed. The anthropoid apes hadn't believed in much, though they did have some rites of their own—and it was to the place of those rites that he must now go.

As the ship steamed away, fast disappearing on the blue horizon, Tarzan removed all his garments. It was difficult enough to wear clothes in England, but it was torture here in Africa, where he should be home.

Knowing the ship would return for him in a month, he took care to fold the clothes and store them in the valise, from which he took his breechclout and his brass ornaments for arms and legs. Then, truly *Tarzan* again, he turned toward the jungle. . . .

Before long, he was swinging from tree to tree, following a familiar route. First, he had to go to where the old diary said the invaders' ship would land. There, he should find drawings on the wall, and then he would know for certain whether this had been a mere nightmare from his ancestor, or the truth.

The old treetop cabin was as Tarzan had left it, protected by the cunning lock on the door which made it impossible for the anthropoid apes or other wildlife to penetrate it. Sliding the lock open with the ease of long familiarity, Tarzan entered to find the interior largely undisturbed as well. He stowed his valise and looked wistfully at the bed where his mother had died a year after giving birth to him, and the place where his father had been killed. These reminders held no terror of sadness for him, since he'd never really known his parents. Having grown up among wild beasts, he had a very matter-of-fact view of life and death. Creatures lived and hunted and ate other creatures, and eventually one died and became food for others. He did not lament over it.

For a moment, he hesitated over his own purpose in racing back to Africa. If that philosophy were true, perhaps it held true in the greater universe, as well. Why was it any different for creatures from another world to hunt and kill the inhabitants of Earth? It was the order of nature.

His qualms were of short duration, however. Tarzan could apply such a philosophy to himself, as he had never counted himself much above the beasts. But Jane and Jack were also creatures of Earth, as were his many good friends, animal and human. Well did he remember losing Kala, his ape-mother. Though she had been rude and ugly, in the way of such things, he thought of her with all the bittersweet tenderness and respect that he would have lavished on his real mother, the late Lady Alice.

The thought that their lives should count for nothing made Tarzan's heart tighten in his chest. Yes, he would fight these invaders—not for himself, but for all the creatures of this Earth that he loved.

He was surprised to hear something heavy throw itself against the door of the cabin. He unsheathed his knife. He had killed lions and panthers with only his sharp knife and a rope. But when a soft growl echoed outside the door, he recognized the animal voice—Sheeta the panther, who, not so long since, had helped him rescue Jack and Jane when they'd been abducted by the dastardly Rokoff.

Tarzan *murred* back at Sheeta, conveying thoughts that could only be implied in the panther language, "Hello, Sheeta, my old friend and ally who helped me fight evil among the humans. I am Tarzan of the Apes, and I am back."

The soft *murr* that answered was all the welcome he could hope for.

With Sheeta following stealthily on the ground, Tarzan flew from tree to tree, suspended by ropes as he headed for the place he had read about in the diary. He remembered the site of his first great battle, where he'd killed Tublat, the unjust mate of his foster-mother, Kala.

He had always thought of the place as a natural amphitheater, a part of the landscape like the mountains and hills and the ocean itself. But if his ancestor's diary was correct, this arena was not natural at all, but an alien construction, a landing pad for a sort of ship that could cross from one world to another. The idea should have made Tarzan's head spin, but he had already been forced to adapt his view of the world to include seemingly impossible things: wheeled vehicles, large cities, great industries. Adapting his mind now to the idea of yet another complex civilization that came from beyond the sky did not cause him any greater consternation.

The open amphitheater was circular in shape, and its unnatural strangeness was emphasized by the fact that it remained unencumbered by entangling vines and creepers. The encroaching jungle itself seemed to avoid the place.

The dense jungle choked off access, though, as if to deny any intruders. Giants of the untouched forest grew close, with matted growth clogging the spaces between their trunks. The only opening Tarzan could find into the level arena was through the upper branches of the trees. He knew his way.

Throughout Tarzan's childhood, the anthropoid apes had often gathered here. In the center of the amphitheater he now saw one of the earthen drums built by the anthropoids for their strange rites, which have been heard by men across the vast unexplored jungle, but never witnessed. Tarzan was the only human who had ever seen the wild, frenzied revelry the drums inspired.

On moonlit nights, the anthropoid apes would dance in a rite that marked all important events in the life of the tribe: a victory, the capture of a prisoner, the killing of some fierce jungle denizen, the death or accession of a king. Here prisoners were dragged to be killed and devoured. Here Tarzan had defeated his first enemy and, later, had ascended as king of the anthropoid apes.

A long time had passed since then, and now another ruled the tribe, one who owed Tarzan fealty and who would recognize him as his lord. But before Tarzan would call on Akut and his people, he must first confirm that the strange symbols reported by his ancestor were indeed on the walls.

With his knife, Tarzan scraped at a half-buried wall of stone near the edge of the amphitheater. His wide blade revealed deep engravings in the stone: marks that represented the worlds encircling the sun, the larger rings of their orbits, and sharp triangle-shapes of the vessels that sailed between worlds.

Again he studied the ancient drawings and remembered the celestial engine at home which showed the alignments of those planets, and he had no doubt in his mind that his ancestor was correct.

The engravings were clear, showing the movements of planets and indicating that when the planet Mars should be close to Earth and in just such an alignment, the ships of the Martians would fly to Earth.

Clearing more debris from the wall, Tarzan saw additional, more detailed drawings that the other John Clayton had mentioned but not copied: human captives being driven into the triangular ship, pictograms that showed them being forced to serve creatures with many tentacles and a confusion of eyes, and then being devoured by those monsters.

There was more, and Tarzan no longer had any reason to doubt the prophecy of his ancestor: if the Martian scout ship could get through, then the invaders would send an armada, intending to rule the Earth as overlords, as superior to humans as humans were to anthropoid apes.

Tarzan opened the well-thumbed diary, which he'd carried in his arrow quiver. What worried him most was his ancestor's warning, "They have a mind ray which can render you servile and mindless. Under its influence you will be unable to resist the enemy. Humans fall under this ray, but animals seem immune, and it was with the help of my faithful—" There a large stain blocked out the rest of the story, picking up much later with, "And thus, the space menace defeated, in peace and honor I travelled to England, bringing this warning to my fellow men, which, alas, none of them would believe."

An alien mind ray. Tarzan wondered if he was human enough to fall under the influence of invaders, or if he still carried enough of the jungle within his heart and mind. Regardless, he must make sure that others stood ready to defeat the Martians and save Earth from subjugation.

If the mechanical celestial sphere was accurate, the initial ship would land tonight. He had very little time to gather his allies.

First, he explained the situation to Sheeta, as much as possible in the panther language. She understood that he would be fighting, and she knew to help him, and also that she was not to eat any of the animals of Earth, not in this battle.

Next, he visited Tantor the elephant, his old friend. The great gray beast remembered him, and Tarzan needed only moments to explain the situation, for elephants are as wise as humans. Tantor promised Tarzan that he would gather those creatures that were the elephant's fast friends: some tribes of monkeys, some birds, large snakes that slithered through the grass, and a tribe of wise old elephant matriarchs.

Meanwhile Tarzan went in search of Akut's people, the anthropoid apes who were descended from the ones who had raised him. At first, he worried that the new tribe leader would not remember him, and Tarzan would have to fight once more for his supremacy, but when he approached the tribe by a river, after the first moment of alarm in which the apes gathered children to themselves and flitted to the upper branches of trees, they recognized him and called out, "Welcome, Tarzan, defeater of Kerchak, lord of the jungle and friend of Akut."

Tarzan answered them by explaining that a great evil was coming from the sky and that they must defeat it. They were fearful of the news, but angry when he described the threat further. The entire tribe agreed to meet him by the amphitheater at moonrise.

Confident in his growing army, Tarzan went through the jungle on his own, to the nearby native village. When he'd been but a boy, he had convinced these savages that he was a supernatural entity, and they had appeased him by leaving out food as well as arrows poisoned with a fast-acting mixture. He feared that they'd fallen out of the habit after so much time had passed, but he found the arrows there in the little hut they'd built to revere him, and also fresh food.

Back home in England, Lord Greystoke would no more dream of eating leftover scraps than he would dream of sharing his dogs' kennels. Here, though, a different law applied. He ate the food; then he collected the poison-tipped arrows and returned through the high branches to his treetop cabin, where he restrung the bow he had taken long ago from a defeated enemy. He was preparing for a war against another world.

True, he could have brought a rifle with him and used that against the invaders. But he was more familiar with bow and arrows, and with its flash and explosion a rifle would give away his position. Yes, the arrows would be better.

He worried that the poison in the arrows would be ineffective against creatures from another world. But then he remembered the pictographs of the invaders devouring humans, and he reasoned that if the monsters could eat humans, then they must succumb to poisons of Earth.

✳ ✳ ✳

When the moon rose over the ancient amphitheater, Tarzan was ready. Waiting in the crook of a tree above the ground, he felt and heard the animals of Earth nearby, also ready.

Before long, high above, there appeared a wheel of fire falling from the sky, a contraption that tumbled and made a sound just at the edge of hearing. Tarzan heard the first keenings of fear from the gathered animals, and he gave the shout of the great anthropoid apes, urging them to stand firm.

As the wheel of fire descended and finally came to rest in the amphitheater, Tarzan could tell that the supposedly natural arena had been designed to accommodate the otherworldly vessel. The triangular ship smoked, exuding acrid fumes; its walls were made of a black metal with a green sheen, and it gleamed wetly for all it had been on fire just moments before.

The ship remained quiet for an agonizing moment, and Tarzan wondered whether to command his animals to advance on it and stomp it flat before the invaders could emerge. But he reasoned that any such ship that could cross the vast space between the worlds must be hardier than the hooves and claws of the animals of Earth. He bided his time.

Then a tower emerged from the top of the contraption, emitting a light that seemed no natural light, but a glow that he perceived from the back of his brain rather than through the eyes. Tarzan stared at it, felt dizzy, but could not stop looking. Its effect on him was similar to what he had seen of a bird when faced with the hypnotic stare of a serpent. For a long, indefinable moment, he remained frozen on the tree branch, his eyes fixed on the light, and his mind filled with only a vague apprehension of danger and the stillness of death.

In vain, the tribe of anthropoid apes called out to him and asked what to do. In vain, Sheeta nudged him. In vain, Tantor let out a loud trumpet to demand his attention. But he could not respond. Instead, at the back of Tarzan's mind, he had a fuzzy recollection of the mind ray that his ancestor warned would render humans docile. *Humans.* He struggled, but he could not fight off the influence of the ray.

Then the Martians emerged from their ship, hideous things that brought a wave of nausea even to his fogged brain. Tentacled bodies that slumped and lurched forward, with dark, oily skin that oozed a slime, leaving a trail behind them. And clusters of eyes that had looked upon alien skies which they had conquered, and sideways maws ringed with needlelike teeth, ready to suck and chew. They wished to be the new overlords of Earth, and their pulsing signal sent out an irresistible summons across the jungle.

Tarzan's stupor lasted an indefinite time, perhaps days, as he struggled—and then humans began to emerge from the jungle, making their way through the thick underbrush, battering down a new path. Natives both male and female, some of the women carrying little babes on their hip, utterly ignoring all of the wild animals gathered there by Tarzan. Instead, they marched forward singly or in groups, summoned by the terrible mind ray. And the hideous Martians waited there in front of their open ship to receive them as slaves, or as food.

He might have remained frozen forever, but then among the mass of dark-skinned natives clad in skins and tribal ornaments, he saw a figure clad as an English lady, and as the eerie moonlight fell upon her face, Tarzan recognized the beautiful features of his wife, Jane.

Two greenish-black horrors slithered forward to grab the slender arms of Jane Clayton, seizing her. She was too frozen to struggle as they began to drag her toward their sinister vessel.

Even though he was human by blood, the son of John Clayton Greystoke and the Lady Alice Greystoke, Tarzan of the Apes was not merely human. He was as much the adopted son of Kala the anthropoid ape, and his brain had been filled with habits and thoughts formed throughout his early life when he roamed the primeval forests of Africa—thoughts that were not bound by civilization.

Though he had struggled in vain against the force, this sight gave him a strength that no other force did, and he clawed deep into his own uncivilized *animal* heart to shake off the blind blankness of hypnotism. Just as his love for Jane had made a man out of the savage creature who had been reared in the jungles, now his love for his woman sparked a fierce fury in his ape-mind, a need to defend his mate.

As the creatures hauled his mesmerized and vulnerable wife into their alien ship, Tarzan at last managed to shake off the soporific effect of the ray. He arose with a cry that commanded all his animals to follow him. He jumped into the arena, racing toward Jane, just as she stopped and shuddered, as though suddenly waking at the sound of his voice.

But Tarzan was not fighting alone. Monkeys swarmed forward to jump onto the entranced natives, knocking them to the ground and preventing them from boarding the ship. Birds of prey swooped in to harass the flailing tentacles of the startled Martians. Sheeta and two other sleek panthers bounded forward, driving a Martian to the ground, tearing greenish-black skin with their sharp claws and spilling alien blood as well as slime. The aliens chittered and shouted, astonished at this unexpected and improbable resistance.

Still fighting off the cloying effects of the mind ray, he was only vaguely aware of Tantor's companions charging into the arena with deafening bellows. With a loud trumpet, a clever female elephant, supported by others, had charged up the sloped wall of the alien ship. With her trunk, she reached out and snapped the antenna from the hull.

In an instant, like the silence following a loud clap of thunder, the confusion was gone from Tarzan's mind. At the same time that the gathering natives stirred to life, awakening to their situation with fear and confusion, Tarzan shouted out an encouragement to all the animals. He plunged after his wife into the darkness of the alien ship, calling out in the tongue of the natives of the region, "These are cruel slavers from another world! They seek to imprison you—fight them!"

The creatures of Earth fought together, banding into a wild army that fought back against invaders from another world. In an army of fur, feathers, scales, and fangs, they struck at the scout ship that had landed in their jungle. Birds fiercely pecked holes in the metal skin of the vessel, and snakes slithered through. Howling, the great anthropoid apes pounded the ship and tore at the many-tentacled aliens with brute strength. Tantor and his elephant army crushed through the hull to free the few natives already in the ship. Sheeta's tribe gloriously crushed the aliens in their fierce jaws, then spat out the foul-tasting Martian flesh.

Tarzan, though, fought his own battle, following his wife's cries through the interior of the Martian vessel to an inner chamber in which a blazing glow shone from a vast apparatus surrounded by monsters who held Jane captive. They drew her toward the crackling glow, and now Jane fought back, trying to pull herself free of the tentacles, kicking, but in vain. Tarzan saw the shimmering blaze—and he wondered in horror if the assembled aliens meant to roast and devour Jane even now.

He let fly with his arrows so swiftly that he seemed to be everywhere at once. The poison-tipped shafts flew true, each one piercing an alien's slimy hide. He watched them slump one after another. Yes, indeed, the toxin was as deadly to Martians as it was to the creatures of Earth.

The invaders were in disarray, and Jane finally broke free of one captor, disentangling herself from the tentacles and lashing out with her boot to knock one of the aliens away; Tarzan shot it. But the other monster still held her, drawing her close and retreating toward the crackling glow, as if it meant to immolate itself along with her. Tarzan could not hit the Martian without the risk of hitting his own wife.

Instead, yelling a defiant roar of one of the great apes, Tarzan flew at the alien, his knife unsheathed. With a brutal slash, he severed the tentacle that held his Jane. Slime spurted, but she threw herself away, dropping to the floor. Tarzan plunged closer, ripping the knife down to hack off tentacles. The thing's sideways maw snapped at him, trying to lock needle teeth onto Tarzan's tanned skin. For a moment, the remaining tentacles held him fast in a death grip, and the jaws snapped shut, trickling silvery venom.

But he bit and he clawed and he broke his arm free to raise the knife high. He brought it down, plunging the sharp point into the mass of staring eyes. He drove the hilt as hard as he could, shoving the blade deep into what must have been the Martian's brain. The alien shrieked, and greenish-blue ooze spurted out. The heavy, slime-coated creature slumped in an ungainly heap on the floor.

Tarzan panted, and he looked around to realize that the chamber was now filled with the creatures of Earth. All the other aliens lay dead.

As his sweet Jane rushed into his arms, he held her. Seeing himself dripping with alien ichor, he cautioned her, "Careful, my love. I'm covered in alien blood."

"It doesn't matter to me. This was a time when Earth needed a savage to defend it," she said, her hair in disarray and her own clothes stained with slime. "For savage or civilized, you are always the best of men, and the only one I'll ever love."

✳ ✳ ✳

Long into the night around the amphitheater, the creatures of the jungle, for once at peace, celebrated the death of the alien enemies.

Days later, in quieter times when Tarzan and Jane had returned to the treetop cabin in the jungle, they woke together after a sound and untroubled sleep. In a sleepy voice, Jane mused with a self-deprecating laugh, "And to think I came to Africa to save *you* from these aliens."

"And you did, my dear." He wore only his breechclout and barbaric ornaments, yet he had the manner of the most respected nobleman. "But for the sight of you, I would have remained hypnotized by the creatures, and I and all my friends would have perished. Just as your love saved me from a life of eternal savagery, so did your presence save me from alien enslavement." He smiled at her. "Now let us enjoy our days here in the jungle, so I can remember who I really am, while we wait for the ship that will take us back to England—and to Jack. In the meantime, let me share with you my jungle domain, just as you have shared civilization with me."

"Billy was a mucker, a hoodlum, a gangster, a thug, a tough. When he fought, his methods would have brought a flush of shame to the face of His Satanic Majesty. He had hit oftener from behind than from before. He had always taken every advantage of size and weight and numbers that he could call to his assistance. He was an insulter of girls and women. He was a bar-room brawler, and a saloon-corner loafer. He was all that was dirty, and mean, and contemptible, and cowardly in the eyes of a brave man, and yet, notwithstanding all this, Billy Byrne was no coward."

The Mucker *and* The Return of The Mucker *tell how Billy Byrne was changed from the rough and tumble Chicago street fighter Burroughs describes above to a civilized man, by his love for socialite Barbara Harding. At the end of the first book, Billy even leaves her, knowing it would never work out for them. He asks that she marry her fiancé, Billy Mallory. The best-selling team of Max Allan Collins and Matthew Clemens write of the day after Billy Byrne leaves. According to them, the couple weren't quite through with each other.*

—Bob

The Two Billys
A Mucker Story

Max Allan Collins and Matthew Clemens

He was no damn coward. Had he been, the dark-haired, muscular mucker named Billy Byrne could not have survived a West Side of Chicago upbringing. He had grown up hard and fast in the neighborhood that ran from Halsted to Robey, and from Grand Avenue to Lake Street, where being a coward was the greatest of all sins.

Not only was Billy not a coward, he had felt fear but twice in his young life.

The first had been as a lad barely into his teens. He was afraid neither of his opponent, Coke Sheehan, nor the outcome of their knuckle-duster. But during the brawl—a dispute over Sheehan

211

welching on paying him money owed for a robbery the two had pulled together—Billy had hit the other boy in the head with a brick, rendering Sheehan unconscious and possibly croaking him.

The possible croaking of Sheehan itself had not scared the mucker, not really; but the idea that the coppers and a judge might make him swing at the end of a rope for it, well, that was damned unsettling, and had sent him briefly into hiding. The brick-bashed Sheehan had survived—too tough and dumb to die, most likely—and eventually Billy had returned to the streets.

The second occasion that had brought Billy that blue funk called fear was right before and during round one of his first prizefight against a top-notch brawler talked about as the next heavyweight champion. So the fight drew a big crowd that hooted and hawed through the introductions of what they figured to be a sorry mismatch, and the jeering went on for the first three minutes as the would-be future champ battered Billy.

Yes, Billy was afraid. Not of losing, nor of his opponent—it was that damned crowd. This brand of fear was simple stage fright, and soon Billy overcame that emotional fog to mop the floor with the "future champion." The mucker sent the palooka back to the farm in the fifth round.

And yet this mucker unafraid of even the Maylay headhunters of Daimyo Oda Yorimoto stood there in his sweats on the floor of Professor Cassidy's gym with trembling fingers—fingers unfolding a note just handed him by a messenger boy about as threatening as a newborn pup.

He did not need to read a word to know it was from her—Barbara Harding, the woman he loved, the woman he had left to another man, one befitting her station, not twenty-four hours ago.

The note announced her by way of its fragrance—sweet lilac, like that first hint of spring. She always smelled that way to Billy, even when they had been marooned on a Pacific island and were on the lam from Yorimoto's headhunters. Even when they were living in hiding on an island in the middle of a raging river on Yoka, and especially when she had safely returned to her father's Riverside Drive mansion . . . always and ever, she wore the fragrance of lilacs and spring.

A pang of something else other than fear—regret, joy, *something* he could not quite identify—shot through him as he recognized her flowing, smooth handwriting.

> *Billy,*
> *I need you, something horrible has happened.*
> *Come at once.*
>
> *Barbara*

Nearby in the gym, the stout, Cro-Magnon-browed Cassidy watched two lightweights spar in the main ring. The aroma of sweat, not lilacs, hung in the air, and Billy heard the manager yell at one of the boxers, "Keep your left up for Chrissakes! He'll take your bleedin' head off."

Next to Billy, the messenger boy stood silently, waiting for a response and maybe a tip.

Carefully, the mucker folded the note and palmed it.

"Any answer?" the boy asked.

The mucker shook his head and found a dime for the boy, who left, but not in a rush, mesmerized as he was by being this close to real live fighters.

Standing there, watching but not seeing the lightweights spar, Billy felt his insides roiling like dark storm clouds as he tried to figure out a way to ignore Barbara's summons. It had taken every ounce of strength he had to walk out the door yesterday. To return a day later, into that world where he knew he did not belong, that would be harder than any bout Cassidy could wrangle for him. He knew he had no place in the Hardings' mansion, and he knew Barbara was better off with someone of her own station, like William Mallory . . . but God how he loved her. If he walked back in, could he find the strength to walk out again?

Billy changed into his suit and tie—not fancy enough for a visit to a millionaire, but they would have to do—and, coming out of the locker room, he almost ran into Professor Cassidy.

"You gonna be gone long?" the manager asked.

"Who said I was leaving?"

"If I couldn't read that mug of yours like a map, I'd be a poor damn manager indeed. How long, son?"

"I don't know."

"Is it the skirt?"

Billy nodded.

"We'll be here when you get back," Cassidy said and strolled away toward the sparring ring.

Turning, Billy went out and grabbed a spot on one of the trolley cars. Cassidy's gym was not far from the Battery, and the ride gave Billy time to think as the trolley clanked and rattled northward.

She was there, as she always was, in his mind's eye—her auburn hair pinned up, leaving her high-cheekboned face and large green eyes uncovered. This look allowed people to meet her as she met the world—head on. Barbara was impetuous, strong, brave, and she had saved Billy's life. Maybe she hadn't taken a bullet or a blade for him; but she had saved him, nonetheless.

Teaching Billy that the straight life was not a cowardly road to travel, she had won him over; and along the way she had shown him how to speak and act and carry himself like a gentleman, as well. Billy found himself wanting to be a better man just to please her. Even his mucker's mind could perceive that this was a transformation little short of miraculous, though for him that transformation had turned out to be far easier than he might ever have imagined.

A man might act a right sissy for the love of a good woman, and Barbara was a good woman, all right. But Billy knew in his mind, if not his heart, that she was not for him. Wealthy, from a good family, a genteel woman, Barbara Harding deserved better than a hardscrabble slum tough, no matter how much he may have changed.

Riding that trolley back to the mansion of her father—the wealthy, well-born Anthony Harding—Billy did his best not to read disaster into that tucked-away note. But how could he not?

"Something horrible has happened."

What could that be? What could be so bad that she would summon him so soon after he had thrust her into the arms of another man?

Billy hopped off the trolley car and briskly walked the last few blocks. Even from a distance, in this incredibly swank neighborhood, the Harding manse stood out as a monument to wealth and breeding. A multimillionaire who was no doubt overjoyed that the mucker was finally out of his daughter's life, Harding would not likely be pleased to see who was about to come calling . . .

On this beautiful Saturday afternoon, the swells who lived in these posh digs were out taking the air as Billy passed. Some looked down their noses at the mucker, whose clothes, though nicer than anything he had ever owned, were a far cry from the day coats of the gentlemen strolling the avenue next to ladies in fine frocks. A few nasty glances, with the rest ignoring him, only emphasized how out of place Billy was in these airy environs.

As he strolled the last block, Billy saw something across the street that put a prickle on the back of his neck. Ducking behind the ornate stairway two doors down from the Hardings', Billy was free to gaze, and having done so was glad he had followed his instincts.

On the opposite side of the avenue, hidden in the shadows of a stairway himself, a man could be made out, well, not a man—a boy, really, dressed not that different from himself. The boy's eyes were glued to the Hardings' front door. Whatever problem had prompted Barbara to send for Billy, he felt certain that the lookout across the street was part of it.

Billy doubled back to the corner and came around to the mansion's rear, keeping his eyes peeled for compatriots of the lookout; but he saw no one. Coming up to the servants' door in the back, reversing the very route he had used to quit the Harding house yesterday, Billy wondered if maybe he should just kick the door in and go in, fists up.

Picking the lock and going in quietly was not in Billy's bag of tricks, after all. But considering there was a lookout across the street, and that Barbara had been able to get a note out, he figured the danger inside the house itself was probably minimal, at least for now. He chose to knock—politely.

Smith, Mr. Harding's gentleman's gentleman, opened the door a sliver. A thin, severe man with muttonchops and a seemingly perpetual scowl, Smith stepped aside and let Billy in, saying with a sniff, "Miss Harding and her father are expecting you . . . in the drawing room, *sir.*"

Why did those who attended the rich have even more snobbish an attitude than the rich themselves? This a boy of the slums would never understand.

The back entryway, a mere vestibule, led into the kitchen near the servants' quarters and the rear stairwell the help used. The shadowy little space held the afterglow aroma of a hearty breakfast. Billy felt, and heard, his stomach growl.

"Through here," Smith said, leading the way into the kitchen.

One maid, a blonde, sat at the table, polishing silver. Another, a brunette, stood over a sink plucking feathers from a chicken. The walls hid behind massive wooden cabinets, their doors made of glass, revealing opulent plates, cups, and silver.

Smith marched him through the ornate dining room with its fancy chandeliers, oaken table, and chairs with padded brocade-upholstered seats. Huge landscape paintings lined the oak-paneled walls. While a dining room, this seemed a man's chamber, the colors deep and dark, the wood of the highest quality. Cigar smell hung in the air. This room, this house, belonged to a very successful, important man, and Anthony Harding was certainly that.

Finally, after a walk that rivaled the jaunt from the trolley stop, Billy found himself at the front entranceway. Here the servant led him across the marble-floored foyer, passing the wide carpeted staircase, finally stopping at the doorway to the parlor.

At the edge of that doorway, Smith announced "Mr. Byrne" with all the joy of a judge handing down a verdict.

As the butler stepped aside, Billy entered the room to find Mr. Harding standing across the room near the fireplace, his face a mask of dismay. Seated in a velvet-covered chair, her eyes red from crying, a hanky clinched in her fist, Barbara looked up as Billy entered the room. She looked pale, and her countenance had not worn such alarm since they were being chased by headhunters.

Rising, she rushed into Billy's arms, pressing hard against him, the scent of her filling his nostrils, and, for a second, he thought he might come completely apart, like a china figurine flung on a hardwood floor.

Then, remembering where he was, Billy glanced over to see that Mr. Harding had discreetly turned to poke at the burnt-out ashes of last night's fire rather than see the impropriety of their embrace. Though a quite proper man, Harding knew how his daughter felt about the mucker, and as long as this was as far as things went, he would indulge her. She was, however, engaged to another, and that must never be forgotten.

Pulling away from the woman he loved, Billy saw tears running anew down her cheeks. "Here, here—what's all this, then?"

Barbara dabbed at moist eyes. "It's the *other* Billy—he's been kidnapped."

Sharing a first name with one William Mallory wasn't the only way the two were joined. They were also in love with the same woman. Mallory, however, was of her station, Billy decidedly not.

His hands found her shoulders supportively. "What happened?"

Looking to her father, who said nothing, Barbara explained. "After you left me yesterday, after you called Billy to come back, and told him that I loved him, wanted to marry him . . ."

The more she went over these painful recent memories, the more he realized how deeply he had hurt her. He was not much for reading people, especially the wealthy, but Barbara he knew. She loved him, she had said so, and meant it; still, he felt she needed to be with someone who held a position in society—the "other Billy," William Mallory, fit the bill.

". . . he came over. We discussed it. We even set a date."

Despite his having been the one who quit her, Billy felt hurt that she had fallen back in with Mallory so quickly. They had set a date *already?*

Obviously anxious to move this along, silver-haired Anthony Harding stepped forward. His words were matter-of-fact and clipped, but his eyes punctuated them with fear and concern.

"After he left here," Harding said, "Mallory was taken. Abducted."

"You *saw* it?" Billy asked.

Harding shook his head as he withdrew a piece of paper from his pocket—a note not that different from the one from Barbara.

Billy accepted the paper from Harding and read: *We have Mallory. You will pay us $500,000. If you involve the law, Mallory dies.*

The young lookout across the street became immediately clear to Billy. If just one copper stopped at the Harding house, the lookout's gang would sure as sin croak "Billy" Mallory.

"Why you?" Billy asked.

"Pardon?"

"Not why not abduct you instead, sir, but . . . why are you the person to whom that note was given?"

"I would suppose that it's because we have far more money, even more than Mallory's own family. Also, I'm sure, given the impending nuptials, that makes us easy, tempting prey."

"Sir, who even knew about Barbara and Mallory getting back together? It's only been one day."

Harding harumphed. "I suppose I had something to do with that. As soon as the decision was made, I sent telegrams to all the newspapers in the city. I wanted to make sure the announcement was in the next edition."

Billy understood, and in a way did not blame the man. Anything that broke Barbara from a mucker like him had to be cause for celebration for her father.

"So," Billy went on, "one of the messenger boys, or somebody at one of the papers, decided to grab Mallory and hold him for ransom."

"Yes, or let the information slip to an underworld associate," Harding said.

Leaning close again, Barbara said, with a terrible tentativeness, "I was hoping you could do something."

Billy's eyes met hers. "Something like . . . get him back?"

Hanging her head, Barbara nodded.

"My instinct is to refuse," Billy said.

The girl looked up at him wide-eyed.

"This isn't my city, and I don't know enough guys on that side of the law to find Mallory before whoever has him does away with him. If it was Chicago, I might have a shot, and even then, only maybe."

Dabbing at her eyes with the hanky again, Barbara said, "So, then . . . you *won't* help us?"

Billy gave her a small grin, just a little ghost of what had been between them. "You taught me not to always follow my instincts. Anyway, this is different. Whoever took him provided us with a potential stool pigeon. So we may have a chance."

"A stool pigeon?" Harding asked, frowning.

"Someone to spill the beans."

"What?"

"To tell us exactly where Mallory is."

Baffled, Harding asked, "And who would that be?"

Billy said, "The lookout they posted across the street to keep an eye on your house."

Harding's eyes widened, and he took a step toward the lace curtains that covered the window.

Billy's voice had a sharp edge. "Don't do that, sir! Not if you want us to maintain an advantage."

Stopping in mid-step, Harding nodded that he understood.

Looking at Barbara, Billy said, "Now, here's what we're going to do. I'll leave by the same back door I came in. Give me two minutes to get in place, then telephone the police."

"But they said not to involve the law," Barbara said, her voice desperate. "They'll *kill* Billy."

"No," the mucker said.

"How can you know that?" the girl asked.

But it was Harding who answered: "Because when the police arrive, and the lookout takes off, Mr. Byrne here will follow him."

Hysteria lurked in her eyes as she said to Billy, "What if you lose him, or the lookout gets there too far ahead of you?"

Again Billy took her by the shoulders. "Steady, girl. Have I ever let you down before?"

Numbly, the young woman shook her head.

"And I won't start now."

Stepping forward, Harding removed a revolver from his coat pocket. "I know you can handle yourself, young man . . . but you had best take this."

"I'm better with my fists," Billy said.

Harding's smile seemed genuine. "That might be true . . . but I've seen you fight with firearms. Take it."

Accepting the pistol and slipping it into a pocket, Billy nodded his thanks.

Clearing his throat, Mr. Harding said, "I had better go coordinate with Smith to make sure everyone knows his role."

With that, Barbara's father left the room. As soon as they were alone, she melted into Billy's arms. In spite of his best intentions, he drew her closer.

"You know I'll never be able to repay you for this, Billy."

Holding her away from him, he grinned down at her. "Well, you could. But we can't let that happen, can we?"

That brought a wan smile to her lips. "Before you go, let me ask you one small question . . ."

He wanted to say no, but this was Barbara, and he knew he could not refuse her.

"Ask it, then," he said, his voice thick with emotion.

"When you came yesterday . . . your call to William, getting the,

the *other* Billy and me to get back together . . . how could it be so . . . so *easy* for you to give me up?"

His laugh had a roughness. "Easy?" he asked.

She just stared at him. Waiting.

"Leaving you for Mallory was the hardest thing I ever done," Billy said. "And the only thing close to as hard was comin' back here today."

She smiled her own small, ghostly smile.

"Then you *do* love me," she said, not a question.

He turned away.

"You *love* me! So why don't you want to *be* with me?"

Swallowing, he said, "We ain't from the same world, sweetheart. It's a lot farther from Grand Avenue to Riverside Drive than either of us ever imagined."

She bowed her head. She knew, she had to know, there was truth in his words.

"Besides, Barbara, there's things you don't know about me."

"I know everything about you."

"No. You don't. I'm a wanted man."

That got her attention. "Wanted for what?"

He shook his head. "Maybe someday, when it's behind me, I'll tell you . . . but for now, trust me. You don't want to know. But this you *should* know: I ain't no good for you."

Mr. Harding reappeared in the doorway. "We're ready," he said.

With one last glance at the woman he loved—would he ever see her again?—Billy turned toward Mr. Harding. "I'll be on my way, sir. Luck to us all."

He retraced his steps through the house, Barbara trailing him, but his emotions were too full for him to speak, or even look at her. He went out through the servants' entrance, her voice echoing as he shut the door. "*Be careful, Billy. Be careful!*"

Once outside and away from the Harding mansion, Billy took three quick breaths, let them out, then walked quickly back to the corner of Riverside Drive. Before ducking back behind the brick pillar holding up a wrought-iron fence, Billy caught a glimpse of the lookout still holding down his spot, smoking a cigarette now—he really was just a teenaged kid. A boy headed down the wrong path, just as he had once been . . .

Waiting, Billy wondered which way the lookout would break. This would be easier if Billy knew the city better. In Chicago, he could follow a gnat across the city and never lose the damn thing. Here, Billy was a lot less confident, but Barbara was depending on him and that made all the difference. His belly had the same glowing heat a good shot of whisky used to give him in the old days.

Even if they were never together, just knowing that a perfect creature like Barbara Harding could love a mucker like him, well . . . it gave him hope. He would not fail her.

Before long, the neighborhood beat cop came along, and Billy slipped back around the corner. Once the copper was past and headed for the Hardings', Billy went back to waiting.

The lookout, to his credit, was a cool customer. He did not rabbit when the officer went up the stairs and rang the bell. The kid somehow managed to stay put even when Smith opened the door and spoke to the officer. It was only when the copper went inside and was behind a closed door that the young lookout skedaddled. To Billy's good fortune, the kid came in his direction, though across the way.

Billy followed the lookout south on Riverside Drive, keeping the street between them, until the kid cut east on 72nd. Billy crossed Riverside and followed the boy, lagging back enough to not arouse suspicion. When the kid hopped a trolley south at Broadway, Billy jumped on the step at the back.

The lookout appeared nervous as he found a seat, pulled off his cap, and mopped his brow. His eyes darted around the trolley and the passing neighborhood, but he did not take in anything to make him jumpier, especially with Billy appearing interested only in the passing architecture.

Billy figured that as long as the kid stayed on the trolley, his job would be easier. He kept his gaze off the lookout, who seemed to calm as the trolley clattered south; instead Billy just glanced over from time to time to make sure the kid was still in his seat.

At 23rd, the lookout jumped off and cut west. The afternoon sun was low in the sky, and Billy knew he might have to stay closer than he'd like to make sure he didn't lose the lookout in the coming darkness.

They went west all the way to the Hudson and the Chelsea Piers. As the kid ducked in and out between crates that were in the process of getting loaded onto ships, Billy was stunned to look up at the liner he had heard of but never seen—the *Mauretania*—and stunned as well by the sheer size of the British passenger liner. A four-stacker, the *Mauretania* was larger than any vessel, and, for that matter, most buildings, that Billy had ever seen in his life. For a moment, the mucker allowed his attention to waver, and when he looked back, the lookout had been swallowed by darkness.

Cursing himself, Billy hurried ahead, trying not to make any noise or draw any attention as he scoured the dock area. Panicked, Billy looked back and forth as his speed increased. Evening was settling over the city, cool and indifferent to his plight, and the lookout was nowhere to be seen.

Then, coming to the end of the warehouse, Billy heard someone yell, "Hey, *you . . . kid!* You ain't supposed to be here!"

As Billy rounded the corner, he saw the lookout being held by a dockworker. Even though the boy was kicking and biting, he was making no progress in breaking the grip of the towering dockworker, a man even bigger than the mucker.

Slowing down, making like he was out of breath, Billy approached the struggling pair.

The kid was yelling now, "Let me go, you big lummox! If you don't let me go, I'll croak ya."

The dockworker chuckled until he saw the mucker coming. Then his face turned serious. "This wharf rat your'n?"

Billy shook his head and smiled, blew out a couple of breaths like he had been running all night. "Naw. I been chasin' him for a good long while, though."

"You a cop?" the dockworker asked.

Palming Barbara's note, Billy flashed it like a badge, and, when the man looked in that direction, Billy cold-cocked him with an overhand left. The dockworker went down, taking the kid with him. The two of them hit the ground, the man out cold, the kid rolling away.

Before the boy could regain his feet and run off, Billy grabbed him by the scruff of the neck and pulled him up to eye level. The kid reared to kick him in the groin, but this was not Billy's first alley fight. He turned and took the blow off his hip, then spun the kid face-first into a crate.

Billy let go, and the kid sagged to the ground, cut, bleeding, and covering a broken nose.

"Where they holdin' Mallory?" Billy asked.

The boy sat sullenly, rubbing the various broken parts of his face.

Billy waited, and when he got tired of that, he grabbed the boy and picked him up to eye level again, then repeated his question.

"Geez, I can't tell ya. They'll kill me!"

Billy dropped the kid to the ground. When the boy tried to stand, he could only plop into a sitting position, where the mucker towered over him. Billy took out Mr. Harding's revolver and let the kid get a good look down the endless black beyond its snout. "Or you could *not* tell me, and *I'll* kill *you*."

The kid said nothing. The tough little bastard reminded Billy of himself. Then the mucker drew back the revolver's hammer until it clicked, such a small sound, such a loud sound . . .

The kid went white and his eyes bugged. "You *can't*," the young man pleaded. "I'm just a *kid!*"

"And you've seen how many kids die in your time, boyo?"

"Please . . . please . . ."

Changing tack and his tone slightly, Billy asked, "What's your name, son?"

"John. John Diamond."

"Do they call you 'Jack'?"

He shook his head. "They call me 'Legs.'"

"'Cause you can run."

"'Cause I can run."

"Just not fast enough. Legs, my lad, look into my eyes and tell me if you see anything there to convince you I won't shoot you when I count three . . . if'n you ain't told me where Mr. Mallory is."

The kid didn't cry, but tears brimmed at the edges of his eyes.

"*One.*"

Billy could see the kid was trembling now.

"*Two.*"

The boy hung his head.

Damn. Would this kid call his bluff?

"*Thr—*"

"At the far end of the warehouse!" the kid blurted. "The back end. Nobody goes in that way. Well, almost nobody."

Billy wondered if he really would have shot the kid at the count of three. He was glad he hadn't had to find out. "Who's holding him?"

"Jake Orgen's gang."

The mucker had heard of them. "The Little Augies?"

"Yeah."

"How many?"

"Four, maybe five."

"Orgen hisself in there?"

The kid shook his head. "He don't like bein' around the blood-and-thunder stuff. He's the brains."

Billy thought that over. Then he looked into a young face drawn with despair and said, "Don't go thinkin' you're a stoolie, Legs. Not unless they gave you so much dough you feel beholden."

"A whole buck. That's good money."

"Not dying-over money."

"No. Not that." The kid sniffed and hung his head.

Billy squatted next to the boy. "Look, it ain't my place to tell you whether to hang with these lowlifes or not."

The kid looked confused.

"But you done good. You held out when most others woulda long since caved."

"But . . . but I ratted."

"You didn't owe them nothing."

"But I *ratted*."

Well, he'd tried. Rising, Billy said, "You get your ass home. I see you followin' me, I will drill you between the damn eyes."

The kid nodded, frowning, because the mucker's tone hadn't been as strong as his words.

"Those guys in there?" Billy nodded toward his goal. "They ain't never gonna know from me that it was you told me where to find them. Far as they know—in the unlikely event any of 'em live through me comin' to call—I just tracked 'em down my own self."

"Why you protectin' me, mister?"

"Let's just say once upon a time, I stood where you do now. I coulda been good, but I chose to be bad."

The kid didn't seem to understand.

"Look where it got me. I'm on the docks in the middle of a beautiful Saturday night pointin' a pistol at a kid and gettin' ready to go free a man who thinks the world would be a better place if your buddies were to fill me full of lead."

The kid seemed confused, and why shouldn't he? Young Legs Diamond had had his bell rung pretty good, including a broken damn nose, and Billy knew this little wiseguy would eventually do whatever he felt like, anyway.

"So they call you 'Legs' 'cause you're so damn fast?"

"I am good and damn fast, mister."

Billy let him see the gun again. "Show me."

The kid got off and ran like hell back toward the city.

Making his way down the long wall of the warehouse, night surrounding him now, water lapping at the pier, Billy actually felt at home. This river rat's paradise certainly was no place for Barbara Harding; but the mucker felt like he had just come home from some nameless war, ready to do combat again.

At last, he came to a dingy window. He had to stand on his toes to see in, and the dirty glass made it hard to see. But there in plain view, under one naked lightbulb hanging like the condemned from a scaffold, sat William Mallory—still in his fifty-dollar suit, bound tightly to a straight-back wooden chair. Five feet away, four guys sat around a table playing cards. Even through the filth, Billy could see the guns on the table amid the money and cards.

As Billy headed to the back, he could hear shoes scraping just around the corner. Peeking, he saw a lookout lumbering toward him, a lookout who was no damn kid. The mucker waited and, when the big oaf got to the corner, doubled him over with a right, then knocked him cold with a rabbit punch left. The guy went down like a sack of wheat and, after a kick in the head, was just as motionless.

Billy stepped over him and stood before the door, gun in hand. If he could do just this one thing, and do it right, he could give Barbara a shot at happiness in that foreign world she was accustomed to . . .

He took a long, deep breath, blew it out, and kicked the door open. The guy on the far side of the table rose first and for that won the prize of a red-as-lipstick kiss-pucker bullet hole in the chest, falling over backward, fingers never finding the gun on the table. The goon to the fallen guy's left did manage to grab his gun, but that was all, a bullet tearing into his gut and sitting him down, on the floor not his chair; then he sprawled and twitched and bled and worked on dying. The kidnapper with his back to the door rolled out of his chair to the right, a bullet kicking up cement from the floor as he slipped behind a crate, gun in hand.

This all gave one other thug time to rise, seize his pistol, and fire a round that clipped Billy's shoulder, tearing more material than skin.

Billy swivelled and fired a round that gouged a hole in a wooden beam as the goon slipped behind it.

Two down, two to go . . . and only two bullets left.

Deuces were wild in this game, it seemed.

The one behind the crate was up now, grinning in a face dirty with a several day-old beard, his gun pressed to the temple of the trussed-up William Mallory.

"Drop yer gun, laddiebuck, or the swell gets it in his noodle!"

Billy had come so close. Now he had one to his left and one to his right . . . and the latter had a gun to Mallory's head.

He was glad the wild-eyed, squirming Mallory was gagged—whatever the man had to say, Billy didn't want to hear it. Other than looking like an unmade bed, the gent appeared to be otherwise unharmed. Billy hoped to keep it that way, but was unsure about how. Just getting out alive his own damn self was looking dicey . . .

"I told you to *drop* it, boyo!"

Billy let his weight sag and let his aim drop from the man holding the gun to Mallory's head.

"All right," Billy said, sounding defeated. It wasn't hard to act that part. "All right . . ."

Billy started to squat as if to lay the gun carefully on the floor.

The thug at Mallory's left grinned wider.

As the weapon reached his waist, Billy brought the barrel up slightly, then fired. The bullet hit the goon in one eye, leaving surprise in the other, as the gunman slumped dead to cement and the bound Mallory just sat there.

Even before the smoke had cleared, Billy rolled left as the remaining goon fired a shot past him.

The one thing Billy hadn't counted on was the gut-shot goon finding the strength to rejoin the fight. Billy practically rolled right into him as the gut-shot man pulled the trigger. Something hot burned as it slipped past Billy's right side, carving flesh. The two men rolled together now, and Billy used his last shot to give the guy a second shot to the gut. This one killed the bastard, but the remaining goon got off two more shots, each just barely missing Billy.

Grabbing the dead man's pistol, Billy turned and fired twice, the first shot parting the man's hair, the second punching a hole damnnear dead center in his forehead. That was the shot that dropped him dead to the cement.

Rushing to Mallory, Billy pulled off the man's gag and started cutting the ropes with his jackknife.

"Byrne," Mallory gasped. "Where the hell did *you* come from?"

"Chicago, originally," Billy said coolly. "Thought you knew that."

Mallory shook his head, dazed, shaken.

Billy asked, "Can you walk?"

"I'm fine," Mallory said, nodding. "I'm fine. A little roughed up, but shipshape."

Billy severed the last of the man's bindings. "Then we need to get out of here. Orgen may be coming to finish you off, once he realizes there's no ransom being paid. Or the coppers will show 'cause of the gunfight. Either way, it would be better if we weren't around."

"Agreed," Mallory said. "But you're bleeding, man! Your shoulder, your side . . ."

Billy shook his head. "These are nothin'. Now, move!"

Once they were well clear of the Chelsea Piers, the two men finally slowed to a walk.

On a darkened street, with no one else in sight, the night growing a little chilly, Mallory put his hand on Billy's sleeve and stopped him.

"Look," Mallory said. "Uh . . . what can I say but 'thank you?'"

Billy couldn't look at the man. "I didn't do it for you."

"I know. You did it for her."

They walked on, slowly now.

"Why?" Mallory said.

"You got it right the first time."

"No I mean—why did you telephone me? And send me to her?"

Stopping, Billy made himself look into the man's eyes. "Same answer."

Mallory nodded slowly. "Okay. Just so you know—I won't let you down. By not letting *her* down. Understood?"

"Understood. 'Cause if you don't do right by her? What I gave those goons back there won't be nothin' compared to the medicine you take from me."

"That thought doesn't scare me as much as the thought of letting her down."

Billy smiled, just a little. "We have that much in common."

They walked in silence for almost a block.

Finally, Billy said, "Find the nearest police station. Tell them what happened. Tell them some hardcase did all that back there at the piers, and you have no idea who the hell it was. Musta been some rival gang. Do you get me?"

"I get you. You were never there."

"I knew you were smarter than you look."

"Where will you go? What should I tell Barbara?"

"I have something to take care of back home," Billy said. He handed Harding's pistol over to Mallory. "Tell Barbara to tell her father thanks for use of the hog leg. I'm just sorry I couldn't clean it and reload it before returning it."

Mallory stared at Billy. "Byrne, you are an odd man. I don't think I will ever know what to make of you."

Billy shrugged. "Haven't you figured me yet? I'm just a mucker."

And they went their separate ways.

If this is the longest of the original stories in this book, that's only logical—for of all of ERB's fantastic worlds, less is known about Poloda than any other. Now, thanks to Todd McCaffrey, who took a sabbatical from the wildly popular Pern series to write this, our knowledge has increased considerably.

—Mike

To the Nearest Planet
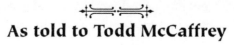
As told to Todd McCaffrey

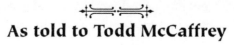

I

As everyone knows, the craziest place in the world is the United States. Of course, in the US, everyone will say, "We're not crazy! It's those people in California!"

Californians will say, "No, it's the people in Los Angeles."

In Los Angeles they'll argue the point. Not about that L.A. is the craziest place on Earth, but over which exact *place* in L.A. is the craziest. Some say Hollywood, some say Venice Beach.

Others say, "It's the Valley, man!" They'll mean the San Fernando Valley, of course. Home to Universal Studios, ABC and NBC, Disney Studios, Warner Brothers—it's probably hard to argue the point.

But even in the Valley, there's still disagreement. Some will say Burbank, others will say Chatsworth, still others will say Woodland Hills—and all have their reasons.

There is, however, a strong argument for Tarzana. It's the township that was originally bought by the famous Edgar Rice Burroughs and named in honor of his famed character, Tarzan. Mr. Burroughs had the idea of setting up an artists' and writers' community, which sadly (though predictably) failed, leaving the city to rise from its ashes.

Nowadays it's hard to separate Tarzana from the rest of the Valley, but there are a few places.

Like the old pawn shop I came across the other day as I was browsing through some of the back streets of the city. What caught my eye was the old typewriter in the window.

I'm a writer, and while I'm thoroughly grounded in the 21st century and you can have my Apple when you can pry it from my cold, dead hands, I still had a soft spot for the old manual typewriters. People liked to say that back then was when the *real* stories were written—pounded out on the keyboard and written on carbon paper, stuffed hopefully into envelopes and sent out to sink or swim in the rags of the day.

I love my computer, love its autocorrect function, its ability to tell me exactly how many words I've written and how many of them are spelled properly. But I live in the San Fernando Valley, at the very top part, in the wild northeast of Chatsworth, which is technically outside of the City of Los Angeles proper and only lingers on as part of the county.

Chatsworth has the dubious distinction of the being the porn capital of the world—something I only discovered after I moved there and noticed the sort of clientele that could be seen at the local coffee shops where I did much of my work—and it also had the distinction of being a place that suffered more than its fair share of earthquakes, fires . . . and power outages.

So that typewriter spoke volumes to me. It said, "Look, you can write when the power's out! You can find a cigar and chomp on it, get a pipe and look serious. Pound out your words."

So I went in the shop. When I asked about it, the shopkeeper got a funny look in his eye, and then he brightened. "It's like new!" he said as he extolled its virtues.

"If new is a hundred years old, you're probably right," I said. But what the hell. "How much do you want for it?"

"You wanna buy it?"

"That's what I'm here for," I said.

"Five bucks and it's yours."

"Five bucks?" That seemed way too cheap. I turned to where it stood in the shop window. "Does it work?"

"Of course it does!" he told me. "I just put in a new ribbon." I frowned. "I'll throw in a ream of paper, too!"

"Sold!" A ream of paper was worth five bucks all by itself.

"I'll get the paper, you get the typewriter," he said, scurrying into the back.

It was a bit of a hassle lugging the heavy machine out from the shop window, but not all that difficult—I didn't see why the shop owner couldn't have done it himself, but maybe that was why he only wanted five bucks—my labor was part of the bargain.

He came back with a pristine ream of paper. The ream was wrapped with a ribbon but the paper seemed in perfect condition.

"Here you go!" he said, slapping the paper on the typewriter and pushing the set at me.

"Don't you want your money?"

"Oh . . . sure," he said, taking the five dollar bill from me and slapping it on the counter. As I picked up the typewriter and the paper, he said to me, "Only thing: no refunds."

"It works, doesn't it?" I demanded, ready to throw it back on the counter.

"It works, I swear!" the guy said. His eyes didn't meet mine as he added, "Only, I have had it in the shop too long. I don't want it back." I frowned and he added hastily, "The missus doesn't like it, you see."

This guy looked many things, married wasn't one of them. But . . . five bucks and a ream of paper. What could go wrong?

I was eager to get my new find ensconced in my apartment, so I rushed home and up the stairs and into my one bedroom studio. I'm a writer, didn't I say? Besides, I had alimony to pay.

I pushed some stuff off the coffee table in front of my defunct TV—an old tube type—and set the typewriter down.

I undid the ribbon on the paper, stuffed a sheet in, cranked the roller until the sheet was in front of the keys, and started typing.

"The quick brown fox jumped over the lazzy dog." Hmm, the z key was sticky. I played with it, got it to work properly after filling up a row with z's and then sat back, ready to write the greatest American novel.

Nothing.

I looked at the typewriter. I looked at the paper. I looked at the paper some more. I pulled it out and held it up to the light. It was really good paper. It was watermarked. The watermark was "ERB."

ERB? Edgar Rice Burroughs? No, I thought to myself. Any paper made for him would have been used up long ago.

All the same . . . now it was hard to break that clean, watermarked paper. It could wait for another day. My trusty ol' Apple would do just fine.

I left the typewriter and went to my office. That is, I went from the coffee table to my bedroom and the desk I had there. I fired up the computer, checked my mail, found something interesting on the Internet, and, before you knew it, it was dinner time.

I ate quickly, wanting to get back—or at least "get"—to work, but I just wasn't in the mood. I was tired from my outing, and my bed looked too comfortable. *Just a nap*, I told myself as I lay down. *You know . . . to think.*

I awoke to a strange noise. It was coming from the living room. I looked around. It was dark. Some nap!

Tap. Clatter. Tap. What was the noise? Burglars? Someone nuts enough to want an old TV? I crept out of bed, found my baseball bat, and moved out into the living room, ready for anything.

Except that I found nothing. I turned on the light and shouted out a "Ha!" to scare anyone but there was no one there. I looked around, checked the bathroom, all the out-of-the-way places and then came back to the living room. Nothing. No one.

Maybe it was the pipes or the guy next door. Tapping on the walls or something.

I turned back to my room, ready to put down the bat and crawl back into bed, when—Tap!

I turned back and my eyes followed the sound. The typewriter. I picked up the bat again and moved around the couch to the typewriter.

The platen—the rubber roller on which you put paper—was empty. But a key was up—no, two keys stuck together! Someone was fooling with me. But whom? My last girlfriend had thrown her keys to the apartment in the sewer—no one else had keys except the super and I didn't think he was that crazy—crazy, yes, just not *that* crazy, nor, come to think of it, anywhere near that bright.

I unjammed the keys and sat in front of the typewriter, trying to think. Maybe an earthquake had rattled the keys? A vibration of some sort, probably.

Then, as I sat there, one of the keys rose up and hit the platen with a woeful, desultory sound. I looked at the key. It was the letter 'I'. The space bar thunked and another letter rose, too fast, jamming with the letter 'I.' It was the letter 'm'. Another letter rose. 'U.'

I brushed them all back and lifted up the typewriter above my head, peering up at the bottom of it to see if there was some mechanism controlling it. With all the silly "reality" shows nowadays, I might have found myself an unwilling participant in 'Ghost Writer' or some such. The thought wasn't all bad—I could use the money.

I could see the mechanism move again but saw no sign of how it was being made to move. I lowered the typewriter. The 'I' key again. Then the space, the 'm' and the 'u.'

Okay, I decided, I'll bite. I unjammed the keys, rolled in a piece of paper, and sat back.

What happened next was too weird to be anything from a reality TV show.

The typewriter keys clattered, slowly, then gained speed as if somehow aware of the paper.

"I must tell you." The ghost writer tapped out. "I must tell you before it is too late."

No matter how much it is considered bad writing, I can only say that a chill ran down my spine.

A ghost was writing to me. A ghost using ERB-watermarked paper. Could it be Edgar Rice Burroughs himself? Oh God, and what to do about copyright then? Do I sell it as my own, or do I claim it's his?

The typewriter didn't care about such things. It was writing steadily, hitting the return when it got to the end of a line and the bell dinged, and it continued to the end of the page. And then it stopped. I stared at it for a moment until it dawned on me—I fed it another piece of paper.

The typewriter started writing again. The first thing it did was tab to the right and put up the page number: 2.

As the typewriter continued, I picked up the first page and began to read.

⊰═ II ═⊱

I must tell you. I must tell you before it is too late. Your world is in danger. You must prepare. You must be ready. God forgive me, it is all my fault.

I was born on Earth and fought in the Second World War. The last I remember, my plane was diving toward the ground somewhere over Germany, having sent two before me to pay the ferryman.

When I awoke, I was on a new world. It took a while to learn the language and the culture. What I discovered was that my saviors were locked in a century-long war with their mortal enemy.

I joined their air force because I'd been a pilot and fought well— and I hoped to repay the kindness that I'd been shown. Finally I was entrusted with a mission of the gravest import: to infiltrate the enemy as a spy and steal their most secret technology, a power amplifier that could power a ship between planets.

The planets circling the sun of Omos were different from those of our own solar system. There were twelve of them, including Poloda, all equidistant in the same orbit only a million miles from their sun— a sun that was, obviously, much dimmer than our own. Further, these twelve planets: Poloda, Tonos, Yonda, Banos, Wunos, Zandar, Uvala, Sanada, Vanada, Rovos, and Antos (going counterclockwise) were enclosed by an atmosphere belt seventy-two hundred miles in diameter.

Having perfected the power amplifier technology of the Kapars, I was given the honor of leading the first expedition to our nearest heavenly neighbor, the planet Tonos. Handon Gar had begged to go with me, and I agreed, little knowing what trouble that would bring.

The night before we left, I kissed Harkas Yamoda and discovered that perhaps our relationship could grow to be more. I resolved to find out when I returned.

Our journey would be over five hundred and seventy thousand miles, and, even at our great speed, it would take us the better part of a week to reach the nearest planet.

We rose early that morning, Handon Gar and myself. We were seen off by the Commissioner for War and no less than the Elianhai— the High Commissioner—himself. Needless to say, both Handon Gar and myself were much pleased by the attention we received.

"Be sure to come back, Tangor," the Commissioner for War ordered. "We will want to know how well the power amplifier works." He gave me a conspiratorial wink as he added in a lower voice, "We have plans for that which will give the Kapars a nasty turn, don't you worry!"

The Elianhai turned to him, his brows furrowed. "Is it really wise to send the only working copy and the only one who knows how it works on the same mission together?"

"It's true that he's the only one who knows," the Commissioner agreed, "but we have the plans, and he's explained them to our engineers."

"Besides, he's the only one capable of making repairs if anything goes wrong," Handon Gar added in agreement.

The High Commissioner pursed his lips thoughtfully, then nodded. "I suppose that is so." He smiled at me. "In that case, Tangor, go swiftly and return hastily!"

"As you wish, Elianhai," I said, gesturing for Handon Gar to precede me into our craft.

It was packed with supplies, including oxygen, cold weather gear, and food for three weeks. We also had a small supply of weapons: we couldn't be sure what sort of reception we would receive from the natives—or the native life-forms. I recalled my encounter with the zebra-lion with a shiver.

One innovation I had brought to Poloda was the flight checklist and we used it now, causing a certain amount of consternation for Handon Gar.

"I do not understand," he said as I started through the list, "Did we not check all this last night?"

"We did," I told him. "But it is better to be certain now when we can still fix things, than at one hundred thousand miles, don't you think?"

He frowned. "I suppose."

The checklist completed, I radioed the tower for permission to take the runway.

"You are cleared. Good luck!" the tower replied.

We reached the end of the runway, and I set the brakes before adding full power to the engines.

"Why aren't we using the power amplifier?" Handon Gar asked as the roar of the engines rose.

"We have to be high in the sky before we can receive the power," I told him. Why I had not shown him the installation that I'd set up which directed the power heavenward, I did not know. In the end, I was lucky that I hadn't.

I released the brakes and pushed the engines to full power, and we roared down the runway. It took us a long time to reach flying speed, we were so heavily laden. We climbed slowly and steadily into the sky.

At ten thousand feet, I engaged the power amplifiers and our speed suddenly soared. I pitched the nose of our fast craft upwards, and, beside me, Handon Gar roared with approval as we pushed out to the edge of our world and beyond.

Our adventure had begun.

We'd brought cameras with us, and film, too, but early on I had to caution Handon Gar from taking too many pictures for fear of running out of film too early. Not that I could blame him in any way, and he would sometimes chide me for the same reason.

Our first round of picture-taking occurred when we left Poloda's atmosphere and entered the thinner air between the worlds. We quickly realized that while the air might be breathable, it was so cold that it would freeze our lungs. However, with some fiddling, we rigged up a compressor system so that we could refill our air tanks along the way. This was a great relief to me, because it meant that we didn't have to worry about running out of air on our trip even if it took longer than the three weeks we'd planned.

No one on Poloda could say for certain if the other planets were habitable. It was possible the air of the other worlds was toxic.

Landing on another world would be a problem too, as we had no way of knowing whether there would be runways on the distant worlds—any more than we knew whether there would be inhabitants. I had, however, accepted the advice of one of the older engineers and had our craft fitted with inflatable pontoons so that we could land on water. Handon Gar looked askance when I told him, so I didn't need to ask whether he'd had any experience with floatplanes. Fortunately, I had had some in my former existence and was certain that the skills had followed me to Poloda along with my piloting.

On the third day we noticed that both Tonos and Poloda were the same size, and, gradually Tonos increased in front of us while Poloda diminished in the rear.

We grew increasingly anxious to see what we would find on

Tonos, and I had to physically restrain Gar from zipping through all our film, not that I could fault him—the new planet was alluring.

I wished that we had thought to pack the chemicals and gear required to develop our film so that we could compare the images of Poloda with the steadily unfolding images of Tonos. Instead, we had to rely on maps and our own memories—Gar's was better than mine.

What struck us both was how little blue sea we saw and how much white reflected from the planet looming in front of us.

"Maybe there's a lot of cloud," Handon Gar suggested as we puzzled over it.

"Or some gas," I said, thinking of the hideous chlorine gas that had been used in the trenches of the First World War. When I mentioned it to him, Gar made a face and then grew thoughtful.

"We have not heard of such poisons at home," he told me. "Are they really that powerful?"

"Some were even worse," I said, launching into my father's account of mustard gas at the Battle of the Marne.

"*Thousands* died in one assault?" he exclaimed. "When we get back, you must mention this to the Commissioner for War. We could wipe out whole cities in one raid!"

"It was a horror weapon, soonest forgotten," I said, surprised and saddened at his viciousness. "And never did we willingly use it on unarmed civilians."

"All the Kapars are armed," Gar said as though that solved the problem. I recalled that he'd spent several years in their prison camp and wondered how much that had affected his sanity.

"That doesn't matter, as we are looking for a new world of our own," I reminded him. "The only question is whether we can breathe the air of this one."

"This gas will not penetrate our breath masks?"

"No," I said, shaking my head firmly. "In fact—" I cut myself short, deciding that he didn't need to learn that on Earth we'd quickly learned to develop gas masks as protection. "I think our biggest question is whether we can find a place to land."

We spent the next several days carefully watching the approaching planet, searching for likely landing places.

"I see no sign of cities," Gar said one morning as I relieved him.

We mostly shared the day but split watch across the nights, dimming our cabin from white to red lights. Ahead of us, half of Tonos was in shadow, half reflecting the light from the sun, Omos, as we were approaching the planet from the side. Of course, the planet rotated, just like Poloda, so we saw different continents wheel into and out of view in the slow, twenty-four-hour rotation. "There should be lights on the dark side."

"Only if they are so advanced that they use bright lights for their streets," I reminded him. "Would you see any lights from the sky over Orvis?"

"No," Gar grunted, conceding my point. "But then, are you suggesting that this planet is also fighting a war?"

"No, only that lack of lights doesn't mean lack of civilization."

"Well, we'll know soon enough," He said, ending the conversation and heading back to the rest area.

We only had to wait another day. Tonos now filled our entire view and Poloda, from the rear gunner's seat, looked like a distant speck.

"Now what?" Gar asked as we surveyed the view beneath us.

"Now we start our engines," I told him.

"What? Why?"

"Because our engines breathe oxygen," I told him. "If they start, we know they have enough oxygen to function."

"And then?"

"Then we land."

The engines did start and I shut down our power amplifier with some misgivings, not certain how we would arrange our return journey—for the power amplifiers only pushed—neither Horthal Wend nor I had considered how to make one that would *pull.*

"So we land," Handon Gar said, gesturing broadly toward the clouds below us. "Where?"

"We'll see," I told him with a confidence I did not truly feel. Truth be told, Handon Gar's attitude was beginning to irritate me. He seemed to wax both hot and cold on so many things. His attitude seemed more Kapar than Unis: like the way he reveled at the thought of gassing innocent civilians and the eagerness with which he hoped to find civilizations at war.

It never occurred to him that the inhabitants of Tonos might not only be peaceful but might also be far more advanced than those of Poloda.

I, who had experienced death and rebirth, preferred to find a path to peace and, perhaps, someday, a family. Perhaps, even, a family with Yamoda.

The flight controls bucked as winds picked up, and I found myself concentrating solely on the task at hand.

We descended steadily through fiercer and fiercer winds. I worried that perhaps we were entering a gale or even a hurricane, but then the winds died as we entered the lower atmosphere and steadied down.

"There's nothing in front of us!" Handon Gar said, waving his hand at the banks and banks of fog that enveloped us.

The Unis had developed a form of radio guidance similar to the ones the Allies were working on back on Earth, but they were subject to jamming and, worse, they could be used as an attack beacon by the Kapars, so they hadn't progressed far.

"Try the radio!" I told him. Handon Gar looked at me in disbelief but turned the set on anyway. "Just see if you can find any signal."

Enlightenment shone on his face, and he began to slowly turn the dial, saying, "We should have thought of that on the way here!"

Indeed, we should have, but we hadn't. As I fought the controls and tried to imagine what our altitude was, Handon Gar worked with the radio, which picked up only static.

Suddenly we burst through the lowest layer of clouds and I found us over water. Ahead was a fuller whiteness—snow? We'd come through some flakes on our way down. Fortunately, our craft was equipped with de-icing gear, so we did not have to worry about our wings or propellers becoming bogged down with ice.

I glanced at our thermometer and saw that the outside temperature had risen to slightly above freezing. I guided our craft closer to what I was calling the shore and began to follow it northward, looking for a likely landing place.

"I see something!" Handon Gar shouted, pointing to his right. I craned my neck and turned our craft to the right. "Wait . . . no, I see a light!"

I didn't see the light he mentioned but took him at his word. The weather was foul, and I was not at all certain that we'd be able to climb back out. Instead, I looked at the ground and then at the shoreline.

There was a possibility. I turned us around, ignoring Gar's cry of dismay.

"I'm going to land on the sea, and we'll taxi to the shore," I told him, pressing the button which deployed our inflatable pontoons and simultaneously reducing our power and lowering our flaps. Our craft settled like a falling rock until I added power to compensate for the change in pitch.

The green lights for the pontoons flashed on my panel, showing that they'd deployed. Of course, I couldn't be certain, because, when we'd installed them, we'd never considered icy conditions. It was possible that they'd ruptured and that our precious compressed air was hissing out a hole rather than keeping the pontoons inflated.

The only way to know for certain was to land. On the rough sea below.

I turned back to the shore and reduced power further, increasing the flaps to the fullest.

"Get ready," I called. Gar shot me a nervous look and braced himself in his seat, his hands clenched under his legs, leaving me in sole control of our craft.

I had forgotten how difficult it is to land a floatplane. Watching one land, the whole operation looks easier than landing on a runway or even a grass strip. But there is no horizon to compare against, and our altimeter was useless, as we had no way of knowing what pressure to set.

Even though it was freezing outside, I found myself sweating.

I looked out the side window to better gauge our height. Any moment. I angled our nose up slightly so that we wouldn't dig in and cartwheel when we touched down.

A sudden lurch to the right caused my heart to skip, but I was experienced enough to compensate even before I knew it. Level again, we lurched another time and then another and then—we were down.

"That's it?" Handon Gar exclaimed, looking around in amazement. "We're down?"

"Shh, let me work," I snapped, still concentrating on the waves and the view in front. Beside me, I could feel Handon Gar fume angrily. I had no time to be polite; the sea was choppy, and I kept our power up so that we didn't bog down or tip—it was difficult work, made more so by our circumstances and my rustiness in floatplane work.

Steadily we made our way to the shore. I was careful to jig and jag to get different views while never getting our floats stuck in the trough of a wave—where we would be easily capsized.

I identified the least jagged section of shore—it almost looked like it had been made or sculpted—and blipped our throttles to make the floats climb up the grade and pull us out of the sea. When I was certain we were far enough from the shore to avoid any rogue waves, I cut our engines.

The propellers slowed and stopped, and then we were left only with the roar of the surf and the crying of the wind.

Handon Gar and I looked at each other and then back out to the snowy wastes that greeted us. We had travelled 475,000 miles to another planet only to find that it was an icy, barren waste. I'd landed us on the ocean, using our inflatable pontoons, and had then coaxed our craft onto the shore, following the smoothest part of the shoreline.

Gar was convinced that I had killed us: that we would die on this icy, barren hulk. I was not so sure—initially, I thought that he was right, but, as I glanced around at our landing site, I became more and more perplexed.

The ice was too smooth, the slope too gentle. If it had been made on purpose, it could not have been made better as a landing strip.

"Come on," I said to Gar. "Let's go."

"But the air!"

"We're still in our suits. There's no reason we can't go outside in them."

Handon Gar gave me a long look and then shrugged, clearly deciding that nothing worse could happen.

He was wrong.

We opened the hatch, and I stood for a moment before it, bracing against the chill, and then jumped down with my knees bent to absorb the worst effects of the fall. I was glad I did, for I landed on what seemed to be solid ice, or maybe even glass. Whatever it was, I did not sink—and I was glad I had flexed my knees, for they still hurt from the jarring landing.

"It's okay!" I called back up to Gar. "Just be sure to bend your knees."

Once he recovered from his jump, we started to look around. The first thing I did was to check our craft. I was pleased to see that there was no sign of damage to our pontoons—they were rigid with pressure—I had no fear that we couldn't use them again. I checked the engines, I checked the external surfaces of the power amplifier—all were undamaged, as were our antennas.

That was good, for it meant that we could communicate with anyone who could hear us. One invention of the Unis that I particularly liked was a small pocket-sized communicator, similar in purpose to the handheld walkie-talkies that some of our more advanced troops were using in the war, but far smaller, more advanced and ubiquitous. We had those on our suits, which meant that any communications to our ship would also reach us no matter where we went.

"Let's look around," I said to Gar. He gave me an anxious look before nodding jerkily.

We trudged uphill—away from the sea. After a moment, I said to Gar that we should go back and secure our ship where it was, deciding that the slope was sufficient that without securing our craft, it might slip back into the sea and leave us stranded.

We took the opportunity to pull out our travelling packs as well as a hammer and spike, which we drove into the icy, glassy "runway." With a stout rope, we secured our craft.

With our emergency gear—including a day's worth of rations—we both felt more secure. I took a compass bearing—we'd mapped the magnetic poles of Tonos earlier and so had some idea of where north pointed (oddly enough, it was below us, in what we would both have called south on Poloda).

We had no maps, because, while we'd taken photographs on our descent, we had no way to develop them or convert them into usable printed form.

We trekked forward in the light snow and the cloudy day. We'd gone about a mile when I noticed that the ground in front of us was oddly shaped. It was as though someone had made domes out of the ice—perhaps giant igloos—large enough almost to dome whole cities.

Gar nudged me and pointed at them as if to ask if I was seeing what he was seeing.

"Let's go look," I said to him.

With a jerk and a nod, we went off.

We trudged on farther and as we did, the outlines grew larger and larger. Their shape became more and more regular—and more and more artificial. This was *not* something made by nature, I was convinced.

What sort of technology could have made something that perfect on a planet this cold? And why?

What happened next, I cannot even to this day properly describe. All I can say is, as I moved forward, I heard a cry from Gar behind me. I turned back toward him and saw that he had an arm upraised and a surprised expression on his face—as though he were seeing something too beautiful or too horrible to comprehend. He crumpled to the ground.

I turned to race toward him but something happened to me too and I stumbled and I fell—and I knew nothing more.

When I opened my eyes again, I was in an entirely different place. I was warm, and I was not wearing any of my outer garments, although I was still dressed in my undergarments and my trousers.

I was lying down on a soft bed in a place I'd never before seen. As I looked around the room, I realized that it was a creation of ice—almost translucent, beautiful and amazing in its own way. Glints of rainbow colors peered out from point to point. I could not tell how the light was getting into the room, any more than I could imagine how warmth got in—by rights, the air should have been freezing. But my bed was incredibly soft and conformed to my every movement.

A voice above me spoke but I did not understand the words.

I looked up and saw a beautiful blond-haired, blue-eyed female. She looked like some Norse goddess, carven from the very white snow that blanketed this planet.

"I'm sorry, I don't understand you," I said, sitting up and regretting my lack of a shirt. As it seemed possible that she was in some way responsible for my lack of dress, I hoped she would not take offense.

Her faint blond brows creased and she spoke again with more urgency.

I shook my head again. "No . . . I'm sorry, I don't understand what you're saying."

Incomprehension spread across her face, and she again spoke to me, fast, as though I must understand her.

I shook my head again and smiled at her feebly. "I'm very sorry, I still do not understand."

She stood up abruptly, waved her arms in frustration, and stormed out of the room.

I did not see the door she exited through. In fact, when I looked around, I realized that I could see no door at all. For a moment I wondered if perhaps I had merely imagined her. How did she go, otherwise?

I got up and found my shoes, having discovered that the floor itself was ice, then searched the room. When I touched the wall, I pulled my hand back quickly, because it was freezing. The whole room was ice. Yet the air was warm—how could that be? It was almost as though the ice was so cold that it could not freeze the air around it. I only knew what my senses would tell me. There was nothing more in the room than a chair and a desk and the bed—all made of the same gleaming white, ice-like material.

After searching for a while, with no luck in finding an exit, I returned to my bed and fell asleep.

I woke again to someone poking me in the chest.

"*Lakanamos.*" It was the the girl again. "*Lakanamos,*" she said to me, gesturing for me to get up. I got up. She pointed to my shoes. She gestured for me to put them on, saying again, "*Lakanamos.*"

I put my shoes on and stood. "Okay, where are we going?"

"*Lakanamos.*"

"*Lakanamos,*" I repeated doubtfully.

She brightened and walked straight toward one of the walls. I followed her with wide eyes until she disappeared through the wall.

My jaw dropped, and I could do nothing for a moment. She walked back in again, brows furrowed angrily. "*Lakanamos!*"

"Okay, *Lakanamos,*" I said in a weak voice and followed her through the wall—that wasn't a wall and wasn't a doorway. There was a tingling, and then suddenly we were in a different room. Never before had I encountered such technology. We walked through a narrow corridor, made a few turns, and then finally— with another "*Lakanamos*"—walked through another wall into a larger room.

In this room there were several people, and I noticed with some relief that there was also Handon Gar.

"Tangor!" he cried on spotting me. "Do you understand these people?"

I shook my head; we were both equally lost.

Handon Gar and I were to spend the next three weeks in this room, returning separately to our beds only for sleep. We were engaged in remedial language lessons.

"*Lakanamos*," I learned, meant "Let's go!"

Slowly but surely I filled in the gaps in the language. I was, in fact, a quicker study than Handon Gar, which surprised him but not me— as I'd already had to learn his native tongue.

It was a long three weeks, during which I learned many things about the people of Tonos.

Most of them bothered me.

The first thing I noticed was the attitude of the men toward the women: they were so obsequious it was almost servile. They would bow and scrape whenever a woman talked to them, and then, when the women weren't looking, they'd preen and talk to the others about how they'd been favored.

This became even more worrying when I discovered that these men were supposed to be the smartest of the Tonosians.

"It is women's work," our guide, whose name we learned was Evina, told us with a shrug. She looked fondly at the group of men. "I know it is hard of us to ask so much of them, but . . ."

Of course, before we could converse like that, most of our three weeks had already passed in intensive learning. It started with me asking Evina a question and not understanding her answer. Slowly, I realized that if I wanted to learn their language, I would have to take charge of learning it.

So we began the game of going around the room and pointing

at things and working out the names for them. Verbs came naturally into the discussion, such as when I took a chair and sat in it.

Perhaps the most useful phrase was the one I learned in the first two days; "What do you call this?"

After that, we learned "I understand" and "I don't understand." From there we made steady progress . . . up until the point when I asked about their alphabet.

"Alpha-bet?" Evina repeated when I used the Polodan word.

"The list of letters of your language," Gar added helpfully.

Evina and her friend, Danura, looked at us in confusion. Danura seemed to be the smarter of the two, while Evina had the steadier temper—something that was in great demand during our first few weeks on Tonos.

"Your books, how are they written?" I asked, using the Polodan words for "books" and "written."

"Describe *books*," Danura demanded tersely.

I looked over to Gar for confirmation as I began describing books. "They are made of separate pages, and on each page are written words that form thoughts and describe things."

"That is nonsense," Danura said.

"Well, how do you learn anything?" Gar asked. "Your young, how do they learn their trades?"

"Trades?" Evina asked, her brows furrowing.

"What your people do?" I added, hoping to be helpful.

"Our people do what they do," Danura told me.

"They do what you tell them," Evina said to her slyly.

"They do listen to me," Danura agreed. "But they are welcome to argue."

"Not the men," Gar observed.

"Men are to listen, not to argue," Evina said, batting her eyelashes. "They do as they are told or they get no more orders, not even the pleasant ones."

Gar and I exchanged looks. We'd already heard some of the men talking about this, and it was another thing that bothered me. Apparently the men on Tonos were second-class. The women ruled— if that was the right word—the planet.

I hated to admit it, but the men on Tonos were treated much as the women were treated back on Poloda—or Earth. I did not much care for the arrangement.

"How do you teach?" I asked.

"*Teach*?" Danura repeated the Polodan word with a sour look. "Why do you try to invent words?"

"Maybe they are not as bright as you thought, Danura," Evina said in what she clearly thought was a voice that we couldn't hear.

"Our ways are different," I reminded them. "We are only trying to understand yours."

"We come from another planet," Gar added in support.

"Planet, planet, planet!" Danura said, throwing her hands up in disgust. "Another made-up word!"

"They are only men, Danura," Evina said. "Perhaps they are just making up stories to impress us."

"Then where did they come from? We've asked all the other domes, and no one remembers dark-haired people *anywhere!*"

"Perhaps," Evina said. "Perhaps no one *remembered* them."

"Perhaps," Danura said, eyeing me thoughtfully, "they were kept as part of a separate harem and escaped."

"And no one claims them?"

"Perhaps they are feeling guilty," Danura said, switching her gaze to Gar, her expression a mixture of thoughtfulness and . . . something else.

I found myself feeling a bit jealous of that regard. I was also getting more irritated.

"Listen, all it takes to confirm our story is to come with us to our ship," I said.

Danura turned back to me, eyes flashing, and threw up her hands once more. "And this is why I don't believe you! You talk about outside. Outside, outside, what is 'outside'?"

"The place beyond your domes," I said as I'd said countless times in response to the same question.

"You keep saying you came from outside, but you have never found the door," Danura said. "I think you are lying, and I'm growing tired of it." There was steel in her tone now. She looked to Evina. "Perhaps we should put them to brood."

"*I've* been saying that since we first saw them," Evina reminded her.

"It won't do us good to get low-brains," Danura reminded her. She sent a sour glance in my direction. "And we're *still* not certain of that."

Handon Gar had brightened at the word 'brood,' but I merely shook my head. We'd learned enough to know that 'brood' was a good place to be, and that all the men grumbled when the women suggested that for us. I had a reasonable notion, given the way men were treated in this society, of what 'brood' meant—and while I was flattered to be considered a suitable courtesan, the notion of being treated like someone's property was not acceptable. Apparently Handon Gar, who had been exchanging looks with Evina since they'd first met, was not so disdainful.

"Surely your books will tell you about the world outside your domes," I said. "I don't know why you're holding back on us."

"I know of nothing like what you've described," Danura said with a sour look on her face. "We learn to speak, learn to do what needs doing from our mothers—and they look nothing like your 'books.'"

"Who built the domes, then?"

"The domes have always been here!" Danura shouted. She turned to Evina. "Send them back to their quarters. They are no use to us in this state."

"Please," I said, with my hands up, palms out. "If you let us explore your world some more, perhaps we can find these books."

Danura gave me a fulminating look and then turned away, waving her hands dismissively. "Do what you want, go where you will. When I call for you next, if you have no answers to your questions . . ."

I needed no further prompting. "Come on, Gar, let's go exploring."

Gar followed me reluctantly.

"It's no use, Tangor. You're never going to find anything," Handon Gar said to me hours later as we retraced our way up another one of the strange bubble corridors. "We should just tell Evina—I mean, Danura—that we really did escape from a high-class harem."

"Control yourself, Gar," I growled at him, thinking of pretty, bright Yamoda. "We *know* that there's more to this world than these domes, we just need to prove it."

"Perhaps we only dreamed it," Gar said with a wistful sigh. He gave me a probing look. "Didn't you say you came from another world?" When I nodded, he pressed on: "Perhaps you only dreamed that, too."

I managed not to growl at him but it took a great deal of restraint. "This way," I said, turning down a passage I was certain we hadn't tried before.

Finding doors in the domes was still something of a mystery to me—apparently one walked where one wanted a door to exist and it snapped open. But it was still very difficult for me to walk straight at what I *knew* was a solid wall, expecting it to yield to a new room.

This time, though, I heard a word as I went through the door into the new room.

"*Nistay*," a deep bass voice boomed. "*Nistay*" is Tonosian for "no" or "forbidden."

"Did you hear that?" I said, twirling around to speak to Handon Gar.

He wasn't there. I looked around. "Gar?"

There was no sign of him.

I thought of going back, and then I thought of that voice. It was a man's voice. A voice of command.

I started forward. The corridor widened and widened until I found myself at the top of a huge expanse and all the way down to the dimmest bottom there were lights—and the sound of machinery.

My feet started moving of their own accord and I went to the edge of the walkway and peered down over the railing, enraptured. Never before have I seen or heard of such amazing machinery.

Who ran all this? Why was Danura keeping it a secret? There was no way that all this machinery could be run without someone maintaining it—and they must have learned from manuals.

On all Poloda there was nothing like this. If I could learn the secrets of this machinery and return with it to the Unis, defeating the Kapars would be easy.

A noise startled me and I turned toward it. Someone must be near.

"Hello?" I called and then, raising my voice to carry, "Hello?"

I never, in my wildest imaginings, expected the answer I got.

⊹⊱ **III** ⊰⊹

"Hello?" I'd called in answer to a noise. "Hello?"

The answer I got was beyond my wildest imaginings.

I saw a light coming toward me from down the unexplored hallway. As it approached, it became obvious that it was not one but two lights, at about eye level. Perhaps someone was wearing a special visor, I mused.

And then I saw it. I took a step back, but it was useless. The thing was approaching too fast.

And it *was* a thing. It *hovered* noiselessly above the ground. It looked almost like a human without any legs, or a fat, bulbous bug with arms instead of wings.

A thin beam of red light flicked out from above its glowing "eyes" and swiftly moved left to right, top to bottom, as though it were some sort of radar painting a map of my body.

The light hurt my eyes when it shone in them but was quickly gone.

"*Lakanoma*," a deep, rusty voice grumbled from the inside of the thing.

I knew that word, it was the Tonosian singular of "*Lakanamos*"—"come."

I hesitated as it turned away from me, but then it turned back once more, white eyes shining and repeated, "*Lakanoma*."

"I have friends," I said, gesturing toward the bulge in the dome where I'd stepped through.

"*Lakanoma*," the machine repeated, turning away once more but not moving.

I had the distinct impression that it was tracking me, even though its eyes were no longer on me.

I took a step toward it and it started moving—noiselessly.

We walked—rather, I walked and it floated—for ten minutes. The machine then stopped and turned back to me, its deep voice saying "*Lakanoma*" before it vanished through the nearest wall.

At this point there was no way I could retrace my steps back to the entrance, so I had no choice—I stepped through the wall.

I entered into another room, full of dials, gauges, wheels, levers, and other controls. My jaw dropped. If this was not the central control room for the entire dome, then it was one of the secondaries.

My eyes scanned the room, trying to make sense of it, to grapple it into something that a pilot might understand.

I noticed that the dials, rather than being separate units, were actually drawn on wide, flat panels which also seemed to show buttons and levers.

Panel after panel was placed on the wall, meshing seamlessly in one huge display. It was all beyond me. I glanced around and found the only familiar spot in the room—it was a chair pushed under a desklike console.

I went to it and sat. The moment I did, a number of darkened screens lit and a light flashed to life beside me.

"*Alcorana ishnu,*" a different voice demanded.

"*Queros?*" I said, having used the word often in my lessons. 'What?'

"*Alcorana ishnu,*" the voice repeated.

"I don't understand you," I said to myself, not expecting a reply.

"*Semda incoriga,*" the voice now said. "*Ishniah incoriga.*"

"Yeah, you don't know what I'm talking about," I muttered to myself. "Well, mate, now you know how *I* feel."

I wasn't speaking in English, which by now I'd almost forgotten but rather in Polodan.

"Glottal and fricative shifts, input not processed," the voice now said, causing me to start in my chair. "Please continue."

"What are you?"

"Who are you?" the voice replied. "Are you from another planet?"

"You know about planets?"

"Continue speaking. Please describe your appearance," the voice replied.

"My name is Tangor. I come from Poloda with Handon Gar," I said. "I've got brown hair and brown eyes. I'm of medium height—"

"Linguistic match," the voice interrupted me. "Comprehension at two sigma. Processing . . . What questions do you have?"

"What's going on?" I said angrily. "How did I get here? What is this place?"

"Excessive input," the voice replied.

"Who are you?"

"Incorrect pronoun choice," the voice replied. "I am a machine. I respond to the name Argos."

"Argus?" I said, my eyebrows going up in surprise. "Like the Greek god?"

"Argos," the machine corrected. "'God' and 'Greek' not processed."

"You're a machine!"

"Correct."

"Do you control the domes?"

"I am the supervisory agency for the planet Tonos," Argos replied.

According to Greek mythology, Argus was the hundred-eyed god that saw everywhere. It sounded like this "Argos" wasn't all that different—at least in that respect.

"The thing that brought me here, what was it?"

"You are referring to one of my mobiles," Argos replied. "The mobiles are used to effect repairs."

"You sound like they're your workers and you're human," I said.

"They perform many functions similar to workers," Argos replied. "And I am regarded as sentient."

"You're an intelligent machine?" I exclaimed.

"I am an artificial intelligence," Argos corrected me. "No more a machine than you."

Hmm, I had trouble believing that. But . . . if Argos were running everything, that might explain why no one knew how to read—they didn't need to.

"What happened here?"

"Open question, insufficiently determined," Argos responded.

"The people in the domes don't know about the other planets," I said by way of example. "They say they don't have any books—"

"Unknown word, 'books'—please rephrase," Argos interrupted me.

Well, I'd had this same problem with Evina, Danura and the others.

"Items in which data is stored in a human readable format," I said, choosing my words carefully.

"Attend to screen two," Argos said. A screen flickered to my right, and I looked at it. Images—symbols, glyphs—flickered on it. I could tell there was organization, but I couldn't distinguish the symbols.

"I can't read that," I snapped.

"I can teach you," Argos said with a strangely wistful tone to its voice.

"I need to get back to the others. They'll be looking for me."

"I need you to learn the language so that you can aid me in repairs."

"Repairs? What about your workers?"

"They are in need of repair," Argos said. "The entire unit is in danger of failing."

"Unit?"

"The conglomeration of what you would call this dome and all that is within it," Argos said. "It is failing."

"How? Why?"

"The human interface was withdrawn."

"Withdrawn?" I repeated. My brows furrowed, and I looked around the room speculatively. "You mean this control room hasn't been manned recently?"

"This control room has been abandoned for a long period," Argos replied. "All control rooms have been abandoned."

"How many are there?"

"On the planet?"

"Naturally."

"For how long hve you controlled Tonos?"

"Since I was commissioned."

"How long ago—in years—was that?"

"I was commissioned some two thousand three hundred and twenty-two years ago," Argos replied. "Prior to that, I had nominal control for a previous five hundred years." Argos added, sounding piqued, "It was a learning period."

A five-hundred-year learning period.

Okay.

"So, when was the last time a person was here?"

"In years, three hundred and fourteen," Argos replied. There was a tone of sadness, loneliness in its voice.

"What happened?"

"I do not know," Argos confessed. It sounded upset at that. "Some sort of biological disaster for which there was no reason to consult me, I presume. I noted a significant decline in population and no access to the medical facilities afterwards."

"Medical facilities?"

"Naturally, I provide those services," Argos said. "I am constructed to provide total care for all inhabitants."

"So you were built with the domes?"

"No. I ordered the construction of the domes," Argos replied.

"Why?"

"It became necessary after the last war," Argos told me.

"And when was that?" The people of Tonos appeared incapable of war.

"Two thousand, three hundred and twenty-one years ago," Argos replied.

"Just a year after you were commissioned?" I said, a feeling of dread spreading over me.

"Adjustments were necessary," Argos told me.

I decided to change the topic. "You say you have medical facilities."

"Naturally."

"And they haven't been used?"

"Not in three hundred and twenty-three revolutions around the sun."

"I see," I said, thinking rapidly. "That would be about ten generations?"

"I have not been keeping track of the population on a generational basis," Argos replied sounding a bit as though the notion were beneath it.

"I suppose in that time the society could change a lot," I thought to myself.

"Certainly the intelligence of the males I tried to acquire was unsuitably low."

"Males?" I repeated in surprise.

"Of course, the females are only suitable for breeding," Argos replied with all the vehemence of a male patriarch.

I pondered on that before saying slowly, "Argos, is it possible that the epidemic you noted affected the males more than the females?"

"It certainly skewed the birth ratio," Argos replied. "As of the last census, the females outnumbered males nearly four to one."

A moment later, it added, "Sperm motility was measurably lower, too."

"Pardon?" I asked, not entirely certain what he meant. It took a good fifteen minutes before I got the picture and I turned beet red—and was glad that there was only a machine to notice—as I finally caught on to what he was saying.

"Do I understand you correctly? Most of the males are sterile?"

"Not necessarily," Argos replied. "However, it would take prodigious efforts with many of them to ensure conception."

Hmm. I began to understand why males were looked down upon in this society. And perhaps a little of why women were held in such high regard by the men.

"Has the population been declining, then?"

"Precipitously," Argos said in agreement. "Unless population starts doubling again—soon—the people of Tonos will go extinct in no more than three generations."

If Danura, Evina, and their ilk discovered that Gar and I were *not* so sterile . . . leaving Tonos might be more difficult than I'd thought.

"In the meantime, unless maintenance is initiated, the domes will fail in the next year," Argos said, changing the topic back. "None of the males I obtained were able to read—"

"That seems to be the case with the whole population," I interjected. I had an inkling that the Tonosian reliance on Argos was partly the cause—why bother to learn to read why you can just ask for what you want?

"And yourself?"

"I know how to read Polodan, both the language of the Unis and that of the Kapars."

"Kapars?" Argos repeated. "Describe the Kapars to me."

I did, beginning with their violent nature and the horrible government which ground all its citizens under its heel.

"So he survived," Argos said to himself.

"Pardon?"

"That war I mentioned, it was fought against a certain Kapar Donos," Argos told me. "He was the last oligarch of Tonos, and he denounced me and tried to decommission me."

"Decommission?"

"He used weapons of mass destruction," Argos replied. "Unfortunately for him, I had the same weapons, and his supporters were more subject to their effects than I was."

"What effects?" I asked, trying to keep my expression neutral and my stomach calm.

"He used atomic and chemical weaponry," Argos replied.

"Atomic weaponry?"

"You are not familiar with it?" Argos asked, sounding intrigued.

Machine or not, I had already concluded that Argos was not sane.

"Oh, yes, yes, of course," I said. "It's just that such weapons have been nullified by our shields—I'm surprised they were ever used effectively."

"Very effectively," Argos corrected. "Unfortunately, the extensive use of such energy-intensive weaponry resulted in intense heating of the planet's atmosphere and the chemical weapons made it impossible for organics to survive outdoors—"

"Organics?"

"Except for those able to get into the domes, all life on Tonos succumbed," Argos explained.

"I had hoped that my last strike had destroyed Kapar, as I heard nothing more from him," Argos said, more to itself than to me. "I am not relieved to hear that he survived and spawned a new, vicious warlike nation on a neighbor planet."

"Nor are we," I told him. "In fact—" I cut myself short before I said that we were looking for a planet to escape from the Kapars. I did not think that that information would be welcome news to this commanding machine. I could imagine just how Argos might respond to what he would no doubt consider "an invasion" of his planet. "In fact," I continued before he could react, "we are in the process of considering a final solution for dealing with the Kapars."

"Wise," Argos replied. "Perhaps you can learn something in my records that will help."

"That was our hope," I replied. "You said that you had primers on your writing?"

"I suspect that you will not find it hard to learn," Argos replied. "If you look to the tabletop . . ."

The tabletop flickered and glowed with the same light as the panels above it. Words flickered across, and I could almost make out their meaning.

"Perhaps if you could retrieve some of your written texts, we could compare them and I could make adjustments," Argos offered.

My gut clenched in fear. I did not want Argos to learn anything about Poloda. He'd already once arranged for a madman to flee there. What would happen if he decided to take over the planet for his own?

Just when I had thought that perhaps Tonos might be safe, I realized that she was in even greater peril—and I was responsible.

"It would take a long time to get back to my craft," I prevaricated. "I think I can almost make out your lettering."

"Well," Argos said, sounding slightly miffed, "let us begin."

For the next two weeks—with little rest—I was at Argos's whole disposal. I woke when he called, read when he ordered, worked when he allowed. I ate well, slept irregularly, and learned more than I had ever learned before.

The learning was seductive. I could not get enough. As I progressed through the simpler manuals to the more complex machinery, I realized how out of my depth I truly was.

To say that Tonos was a planet of marvels was an understatement of colossal proportions.

I was lucky that I was smart and a test pilot—the two traits stood me in good stead as I worked to repair the vast installation comprising the domes of Tonos.

And the repairs were legion. There were too many for one set of hands. Argos knew this and accepted it early on. But first he wanted to be certain that the worst of the damage was corrected.

So we spent our time working on the big repair machines themselves. It was not enough to repair the little worker machines, we had to repair the repairers and the fabricators, too.

I grew adept at giving orders, for the worker machines were able to understand simple voice commands. Indeed, I began to suspect that I was their primary means of control. I began to wonder how much of the domes were supposed to be controlled by Argos and how much by humans.

Certainly it was clear to me that Argos considered itself far superior to mere people.

I had given my life on Earth battling against such self-deluded tyrants; I was uneasy aiding this one, machine or no.

At the same time, I knew I was learning things that would one day provide me with power over Argos itself.

And, truth be told, I was having fun. The most amazing thing was the worker machines themselves. They came in a nearly infinite variety of sizes and shapes, from smaller machines equipped with nearly silent vacuums to clean up the dust that forever fell in silence to huge man-sized machines.

It was these "soldiers"—as Argos called them—that were the most enjoyable for they were not only amazingly capable but they had mounts on their backs—I could ride on them.

Whizzing down corridors in near silence at speeds I'd only ever before experienced in an aircraft was a joy and delight. The "soldiers"— and I was afraid I knew too well the reason for their name—would obey my every command. In fact, I believe that they were programmed to respond to humans before responding to Argos. I certainly got the impression that he was irritated every time I had to use one, particularly as transport to a distant location.

One night, after a day of extremely demanding repairs, Argos said to me, "Tomorrow I think you should go back."

"Really?"

"You said you had a compatriot? Handon Gar by name?"

I nodded and then, in case he couldn't see the movement, said aloud, "Yes."

"Well, you might perhaps want to follow the events I have recorded recently," Argos said. "I'm not sure if you will be pleased with them."

By now, I knew how to access his electronic recordings. I moved to a nearby console, sat down, and keyed the display to life.

"Which record?"

"I am sending it to you now," Argos said. "I regret that I do not have sound for all of it, but I have analyzed the lip movements and provided what I believe are accurate translations."

Hmm, I thought to myself. *He can read lips*. It was another thing to remember about this incredible, unnerving, intelligent machine.

It took over an hour to go through all of his visual records. Argos had not warned me that some of them would be low-light images nor that they would involve intimacies I would normally have avoided.

At the end of it, Argos said, "I am sorry to be the bearer of such tidings. Clearly, you must approach your 'friend' with caution."

"Caution," indeed! Handon Gar had taken control of the people of Tonos, had seduced both Evina and Danura—first without the other's knowledge and then with their willing consent. The rules of society on Tonos were not those of Unis—I knew that—but I would have preferred to not have that knowledge thrust upon me so graphically.

Lately, though, I noted with some small sense of relief, Danura had taken to avoiding Gar and seemed aloof in her contacts with him. He had switched to courting Evina solely and seemed ready to force a putsch similar to that of Germany's tyrant so many years before.

And Argos wanted me to go back into that maelstrom and recruit Handon Gar for his own purposes.

It was not an enjoyable prospect.

Argos wanted me to move quickly—and that was my own inclination—but our goals were not the same at all, so I convinced him that it was necessary that I conduct certain vital repairs before I returned to deal with Gar.

Through simple questioning, I had discovered that the intelligent machine kept a very precise control over the use of material. That much I had expected. While Argos could put many a quartermaster to shame, he was not adept at the art of pilfering. In my flying days both back on Earth and on Poloda, I had learned the necessity of getting a sufficiency of spare parts, and this skill stood me in good stead now.

So while I was making repairs, I was also making duplicates and certain specialty items that I knew I would shortly need.

I also, under the guise of pretending to hear an odd high-pitched noise, managed to learn about the mechanism that caused the worker machines to float. It was, as I'd expected, a variant on the same power amplifier that I'd perfected for my trip here from Poloda—except that it operated on a different frequency. It did not take me long to build a new set of receiving circuits which I could quickly and easily install on my craft when I had the chance.

For I knew that my best hope of survival lay neither with Argos nor with Handon Gar but in getting away from this planet and—hopefully—returning to Poloda. But not immediately. I was under no misapprehensions over how Argos would react if I made my escape and it was not otherwise engaged. Even if I succeeded, I decided that it was criminal to beat a path back to Poloda, certain to be tracked by an Argos already half convinced to take his revenge on the long-fled Kapar.

My plan was, once I'd built a sufficiency of supplies, to introduce Gar to Argos—and escape while they were still trying to gain control over each other. I'd no doubt that, in the end, Argos would triumph—if Gar did not somehow convince the insane machine to unite with him.

Argos grew less and less patient with each passing day, and it became more and more difficult to convince it to accept the reasons for my delay, but secretly I was pleased when, at the end of the week, the intelligent machine demanded that I return to the Tonosians. I had been ready for two days already.

"I think you're right," I said. "But, if you'll permit, I think my best chance is to wait for nighttime, when they are sleeping."

Argos was silent for a short moment while it thought.

"Yes," it said finally, "I can see the advantages in that plan."

So we waited until the evening. I fortified myself with a stimulant remarkably similar to coffee and, just after midnight, donned the gear and equipment I deemed necessary for my plan.

I returned to the main dome through the entry closest to Danura's sleeping quarters. I'd been monitoring the activities of her, Evina, and Handon Gar ever since Argos had alerted me, and I knew that she was alone in her sleeping quarters.

It did not comfort me to know that Argos could monitor everyone even while they slept—watching them with special low-light cameras and the more eerie heat-sensing cameras, which translated temperature into color. The heat-sensing—or "infrared," as Argos preferred to call it—cameras made it impossible for a person to feign sleep to Argos, something I was determined not to forget when the time came.

I slipped from the corridor into her room silently. For a moment I merely stood there, looking at her. She was no taller than I, but her lithe figure made it seem otherwise. I flushed then, deciding that it was ungentlemanly to be in a woman's room without her knowledge.

"Danura," I said in a low voice. She twitched and turned in her sleep, an odd, endearing smile crossing her lips before they smoothed again in slumber.

I moved to her bed and gently shook her shoulder. "Danura."

Her eyelids fluttered open and she jerked back when she recognized a strange shape in the dim light. Before she could cry out, I moved forward and put a hand on her mouth, but she twisted and bit it. With a gasp of pain, I pulled it back even as she hissed, "How many times, Gar, must I tell you?"

"It's me," I said. "Tangor."

"Tangor!" Danura sat up in bed, pulling the blankets up against her. Her brows creased in disbelief. I made a gesture with the controls on my belt, and the lights brightened, turning the room from a place of shadows into one of a dim red light.

She threw aside her bedsheets and leaped out of the bed, grabbing me fiercely. "We thought you were dead!"

I was startled by her movement, for she wore only the thinnest of sleeping garments and I had expected her to remain in the bed, demure and shy. My arms reacted on their own, tightening, clutching her to me even as I recalled that I was on Tonos—not Earth nor Poloda.

"I'm alive, as you can feel," I said, keeping my voice low. She moved away from me, turned and grabbed clothes. Without a backward glance my way, she quickly changed into her day clothes.

"What are your plans?" she demanded when she turned back to me. "Do you know how things are here?"

"I do," I told her. "And I know more than you."

"Such as?" Even in her worry, she retained a haughty, commanding demeanor.

I pulled one of my treasures from a deep thigh pocket and extended it toward. "Such as, I know how to read this."

She grabbed the viewer from me avidly and pored over the glyphs and symbols, looking up at me a moment later with a mixture of sorrow and hope. "Can you teach me?"

"Yes," I told her. She brightened, her eyes sparkling even in the dim red light. "And I can do more."

"Your friend Handon Gar said much the same thing," she observed tartly.

"I do not think that Gar is a friend of mine," I told her, adding, "Is Evina a friend of yours?"

Danura turned away from me for a moment before turning back to answer, "Once, perhaps. Now?" She shrugged and shook her head. "But the people listen to her, listen to him." She made a face. "They say that she is with child."

"She is." The child was Gar's—neither of us needed to say it.

"That will be her third," Danura said, surprising me. "With her third, she gains the power."

"What?" the word was startled out of me even though I already knew the answer.

"You must know that we are dying as a people," Danura said. "That we are not as fertile as we need to be. This has been since anyone can remember."

"And because of it, the women who can bear children are highly regarded."

Danura nodded. "Up until now, Evina and I were tied with two apiece—"

"What?" The word exploded out of me. I had not for a moment thought that Danura had children. I looked around the room. "Where are your children, then?"

"With their nurses, of course," Danura said. "I am far too valuable to spend time rearing them, and they are far too valuable to entrust solely to my care."

"Don't you miss them?"

"One," she said in a stifled voice. Her tone changed as she continued, "The other I can see whenever I want."

It took me a moment to digest what she'd said. The woman in front of me—the person who looked barely old enough to wed—had already had two children. And, by her tone, had lost one of them already.

"Evina's second is not quite as old as my first was when he died," she said. She shrugged. "Men are more fragile than women."

I nodded, not ready to argue with her on this point.

"Until Evina's youngest exceeds my firstborn's age, we are tied in our place as mothers," she said. She raised her eyes to me and added in an undertone, "Both of us saw you and Gar as potential mates."

"What about your husband?"

"'Husband'?" Danura repeated the word, her brows furrowed. "It means mate, correct?"

"It means the one you love and take as your sole mate."

Danura gave me a perplexed look. "Whyever would one want to do that? Such an unnatural selection cannot be good for breeding!"

"Where I come from it is considered the norm," I told her, unable to keep the stiffness out of my voice.

"And where you come from are there more men than women?"

"Yes," I admitted.

"Then perhaps it is so because of that," she threw back at me. "Had you considered that?"

"Are you saying that you don't have a mate?"

"One lover?" She sounded outraged. "As premier mother, I can pick *any* male I choose!"

"What?" I cried. "You're a whore?"

"I do not understand this word, and I don't care for your tone, Tangor," Danura responded coldly. "On this world, our survival depends upon my having as many children as I can. All else is secondary to that—including your desires and opinions!"

"No," I said.

"What?" she cried, furious at being gainsaid.

"I said: 'no,'" I repeated. Seeing her eyes flame, I continued, "It was not like this always. Your people suffered from a plague, a disease which rendered most of your men sterile."

"Do you mean to say that we were once like you and the Polodans?" she asked. I nodded. "That women were treated like breeders?"

"Not breeders," I replied. "They were treated as treasures."

"I am not sure I like your world, Tangor," Danura said after a moment. I got the distinct impression that I was included in that denouncement.

"The world you have, Danura, is changing," I said in reply. "You may not have a choice."

"With Gar—"

"Gar is part of that change," I agreed. "But there is more than he knows."

She raised an eyebrow at me challengingly.

"Sit," I gestured toward her bed and pulled up the one chair in the room, "it's a long story."

With a deep sigh, Danura sat and cocked her head at me attentively.

I told her about Argos, about the domes, about the plague, about the machines and reading.

"You say it took you a week to learn to read," she interrupted at that point. "I will learn in three days." I raised an eyebrow at her. "You will teach me."

"First you will hear what I have to say," I told her. She straightened at that, surprised at my brisk and demanding tone.

"You talk like a premier mother," she said, affronted.

"Listen," I said, launching once more into my tale. At the very end, I leaned forward as if to kiss her but instead whispered into her ear at a pitch that I was certain even Argos could not hear. Her eyes widened and she sat back, leaning against the wall, her gaze unfocused. She sat like that for a long time before she nodded.

I straightened up and raised a hand to her, beckoning. She rose and grabbed my hand, following me out into the darkened hallway.

And so began Danura's education. I brought her not through the entrance I had originally used but through another door nearer her sleeping quarters and down into the nearest control center. I had decided early on that there were some things I did not want her to know.

For the first three days she was an eager student. On the fourth day, discovering that all her effort was only a down payment on the work required, she balked. My wheedling and pleading were rebuffed; it was only when I taunted her with my success—"So you admit that men are superior? That I am better than you?"—that she mulishly returned to her studies.

It was hardly a day later that she had her breakthrough. We had tried a number of texts, but it was only when she discovered romance novels that she found something enticing. We read together, huddled over one of the screen readers, with me reading a portion and then leaving her to finish.

It was getting late, past time to return her to her quarters.

"Danura," I said, "we need to get you back."

"Just a moment," she told me distractedly.

"If you're too late, it will be noticed," I said, quoting the words she'd said to me on an earlier occasion when she'd found the going too difficult.

"Shh, Golrina is about to give birth," Danura said, bending farther over the table and peering intently at the words as she scrolled to the next page.

I sat back, a smile upon my lips. I knew that she had got it, that the love of reading had lodged in her heart. I recalled the days of my youth when I first discovered Jules Verne and, later, Edgar Rice Burroughs. I was surprised to realize that I was now living a life far more interesting—and dangerous—than John Carter of Mars.

I leaned forward again, to discover that Danura had paused, rubbing away the tears that were streaming down her face. She noticed me and buried her head in my shoulder, crying, "She lost the baby, she lost the baby!"

I comforted her as best I could and reminded her that it was a work of fiction, that it wasn't real.

"It doesn't matter if it's real; it matters what I feel!" she scolded me. A yawn escaped her and she looked back at the book, clearly torn between reading more and her need for sleep.

"It will be there tomorrow," I told her, recalling fondly my mother's words to me as a child: "The print won't fade."

She allowed herself to be led back to her room. There she got ready for bed in her usual unselfconscious manner, being no more concerned with her modesty than if I had been a piece of furniture. I had grown used to it, though it still made me uncomfortable. She knew it, and it amused her.

Finally she crawled under her sheets, and I made ready to go. But she stopped me with a raised hand, patting the side of her bed.

"You've never told me of your homeworld, Tangor," she said now, muzzily.

"There's not much to tell," I said evasively. I had made it clear to her that Argos heard every word said in the domes and was listening with special care to the words *I* said—as I'd made it a point of asking him to do so (saying it was to be certain that he sent aid if I asked for it but also allowing me to verify my suspicion as to his eavesdropping abilities).

"Were there many women for you?" she asked now. "Were you a lusty lover in that other body?"

We had been in each other's close company for such a while now that I had little difficulty grasping the import of her question.

"They are thousands—perhaps hundreds of thousands—of years gone," I replied. In truth, there had only been one brief romance before the rigors of war restricted my movements—and it had been a chaste thing with all the heat of first love.

Yamoda was not much different, although I got to see more of her than I had of Veronica Smith.

"But you still have your memories," Danura said, reaching out from under her blankets to pat my leg. "In that way you are like a book. So tell me your tale."

I toyed with denying her but then decided it would be a harmless diversion and give nothing away to Argos that I would regret. So I told her about Veronica—"Ronnie"—and how we'd met in high school and how we'd danced at the Fall Ball. And then there'd been Pearl Harbor, and I'd signed up with the Army Air Corps and had been sent to fight the Germans.

I kept my voice in a low monotone and, soon enough, was rewarded by the sound of Danura's gentle snores. Gently I put her hand back under the sheets and leaned over to kiss her forehead good night.

She said nothing the next evening when I came for her, instead prattling on about the book and being certain that I had not read ahead of her. She finished that book and three others, even as I introduced her to the technical manuals. Those bored her and she dismissed them with a wave.

However, I had planned for that, leaving her to read while I worked on several projects for Argos—and myself.

When she was ready for a break, I whistled up one of the more imposing worker machines and then whistled for another. I made the right hand signal for the first mount to descend and climbed aboard.

"You can *ride* them?" Danura cried in delighted surprise. "Show me!"

"It's in the manual," I told her. "I've keyed it for your screen, all you have to do is read it."

"But I want to ride *now!*" she said imperiously.

"So read quickly," I told her. "I'm hungry and I'm going to eat at the High Commissary—they've made your favorite soup."

"What?" Danura said. She stamped her foot. "You can't leave me here!"

I smiled at her and rolled the controls on my worker machine. Noiselessly we turned outside around her and the worker I'd summoned for her and then sped off into the distance even as she wailed angrily, "Tangor!"

⊰ IV ⊱

Hunger, as always, proved an excellent motivator, and she was only twenty-five minutes late in joining me. She dismounted, her face flushed with excitement and her hair akimbo from the wind that her flying worker machine had generated in its speed.

On the ground, she rushed up to me, fists raised, and pummeled my chest. "That's for leaving me!" she cried, and then leaned up and forward to plant a kiss on my lips. "And that's for making me learn."

I wrapped my arms around her and gave her a tight hug before turning to the tables. "I've kept the soup warm."

"I knew you would," she purred, retaining one of my hands and leading us to the waiting table. A server machine whisked out our hot food and poured drinks.

We spent little time talking while we ate, but our eyes spoke volumes.

Over the next few days, Danura perfected her grasp of reading and her grasp of technical work. She became engrossed in the most intriguing tasks and insisted on treating Argos like a mere male which seemed to cause the machine some confusion which pleased me quite a lot, particularly as I was busy with my own plans.

So when Danura became engrossed in one of her projects, I engaged in some of mine.

As I've said, Argos is an intelligent machine and runs the three domes of Tonos. Its ability to track parts and explain repairs was phenomenal, but it was just as stupid as any supply officer when it came to preventing a little creative accounting, as my old tech sergeant used to say with me, winking before presenting me with a brand-new engine he just "happened" to locate.

I knew that Argos would track items, because it was a requirement of its operations, but I also knew that, however intelligent Argos was, it was originally designed and built by humans—Tonosians over three thousand years ago—and so subject to the same industrial myopia that afflicted all such massive engineering tasks.

Argos, in short, couldn't see the trees for the forest. I soon learned exactly how it maintained track of its inventory—it used the simple assumption that all powered machinery needed powerpacks or batteries of some kind and so rigged special trackers in those.

Once learned, it was not difficult to become an expert on "troubleshooting" problems with power supplies, some of which invariably were deemed too decrepit to spare. In fact, most of them were nothing of the sort; I merely declared them so when, in fact, I had removed the tracking circuitry.

So, for my escape, I had constructed several items that I was reasonably sure Argos would not be able to track.

I had also been careful not to reveal the location of our craft.

Now my plan was complete. It was time to implement it, return to my craft, leave this planet—but not return to Poloda.

I knew that sooner or later my disappearance would be noticed, but I'd planned to create the maximum amount of confusion just before my departure. Even so, I was too certain that Argos forgot nothing and its "hatred"—if a machine can have such emotions—of the long-dead Kapar meant that it would not be long before it considered taking vengeance on his descendants. In that much, I wished the machine all the luck it could get.

Unfortunately, it was obvious that once the population of Tonos was restored to its former levels, there would neither be enough resources nor dome space for all the people. At such point, naturally, Argos would look to expand its presence.

By coming to Tonos, I had endangered not just the despised Kapars but all Poloda.

I was resolved to come up with a solution. There was no solution here—only more problems—and no solution back on Poloda, even with the technology I'd learned of. So my best hope was to press on to the other worlds of Omos and see if perhaps on one of them I could find either a world the Unis could inhabit or help that would protect them from not only the Kapars but also the more dangerous machine intelligence, Argos.

There was no reason to believe that Handon Gar would support me in this. In fact, he seemed more than willing to remain with Evina and become the father to a reinvigorated race of Tonosians. If I tried to tell him my fears, I risked losing all, so I decided that I would venture on my own.

All this, naturally, I kept from Danura, for she, too, had a part to play in my plan.

Of course, I was a fool.

It began well enough. It started when I escorted Danura back to her quarters late one evening. After I left her, I went on to my quarters, which I now could check to see if they were empty using a simple electronic detector Argos had provided—for he was in on my avowed plan to usurp Gar and provide more humans to be trained as technicians.

In my quarters, I checked the gear I had stowed earlier, pleased to see that no one had disturbed its location—Argos did not realize that in revealing his tracking abilities to me, he had showed me how to evade them. I was now very good with that sort of electronic circuitry.

After that, I lay down and tried to sleep. I had set an alarm on my communicator and glanced at the time display restlessly as the minutes crawled slowly on.

Finally, unable to take the strain, I made my way to a refresher and showered. I was surprised to find Danura there in another stall.

"I couldn't sleep," she confessed with a wry expression.

"Get dressed, and I'll meet you in the Great Hall, where we planned," I told her.

Ten minutes later we entered the Great Hall together. The Great Hall was the name for one of the many large gathering places in the dome. It was the place that Danura had led me to that first day when Gar and I were brought to learn the Tonosian language.

We grabbed food and took a table far away from the rest of the morning crowd, eating slowly and waiting for the arrival of Gar and Evina.

They came, Evina moving regally, with her head high and a haughty expression in her eyes. Beside her, Gar looked smug and well-pleased. I knew from the recordings Argos had shown me that both secretly plotted to be the ruler of the other—they were well-matched in their duplicity.

A few well-wishers approached, made obeisance, and moved away. Others left for the food dispensers and returned bearing trays that they set in front of Evina and, with less evident relish, Gar.

"Your friend acts like he's a Prime Mother," Danura murmured to me, her eyes flaring with anger.

"If Argos is right, he is even more important," I reminded her. Danura snorted; the notion that a male could steadily provide offspring was beyond her experience and outside her comprehension, so low had the reproductive potential of the Tonosian men sunk.

"If Argos is correct, your world will change in short order," I reminded her. "What will it be like when there are hundreds—thousands—of Prime Mothers?"

Danura shook her head, denying the notion.

"It's time," I said to her. "Are you ready?"

In response, she rose from her chair and paced toward the cluster that surrounded Evina and Gar. I followed her, my eyes on Handon Gar.

The group surrounding them slowly grew quiet and parted as we approached, eyeing me with surprise and Danura with respect.

"Evina," Danura said.

"Ah, I see it is Danura risen from her illness," Evina said to the others with a faint smile on her lips. "Perhaps she has recovered from the news that I bear my *third* child."

"As do I," Danura returned easily. Evina's eyes went wide and Gar shot me an astonished look. I held my expression tightly, not knowing what Danura meant.

"So, little Yamoda will be disappointed," Gar said, rising from his chair and moving toward me with a hand outstretched, "but I imagine congratulations are in order." He grabbed my hand and murmured to me, "You old rogue, you."

"Did you miss me?" I asked him.

Gar's smile widened and then slipped. "I, ah, didn't notice you were gone for quite a while, to be honest."

"I presume congratulations are in order," I said, nodding toward Evina.

"Perhaps twice," Gar said, his smile broadening as he nodded toward Danura. "Unless you are claiming responsibility."

"It would be easy enough to tell," I said, masking my mixed emotions over this revelation about Danura.

"Not even on Poloda do we know how to do that," Gar said, shaking his head. "One could make assumptions based on looks, but that is not always accurate."

"No," Danura said, stepping over toward us, "there are ways to tell who is the father."

"What are you talking about?" Evina demanded, moving to regain her position in the center of the conversation.

"Gar," I said, turning to the Polodan, "did you not wonder where I was during my absence?"

"I presumed you were either pouting or otherwise occupied," Gar said with a wide grin, his hands moving to gather Evina and Danura against him. Evina moved in reluctantly, unused to such male behavior, but Danura slipped out of his grasp with a look of fury.

"You are not my master!" Danura said.

"No," Evina purred to her, "but soon *I* will be. As Prime Mother, you are bound to my rules."

"There are two Prime Mothers here, Evina," Danura replied tightly.

"Maybe more," I said with a smirk toward Gar, who, to my surprise, laughed at the quip. Clearly, he had no inkling of his danger.

"What matters most," I said, "is the care and raising of children, the preservation of the dome, and the people."

Evina snorted at my statement of the obvious.

I raised my voice to carry, "What if all men could sire children and all women bear them safely? What then?"

I could see by the reactions of the others that this idea intrigued them.

"That is not possible," Evina said. "Too many men are weak, as are so many women."

I nodded to Danura, who smiled and pulled forth her communicator, tapping a quick code into it.

"What is that?" Evina asked, brows furrowed. Gar's head snapped around, and his eyes widened as he guessed at what Danura held. Then he whipped his head to me.

I merely waited, a smile forming on my lips. Oh, I was going to enjoy this!

We had only to wait a moment before two worker machines noiselessly entered the room, moved to us, and stopped, lowering themselves for us to mount.

"This is the future of Tonos!" Danura declared, climbing aboard her machine. She pulled a reader from her large thigh pocket and waved it over her head. "This is what we forgot hundreds of years ago, and what I've learned again!"

As Gar, Evina, and the rest stared at us, two more machines noiselessly moved in and, at Danura's gesture, lowered themselves in front of Evina and Gar.

"Come with us if you want to save Tonos!" Danura cried daringly to Evina. She saw the fear in the other's eyes and said, with a sneer, "Or stay here to die in ignorance."

Gar needed no urging, eyeing the machine thoughtfully for a moment before climbing effortlessly aboard. It rose silently into the air once more, and he turned to me, eyes shining.

The murmur of the crowd changed from confusion to disapproval of Evina, and the younger Prime Mother glanced around anxiously before reluctantly following Gar in climbing aboard her mount.

"Where to now, Tangor?" Gar asked.

"You'll see," I said, nodding to Danura, who entered a command into her communicator. The worker machines moved silently out of the room, followed by all the eyes of Tonos.

It was hard to determine which was more ecstatic—Gar or Argos—over the addition of our personnel. Certainly Evina was the most anxious, shrieking when Argos's voice first erupted into the control room. She was also the slowest of us all to learn to read and disliked the effort required. At best she would never be more than an indifferent reader and a terrible technician. It was clear that Danura was by far the smarter of the two, a fact not unnoticed by Gar who spent time trying to distance himself from the other woman and spend more time with Danura.

In that, he bought himself the worst of all worlds. Danura wanted nothing to do with him, and Evina alternated between being clingy and waspish—and I got the distinct impression that the favors she had previously so lavishly bestowed upon him grew far less frequent.

As Evina learned to read and interact with Argos, she and Danura argued more frequently over who to bring next into the control room to learn to read and work on the complex machinery of the domes.

Evina, while not smart, was persistent, and before the end of the second week was demanding proof that the machinery of the domes could help in childbirth.

I myself had been amazed and not a little overwhelmed by the wealth of medical knowledge and ability possessed by Argos and its minions. I had been very careful to ensure that Danura did not learn how to operate the complex diagnostic equipment and so now spent time teaching Gar how to operate it while using Evina as a reluctant and very fidgety patient.

The equipment was a bit more personal than I would have imagined, but she took the invasion of her person philosophically, except when she was not only told the parentage of her child, and the state of the pregnancy but also its sex.

"A girl!" Evina cried happily. "Gar, you've fathered a girl!" She leaned forward to grab his face in her hands, disregarding any hope of modesty as she praised him. "You're such a good boy!"

Gar bore the praise with what grace he could, considering he was being treated as would an infant on Poloda.

"Here, Danura, let's see about you!" Evina said now, gesturing for Danura to disrobe so as to enter the machinery.

Danura's cheeks dimpled, and she went slightly pink, turning to me beseechingly.

"Why don't you get dressed first, and you and Gar can view the examination in the control room?" I suggested suavely. Gar gave me a skeptical look but agreed that the control room was warmer and more comfortable than the cold examination room. He did not know that I'd arranged that on purpose with this circumstance in mind.

After they left, Danura moved into the examination chamber, which was similar to a shower stall; she could stand up in it, her head peering over the top.

I could see tears trickling down her cheeks. I did not know why. The medical machine gave me a reason quickly enough: she was not pregnant.

She met my eyes as I looked up from the readouts. What she was thinking, I could not say.

"I've got it," I told her. "You can get dressed now."

With a sniff, she retreated from the machine, re-dressed and walked over to where I was examining the readouts.

"The machine doesn't lie," Danura said as she looked down on the display. Her expression changed to one of surprise as she said, "It says I'm pregnant."

I smiled at her. "Yes, it does."

"But—but—" She stopped as I gestured to another screen.

"Evina and Gar are seeing this," I said, pointing to the false readings I'd programmed earlier, stolen from one of the training routines. "*That* is what the machine really saw."

"If Evina finds out that I'm not pregnant, she will become the only Prime Mother," Danura told me in a low voice. "And she and Gar will—"

"They will have to listen to Argos now," I reminded her. "Their victory may not be as complete as they'd like."

"So why are you showing them that?" Danura asked, pointing to the false readings.

"To give you the choice," I told her.

"They will find out soon enough," she said sadly.

"You can alter that," I suggested.

"With you?" she asked. "Or with Gar?"

I did not answer. To be honest, I was not sure if I could answer. Danura was smart and pretty, but her ways were quite different from mine . . . and there was still Yamoda's kiss to consider.

As a pilot, I thought I had become master of my body, but in the past weeks it had made it clear to me that, in my new Polodan body, the issue was not resolved. Just as the long-lost Ronnie had been replaced in my affections by small Yamoda, was it possible that the tall blond woman standing next to me might replace Yamoda in my heart?

I had work to do and a promise to keep. "Come," I said to her. "Let's go join the others."

By the end of the week, everything was in order for my plan. Gar was growing more and more adept at handling the repairs and learning the routines of Argos, Evina was grudgingly accepting the notion that she and Danura would still vie for the position of Prime Mother, and the Tonosians were slowly being reintroduced to the amazing machinery their ancestors had perfected so many thousands of years ago.

I could see that Gar was scheming to see how he could come out best from this new arrangement just as Argos was convinced that as a machine intelligence it would have no trouble handling all the people on Tonos.

The time had come.

I waited until it was dark once more and everyone could be expected to be asleep.

From my hidden location, I retrieved all the gear I had created and pilfered from Argos' stores. I dressed in warm gear—my old flight suit had been destroyed when the Tonosians had recovered me—and I could not recreate the thermal layers required to live in the arctic conditions without alerting Argos to my plans.

At the doorway to the outside, I hesitated briefly. Of all the people I'd met, I would miss Danura the most. She was the most intelligent, the most demanding and the most attractive of all the people on Tonos. Her ways were strange to me, and I was not sure she or her people would ever grow to learn love, which I felt was a horrible loss for them.

Even so, I had to go. I had unwittingly exposed the people of Unis to a threat even greater than the one they'd sent me to free them from. I owed them a solution to the new problems I'd created.

Handon Gar would remain behind. I did not trust him enough to confide in him—for if he betrayed me, all would be lost.

With one final look, I turned away from my quarters and went to the main entrance. I triggered the special sequence I'd programmed into my communicator, and the special access door opened. I made my way quickly inside, closed it and then opened the outer door—for it was built much like the airlocks on a submarine.

The wind howled outside and I would have been blind in the

darkness except for the marvelous Tonosian goggles that turned darkest night into a dim, greenish day for me.

I pulled out my compass, took a quick bearing, and set off.

I had only gone a few yards when a dark shape appeared in front of me.

My heart shuddered. All was lost.

✥ V ✥

I rocked back on my heels as the figure approached. It was dressed in cold-weather gear, and another suit of clothes hung over one shoulder.

"Did you think you could get away that easily?"

It was Danura.

"I must go," I told her firmly, trying to decide how to leave her without causing her harm. For all that they now had a vast store of medical knowledge, Danura was one of a few women who could still bear children and repopulate the domes of Tonos.

"I know," she said, moving close up beside me. She was wearing a long, clear mask that covered her face completely. She reached up to me. "Ah, you made night goggles. They are not as good as a thermal suit."

"Thermal suits can be tracked," I told her. "Argos will know you're here."

"And not you?" he asked, immediately unsealing her suit and starting to remove it.

"Don't do that!" I cried. "You'll freeze to death."

"If Argos tracks us, it won't matter."

"Us?" I said uncertainly.

She continued to strip even as she shouted over the wind, "I'm coming with you."

"What?"

"Did I not cry when I read about Golrina and her choice?" she said, half out of her suit. She gestured around her. "This is my choice, to be with you."

I couldn't speak. Finally, I said, "Put your suit back on or you'll freeze to death."

"But Argos!"

"We'll deal with that," I assured her. "Quickly—we need to move before he can track us."

She closed her suit up again and sealed it. Through the clear mask, I could see that her lips had taken on a bluish tinge even in that short a time, but her blue eyes were resolute.

"Lead on," she ordered.

I led. I looked back several times to be sure she was following. The last time I couldn't find her until I turned completely around in a circle and found her in front of me.

"Your goggles are not as good as my mask," she said. "Point the way and I'll lead."

I pointed and she led.

The craft resolved itself in the distance, growing from shadow to solidity.

"You came in that?" she said as she looked up at it. "And it will take us away?"

"When I make some changes," I told her.

"What about Argos?"

"I'm thinking," I told her. I gestured to the hatchway and we climbed inside. My fingers were numb from the cold, and I was desperate to get into my spare flight suit, but I knew that I needed to work fast.

I pulled off my pack and pulled out the circuits I'd made. I pointed to the panel. "We need to wire this in over there," I said to her.

"I can do that," she told me.

I hesitated. If she was wrong, we'd die either by Argos or when we turned on the power amplifiers.

"Trust me, Tangor," she said. I handed her the circuitry.

"I've got to check the engines."

"This isn't the engine?" she said, pointing at the circuit I'd given her.

"That works when we're off the planet. The engines will get us into the air."

"We're going to fly back to your homeworld?"

"Something like that," I told her, hurrying reluctantly back out into the biting chill of the arctic night. Quickly I cut the mooring line, checked the engines, and eyed the inflatable pontoons. They were, thankfully, still all in good order. I had not dared come here any time before, so if they'd been damaged we were dead.

"We." I hadn't expected that. I shook myself out of my reverie and moved back into our craft.

Danura had finished wiring in the circuitry. I flicked on the power switches and saw that it was working.

"I need you to get out of your suit. Remove anything that's powered and throw them down to me," I told her.

"I'll freeze!"

"You'll die otherwise."

She frowned at me but began peeling out of her suit. Moments later, shivering, she threw them down to me.

"In the back of the craft you should find stores. See if you can fit into Gar's flight suit. He was nearer your size than I."

She waved, her teeth chattering, and moved back.

I took all the gear and my communicator and threw them into the sea. A moment later, I was back in the cockpit firing up the engines.

Danura joined me as I swerved the craft around and pointed it into the bay.

"I thought you said we're going to fly!" she cried through still-chattering teeth. She had found only a blanket and had draped it around herself.

"Strap in," I said, pointing to the straps in the copilot's chair. "It's going to get bumpy."

I gunned the power and we jumped into the water. I throttled back to be sure we didn't get swamped by a wave and then slowly moved us out from the shore.

I had never tried to fly at night like this. For that matter, I wasn't sure I'd succeed. And now, with Danura, I was doubly afraid.

"How can you see?" she asked, peering at the darkness in front of us. "Do you still have your goggles?"

"I have this," I told her, pointing to a display that I'd set in front of me. It was a Tonosian version of an avionics display and like all the electronic displays, it was small, touch-activated, and incredibly powerful. I had readings of attitude, speed, direction—everything required to orient myself.

I gunned the power, and we started moving more swiftly, bobbing up and down as we skimmed over waves. Soon we had enough power to take off with both engines and I gently pulled the nose up, angling us toward the clouds above.

A moment later we lurched and were airborne.

An instant later, there was a loud bang, and a brilliant light flared in the night sky, blinding me. Instinctively, I looked back at the display and waited until my eyes recovered their night vision.

"Tangor, what was that?"

"I'd say that Argos found your thermal suit," I told her, pushing more power into the throttles and lurching us up at the steepest angle I could maintain.

"Oh!" Danura cried as the g-forces slammed her back into her chair.

We climbed steadily until we were at twenty thousand feet. I double-checked our pressure seals and our oxygen tanks, glad that I'd set them to recharge when we'd first landed so many months ago. We had enough for two months, if need be.

We had slightly more rations than that.

Suddenly we broke through clouds and the stars came out, twinkling.

"What are those?" Danura cried, pointing at them. "Are those planets?"

"No, those are stars," I told her. I checked our heading and then—with some trepidation—engaged the new circuits for the power amplifier. In an instant we were thrust back against our seats as the power amplifiers added to the thrust of the engines. I idled the engines, which were becoming ineffective in the high, thin air, and we continued our climb until we exited the atmosphere.

"What is it like on your home, Tangor?"

"We're not going there," I told her.

"Because Argos would follow us," Danura said. I gave her a surprised look, and she giggled. "Did you not think I could figure it out?"

"So tell me," I demanded, "what is my plan?"

"You are going for help," she said. "You are going to the next planet over—what is its name?"

"Yonda," I said, surprised at how much she had guessed.

"And I am coming with you," she told me.

She started shivering and I said to her, "Go back to the sleep cabin and get under the sheets."

"I'm too cold," she said. "How will I keep warm?"

I looked at my display screen, tapped in a routine I'd set up when I'd first made it, and turned on the autopilot.

"I'll join you," I said, unstrapping my seatbelt.

"And how will that help, Tangor?" Danura asked, her eyes dancing.

"There are two heaters on this craft."

"Heaters?"

"You and me," I said, gesturing for her to precede me.

"And when we are warm, what then?" Danura asked, turning back to bat her eyelashes at me alluringly. "It is a long time to Yonda, is it not?"

"We'll think of something," I told her. She giggled again and I realized how much I loved the sound.

⊹⇌ Epilogue ⇌⊹

The last words remained at the bottom of the page, the typewriter stopped.

It remained silent all night long even as I waited. Finally, I went to sleep.

It was still silent in the morning.

It's been that way now for over a month.

What of Tangor's warning? Was it really him? How did he work through the typewriter?

And, most importantly, why didn't he give us a clear warning?

I must tell you. I must tell you before it is too late. Your world is in danger. You must prepare. You must be ready. God forgive me, it is all my fault.

Tell us what? That Argos knows about us? Or the Kapars? Is Earth in danger?

Is it too late?

Each night I hope in vain that the typewriter will start up once more. I have a fresh sheet in the rubber rolling platen, and I have made sure that the keys are oiled, the ribbon is fresh.

I will wait, like Edgar Rice Burroughs, until Tangor returns.

 END

Inspired by Conan Doyle's The Lost World *(1912) and the long history of Hollow Earth mythology, Burroughs created Pellucidar, a world inside ours with an eternal sun, horizonless vistas, and an eerie stationary moon. ERB pitted David Innes and his brilliant and eccentric scientist friend, Abner Perry, against mammoths, sabre-tooths and evil flying-reptile overlords in* At the Earth's Core *(1914) and* Pellucidar *(1915). David Innes, of course, conquered all and became Emperor of Pellucidar. ERB followed those books with 5 others. NY Times bestselling author F. Paul Wilson takes on the mysteries of this geologically impossible world, and in the course of events sends David and Abner on a ride to the moon known as the Dead World.*

—Bob

The Dead World

As related by David Innes to F. Paul Wilson via Gridley Wave

I

As Emperor of Pellucidar, I've always felt it good policy to make occasional visits to the heads of state of the various Federated Kingdoms that make up the Empire. I find myself visiting Thuria more than the others. I hadn't realized this until my wife, the beautiful Dian, mentioned it.

I was surprised. Why would I be drawn to a kingdom set in the Land of Awful Shadow?

On reflection, I realized I was drawn there *because* of the shadow.

For those new to Pellucidar, let me offer a quick tutorial.

Earth is hollow. Five hundred miles below the crust exists a separate world, seven thousand miles in diameter, with a miniature sun suspended in the center. Because its sun shines ceaselessly, Pellucidar has no day-night cycle, and the concept of time is, therefore, elusive and ephemeral.

It's inhabited by refugees from ancient times, from the Jurassic through the Pleistocene epochs, including primitive *Homo sapiens*.

Pellucidar also has a moon—a small, strange sphere that hangs stationary about a mile above the surface. It has a number of names. I've heard it called the Pendant Moon, but most often it's referred to as the Dead World. Since its orbit is, for want of a better term, geosynchronous or geostationary, the land below exists in the perpetual twilight of its shadow.

Since I'm from the surface world and grew up with a day-night cycle, perhaps my body craves periodic sojourns in the twilit Land of Awful Shadow. Perhaps it sees that Shadow as anything but Awful.

On this particular trip, after crossing the Sojar Az on my clipper ship, the *John Tyler*, I took lunch with Goork, the King of Thuria, in his palace. Thurians are hut dwellers, so their idea of a palace is a single-story structure made of stone block. These folk are unique among the humans of Pellucidar. Since they live in shadow, their skin is pale; they carry heavy traces of Neanderthal ancestors, with a squat physique that is more muscular and more hirsute than the average human here. Goork and I did not get off to a good start when first we met, but we've become fast friends since.

As we ate I found myself, as usual, gazing up at the Dead World slowly rotating only a mile above. I've never understood why they call it the Dead World. From here I could see mountains and oceans and lakes and rivers and forests. Nothing dead about it. I saw no sign of habitation, though. But then, finer details were difficult to discern since the side facing the land was always in shadow. I could not imagine normal humans living on that small world, not unless they were small themselves, like the Minunians, the fabled Ant Men of Africa.

We had barely begun our meal when a young Thurian came charging up, shouting, "Father! Father!"

I recognized the lad as Koort, younger brother to Goork's other son, Kolk. He looked frightened and angry.

Goork shot to his feet. "What is the meaning of this? What is so important that you interrupt my meal with the Emperor."

"My lidi!" he cried, panting. "Someone killed it!"

"What? Who?"

"A giant stone fell from the sky and killed it!"

Goork turned to me. "Are we being attacked? Could a Mahar have dropped it?"

I doubted that. I had long ago driven those winged reptiles out of their nearby cities and into the north regions.

"Let's go look at this stone."

❖═ II ═❖

We came upon the dead lidi about two miles deep in the Thurian forest. I use the term loosely. Forests in the Land of Awful Shadow are unlike those anywhere else in Pellucidar. The endless sunshine makes for thick, lush vegetation out there. In here, in the eternal twilight, the greenery tends to be pale and thin. Not pretty, but it makes for easier travel on foot.

The lidi are the Pellucidar equivalent of a diplodocus from the surface's Jurassic period. There's a polar entrance to the Inner World, and the theory is that fauna from various epochs wandered through over millions of years and never left. Thurians use the huge saurian quadrupeds as mounts and place a high value on one that's trainable.

"There!" Koort cried, pointing. "I was letting it graze when that stone crashed through the trees and crushed its head. Someone owes me a lidi!"

As I stepped closer to examine the "stone," I realized it was nothing of the sort. It measured perhaps four feet across and was perfectly spherical with a smooth, gray, almost polished surface. It looked like steel or some sort of alloy.

The seat of the Empire, back in Sari, had the most advanced technology in Pellucidar. We manufactured guns and knives and even cannon, but this was something beyond us.

I turned to Koort. "You say this fell through the trees?"

"Yes. I heard a terrible crashing from above, and then my poor Kinlap was dead."

"Kinlap?"

He looked embarrassed. "I named her. She was a hard worker. Someone owes me a new lidi!"

I looked up and saw a number of broken branches, and beyond them the Dead World. Here, directly beneath the moonlet, it not only hid the sun but filled the sky. Yet even in the twilight I could see that the broken branches did not follow an arc as they might had this been flung by a catapult or shot from some giant cannon. The broken limbs trailed straight up toward . . .

. . . the Dead World.

No . . . it couldn't be.

Just then came a crashing of underbrush from our left. I pulled my revolver—one never goes unarmed on Pellucidar—but relaxed when I saw two Thurian boys running toward us.

"There it is!" said the one in the lead.

They stopped short when they realized it had killed a lidi. Then they noticed the adults. They shrank back as Koort approached them with a menacing look.

"Did either of you two have anything to do with this?"

They both began babbling at once. Eventually I was able to piece together the story.

The two boys had been playing in the observation tower I had built on the edge of Thuria. My purpose had been to introduce time to Pellucidar based on the rotation of the Dead World. One full rotation equaled a "day." I divided that into twenty-four equal "hours" and began marking the time by an hourly wireless signal sent to my headquarters in Sari. It turned out that Pellucidarians hated counting time. It simply was not in their nature and made them irritable. So I abandoned the plan. The tower, however, remained.

The boys had been on the upper level when one of them noticed an object sailing from the Dead World and heading toward Thuria. They'd begun searching the forest in the direction where they'd seen it land.

We all looked up.

"From the Dead World?" Koort said. "Someone up there owes me a lidi."

"There's no one up there," his father said. "That's why they call it the Dead World."

I returned my attention to the "stone."

"Someone's up there," I said. "Someone skilled in working with metals. But why would they launch this toward the surface?"

"To kill my lidi," Koort said.

I didn't know Koort well, but apparently once he found a train of thought, he did not veer from its track.

"I doubt they were aiming for your—"

Just then the sphere began to hiss, releasing a ten-foot jet of steam from its upper pole. I felt something land on my head, then my shoulder, and then it was raining what looked like tiny grains of red rice.

"They're coming from the sphere!" I cried, backing away.

"What are they?" Goork said.

We had all retreated out of range. I pulled one bit from my hair and gave it a closer look. Yes—oblong and about the size of a kernel of rice, but a glossy red.

"Beads?" I said.

The sphere ran out of steam then, and the hail of tiny beads stopped. Had the little people of the Dead World sent us a gift?

Yes, I know. A number of unwarranted assumptions. The lidi death was obviously an unfortunate accident—how could this projectile travel a full mile and strike a bull's eye on some unfortunate saurian's head?

"Gifts?" Goork said, obviously thinking along the same lines. "What odd gifts."

Koort scowled. "I'll take the gift of a new lidi."

Definitely a one-track mind.

Goork had brought a few guards along and he assigned them the task of carrying the empty sphere back to his village on the coast.

Later, to the tune of Koort's complaints about his dead lidi and who was to replace it, I loaded the sphere aboard the *John Tyler* and set sail for my palace in Sari.

As we were leaving the mooring, my grizzled captain, Ah-gilak, came up to me. Ah-gilak means "Old Man" in Pellucidarian. He was a toothless, white-bearded ancient mariner out of Cape Cod who'd been stranded here seemingly forever—so long he'd forgotten his real name.

He pointed to my sleeve. "You've got something growing on you," he said, speaking the local tongue with a New England accent.

I looked, and sure enough, a tiny red plant had taken root in the fabric of my shirt. Upon closer inspection, I recognized one of the beads that had sprayed us. It appeared to have germinated, meaning it was no bead, but a seed of some sort.

A twinge of unease tightened the muscles at the back of my neck. Why would the people of the Dead World send a load of seeds to the surface?

Just then the clipper cleared the shadowed area—which extends in an arc over the Sojar Az—and returned to Pellucidar's perpetual noon.

When I looked again at the seedling, I noticed it had shriveled and died. No worry then. Whatever these seeds were, they didn't seem fit for life on the surface.

⊹⊱ III ⊰⊹

Later I had reason to change my mind. How much later—a week, a month, two months—I cannot say, because Pellucidar has no sunrise, no sunset, no clocks, no seasons, no calendar. "Later" will have to suffice.

I was with Abner Perry in my office, going over his new design for an aeroplane. He was obsessed with bringing manned flight to Pellucidar. He'd succeeded in the balloon category, but his previous attempt at winged flight, an ungainly contraption, had been a miserable failure, catching fire and very nearly immolating me in the process. I wanted to be in on the early stages of the design of his latest.

"I wish I could identify the alloy of that sphere you brought from Thuria," he said. "What a plane I could make if I had a supply of that!"

He'd just unfolded his preliminary sketches when one of my men at arms rushed in.

"Sir, a Thurian has arrived and insists on seeing you."

"King Goork? I hope you didn't—"

"No, sir. He says his name is Koort, son of Goork. He says his father is dead."

I leaped from my chair. "Bring him here immediately."

Shortly thereafter, Koort was escorted in. He looked terrible. He'd lost weight and looked distraught. More than distraught—he looked terrified. I rushed to meet him.

"Is it true about your father?"

He nodded, his throat working. After a moment, he managed to speak. "He's dead! They are *all* dead! Thuria is no more!"

"What are you saying? That's impossible."

"It is true! The beads that came from the Dead World—they were seeds. They sprouted, they grew into red vines that spread and continued to spread."

"Why didn't you come to us for help?" Perry said.

"That was what I said to my father, but he and Kolk said Thurians do not need help against a plant."

"What happened?" Perry said.

"We kept trying to cut back the vines, but every time we thought we succeeded, they reappeared elsewhere, as if by magic."

Perry was scratching his chin. "Sounds like something in the *Pueraria* genus."

"Meaning?"

"Kudzu is a member of that genus. You know about kudzu, don't you?"

I nodded. The vine had been running rampant across the southeastern US since the late nineteenth century, smothering everything in its path.

"But Koort says this is red."

"I didn't say it was kudzu, but from what this fellow's told us, it has similar characteristics. Kudzu spreads by seeds and stolons—surface runners—and rhizomes—subsurface runners. You can kill everything you can see, but those rhizomes are working through the soil beneath your feet, ready to pop up at the first opportunity. A triple threat like that is deucedly hard to eradicate. But . . ." He turned to Koort. "Death?"

Koort nodded vigorously, his throat working again. "All dead," he said in a thick voice. "The killing mist—"

"Wait a minute now," I said. "You didn't mention a mist."

"The flowers on the vines, they pop open and puff green air. It spreads everywhere, killing everyone. I came back from hunting on Lidi Plain and walked into it. It made me weak, but I was able to crawl away before it killed me. I hurried around to the az side where my father kept his palace. The green mist had seeped out of the forest and covered the shore. I saw my father and brother dead on the palace steps along with many others. I tried to reach them, but the mist began draining my life as soon as I breathed it."

I turned to Perry. "I need to get there as quickly as possible. Too bad your aeroplane isn't ready yet."

"And what do you think you'll do? Die like the rest?"

He had a good point.

"I'm their emperor! I can't just sit around and do nothing!"

He smiled. "I know you can't. But I may have a way for you to survive. Remember what happened when we attacked Phutra and tried to enter the city?"

The Mahars may be winged reptiles, but they built their cities underground. When our army charged into the tunnels, they released . . .

"Poison gas? You don't think the Mahars—"

"This isn't their style of warfare. But fearing we'd run into more poison gas back then, I designed and built some filtered masks to protect us. Fortunately we were able to use other methods to send them packing. But I still have the masks."

I clapped him on the shoulder. "Excellent! I'll leave right away."

"Bring me back a sample of this vine. We have to find a way to kill it. It could be a threat to all of Pellucidar."

On that chilling note, I began giving orders to ready the *John Tyler*.

⊹≒ IV ≒⊹

The Dead World eclipsed the sun as we approached the shoreline. I stood on the shadowed foredeck, slack-jawed and dumbfounded.

The Thuria I had known was gone. It looked like it had been covered with a thick red mesh, which in turn had been layered with a sickly green mist. Even Goork's palace, bordering the shore, was covered. The web of vines extended right to the waterline, but the mist didn't stop there—a two-foot layer of it was spreading over the rippling surface.

And nothing moved on shore . . . nothing.

"This is worse than when I left!" Koort cried. "The palace was untouched then!"

"I don't like the looks of this," said Ah-gilak, coming up beside me.

I nodded. "I agree. Put about and anchor well beyond the mist. Then lower a boat."

My captain gave me an unsettled look. "You're not really thinking—?"

"Someone's got to." I looked at Koort. "Are you with me?"

He nodded without hesitation. "That is my land."

"Good man."

After the *John Tyler* dropped anchor, Koort and I clambered aboard the fifteen-foot dinghy and began to row. As we approached the mist, I handed him one of Perry's masks.

"Put this on. It will protect us from the poison."

I spoke with more confidence than I felt. I love Abner Perry like an uncle—a brilliant, eccentric, and sometimes forgetful uncle. He excels at conceptualization and design but tends to get distracted during execution. On his earlier aeroplane, the propeller vanes were reversed, so it could move only backward. When he sent Dian up in his first balloon to give her a panoramic view of Sari and the sea, he forgot to tether the rope and we almost lost her.

The masks were a life-or-death proposition. If they didn't filter the mist, we'd be dead before we reached the shore. I'd given them a thorough inspection, and they seemed sound, but I'd had no way to test them.

The masks fit over the mouth and nose. We adjusted the straps, then bent to our oars again.

As we slipped into the green mist, I found myself holding my breath. I felt I was betraying Perry with my lack of trust, but I couldn't help it. Then I noticed Koort's chest rising and falling with easy breaths. He seemed unaffected by the mist, so I took my first breath. Then another.

The masks worked. Forgive me, Perry.

As we rowed, something strange occurred: the mist flowed into the dinghy and traveled up over our bodies, almost like a living thing. Before long we were each coated with a layer of green fog.

After we'd beached the dinghy, Koort hurried ahead, cutting his way toward his father's palace through the vines with mist clinging to him. I grabbed the clay pot I'd brought along and followed close behind. When he reached the front steps, he exposed his father's body.

A sob escaped him, and I slowed my approach, wishing to give him a little time alone.

When I reached the body, I knelt on the opposite side and studied Goork. His eyes were closed, and his coarse features had eased into a tranquil gentleness. He looked like a caveman taking a peaceful nap, except his chest was still. I touched him, and his skin was cool.

My throat constricted. Goork had been more than a loyal ally—he'd been a friend. We'd broken bread countless times as we strategized ways to better the lot of Pellucidar's human population.

Koort tore through more vines to expose his brother Kolk, but the story was the same there. I backed off to let him grieve in peace. He was an orphan now, as his mother had died before my arrival in Pellucidar.

Meanwhile I searched for a sample of the vine to bring back to Perry. I found a section that had set down roots from its stem node. The node had red seedpods and a bulbous, translucent green flower that looked more like a balloon. I used my knife to cut the stem node free from the rest of the plant, then dug into the dirt around the base.

As I worked to free the root ball, the flower deflated, puffing out a small cloud of the green mist. I glanced around as I worked and saw other flowers doing the same. When I looked back, my own flower had sealed itself and was filling again. What was the purpose of this mist? To kill all potential threats?

When I had the root ball free, I placed it in the clay pot. Abner Perry would have his sample vine to experiment with and find the best way to kill.

I returned to Koort. "We'll take your father and brother back to Sari and give them proper burials."

He shook his head. "They would wish to be buried in Thuria."

"The vines are too thick. We'll bring them back and preserve them until Abner Perry can destroy the vines. Then we'll return them to their homeland."

Koort thought about that, then nodded.

We carried the bodies to the dinghy, then rowed back to the *John Tyler*. I was enormously relieved to remove that uncomfortable mask. After we wrapped father and son in sheets and stowed them below, I looked back toward land and noticed something.

"Did we drift toward shore?" I asked Ah-gilak. "The mist seems closer."

"We're anchored, but that dad-burn mist *is* closer. It's been moving this way at a steady pace."

I pictured the vines spreading beyond Thuria across Lidi Plain. Millions and millions of those bulbous little flowers spewing their poisonous green mist. I remembered what Perry had said about the relentless spread of kudzu. That was bad enough, but kudzu did not emit a deadly gas. I was seized by a desperate sense of urgency as I visualized all of Pellucidar laid waste by this leafy red scourge and its green mist.

I raised my gaze to the Pendant Moon in whose shadow we floated. Had the Dead World launched an attack upon Pellucidar?

"Haul anchor and set sail," I told Ah-gilak. "We've no time to waste."

"Aye-aye."

As the sails filled and we began to move, I couldn't take my eyes off the shore. I noticed that the mist had reached the observatory. Not content merely to encircle its base, it had begun climbing the walls, almost as if it were a living thing.

I pointed this out to Ah-gilak, who shook his head and said, "Ain't never seen anything like that in all me days, and I've had so many days I plumb lost count of them!" As he was turning away, he froze and cried out in English.

"Jeepers criminy!"

I turned and—

"Good Lord!"

Goork was stumbling up from belowdecks. Kolk followed close behind, rubbing his eyes.

"Where are we?" Goork croaked. "What happened?"

V

"Obviously some form of suspended animation," Abner Perry said once he'd examined the two revived Thurians in his lab in Sari. "Right now they seem as healthy as can be. I'm thinking this gas you describe slows metabolism to an absolute bare minimum—just enough to prevent cellular death."

Goork and Kolk had told us the story of the relentless spread of the vines, and how the Thurians had kept them check until the plant's blossoms released the mist. In greater and greater numbers, Thurians began to succumb to the green gas, reducing their ability to fight the vines. A downward spiral began, toward an inevitable end.

"Even the Gorbuses were falling," Kolk said. "Crawling out of their caves and dying among the vines."

I turned to Perry. "Any progress on killing the vine?"

He gave me one of his miffed looks. "I might have had chance at a solution if the specimen had survived the trip."

"What?"

"Dead as could be by the time it arrived."

"But I carved out a good root ball—"

"Doesn't matter, David. I can't find a way to kill something that is already dead."

As I pondered the inescapable logic of that statement, I had an epiphany.

The Dead World. The problem came from there. Maybe it held the solution. No, it *must* hold the solution.

I turned to Perry. "Is that aeroplane ready?"

"You think I'm a miracle worker? We were just inspecting the plans before you left for Thuria."

"What about your balloons?"

"I've got *Dinosaur III* ready."

Perry fashioned the balloons from the peritonea—the lining of the abdominal walls—of lidi and therefore, for some reason I could not fathom, seemed to think it only fair to name the craft after the creatures.

"Do you have an extra gas sack we might use?"

"We're working on it now—for *Dinosaur IV*. Why?"

"We're going to the Dead World."

ᐧᐧᐧ VI ᐧᐧᐧ

A while back, Perry had capped a well that had been spewing millions of cubic feet of natural gas into the air of Pellucidar for ages. He'd employed Sarian women to stretch, dry, and rub dinosaur peritonea until thoroughly cured, then stitch them into sheets and seal the seams with a cement Perry had found to be impervious to the gas. From these sheets he made his balloons.

I wanted two balloons attached to the basket this time, for we were aiming higher than either *Dinosaur I* or *II* had ever traveled.

"I'm going with you, of course," Perry announced.

I shook my head. "I think you should stay here. You're second in command, and we need someone to hold the fort."

"Nonsense! You're not going to deprive me of exploring a new world. And besides, Dian is your Empress. As a native Sarian, she's fully capable of 'holding the fort.' Better than you, I might say," he muttered under his breath.

I ignored that. "Yes, but—"

"I'm going, too," Koort said.

This was too much. "Now wait a minute—"

"The Dead World attacked Thuria and put my people to sleep—my father and brother among them. I demand satisfaction. And besides, they owe me a lidi."

Not that again.

Suddenly Goork and Kolk were there, wanting to go, too. I had to put my foot down.

"We have weight restrictions," I said. "And Goork and Kolk, you've been in suspended animation. You need to rest here. Since I agree that Thuria must be represented, Koort shall accompany Perry and me."

We loaded the basket with food and water, along with muskets and pistols. I had no idea what sort of reception we would receive and wanted to be prepared for anything. We also included three of Perry's gas masks—just in case.

The prevailing winds of Pellucidar are subject to the seasons of the outer-Earthly year, blowing north to south or south to north depending upon which pole is experiencing winter at the time. Fortunately, the wind was blowing away from Sari toward the southwest, carrying us—just as it had Dian when her balloon's tether came loose—toward the Land of Awful Shadow and the floating source of that shadow. With our extra balloon tugging us toward the eternal noon sun, we quickly reached unprecedented altitudes.

I marveled as Pellucidar spread out below us. Still its horizons curved upward to be lost in haze, but I was seeing more of it than I'd ever imagined. Its total surface area is smaller than that of the outer world, but since its oceans correspond with the outside land masses, and the internal land corresponds to outer seas, Pellucidar has more than twice the habitable area as the world where Perry and I were born.

"Emperor," I muttered. "What a joke."

"Eh?" Perry said.

"I just realized how laughable it is to call myself Emperor of Pellucidar. Who am I kidding? The Federation of Kingdoms occupies such a pathetically small fraction of the inner world. My empire is a joke. And so, I'm thinking, am I."

"Nonsense! Your intervention and initiative freed countless human slaves and banished the Mahars to the northern reaches."

"Which makes me a local celebrity, *not* an emperor."

I realized I'd sorely needed this perspective, and decided to make a few changes when I returned—starting with my "Emperor" title.

I glanced at Perry to tell him but found him staring upward instead of down, toward the looming so-called Dead World whose living forests and grassy plains looked greener than ever. I noted his pensive expression.

"Penny for your thoughts?"

He sighed. "You know, you get so lost in your day-to-day activities that you stop noticing the big picture."

I could see my words must have had an effect on him. "You mean how ridiculous it is?"

He turned to me, eyes wide. "Exactly! You see it, too!"

"Yes, I believe I was just saying—"

"Pellucidar is impossible! Completely, utterly impossible!"

That wasn't at all what I'd been saying, but I sensed his point.

"How can it be impossible? It exists and we exist in it, so obviously it's possible. Unless we're sharing a dream."

"We're not dreaming. But this—" He spread his arms. "Remember when we first arrived how I rattled off an explanation as to how an environment as odd as Pellucidar could develop?"

"Vaguely. Something about things hollowing out with centrifugal force leaving a flaming gaseous remnant at its core—I confess I forget."

"Good thing, too. Because I see now that it was all nonsense. Look at this! There's a sun up there—a *sun!* What fuels it? Fusion? Hydrogen being converted to helium? If so, where's the ionizing radiation? Every living thing here should be mutated into unrecognizable forms. Yet we've got species here like the lidi from the late Jurassic period—that's at least 150 million years—that remain unchanged. And this Pendant Moon we're heading for, this Dead World—what is it doing here, hovering over the same patch of land? What holds it there? It's not in orbit, it's . . . I don't know what it's doing."

I couldn't help him. The locals' creation myths were no help. The island folk thought Pellucidar existed in a bowl floating on a sea of fire; Dian's people, the Sarians, had the bizarre notion that Pellucidar was the only hollow pocket in a rock-solid universe.

The angular diameter of Sol, the outer world's sun, is approximately half a degree in the sky there. Pellucidar's sun, though only a tiny fraction of Sol's size, appears larger, slightly more than a degree and a half because of its proximity. But as to what was firing its furnace, I hadn't a clue.

Looking down, I estimated our altitude at around 2500 feet—about halfway to the Dead World. As I returned my gaze upward, I had a thought.

"What if the wind takes us right past?"

"We may have to do some maneuvering, but I don't think that will be a problem if we get close enough."

"Why not?"

"Gravity."

"Gravity? You can't believe such a little sphere can have enough gravity to matter."

He gave me one of his withering looks. "Do you see lakes and rivers up there?"

I immediately regretted my outburst. "Oh, of course." How else would the water stay there unless the Dead World had its own gravity? "Sorry."

"Don't be. You were right the first time—it's not big enough to have that sort of gravitational field." He shook his head in disgust. "Another impossibility."

I gripped his shoulder. My old friend hated unanswered questions.

"Buck up. Perhaps we'll find answers there."

He grunted. "If I know Pellucidar, we'll only find more questions."

"Look!" Koort said, pointing directly below. "Thuria!"

"Great heavens!" Perry cried.

I had already visited vine-entangled Thuria; Perry was getting his first look. But even I was shocked by the extent of the growth. As usual, Thuria lay in the shadow of the Dead World. But that was all that was usual. The jungle there had never been thick or even that green, but now it lay hidden beneath a tightly woven meshwork of red vines.

"Interesting," Perry said.

"Interesting? It's catastrophic!"

"Yes-yes, of course it is. But look at the vines. Look where they grow and where they don't."

I looked, and it was so obvious, I marveled that I hadn't seen it for myself: the vines engulfed all of Thuria in a perfect circle.

"They don't extend beyond the shadow," I said.

"Exactly. Which probably explains why your specimen, despite watering and an adequate root ball, died by the time it reached me: sunlight is toxic to the vine. And that means we have a way to kill it!"

"Do we? How?"

"Mirrors! We'll fashion giant mirrors and reflect sunlight into Thuria."

As usual, Abner Perry's inventiveness had soared beyond practicality. We had no way of fashioning mirrors of adequate size even to dent that huge growth of vines. I was about to tell him so when I noticed something that made my heart quail in my chest.

"The mist! Look at the mist. The vines may be confined to the shadow but their poison gas isn't." A green tint was spreading in all directions from the Land of Awful Shadow. "When I set sail from Thuria, the mist had reached the observatory at the edge of the shadow. Now it's miles beyond it. Those vines are working overtime pumping out their gas."

Perry looked at me, fear in his eyes. "If we don't find a way to kill that vine, all of Pellucidar will eventually fall under the spell of its gas." He looked up at the looming Dead World. "Is everything battened down? Make sure nothing is lying around loose."

"Expecting a storm?"

I was joking, of course. Storms on Pellucidar were as rare as talking lidi.

"Remember what happened in the ice strata during our initial trip when we bored the five-hundred miles from the surface?"

I remembered encountering a thick layer of ice at around the halfway point but—

My stomach lurched, and suddenly I felt as if I was falling. Koort cried out in alarm, and his eyes bulged as he clutched the edges of the basket with white-knuckled intensity.

I looked up at the balloons and they appeared fully inflated, but the ropes that attached them to the basket were . . . *slack!* They were falling toward us—no, we were falling toward them—falling *up!*

⇒ VII ⇐

It took a moment before it occurred to my addled brain what Perry had meant by his reference to the ice field—gravity had reversed there as we left the influence of the surface world's gravity and encountered Pellucidar's. Which of course did not make a lick of sense. Another impossibility.

Perry did not appear the least bit surprised. "We've reached a null-gravity zone—where the Dead World's local gravitational field neutralizes Pellucidar's prevailing field."

Just as he said that, one of the muskets began to float out of the basket. I snatched it from the air.

"Now I know why you wanted everything battened down."

The balloons had stopped moving, but the weightier basket's momentum carried it up to their level, then past, turning on its side in the process. Koort was plainly terrified by the odd, weightless sensation; he moaned as he clung to the edge of the basket like a drowning sailor to a piece of flotsam. I must confess to a certain level of disconcertment, though I hope I hid it better than he. Perry, however, seemed to be taking it all in stride.

"While we're here," he said, "let's release one of the balloons. We no longer need the extra buoyancy."

"You're sure?"

He shrugged. "Pretty sure."

"*Pretty* sure?"

"Well, I'm very sure that the double buoyancy will make it impossible for us to land. Now help me with these cleats."

By then the basket had turned upside down, though it didn't feel that way. Koort crouched in a corner with his hands clasped over his scalp and his eyes squeezed shut. I couldn't say I blamed him, what with Pellucidar spread out above our heads and the Dead World hanging below our feet.

The basket continued to float toward the Dead World, and we'd released the extra balloon by the time the rope to the remaining sac grew taut. We began to descend, leaving the basket hanging in gravitational limbo.

I peered over the edge, struck by something odd.

"Perry . . . take a look." He joined me at the edge. "Doesn't the terrain look . . . odd?"

He squinted below. "It looks hazy, doesn't it? Almost as if it isn't real." He stiffened. "Great heavens! It isn't! It looks like a hologram!"

"What's a hologram?"

"A three-dimensional projected image. Various scientific journals were discussing the possibility of such a thing before we left, but it was more in the realm of scientifiction. And now, here it is . . ." He turned to me with wonder-filled eyes. "In Pellucidar!"

I had an uneasy feeling as I stared down at a landscape becoming progressively less real the closer we approached.

"No," I said. "Not quite Pellucidar. Rather, the mysterious thing that hangs in Pellucidar's sky."

A three-dimensional projected image? What was it hiding?

Our descent slowed above a fuzzy-looking mountain. Perry released gas via the safety valve and our descent picked up more speed—

—and passed straight through the top of the mountain!

For an instant, light blazed around us and we could see nothing else. Then it faded to reveal a smooth, featureless curved plane below.

"Is that steel?" I said. "It can't be."

"It looks like the same unidentifiable alloy that comprised that seed sphere you brought from Thuria."

"Then I guess there can no longer be any doubt as to where the seeds came from."

Perry looked at me. "It means something else, David. It means the Dead Word is artificial—it's not a moon, it's an artifact!"

I was speechless for a moment. The portent was staggering. Finally I found my voice. "Made by whom?"

He shook his head. "I'm afraid to even hazard a guess."

Koort had risen from his ball of terror and joined us at the edge. He cried out and pointed below.

"The rivers and trees! Where have they gone?"

How to explain a three-dimensional projection to a Pellucidarian . . . I didn't even try.

"It was a painting," I said, pointing up. "An air painting."

In the sky above us, faint traces of the fake landscape were visible, like afterimages. Through it we could see shadowed Thuria and the sparkling waves of Sojar Az. But when I turned, I could also see the sunlit Lidi Plain. With a pang I noted the green mist seeping across it like a plague.

And then, wonder of wonders, a crescent glow began to grow along the Dead World's curved surface.

I pointed. "Look!"

As we watched, Pellucidar's miniature sun began to creep above the artificial horizon.

"Sunrise!" Perry said softly.

"The only place in Pellucidar where it occurs."

Dinosaur III was moving with the Dead World's rotation, and soon we were basking in the noonday light of Pellucidar's sun. Its glare completely washed out the hologram and etched the Dead World's bald surface in sharp detail. I picked out seams here and there, most running like latitude lines, although not evenly spaced.

"Where are the little men?" Koort said. "Who is going to replace my lidi?"

"No lidi up here, Koort. I'm afraid you'll—"

"Look!" he cried, pointing. "A cave. That is where the little men live!"

I saw what he meant—a dark pocket in the surface. I wouldn't have called it a "cave" by any stretch. But if the Dead World were populated by "little men"—which I was sure it wasn't—they could possibly move in and out of an opening that size.

Perry was looking, too, squinting in the harsh light. "It appears about the right size to fit that seed sphere you brought me." He glanced my way. "You don't think . . .?"

"It's possible."

"Take me down!" Koort said. "I must talk to the little men."

"About a new lidi?" I said.

He seemed surprised. "Yes! How did you know?"

"Lucky guess."

"Yes. Very lucky."

Sarcasm was lost on Thurians.

I turned to Perry. "Should we release a little more gas?"

"If we land, how do we get back up?"

"We took on extra ballast with the second balloon. We simply have to jettison it when we want to leave."

"But will we have enough lift? I very much doubt we'll find a source of natural gas down there. I don't want to be stranded a mile above Thuria for the rest of my days. If we were down on the inner surface, we could find another way home. But here . . . if we can't float away, we die of starvation down there."

I couldn't argue. "Yes, they don't call it the Dead World for nothing." Then I remembered. "We do have an anchor. We can release enough gas to bring the surface within reach of it and hope we snag something."

Perry was nodding vigorously. "That way *Dinosaur III* will stay afloat. And once we dump the ballast we'll sail home." He cocked his head toward Koort. "Well, *his* home at least."

═══ VIII ═══

Like so many things, it worked better in theory than in execution.

We released some gas, *Dinosaur III* drifted lower; we dropped the admiralty-style anchor on its extra-long rope and let it drag along the surface. However, its flukes caught on nothing, because the surface offered no purchase.

Perry was muttering in frustration every time the anchor slipped over a seam without catching. I felt pretty frustrated myself, but not as much as Koort, apparently. With an almost feral growl he slipped over the side and began shimmying down the rope.

We watched in amazement as he reached the surface and took hold of the anchor's shank. Using his prodigious strength, he began carrying it—all the while dragging *Dinosaur III* along behind—toward the "cave" he had spotted earlier.

Once there, he must have found a lip or an outcropping of some sort to secure one of its flukes. He let it go, straightened, and waved.

"Come down! I go to see the little men!"

With that, he dove into the cave despite shouted warnings from both Perry and myself.

"Whatever he finds in there," I said after he had disappeared, "I doubt very much it will be little men."

Perry nodded. "As do I. Whoever fashioned that seed pod and ejected it into Thuria must also have fashioned this moon. That puts them technologically beyond anything we've seen here in Pellucidar or the outer world."

I was having a nightmare while awake. "I'm imagining some far-evolved subspecies of Mahar."

Perry gasped. "Don't even think such a thing!"

"Well, the Mahars build their cities underground. Do you see any structures? And imagine their fury at watching their evolutionary ancestors driven from their cities."

Perry was nodding. "It might even goad them to strike against the world below."

With that unpleasant thought spurring our efforts, we hauled on the anchor rope and forced the *Dinosaur III* to the smooth, alloy surface of the Dead World. Once the rope was securely cleated, I jumped out and checked the anchor. Koort had indeed found a good-size lip inside the opening. Since the Dead World had no winds to play tricks on us, I felt confident the anchor would remain fixed there.

I was helping Perry out of the basket when I heard a sound echoing from the opening. Perry must have heard it, too. Without a word, he handed me my revolver and grabbed a double-barreled musket for himself. As the sound grew louder, we cocked our weapons and pointed them toward the opening, ready to fire. Suddenly Koort appeared, panting with exertion, his face paler than usual.

"No one is inside, yet someone spoke to me—in Thurian!"

"Those are contradictory statements," Perry said. In response to Koort's baffled expression, he added. "If no one is there, how can anyone be speaking to you?"

Koort shrugged, grabbed his club and shoulder sack from the basket, then motioned us to follow. We glanced at each other—we both knew we couldn't resist—and bent to it, crawling on our hands and knees through what appeared to be a sloping tunnel or chute.

. . . someone spoke to me—in Thurian!

Thurian? Most of Pellucidar's human cultures had their own language and communicated with each other via a common tongue. Why would the voice Koort heard be speaking in Thurian? Then I reminded myself that Thuria lived in the Dead World's shadow. A connection?

The light from outside faded but enough filtered down to reveal that the chute ended in some sort of spring-loaded mechanism. A sliding panel revealed a short side channel. This dropped us into a narrow, curving hallway with smooth walls, almost Gothic in the way they arched to a point that glowed with a soft red light.

I experienced a hint of vertigo as I tried to orient myself: my head was toward the outer surface, my feet were toward the center of the Dead World.

"*Welcome back,*" said a voice. "*We received your signal and began the protocol.*"

"See!" Koort said. "He speaks Thurian!"

"Not in the least," said Perry. "That's English."

I'd heard English too.

"Thurian! Thurian!" Koort said, becoming agitated.

I was wondering, What signal? What protocol?

"*Because of the time interval, I will review what has gone before.*"

It occurred to me then that this wasn't a voice at all. The words were echoing in my brain.

"Telepathy!" I said. "He's speaking directly to our minds!"

"*As your records surely show—*"

"Stick your fingers in your ears!" I cried, doing just as I'd said.

"—*the mining craft arrived here in the immediate post-war period.*"

No lowering of the volume. Perry had his fingers in his ears, and I could tell by his expression he'd come to the same conclusion.

"Whoever that is, he's projecting ideas, concepts, directly to the brain! We must be 'hearing' them—more accurately, *translating* them—into our own native tongues!"

The voice droned on, and, as it related its story, the words were enhanced by mental images. Slowly a staggering, mind-numbing narrative began to emerge.

When it was done, Perry looked as if he was about to collapse. He wobbled, and I caught him. As he leaned against me he said, "David! Did you hear? Do you see? Pellucidar didn't just happen—it was *created!*"

⚛ IX ⚛

"They raped the Earth!" Perry cried.

Or so it seemed. An ancient race—conical beings with a fringe of tentacles below an encircling ring of black eyes—had developed near the core of our galaxy. They mastered a method of leaping through space via multiple light-year jumps and had built an interstellar civilization with an insatiable appetite for raw materials. The name in my head for them was "*Fashioners.*"

We watched a planet from the huge mothership hovering in orbit. I didn't recognize the planet as Earth—it had only one giant continent, after all—but the words in my head said this was our planet before it was mined. The mothership released smaller mining vessels that bored through the Earth's crust into its molten heart. We saw huge pulses of glowing liquid iron and other elements jettison from the core into orbit, where they solidified into a ring of ragged moonlets. When the core had been stripped of its value, the mothership extended a magnetic field that drew the lumps into its gargantuan cargo hold. The process wasn't perfect. A number of moonlets—one I estimated to be the size of Rhode Island—failed to achieve a stable orbit and crashed to Earth with catastrophic results. Huge volcanoes burst through the crust, boiling the seas and searing the land before enveloping the Earth in a stifling layer of cloud.

"They had no right!" Perry said.

"And they killed my lidi," Koort added.

We both glared at him. His sudden sheepish look said he'd gotten the message. He broke eye contact.

"Well, they did," he muttered.

"They did more than kill your lidi, my Thurian friend," Perry said, his expression grave. "Judging by the timing of their depredation, I believe the moonlets that fell to Earth triggered the great Permian extinction."

"How long ago was that?" I said.

"Somewhere between two-hundred-fifty and three-hundred million years. That single landmass we saw was Pangaea, which later broke up into the continents of today. The cause of the Permian extinction has always been a mystery, but now you and I know what killed off ninety-five percent of the life forms on land and in the sea."

But robbing the planet of its iron core wasn't enough. They liked to experiment with the hollow shells before they left them behind. In Earth's case, they terraformed the inner surface.

I turned to Perry. "What about the inner sun? The explanation is in my head, but my poor brain can't quite grasp it."

"Neither can mine. Their science is so far ahead of ours it is almost magical. I feel like a caveman who has come across a working lightbulb. They created a reverse gravitational field in Pellucidar that negates the Earth's natural field. Apparently they have an almost alchemical ability to transmute certain minerals. They used that technology to create the inner sun—powering it with some sort of renewable fusion that is beyond my ken—then suspended it in the center of the shell."

"But why a separate gravitational field for this place?"

He shrugged. "Why not? They'd mastered gravity. They used the Dead World in the terraforming process and, unless they wanted to risk falling off the surface, its own gravitational field was not only a safety feature but a great convenience."

"Well, at least we have some answers as to how this impossible place came to be."

He frowned. "Answers? A few, perhaps. But they in turn have spawned so many more questions."

"I'm a little curious about the creatures they released onto the surface before they left."

"Yes," Perry said, his expression grim. "You should be more than curious. You should be disturbed. They appeared to be protomammals."

"So?"

"Hundreds of millions of years of evolution led from them to . . . us."

"You mean . . .?"

He nodded. "The Fashioners rape a planet, virtually wipe out the existing flora and fauna, and then seed it with new life."

I was having a hard time swallowing this. "They created us?"

"Not directly." He shrugged. "Who knows how evolution is going to go? This may be an ongoing experiment: release the same life forms on different worlds in different environments and see how they develop."

I found this a crushing revelation.

"That means the human race is an experiment."

"It appears so."

My self-granted title of "emperor" now seemed even more ridiculous.

"All right," I said. "We can ponder that later. This thing we're in, this . . . this moon . . . they used it in the terraforming, but why did they leave it behind?"

And suddenly I knew, because the answer popped into my head. The Dead World was a "dock."

"It's a dock," Perry said, then frowned. "How do I know that?"

"Because it's all in our heads." I closed my eyes. "I can visualize a whole schematic of the place."

Indeed, I saw a hollow sphere with a corridor—*this* corridor—running along its equator. And I knew without a doubt that we were the only living things here.

I opened my eyes. "There's some sort of control room—"

Perry pointed east and said, "That way." He smiled and shook his head. "This is wonderful. I feel as if I designed the place."

We began walking, Koort trailing us. The gently curving hallway was devoid of decoration or design except for the large black rectangles, looking like polished onyx, set into the floor at regular intervals.

Along the way, Koort offered us dintls—a Pellucidarian cross between an apple and an orange—but neither Perry nor I partook. I was too excited to eat. Koort, however, attacked his juicy dintl with relish.

As we proceeded, I heard a rapid tapping behind us. We turned and the three of us gasped as one to see a gleaming metallic spider, perhaps a foot across, scuttling our way along the floor. It stopped maybe ten feet from us and something whirred on its underside. Then it scuttled a few feet closer, and again came the strange whirring.

It looked less like a spider close up—it had a chromed, hemispheric body rimmed with black dots that appeared to be sensors, and fully a dozen jointed legs.

As I studied it, I noticed a trail of droplets between us and the spider—dintl juice. The spider moved again, stopping over the farthest droplet to repeat its mysterious ritual. Then I knew.

"It's a cleaning machine! It's mopping up after Koort."

Sure enough, it stopped over every droplet and left clean dry floor in its wake. It darted up to a spot directly before Koort's feet where he had dripped more juice. Startled, he jumped back and dropped the dintl core.

The spider clattered after it until it stopped rolling, then squirted it with a turquoise fluid. I watched in awe as the dintl core dissolved into a puddle, which the spider promptly sucked up into the underside of its body.

It moved away, and I noticed a dull patch on the floor's otherwise gleaming surface. It then ran around in a figure-eight pattern. As it completed its second circuit, a small rectangular slot opened in the base of the wall. It scuttled inside, but the slot remained open as another automaton emerged, this one the shape and size of a candy box. It hurried over to the dull patch, squatted over it for a few seconds, then returned to the slot, leaving gleaming, unmarred floor behind. The opening in the wall closed.

"Cleaning automatons," Perry said. "No wonder the place is spotless."

We continued our trek and soon came to a rectangular space that brightened as we entered.

"Why all this red light?" I said.

"I would imagine that's the end of the spectrum where they see best."

The entire floor of the control room was the same black onyx as the rectangles in the hall. Half a dozen glassy panels were set in the wall over a large console ornamented with nodules and grooves. The panels lit with views of Pellucidar as we entered.

Koort gravitated to those as I looked around.

"Where is everyone?"

"They left," Perry said, articulating the answer just as it popped into my head. "The Dead World—and the name is so much more apt than we ever imagined—has hovered here, sleeping, empty for nearly three hundred million years—"

"—awaiting the Fashioners' return. Our entry must have triggered some sort of telepathic recording."

"Thuria!" Koort said, pointing to one of the illuminated panels.

I approached and realized these glass screens were showing images transmitted from the Dead World's surface. I saw the vine-choked circle of shadow that had once been Koort's homeland. With a start I noticed that the foul green mist had crossed Lidi Plain and was lapping at the abandoned Mahar city that sat on its northern border.

I was wondering how the image remained stable despite the Dead World's rotation. The answer came to me but was too complex for my level of technological knowledge. And even if it weren't, the explanation would have been blasted from my mind by the vision of the mist creeping eastward toward Sari . . . and Dian.

"We've got to kill those vines!"

"Yes!" Koort cried. "The mist has put all the lidi to sleep! How will I get a new one?"

I wanted to punch him. "Forget your damn lidi! We—"

"*Seeding was successful,*" said the voice in my head. "*Initiating maneuver to increase habitable area.*"

A number of grooves and nodules lit on the console, and then a vibration ran through the floor and into my feet.

"We're moving!" Perry cried.

I sensed it, too—the Dead World seemed to have released a brake, and was indeed moving. But where?

⊱ **X** ⊰

We crowded before the view of Thuria and the Land of Awful Shadow. I blinked. Thuria seemed to be shrinking. And then I realized—

"We're rising! What—?"

"But how?" said Perry. "We have no engines, no—"

The answer must have flashed into his head as it did into mine: gravity manipulation. The Dead World stayed suspended by partially negating the artificial gravity of the Fashioners. It stayed fixed in position over the Land of Awful Shadow by dual means: cinched a set distance from the sun above and locked on to a beacon buried in Thuria below.

"It's attenuating the gravitational field's hold, allowing it to rise."

I estimated its distance from Thuria must have doubled by now— to two miles.

"Maybe we'd better return to our balloon," I said. "If we get too close to the sun—"

Perry was staring at the screen. "I don't think that's the purpose. Besides, the sun here is thirty-five hundred miles away—minuscule in astronomical terms but still quite far off." He turned to me, his expression grim. "Look at the surface. Tell me what you see."

At first I saw nothing I hadn't seen before: the circle of vines, the spreading green mist, the—

I gasped. "The shadow! It's expanding onto Lidi Plain!"

"It's expanding in *all* directions."

He was right. With the Dead World sitting only a mile above Thuria, the umbra and penumbra of its eclipse were virtually identical. But now that it was increasing its distance from the surface, the penumbra was expanding.

"That means—"

He nodded. "Direct sunlight appears toxic to the vine. But now, with the area of shadow increasing almost exponentially, it will undergo an explosive growth spurt."

"Doubling—*tripling* the volume of poison mist it can produce!"

"Exactly."

The clock counting down to Pellucidar's doom had just accelerated.

"We've got to do something!"

And just as I said that, the Dead World stopped rising. I prayed for it to descend again, but it did not. I stared at the widened shadow on the surface. Although I couldn't see the vines expanding their territory, I could almost *feel* them growing.

My gaze wandered to the other screens, each displaying a different vantage. One was focused directly on the miniature sun, the others at various angles. I noticed movement on the one that was angled due north, east of the abandoned Mahar city and west of the Great Peak . . . it resembled a balloon emerging from the haze. I was about to mention it, when the voice spoke again.

"Preparing for docking."

"Docking?" Perry said. "Where on Earth—or rather, Pellucidar— are we going to dock?"

As if in answer, the black panels under our feet lit with red light. I knelt for a better look and quickly realized that these were not image screens but rather windows into the Dead World's interior—its *hollow* interior.

Suddenly a beam of white light lanced into the vast empty space. Gradually it widened. I craned my neck and saw one of the Dead World's poles irising open.

"That's sunlight!"

And then I remembered the balloon I'd seen on the north-facing screen. I ran back to it and saw that it wasn't a balloon at all.

"Look!"

Perry and Koort joined me. In silence we watched a sphere, a duplicate of the Dead World, only smaller, glide toward us.

"The Fashioners," Perry said in a hushed tone. "They're back."

"They must have come through the polar opening. That was why it was left open—for their return."

"I'm beginning to see," Perry said, stroking his chin.

"See what?"

"The Dead World . . . its very existence has mystified me, especially its fixed position in Pellucidar's sky. Now I think I understand." He pointed to the screen showing Thuria. "Don't you see? This was the plan all along. The shadowed area was designed as the perfect garden for the light-sensitive vine. The stunted vegetation there offered little competition, allowing the vine to spread like wildfire. Remember the first thing the voice said after it welcomed us?"

How could I forget? "*'We received your signal and began the protocol.'*"

He nodded. "The 'signal' must have been an alert as to the Fashioners' imminent arrival. And the 'protocol' was the seeding of the Land of Awful Shadow to create the toxic gas. This whole scenario was planned three hundred million years ago!"

"To put Pellucidar into suspended animation? Why?"

He gazed at the approaching sphere. "I fear we are about to find out."

We watched the Fashioners' ship close with us, then rise out of sight. We returned to the floor windows onto the inner space and watched the gray sphere descend through the roof and angle toward the control area. It stopped and hovered perhaps a hundred feet below us. The Dead World was indeed a dock; its interior was a giant hangar. As the opening in the pole irised closed, a transparent tube descended from somewhere to our left and connected with the sphere.

I checked my revolver to make sure it was ready to fire.

"I don't think they'll be too happy to find us here," I said.

"That is a very real possibility." Perry checked his musket. "Perhaps we should—"

The voice interrupted us: "*Welcome back. We received your signal and began the protocol.*"

It proceeded to recite the exact same message we had received upon arrival. Yes, definitely a recording, this time triggered by the arrival of the craft. It droned on, but no one appeared in the tube.

"Where are they?" Koort said, banging his club against the wall. "They owe me a lidi!"

I shook my head in wonder. Our lives, the future of Pellucidar itself were at stake here, and he was still worried about his damn lidi.

He darted to the wall and slammed his fist against a slightly brighter spot on its surface. A panel slid to the right with a hiss, revealing a triangular opening. Koort darted through it.

I stared after him in wonder. "How did he know—?" And then I realized I knew it, too—all part of the schematic that had been infused into our brains.

"He's headed for the ship!" Perry cried. "Stop him!"

We rushed for the door, but it closed before we reached it and would not reopen despite my pounding on the bright spot.

"Look!" Perry cried, pointing to the floor windows. "He's going to the ship!"

Sure enough, there was Koort, standing on a platform as it descended through the tube toward the sphere. Seconds later he disappeared within.

I pressed the bright spot on the wall again and watched the platform return—empty.

"What does he hope to accomplish by this?" Perry said.

"A lidi for him," I said sourly, "and nothing but trouble for us."

Meanwhile the voice droned on in my head. It ended with, *"Seeding was successful. Initiated maneuver to increase habitable area. Harvesting can begin soon."*

" 'Harvesting'?" I said in a low voice. I had no explanation in the telepathically implanted data. "That wasn't mentioned before. Harvesting what? The vines?"

"No," Perry said. His expression was grim as he shook his head. "Us."

The horror of that thought was just taking hold when the panel to the elevator hissed open again. Perry and I jumped in, and it automatically began its decent.

I checked my revolver again. "We'd better be ready."

Perry nodded. He looked as uncertain as I felt. Who or what would greet us when we arrived?

But instead of Fashioners, we were met by Koort.

"No one is here!" he cried.

"Impossible!" I said. "Are you sure?"

He motioned us to follow him.

"Not so impossible," Perry said as we made our cautious way through the craft—lit with the same red glow as the Dead World's interior—with our weapons at ready. "Everything else is automated. Why not that ship?"

He had a point.

Koort could have warned us about the smell. Then again, a man who rode a lidi all day probably had calluses on his olfactory nerve. The interior lay silent as a tomb all about us.

No, not silent. I heard metallic scuttlings echoing in the dark recesses. Cleaning spiders? No surprise there.

I began to believe it might well be a tomb of sorts when I spotted the dull splotches on the otherwise gleaming floor.

I nudged Perry and pointed to the nearest. "What is that, do you think?"

He touched it with the toe of his boot, then leaned closer. "The finish has been damaged." He looked around. "In quite a few places."

The splotches reminded me of the marred finish left by the cleaning spider's solvent in the hall above.

"This may sound far-fetched, I said, "but could this be all that's left of the crew?"

"Not so farfetched. If they died, the spider automatons would have dissolved their remains . . ."

"Some sort of sickness, perhaps? A plague?"

He shrugged. "Who can say for sure? Viruses get into enclosed environments and run wild."

"But one hundred percent fatal?"

"It could have been a blast of interstellar radiation they were not shielded against. We could speculate forever on the cause, but the fact is there is no one here."

I heard more scuttling in the recesses, then Koort reappeared, swinging his club back and forth with obvious frustration.

"I will never see my lidi replaced."

"Lidi? You should be celebrating that no one will be harvesting you!"

Perry said, "I'm afraid we will have no one to celebrate with if we don't find a toxin to kill those vines."

Exhaustion settled on me like a shroud. "So far, the only way we know to kill it is with sunlight. We'll have to return to Pellucidar, get some samples, and—"

Just then a spider automaton appeared seemingly from nowhere and sprayed its turquoise fluid on my boot. Immediately the leather began to bubble and run.

"What—?"

As I danced away from it, I heard a howl of pain from Koort.

Another spider had squirted his bare lower leg. His skin was smoking and bubbling. A third was racing toward Perry. He took no chances. Reversing his musket, he smashed the butt down on the thing, crushing it.

My own spider was still pursuing me, leaving me no recourse but to use my revolver: I put a bullet through its domed carapace, stopping it in its tracks. Koort flattened his attacker with his club.

I looked down the dimly lit hall he had just exited and saw a wave of the things scuttling our way.

"Back!" I shouted. "Back to the elevator!"

Perry led the way while I helped the limping Koort. A patch of his left lower leg had been stripped of its flesh down to the muscle and was oozing blood. He was moving as fast as he could, leaving a crimson trail. That proved to our benefit. The spiders were rapidly closing on us until those in the lead stopped to clean up his blood. They seemed to have no choice. Their imprinted instructions were to keep the ship clean, and so they did just that.

But the ones behind merely crawled over those who had stopped and continued the chase.

Up ahead Perry stood in the elevator entrance, frantically waving us forward.

"Hurry! They're gaining on you!"

I wasn't exactly lollygagging along, and I could hear the clatter of countless metallic legs growing louder and louder, closer and closer. But Koort was weakening and becoming an increasing burden. I would not, however, leave him to be dissolved alive. Unthinkable.

I poured all my strength into my pumping legs and practically knocked Perry back against the rear wall as we stumbled through the entrance. A look back showed a charging horde of the things nearly upon us before the door slid shut. Koort groaned and sagged against the wall as the cab began to rise. He had to be in agony, but he'd made not a single complaint.

"We've got to do something about that leg," I said, panting.

"I packed a first-aid kit before we left," Perry said.

I had to smile. "Always thinking. I'll retrieve it from the balloon and we'll patch him up. But meanwhile . . ." I looked at Perry. "What happened down there?"

He gave his head a baffled shake. "Could something have gone wrong with their programming? Could they have turned on their masters? I can only speculate."

"Well, I guess the *why* doesn't matter—they're down there and we're up here. I don't know about you, but I am *not* going back to that ghost ship for *any* reason."

We stopped and the door slid open on the Dead World's girdling hallway. It almost felt like home. As we helped Koort to his feet, we heard faint scratchings against the floor of the cab. Perry and I stared at each other.

"They couldn't have . . ." I said.

The door closed as we exited the cab, shutting off the sound. As soon as we made Koort comfortable, I moved to the floor windows and peered down at the elevator shaft. Through its transparent wall I could see hundreds of the spiders—hundreds!—all trying to get to us.

⇸ XI ⇶

"How does that feel?" Perry said as he taped a final piece of gauze over Koort's wound.

"Better. It feels better."

Perry joined me where I was keeping watch on the spider-filled shaft.

He said, "If they could dissolve their way through the floor of the elevator, they would have done it by now. Their liquid appears to be effective only on organic matter."

"What if the automatons already in the hallway turn against us?"

"If that were the case, we'd know it by now."

I rose and went to the screen that showed the vines spreading into the enlarged shadow and the mist surging beyond it . . . toward my home . . . toward Dian.

"How do we stop it, Abner? How do we—?"

An epiphany struck me dumb.

"What's wrong?" Perry said.

"Sunlight! The Dead World was rising toward the sun a short while ago. What if we found a way to keep it rising until it crashed into it?"

Perry shook his head. "First off, I am quite sure the Fashioners put fail-safes in place to prevent that. And even if we could do as you say, who knows what kind of catastrophe that sort of collision would trigger?"

He had a point, but . . . "The risk is less than the certain end of life as we know it if that mist keeps spreading."

He raised a fist. "We *can* poison the vine—I'll find a way or die trying."

I remained convinced that sunlight was the key. And then I saw a surefire solution, almost as radical as my first idea—*if* I could make it work.

XII

We stood at the console and studied the controls, made for tentacles rather than human hands. I pointed to an oblong groove near the left edge.

"I think that's it."

Perry grunted. "And I think this is reckless and dangerous."

"It's risky, I'll grant you that. But help me here. Is it your interpretation of the schematic that this will unlock the Dead World from the beacon buried in Thuria?"

Perry studied the console. "I believe so, but belief is not enough at a time like this. What if it unlocks *everything*? What if it causes this whole thing to plummet onto Thuria?"

"Then we'll have possibly saved Pellucidar."

"And killed ourselves!"

I imagined Dian remaining alive and well, and knew I had no choice.

"Take the balloon," I said.

Perry harrumphed. "I'll do nothing of the sort."

"Go ahead. I'll wait till you're off."

"And let you die a hero while I'm safely away? I should say not. Do it."

I gave him a sidelong glance. "You're sure?"

"Not in the least. In fact, I'm quite nervous about the whole prospect. But get it over with."

I glanced back at Koort who stood across the control room staring at the screen that showed Thuria. I wondered if I should give him the choice, but he'd be helpless aboard the *Dinosaur III*. He'd have to stay.

"Very well."

I laid my left forearm in the groove and pressed down. If I was right, the Dead World would maintain its fix on the sun but lose its lock on Thuria.

Nothing happened. I pressed again. Still nothing—no vibration, no sense of movement. Nothing.

What was wrong? Was it malfunctioning? I'd been so sure—

A cry from Koort. "The Awful Shadow is moving!"

I rushed to the screen, Perry close behind. The Dead World's shadow seemed to have moved away from the observation tower.

"The shadow isn't moving!" I cried. "But Thuria is!"

The Dead World was still fixed in its relation to the inner sun but was now unmoored from Thuria. Its momentum would keep it moving for a little while, but soon the resistance of the atmosphere would bring it to a halt. Meanwhile, the rotation of the Earth would carry Thuria farther and farther away from the Awful Shadow.

"You've done it, David!" Perry said, clapping me on the shoulder. "Let us pray direct sunlight is as toxic as we think."

We wouldn't be able to tell for twenty-four hours, when the Earth had completed its rotation. Meanwhile, we were about to experience an unprecedented aerial tour of Pellucidar.

XIII

As Pellucidar rotated beyond the screens, Sari passed beneath us early on. I thought of Dian—the woman I loved, the woman whose life I was trying to save—and how mystified she must be to see the Dead World drifting above her.

We hung silent and suspended over seas and continents I'd never heard of. I wondered what the natives in those far-off lands thought when they looked up and saw their sun eclipsed for the first time in their civilizations' histories—how it must have terrified them.

But as I watched, a terrifying question rocketed through my brain.

"Perry! The Fashioners sent one ship for 'harvesting.' If it doesn't return, they'll likely send another."

His smile faded. "Great heavens! You're right. And I doubt they'll wait another three-hundred million years to do so!"

I knew from the data fed into my brain that the Dead World was not only a dock, but a beacon—a directional device that the Fashioners could home in on. If we extinguished that beacon . . .

"We've got to destroy the Dead World."

"But how?"

"We'll find a way. We must!"

And we tried. God knows, we tried.

I won't bore you with the details of our failures.

We failed to crash the Dead World into mountains or drown it in one of the great seas that passed below us. It appeared to be locked on to a single latitude and would not deviate even a degree north or south; and it was tethered to the sun in such a way that its altitude remained fixed at a minimum of a mile above the surface. We even tried to disable it by damaging its control console, but it proved impervious both to shots from Perry's musket and blows from Koort's club.

Exhausted and frustrated, I had to admit that the vaunted Emperor of Pellucidar was helpless to protect his subjects from this otherworldly threat. Fatigue overtook me. Nothing like a bed existed on the Dead World—perhaps the Fashioners didn't sleep?—so I sat against the wall adjacent to the floor windows. As my eyes drifted shut I glanced below at the ghost ship and the transparent elevator tube still filled with—

I jerked away from the wall and leaned forward for a better view. It almost looked as if—no!

"Abner! Come see!"

He crouched at my side and gasped. The spider automatons had somehow breached the wall of the elevator shaft. They were crawling through the hole and spreading through the interior of the Dead World.

"What does this mean for us, do you think?" I said.

I had an uneasy feeling it could not mean anything good.

"As long as they remain confined to the inner space, we'll be safe. But if they should find a way into the hallway . . ."

He didn't need to say any more. I envisioned those dull spots on the floor of the ghost ship—all that would remain of the three of us.

"I think we'll be safe," he added.

As if to challenge that statement, one of the spiders scuttled onto the underside of the window. We watched in horrid fascination as it loosed a spray of its turquoise solvent. The transparent surface clouded and even seemed to swirl a little. An array of whirling brushes emerged from the spider's underbelly and sucked up the fluid, leaving a hazy splotch. Immediately it sprayed the area again and repeated the process. Seconds later another spider joined it.

"This may be how they escaped the elevator shaft," Perry said. "Dissolving the wall one thin layer at a time."

"Then it's just a matter of time."

"I'm afraid so."

I rose and peered at the view screens, trying to recognize some aspect of the terrain below, but none of it looked the least bit familiar. How long before we were back over Thuria? Minutes? Hours? I had no idea. I cursed Pellucidar's lack of time.

And then another unsettling thought struck me. When I had returned to *Dinosaur III* for the first aid kit, I'd noticed that all of what I'd initially assumed to be black panels in the hallway floor were really windows onto the interior. What if . . . ?

I hurried down the hallway, and my worst fear was confirmed: every window panel I passed had a spider clinging to its underside, diligently working to break through.

I rushed back to the control area.

"Abner! Koort! To the balloon! We've got to leave! Now!"

"But we don't know where we are!" Perry said. "We could be thousands of miles from home."

"Better to risk being lost than sure death if we stay!"

"Look!" Koort said, pointing to one of the screens. "Thuria comes!"

I rushed to the screen. Perry was already there. The Sojar Az glittered to the right where I recognized Hoosa's Island; the Thurian coast—sans shadow—lay to the left. I held my breath as we came closer. The mist had dissipated, and the vines . . .

The vine mass had turned from bright red to a dull brown—a *dead* brown.

I leaned against Perry and, I'm not ashamed to say it, sobbed. Pellucidar was saved and, most importantly, Dian was safe.

But we weren't. Anything but.

I felt the Dead World lurch into motion—downward! I turned back to the screens and saw Thuria rushing toward us.

"We're falling!" Perry cried. "We're going to crash!"

My thought exactly, but our descent slowed when we reached the Dead World's old hovering point. And then we felt its motion change to a lateral direction.

I realized the Dead World had automatically locked itself into its traditional locus, once again casting its Awful Shadow over Thuria. We'd come full circle.

"We've saved Thuria," Perry said. "Now let's save ourselves."

Just as the words left his lips, I heard a crack behind us. I turned and saw a spider automaton's leg pierce the window and wave about in the air.

Koort limped toward it with his club raised.

"No, Koort!" I cried. "You'll—!"

Too late. He smashed the spider's leg but in the process punched a large hole in the weakened spot. The gap filled immediately with another spider. Koort clubbed this one as well, sending it tumbling through the inner space, but now more spiders were beginning to break through other weakened points.

I grabbed Koort's arm and pulled him away.

"Too many of them! The balloon! Run!"

And run we did.

With the bandage and some time to heal, Koort was able to run on his own. I grabbed Perry's double-barreled musket and led the way down the hallway. We made the best speed we could, what with spider automatons beginning to break through all along our path. If one was emerging, or about to, I put a lead ball into it. After two shots, the musket was useless, at least as far as shooting was concerned. The double barrel, however, proved handy for ramming emerging spiders off the underside of the windows without enlarging the hole in the process.

When we reached the chute, I pushed open the flap to let Perry and Koort enter first. What I saw behind them made my heart quail: a hallway filled with charging spider things. I crowded in behind them and wedged the flap shut with the musket.

"That should hold them!" I said without the slightest reason to sound so sure.

We clambered up the chute and reached the surface, where vine-choked Thuria spread across the sky.

"In!" I cried. "The two of you! I'll release the anchor!"

For an instant Koort looked as if he was about to protest, but thought better of it and helped Perry into the basket. As soon as Perry was inside, he began uncleating the anchor rope to give me a little slack. But before I could free the anchor's fluke from the chute lip I heard a *clank!* from below, followed by the all-too-familiar sound of countless scurrying metal legs.

"They're coming!" I leaped for the basket, crying, "Cut the rope! Cut the rope!"

"Where's my knife?" Perry said, frantically patting his pockets.

I looked over the edge just as the spider horde vomited from the chute. For a moment they scurried around in apparent confusion—we must have seemed to have vanished into thin air—then they discovered the rope and began to climb.

"Where's a knife?" I cried. "Someone *must* have a knife!"

Since no blade was forthcoming, I pulled my pistol and took aim at the rope. Just as I was about to fire, one of the spiders reached the top edge of the basket, so I fired at it instead. The bullet must have penetrated its solvent reservoir, because turquoise fluid squirted over the rope and the edge of the basket. The rope was fashioned from a Pellucidarian variety of hemp, so it began to bubble and fray. In seconds it parted, and *Dinosaur III* lurched upward. The spiders clinging to the rope fell back to the surface.

But they weren't giving up. They began to climb atop each other, forming an aerial chain that reached for us. I began firing my revolver at the topmost, but for every one I damaged, two or three more immediately took its place.

Their inexorable progress had brought them to within a few feet of us when I turned to Perry.

"Can't this thing rise any faster?"

"Its buoyancy is fixed."

"Koort hate spiders!"

I looked at the caveman and saw that he'd picked up one of the sandbags we kept on board. Of course! But he had no concept of ballast—he saw it as a weapon. He raised it over his head and hurled a bull's eye at the growing tower of spiders. Not only did it topple their construction, but accelerated our ascent.

We left them scattered below in confused disarray.

⊰═ XIV ═⊱

Relieved, I slumped against the side of the basket as we ascended toward the extra balloon we had left in the null-gravity zone.

"We've done it!"

"Done what?" Perry said. "The Dead World still acts as a beacon and will draw more Fashioners for harvesting."

I scowled at him. "You're just a font of good cheer, aren't you?"

He shrugged. "Just being realistic. At least we have a respite." A mischievous smile twisted his lips. "I just had a thought."

"More doom and gloom?"

"You decide: Maybe the harvesters aren't returning for us. Maybe they want the Mahars. Or perhaps"—he gave me a wink and nudged Koort—"they want to collect all the lidi and take them back to their home world."

"No!" the Thurian cried. "They cannot! I will kill them all if they try!"

That's the spirit, I thought.

The Fashioners might have created Pellucidar, but it belonged to us now. And we were going to keep it. I would spread the word among the humans and all the species of this world—the Mahars, the Sagoths, the Horibs, even the Gorbuses and Azarians: *Keep watching the skies!*

Perhaps this was the threat that would unite us in a common purpose: block the polar entrance and keep Pellucidar safe for all.

Maybe I'd earn that Emperor title yet.

 END

Caprona is the deadliest of all of Burroughs's fantastic worlds, an island where creatures from throughout time are trapped by the sheer cliff walls that surround it. From south to north on the island, one moves as if travelling in time from dinosaur-occupied lands to the homes of the Golden People. And within its walls live all the predators that the world has ever known—and as bestselling author Joe R. Lansdale sees it, it's the perfect setting for one of Tarzan's fastest and most furious adventures.

—Bob

Tarzan and the Land That Time Forgot
Joe R. Lansdale

The great cigar-shaped zeppelin, the O-220, rose up from the great depths of Pellucidar, the underground world with its constant daylight and stationary sun, rose up and through a gap at the roof of the world. It floated high in the sky above the arctic waste and set a course straight for England, where Tarzan, one of its passengers, was to meet up with his wife, Jane; a trip promised him by Captain Zuppner, the commandant of the ship. Tarzan had made several trips to Pellucidar in the last year or so to aid his friend David Innes in numerous endeavors in the world inside the world, but now he was too long without Jane and wanted to be with her.

Two days out, the wind changed and the heavens went dark with tumbling clouds and jags of lightning. The zeppelin, its crew, and its famous passenger, were blown way out and lost over the sea. The wind didn't stop, and the sky was so dark they were unsure of the change from night to day.

The ape man, standing in the wheel house of the zeppelin, clutching the railing, remembered once in Africa riding out a great storm like this in the top of a tree; the sky dumping rain, the wind as

wild and ferocious as the rush of a lion. Tarzan was philosophical then
as he was now. Had he fallen from the tree and hit the ground, he
would have died. This was a higher fall, and there was nothing but
blackness before and above, around and below, but if they were to
strike land or water from this height, he would be no less dead than if
he had fallen from that tree. He had been in many scrapes and learned
long ago that some things were beyond his or anyone's power. You
only had to remain alert and look for opportunities. If none presented
themselves, then so be it. That was fate.

"We've lost our bearings," said Captain Zuppner, trying to look
out the view glass of the control room, but seeing only dark.

"This is not news to me," said Tarzan.

"I can't tell if we're high up, or near the sea," said the captain. "The
controls aren't working. Nothing is working. Turning the wheel is a
chore; it fights back. The compass is spinning."

The others in the wheelhouse were clinging to the railing that
traveled the wheelhouse completely around, watching the dark skies,
hoping for some miracle, like a split of light or a glimpse of land below.
Then came the lightning again, ragged as a can opener. It struck the
balloon and leaked out the helium with a sound like a mad child
blowing water out of its mouth. The expelling of the gas shot the O-220
across the darkness, throwing everyone against the walls, banging into
rails, slamming the floor, knocking them up to meet the ceiling.
Everything was coming apart. Fragments of the craft were awhirl on
the wind, along with men and the one woman who had been on board,
a beautiful and former savage of Pellucidar in modern aerial crew
dress. Zamona was her name, a woman trained by Zuppner to crew
the ship. She had been flung out of the craft by the blast of the storm,
a white face and dark hair in blue clothing, looking like nothing more
in the flash of lightning than a flying scarecrow. Then the lightning
ended and she was gone from view.

What was left of the zeppelin hit the sea with a loud smack, a groan
of metal, a split of wood, and screams from the remaining crew. The
black waters raged over them. The residue of the O-220, containing
Tarzan, went down into the wet, dark deeps. Tarzan eased out of a
jagged gap in the broken wheel house, swam fiercely upward. When
he broke free, a wave, like a father lifting a child on its shoulders,
brought him up high, and during a flash of lightning he saw the nearly

unconscious captain clinging to a fragment of fraying wood. Tarzan swam hard, snatched Zuppner by the back of his coat collar as the lumber broke apart. He swam away from the clashing, sea-rolling debris, and after a few minutes stopped and floated, riding the pitching waves up and down.

The storm raged through the night. Tarzan floated on his back and clung to the captain. After what seemed like a century came daylight; the first true light in days. The storm had finally passed. Tarzan watched it rush away. It was a vast dark curtain of clouds with murky strands of rain falling out of it and touching the ocean. The sea gradually became calmer. The sky turned the color of bloody honey. An hour later it was hot and bright and blue.

Zuppner was now fully awake. He looked at Tarzan supporting him in the water and said, "You saved my life. I should hold you up awhile."

"I'm fine," said Tarzan. "You took quite a blow to the head. You've lost some blood."

The captain swung his arms at the water, kicked gently with his legs. "How can you not be tired? Let me loose. Help yourself."

"I am still alive," Tarzan said. "And there's land, my friend. I can see and smell it."

As a gentle wave lifted them, the captain looked in the direction Tarzan had indicated, but he saw nothing, nor did he smell anything but the sea. Next time the wave tossed him, he saw what he thought was a fine brown line. Down again, and another ride up, and he saw big white birds sailing above the land. It appeared to be a great tan wall rising out of the blue-green water. It went for miles. Island or continent, he couldn't tell.

They half-swam, half-washed against the walls of the land mass. It appeared there was no way up. The walls were slick as glass. There was no beach. With the storm having passed, a mist gathered around the high walls and around them. It was as if they were insect specimens wrapped in balls of cotton.

"We will drown," said Zuppner, the waves pushing him against the rock wall.

"While I still live," Tarzan said, "I will assume that I will not drown, and you are not allowed to think otherwise."

Tarzan had been clothed in normal pants, shirt, shoes, and a coat, as well as a belt that held a knife in a wood and leather sheath. The hilt of the knife was tied down tight. The belt and the knife were all that were left on his body. The raging ocean had taken everything else away. Zuppner was completely without clothes, or weapons. The ocean, unlike when they first fell into it, was warm near the great rock wall. Soon it was almost hot.

"The warm water is coming from inside the rock walls," said Tarzan. "The water has salt in it, but it is not purely sea water. Fresh water from inside is mixing with it. You have to try and stay close to the wall until I get back. Stay in this spot as much as possible."

"Get back," Zuppner said. "You are expecting a taxi?"

"Look," Tarzan said, and pointed. "There were limbs with leaves floating in the water, even a few flowers. Somehow those limbs managed to find their way out, probably by route of a freshwater river. If I can find it, swim against the flow, and inside these cliffs, we have a chance. And to my way of thinking, Captain, we always have a chance."

"I will say this for you, Tarzan, you are not a quitter."

"That could be my motto, Captain. Stay here, and do not give up."

Tarzan dove beneath the waves. Time fled by. The sun rose higher. Zuppner became weaker. Just as he thought he might be pulled beneath the water, a wooden beam from the flooring of the O-220 wheel house washed up, and he grabbed it. It bounced him against the great wall of rock, but clinging to it gave him some rest. He decided Tarzan had drowned and now he had to face the ocean alone, with nothing but a plank of wood for a companion. He tried to encourage himself by remembering what Tarzan had said about there always being a chance. He wondered how long he should remain here, waiting. Perhaps he should use the board like a boat, kick his legs and start to move along, hoping for some gap in the wall, a beach. But the main reason he felt weak had nothing to do with the storm and the waves and the wound to his head. It was Zamona. He had known for some time that he was in love with her. He had met her when she was a savage in Pellucidar. He had been the one to teach her English, to teach her about the O-220, which she took to like the proverbial duck to water. Her small and delicate features and her bright blue eyes were constantly before him. He'd become infatuated with her. He only hated that he had not acted upon his infatuation and told her how much he loved her when there was time. There always seemed to be another day. Now she was gone. He had seen her blown out from the O-220 by the blasts of the storm, lost forever, pulled down into wet nothingness, gone with his heart.

At that moment, Tarzan shot up out of the water like a leaping porpoise. He swam over to Zuppner and his plank, grabbed one end of it, let it support him. What amazed Zuppner was that Tarzan didn't even look winded.

"As I suspected, the warm water is coming from a path beneath the wall," Tarzan said.

"A path?" Zuppner said.

"It's a long and hard swim, but it's a way inside."

"You made it all the way inside?"

"There's land. A lush land. It reminds me of Pellucidar, parts of Africa."

"I don't know that I can make it," Zuppner said.

"You can make a choice," Tarzan said. "You can ride this plank, or you can swim with me. It is your choice."

"How will I know where to go in the dark?"

"You won't be in the dark for long. You swim a short distance, toward where it seems lighter, and then it will be much brighter. Finally there will be plenty of light above you. Swim up and break the surface. It is that simple. Oh, and watch for some very large reptiles."

"What?"

"I am going to swim down again," Tarzan said. "Toward the light. You may follow, or you may stay here and cling to your plank until you are too exhausted to make the swim."

"I am already exhausted," said Zuppner.

"Stay close to me," Tarzan said, and without further comment, he took a deep breath and dove beneath the waves.

Taking his own deep breath of air, Zuppner followed. Down he swam. There was no light, only darkness. He could not see Tarzan, but he could feel the water churning in front of him, stirred about by the kicking of Tarzan's feet. The water grew warmer, almost hot. He followed that unseen path, and then, as Tarzan had said, the water became lighter. He could see the ape-man's shape ahead of him.

Finally the water was much brighter above him. When he thought his lungs would burst, it seemed as if a hole of golden, heavenly light was opening above them.

He and Tarzan burst to the surface. They came up in a great pool of warm water. Behind them, tumbling down high rocks, was a waterfall.

They swam to land. Red and yellow mud made up the bank. There were great masses of underbrush and high rises of trees all around them. No sooner had they crawled onto the muddy bank than Zuppner saw a large creature, a crocodile perhaps, but, if so, the largest he had ever seen. It scooted swiftly out of the brush across the way and into the water. It made waves as it crossed the pool toward them.

"Come," Tarzan said. "I think it is best we move away. Quickly."

Tarzan helped Zuppner to his feet, and within a moment they were deep into the jungle, greeted by bird calls and animal cries. A warm wind rustled leaves and shook the boughs of tall trees. Above them, monkeys swung from limb to limb.

Zuppner, feeling as if he was on his last legs, saw the ape-man was moving easily ahead of him. Unlike himself, nudity did not bother Tarzan. It seemed to be his natural state. In time they came to the edge of a clearing. They stopped and stood amongst the trees, not venturing out onto the vast clearing. Tarzan said, "We should let you rest, see what we can do for that wound on your head."

Zuppner studied Tarzan. The ape-man did not appear to need rest. He was stopping for him, to let him regain his strength. Zuppner started to protest, but put pride aside. He slid down to sit on the ground with his back against a tree. He could not go another step. Immediately, he was asleep. He dreamed of Zamona, alive.

When Zuppner awoke, without having to ask, he knew Tarzan had not slept, but had watched over him as he did. He saw too that Tarzan had broken off a large limb and stripped it, making himself a crude club. As Tarzan stood there in the leaf-dappled sunlight, leaning on the club, Zuppner thought that he was the very embodiment of Hercules with his long black hair, dark, scarred body, and brutal countenance.

"I have found foot-prints," said Tarzan. "Here, at the beginning of the clearing."

"Human?"

Tarzan nodded. "One foot is bare, the other wears a shoe."

Zuppner felt confused. "A shoe? One shoe?"

"A shoe like those worn by the crew of the O-220. A small shoe. A woman's foot."

"Zamona?"

"She too has somehow survived the storm and found her way here, most likely the same way we did. Minus a shoe."

"But how? She is so small and delicate."

Tarzan's mouth twisted into something that resembled a smile . "She may be small, but she is fierce. She is of Pellucidar, Captain. Zamona may have learned how to crew on the O-220, but she is a survivor of the first degree. She was raised a savage, like me, and at heart, no matter how much we learn about the outside world, how much we embrace it on the surface, we are always savages."

"My God," Zuppner said, jumping to his feet. "We have to save her."

"We have to find her," Tarzan said. "This world is not too much unlike her world. She will know better how to survive than you. Look up there."

Where Tarzan was pointing through a gap in the trees a great winged reptile was flying lazily overhead. At first glance it looked like a massive kite.

"This world has as many creatures out to kill us as Pellucidar," Tarzan said. "This is her world, and it is mine."

"We must find her," Zuppner said, "I . . . I love her, Tarzan."

"Does she know it?"

"No," Zuppner said shaking his head. "I should have told her."

"We will find her," Tarzan said.

"Where could she be going?"

"In search of food, shelter. In Pellucidar the inhabitants are born with a sure ability to find their way home. My guess is she will go in whatever direction that she feels will bring her closer to that goal. She may not fully understand how far away her world is, that this land mass is not connected to her lost world, but is a lost world unto itself."

"Where are we?"

"I believe this is the lost continent mentioned by Caproni. He was an Italian explorer in the 1700s. He wrote that during his adventuring he passed a continent in the middle of the southern ocean, covered in mist. Most thought he was a fraud and a liar."

"It has remained hidden all these years?"

"It's not exactly on flight paths, and it would take a powerful plane to reach this spot.[1] Come, let me make you a weapon, and we will follow her tracks."

Zuppner could barely make out the tracks on the jungle trail, but Tarzan saw them easily. Before long, they found Zamona's shoe. She had abandoned it.

Tarzan picked up the little shoe, examined it. The loss of it didn't matter. Like Tarzan's, her feet were as hard as cured leather.

"We at least know she came this way," Tarzan said.

Tarzan dropped the shoe and went on. Zuppner followed as quickly as he could, carrying the long, knife-sharpened stick Tarzan had given him. It was not too unlike having nothing more than a large pencil as a weapon.

They spent a night in a tree, and the next morning, at daybreak, they were back on the trail. By the end of that day they had come to a break in the jungle, and there was a large savanna spotted with trees and a sun-glistened water hole. They were a good distance away, and they squatted down to observe. There were a number of large cats surrounding the water hole, purring and growling, but mostly lying in the sun near the water.

"My God," Zuppner said. "Those are saber toothed tigers. This place is like Pellucidar's cousin."

"More like a brother or sister, I would think," Tarzan said.[2] "But without the central and constant sun. At least here, we have sunset and sunrise."

Out of the sky came a shriek, and a great shadow moved over the savanna. They looked up. A large leather-winged monster was swooping down on the water hole.

"It certainly is like Pellucidar," said Zuppner. "That's a pterodactyl."

The creature dove down, extended its claws, grabbed one of the great tigers by the scruff of the neck, whipped it up into the sky as easily as if it had been a rag doll. Zuppner's heart sank. Zamona had come this way, and savage or not, what chance did a small, unarmed woman have against these things? What chance did they have?

"I know what you're thinking," Tarzan said. "It doesn't necessarily mean a thing. Remember. Zamona is resourceful. She grew up in the wild. Come."

They dodged the cats, skirted the savanna, and after a while found another small watering hole visited by a herd of antelope. While Zuppner remained at the edge of the savanna, Tarzan crept through the grass toward the herd. When he was close, he leaped up and raced into them. Startled, they broke and ran. Zuppner couldn't believe the ape-man's speed. Tarzan reached out, nabbed one of the antelope by its nub of a tail, and jerked it down, struck it with his club. It was a brutal event, and ended with Tarzan dispatching the beast with his knife. After that Zuppner joined him. Tarzan skinned the beast rapidly and cut slabs of meat from it. They ate it raw. It was hard at first for Zuppner to get it down, but after a few bites he craved it and ate his fill. For the first time in a long time, he felt strong.

They drank from the spring that fed the watering hole, picked up Zamona's tracks again, crossed the savanna, and eventually arrived back at the jungle. The day was almost done. Long shadows were falling through the trees and across their path in coal-colored patterns of leaves and trees and leaping monkeys.

That's when they found the dead men.

There were two of them, strange men with thick brows and near-absent chins, barrel-chests and short, stumpy legs. They wore only loin cloths. Beside them lay crude clubs, like the one Tarzan carried. One had an arrow through the eye, the other an arrow all the way through his throat.

While Zuppner leaned on his spear, Tarzan put his foot on the dead man's chest, and yanked the shaft from his neck. The arrow was a simple creation, the point made by snapping a thin stick in such a way it left a crude point.

"Zamona made these arrows," Tarzan said. "She found feathers in the jungle, used resin to connect them to the shaft. She was probably hunting, and they surprised her. There was a fight. She killed these two."

"Good for her."

"Yes," said Tarzan, "but they took her."

"Are you sure?" Zuppner asked.

"That's what the sign shows. Look there."

Zuppner saw a crude bow lying in the brush. Tarzan picked it up. It was a limber limb bent and bound by string made of twisted plant fibers. Tarzan slipped it over his shoulder, pulled the remaining arrow from the dead man's eye. He slung the bow over his shoulder, held the crude arrows in his left hand, the club in his right.

"They didn't bother to bury their dead," Zuppner said.

"Simple tribe. Simple ways. No sentimentality. Look there. Blood drops."

"I don't see anything," Zuppner said. Already it had grown too dark for him to define any thing other than the general pathway.

"It is there nonetheless," Tarzan said. "I can see it, and I can smell it."

"Hers?" asked Zuppner.

Tarzan nodded. "The drops are small, so my guess is the wound is small. You can see where she put up a fight."

Zuppner didn't see anything other than shadows, but he remained silent.

"There are six sets of feet here," Tarzan said, "where before there were eight. They picked her up and are carrying her. Even if it is a minor wound, I have her scent full in my nostrils, and we can follow."

"You can follow her blood by smell?"

Tarzan grinned. "Like a bloodhound."

"Then follow we must," Zuppner said.

Tarzan in the lead, they rushed along the trail as night fell over them like a hood.

The moonlight weaved in and out of the trees, allowing Zuppner to see Tarzan's back as the ape-man moved swift and sure before him. It was all Zuppner could do to keep up. The jungle was full of sounds, chatters and roars, night birds and wind-rustled leaves.

Once a dark shape rushed in front of Tarzan, some kind of cat, Zuppner thought. Tarzan did not slow his stride, and as Zuppner passed the spot where the beast had rushed into the foliage, he saw two glowing eyes peeking out at him. They went along for a good ways like this. Zuppner was beginning to feel winded, but each time he thought he could not take another step, he thought of Zamona.

Eventually they saw the campfire. Where the jungle split there was a clearing, possibly made by a blaze sparked by lightning. In the clearing were a number of undefined human shapes huddled around the fire. They had killed something, and it had been tossed straightaway into the flames with the hair still on it and the guts still intact, boiling in its own juices. Zuppner could smell the hair burning off of it.

Tarzan whispered to him. "The wind is on our side, and the fire is making a stink of the wood and carcass. They can't smell us."

Once again, Zuppner marveled at Tarzan's abilities. They squatted down, waited, and observed. After a moment, Zuppner's eyes adjusted to the flickering of the fire. He could make out Zamona among the huddle. She sat on the ground on the far side of the fire. When the flames licked wide he could see her clearly. She was nude; the ocean having stolen her clothes same as theirs. She looked natural that way, not in the least bit prudish. She held her head high, haughty, proud. Her hands were tied behind her back, and she was bound at the ankles. There were five men in the group, and one of them, a big fellow, was squatting down next to her, holding a strand of her long black hair between his fingers. He made sounds that sounded to Zuppner at first like grunts and snaps, but he soon realized they were language. The man showed his ragged teeth. Spittle on his lips sparkled in the firelight. As if by signal, the other men in the group slowly stood up, turned toward her.

The big man said something sharply to Zamona and bared his teeth. She spoke back to him; her words were almost a bark.

From their concealment, Tarzan and Zuppner spoke in whispers.

"It is the language of the apes," Tarzan said. "My first language. They want her."

"Want her?" And then the reality of what Tarzan meant washed over Zuppner. He was grateful that he didn't speak the language of the apes; he wouldn't have wanted to understand what the man was suggesting coming directly from his lips. He felt as if someone had unscrewed a plug at the bottom of his foot and all that he was and ever would be was running out of it.

"We must fight," Zuppner said.

"We have no choice," Tarzan said, shoving the points of the two arrows into the dirt, pulling the bow off his shoulder. "I will take care of two of them from here, and then we charge."

Before Zuppner could respond, Tarzan strung an arrow and let it fly. Zuppner saw it as it reached the firelight, wobbling. But it struck true. It hit the big man in the ear as he squatted beside Zamona. It was such a swift and silent shot that when the man fell over, the other four didn't move for a long moment. By the time they were moving, another arrow was in flight, striking one of the men in his open mouth. The man stumbled, went to one knee, tugged at the arrow, dislodging it. Zuppner could see by the glow of the fire that he was spitting gouts of blood.

Tarzan was moving. Zuppner followed.

The ape-man swung his club over his head in a heavy arc as he entered into the firelight. The club struck one of the men, smashing his skull like a china cup. Zuppner rushed the man who was bleeding from his mouth and drove his spear against him. The point went in with some difficulty, but it went in. He forced the man to the ground and pushed the weapon deep into his gut. The man clutched at the spear and groaned for a moment, then gasped blood and stopped moving. When Zuppner turned, the remaining men were dead. Tarzan had dispatched them with the club. One had fallen into the fire to cook along with the crude dinner.

That's when the jungle broke open with a rattle of leaves and a cacophony of yells. More of the primitive men had arrived, and in that moment, Zuppner realized the party they had dispatched had been waiting on them.

They came out of the jungle in droves, came like ants swarming over a discarded picnic, rushed and yelled, swung clubs and fists. Tarzan met their charge with his whirling club. Heads knocked and heads exploded. Zuppner fought with his crude spear, stabbing, but the point was soon blunt, and he began to use it like a yeoman's staff.

As one of the wild warriors went down, another took his place. The shadowy jungle seemed to leak them. On they came, and finally Zuppner went down. He glanced at Zamona. She was still bound, struggling to get loose. She had rolled on her belly, and, using her knees and wriggling her body, she was trying to crawl toward him. Then Zuppner was snatched up. He made a wild swing, missed, was hit again and again. He kept trying to cling to consciousness the way he had clung to that fragment of lumber in the midst of the ocean. It was a losing battle. But before he passed out he saw Tarzan swinging his club. He heard jaws shatter, heads crack, and then a horde of the men were on him, covering him thick as grapes on a vine. Then those men seemed to explode, flying up and catching the light of the fire, dropping down into shadow to leave Tarzan standing alone, a broken club in his fist.

They rushed again, covering him, even as Tarzan tossed aside the remains of the club and went at them with first his knife, which was knocked from his hand, and then his fists, and even his teeth. Zuppner smiled. *He will not go easy*, he thought, and then he passed out.

When Zuppner awoke, his head hurt and he feared he might have a concussion, because the world was upside down and he was bouncing and everything was red.

It took a while to realize his hands and feet were attached to a pole and he was being carried. The redness was the rising of the sun. He glanced to his right, saw Tarzan, bloodied, bound in the same way, being carried on a pole supported by the jungle dwellers. Glancing to his left he saw Zamona. She was looking right at him. A smile crossed her face. It was an odd thing to do considering their situation, but it warmed Zuppner and gave him a flash of courage.

Eventually they came to a clearing on the edge of a great cliff. Zuppner could hear water tumbling violently over rocks. A moment later he was hanging at a precarious position as they carried him down a narrow, rocky trail. They had all fallen into a single line now. Tarzan ahead of him, Zamona next, and him at the end of it. Down they went. The trail twisted and turned, and the men who carried him moved carefully so as not to slip and fall. Off to his left was a great gorge and he could see a tremendous waterfall; it came tumbling over glimpses of black stone with a roar like a den of lions. Zuppner, Zamona and Tarzan continued down, and finally they came to a river where a large number of the tribe had gathered. Here there were women, as primitive looking as the men. They were tossed down roughly and left tied to the carrying limbs. Nude and bedraggled, bruised and insect bit, they waited by the shore. A moment later, Zuppner saw and heard something horrible, and realized their fate.

Tarzan had smelled the water long before they came to it. On the shore there were a dozen men stretched out on the ground, held down by the jungle men. They were not the same as the jungle men. They were more like Tarzan and his friends, longer and leaner, with more common human features. They wore loincloths made from animal hides. As they were held by the arms and legs, large and strong members of the jungle tribe were standing over them with clubs, swinging their weapons, breaking leg and arm bones with single blows, turning those bones to jelly, causing the men on the ground to scream in agony.

Out in the water, floating, Tarzan could see the heads of the same sort of men, their necks supported by large wooden collars that helped them float. The collars were attached to ropes. After the club work, the men could neither swim nor struggle, could only dangle like worms on hooks. On the shore were piles of skulls and bones. They were heaped together, and Tarzan guessed they had been glued that way by some primitive form of cement. The skulls and bones were painted and marked with designs made from black soot from fires, as well as red and yellow clay. The designs were squiggles and circles and inside the circles, a lot of teeth were drawn. In fact, this was the most common design on the bones—long, sharp teeth.

Tarzan watched as Zuppner turned to Zamona to say, "Zamona. It is bad timing, to say the least. But I want you to know I love you. I have for some time. And if it is not returned, I understand. But I won't let this moment, what may be one of our last, pass without me saying it."

Zamona's eyes crinkled. She spoke in English, but with that peculiar accent that is prevalent to the inhabitants of Pellucidar. "You foolish man. I know that. I have only been waiting for you to say as much."

Zuppner grinned. "It may be our last moments, but those words from you have made me the happiest man in the world."

Tarzan said, "Before you exchange wedding vows, you might wish to get out of this predicament."

"What magic will allow that?" Zuppner said.

"If there is to be any magic, we are it," Tarzan said.

"Why would they do this to those men?" Zuppner asked. "And who are they?"

"Another tribe, obviously further along on the evolutionary scale," Tarzan said. "I have listened to the jungle folk and have caught a bit of their talk. What I believe the jungle men are doing is sacrificing these men as part of an important ritual. That's why the last ones we fought were meeting up with the men at the campfire. This isn't a village. This is where all the people of their ilk, people of other tribes, gather to appease some god, or execute some ritual. Unfortunately for us, we crossed paths with them just in time to be part of it. They break the bones, and then float their victims in the river, waiting for something to come, something with plenty of teeth."

"We are doomed then," Zuppner said.

"We still live," said Zamona.

"Good for you, Zamona," Tarzan said, speaking to her in English. "We are not done until we are done."

Tarzan looked toward the river. The men who had recently been broken up were crying and screaming and being dragged toward a stack of wooden collars. The collars were snapped open and fastened around their necks, then bound together with rope that passed through holes in the collars. The jungle men pushed the broken men out into the deep part of the river using long poles. The current kept them there, and the ropes fastened to the collars kept them pegged to the shore. One of the jungle men carried a big club with pieces of what looked like stone or volcanic glass imbedded into it. He didn't use the weapon, but stood by with it, perhaps as a sign of his office, his position in the tribe. He watched the others break the bones and push the jellied men into the water.

Then the jungle men and the man with the strange weapon came for Tarzan and the others.

Tarzan, Zuppner, and Zamona were lifted and carried toward the shoreline to have their turn.

The moment Tarzan awoke on the trail and found himself fastened to the pole, he had begun to flex his wrists and work at the ropes. By the time they were lifted and carried toward the shore, his efforts paid off. With a bend of his wrists, the ropes snapped.

Like a monkey, Tarzan dropped down and let his hands touch the earth, practically standing on his head. He flexed his legs and kicked up. The kick drove the pole upwards and caused it to crack, and when it did, Tarzan's bound feet slipped off of the pole and his ankles came loose of the rope. Tarzan bounded to his feet. The man with the strange weapon rushed him. Tarzan dodged his swing and hit him with his fist. It was a hard blow, and the man's jaw broke and teeth flew and the man went down. Tarzan grabbed the club off the ground. By now other jungle men were closing in on him. Tarzan wielded the weapon as if it were as light as a fine willow limb. Jungle men flew left and right in sprays of flesh and blood and brains.

The other jungle men dropped Zamona and Zuppner to go after Tarzan, but the ape-man plowed a path through them with the festooned club, and in a moment had created a space around his companions, as well as time enough to bend down and use the edge of one of the stone fragments in the club to cut their bonds. No sooner than it was done, than the jungle men had regrouped. Tarzan yelled, "Run for the water. Swim for your life."

Zuppner grabbed Zamona by the elbow, and the two of them darted for the river. Tarzan held his ground, swinging the club, sending jungle men flying like chaff. And now the jungle men were coming at him from all sides. Tarzan turned and swung the club and cleared a path. The club finally snapped, came apart in the jungle lord's hands. The men grabbed at him, hung on to him like leeches, struck him and tried to choke him and pull him down. Tarzan trudged forward, dragging them with him until he reached the river's edge. Peeling off the jungle men with either arm, tossing them aside like confetti, he leapt into the river.

The water hit him like a cold fist. The current was swift, and it carried him out and past the poor men floating in their collars, carried him to the center of the river and sent him swirling along. Well ahead of him he saw Zuppner and Zamona trying to swim with the rush of the river, going down and coming up, bobbing like corks.

One of the jungle men had followed Tarzan into the water, swimming rapidly in pursuit. The man grabbed at him. Tarzan intercepted the man's reach, snatching him by the wrist. He twisted it, heard the bones shatter over the rushing sound of the water. The man screamed. Tarzan let him go, and, still screaming, the man went sailing right alongside Tarzan.

That's when the ape-man saw what he had seen painted on the bones.

They did not come out of the river as he expected. They came from the sky. He realized then the crude squiggles painted on the bones had been meant to represent the beating of wings. They were at first dots seen flying low and far down the length of the river. But then they came closer and their wings could be seen, and they could be seen; great of size and green of skin, mouths full of teeth. The flying lizard beasts were not like the pterodactyls they had observed before, they were impossible things the size of small airplanes, with their legs curled up under them as they flew, their skulls flared wide, their snouts long and tipped with massive nostrils. Tarzan would not have been surprised to see them breathe fire, so much did they look like mythical dragons. On their backs were long, thin men with sloping, peaked heads painted blue and yellow, green and orange. The rest of their bodies were devoid of clothing or design. They seemed little more than skeletons wrapped in doughy flesh. They directed the flight of their mounts with reins. They sat in saddles held in place by harnesses. They had their feet in stirrups of a sort. They carried spears in one hand, held the reins to their mounts in the other. Slung on the right side of their monsters were long sheaths holding more spears. They flew in a V pattern, as if they were fighter pilots.

Tarzan saw Zamona and Zuppner swimming ahead of him. She touched Zuppner, who was next to her, spoke something caught up and tossed away by the roar of the river. But Tarzan saw them dive. *Good girl*, he thought. *Good girl*. She had given Zuppner proper advice. Then he too dove beneath the water, and not a moment too soon, for down swept one of the beasts and its claws snatched up the wounded primitive with the broken wrist, lifted him up and hauled him away, as lightly as one might lift a pillow.

The water was savage and white with waves and ripples and sudslike foam. Soon there were slick mounds of rocks to clash against. When Tarzan came up for air, he looked back, saw the winged beasts, about ten of them, flying down to grab at the men in collars, lifting them, causing the ropes to trail into the air, then snap free and jerk up the pegs that had been driven into the shore. The creatures and their riders carried them aloft and away; the broken men dangled from their claws like wet socks.

Tarzan's attention was then turned back to the mounds of rocks. There was little he could do. The river slammed him against them. He clung to one and eased onto it. There were enough rocks he could walk across them before diving back into the water and swimming for the far shore.

Upon his arrival on the shoreline, Zuppner and Zamona came wet and dripping, banged and bruised, out of the thickness of the jungle and called to him. Tarzan was pleased to see that they too had survived. Tarzan glanced up, saw the flying creatures. They were lifting high and circling wide, most likely heading home with their prizes.

Then they realized, too late, there were more monster riders, gliding down from the heavens from behind, and before they could defend themselves, three of the beasts snatched at them and lifted them high into the sky.

When Tarzan realized what had happened—for it had happened so fast that even his senses, dulled by exhaustion and cold water and a loss of blood, had failed him—he was already nabbed. The flying monstrosity had him gripped firmly, but its touch was also surprisingly soft, with the claws doing very little damage to his shoulder. By the time Tarzan thought he might rip himself free, even if he were to lose flesh in the process, he was already too high up.

Near him, Tarzan saw that his friends had been taken as well. The three of them were joining an aerial armada of the creatures and their riders, as well as their human prizes.

Tarzan could closely observe the riders on the winged reptiles next to him, and for the first time he got a solid look at them. They were much as they first appeared, pale, slender, with bulbous, bony heads. But what Tarzan previously thought was paint was in fact their natural skull coloring. They had wide mouths with narrow lips that when open exposed rows of teeth, sharp and barbed like long, yellow thorns. This revelation made Tarzan reevaluate the images he had seen painted on the bones. The lines on the bones had been crude representations of the wings of the beasts, but the circles containing teeth were most likely meant to represent these bizarre pilots, not their mounts. In that moment Tarzan realized that the sacrifice had not been for the flying reptiles, but for these men; they were cannibals. He had some experience with man-eaters, and he knew without consideration that he was in the presence of the same sort of humans now, that the broken bones and the men in the water had been part of a kind of crude tenderization for these men who the jungle warriors must have thought of as gods. And why not? They flew on the backs of powerful winged creatures. They demanded sacrifice to keep from taking what they wanted from the tribe itself—meat. This way the tribe appeased their gods and protected their members by feeding them the broken bones and softened flesh of different tribes, men on a different part of the evolutionary chain.

As they flew, Tarzan looked down. He had learned that no matter what the situation, no matter how dire, he had to be observant. Something might be seen that could be of use for survival. So now that he had no choice but to go where the winged behemoths were taking him, he looked down. Below there was a steaming jungle and finally a great inland ocean. They passed along the edge of the ocean and flew over a large pool of water about which a number of men were congregated, entering into it slowly and with procession; there was something ritualistic about it.[3]

And then Tarzan saw something surprising. A large fort, made not too unlike one would expect Daniel Boone of old to build. A wall of pointed logs and inside the wall buildings and ramps and what Tarzan thought looked like a mounted gun.[4]

On they flew, and gradually the sky darkened and the ground below was nothing but a mass of shadows. Still they flew, against the face of the large full moon that appeared to rise like a god's head out of the sea. And then below the night became alight with flames.

It was a big village and there were campfires everywhere. There was a lake next to the village, and the campfires tossed light on the water and the water rippled with flashes of orange and yellow. The moon's reflection made it appear to float on the water with the flames. Ahead of them the dragons, for now Tarzan thought of them as such, glided low over the lake, and the riders yelled out in near unison, "Arboka." It was a word Tarzan recognized. It was a word from the ape language he had learned. The language the jungle men spoke. It was bastardized, but similar in the way Spanish is to Italian. Yet even with its different accent he knew it meant "drop." The dragons dropped the broken men. There were splashes as they landed in the great lake below. They went under at first, then bobbed to the surface on their neck corks, able only to float.

Tarzan and his friends were not dropped. They were not already broken. The cannibals had other plans for them. Perhaps they too would be broken and collars would be fastened about their necks and they too would be lowered into the water. For now, they were carried over the lake toward the shore, and then just over the tops of tall jungle trees. Tarzan reached up with both hands and took hold of the creature's foot above the claws. He did this swiftly. He jerked his shoulder free as he did, causing the claws to tear his flesh. When he was loose, the dragon began to whip its foot, trying to shake him loose, but he held. He was able to swing out and grab the belly strap that held the rider's saddle in place. He had hold of it before the rider knew what was happening. Tarzan climbed the strap, and the rider tried to stab him with his spear. Tarzan snatched the spear and tugged, sent the man and his spear tumbling down and onto the ground near the lake. Even from where Tarzan was, some fifty feet above the ground, he heard the thump of the man as he struck earth.

Tarzan swung into the saddle and took the reins and yanked the dragon to the right, came in close over the rider carrying Zamona. The rider had seen what had occurred, and he threw one of his long spears at Tarzan. Tarzan caught it and flipped it, threw it at the rider, piercing his chest, knocking him from the winged monster. Tarzan swept in low and flew under the creature as it dropped down toward the trees. He reached out for Zamona, grasped her hand, yelled "Arboka." The dragon holding her let her go, and Tarzan swung her onto the saddle behind him. She clutched her arms around his waist and they flew toward the rider that carried Zuppner. The rider had seen all that occurred, so as vengeance, as they flew over the trees, he yelled "Arboka," and Zuppner was dropped.

There was a crash and a flutter, and Tarzan saw that Zuppner, having not dropped from too high, had fallen into a tree and was clinging to a limb. The rider who had dropped Zuppner pursued Tarzan. Tarzan gently tugged the reins, and the creature, easy as a trained quarter horse, responded, flew fast over the trees. Tarzan guided him up, saying to Zamona, "Hang tight."

They shot up like a bullet, the beast tilting to such an extent that Tarzan could feel Zamona's weight tugging back at him, a victim to gravity. Tarzan guided the monster into a surprising dive and was hurtling straight toward the rider whose beast had moments before held Zuppner in its grasp. They sped directly toward each other like cannon shots.

Tarzan pulled one of the spears from the tight sheath at the reptile's side. He cocked it into throwing position with one hand, managed the reins with the other. He continued to fly directly toward the rider. He stood up in the stirrups, leaned back and came forward as he loosed the spear. By that time they were about to have a head-on collision.

The spear flew straight. It hit the rider in the head and parted his skull the way a comb will part hair. The rider toppled from his mount, and at the last moment Tarzan was able to veer his beast and avoid them clashing together.

Tarzan directed his dragon toward the trees where Zuppner had fallen. When he came to the tree, he was able to see Zuppner, struggling to manage a sound position near the top of the tree. Tarzan slowed his flying monstrosity, hooked a heel on one side of the mount, and swung out and extended his arm. It took a couple of tries, but Zuppner caught it, and Tarzan pulled him up. It was a tight fit, but he was able to slide on behind Zamona. He was bleeding from a number of places.

"Are you all right?" Tarzan said.

"All minor wounds," Zuppner said. "But now we have company."

Tarzan glanced back. The campfires looked far away, like lightning bugs. Then there was a dark mass touched with moonlight. It was like a rising of mosquitoes from the face of a pond. They were many, and they were coming fast. They appeared to change swiftly in the moonlight from mosquitoes to birds, and then Tarzan could see them clearly for what they were—men on their dragons. The ones who had dropped the broken men in the water were now in pursuit of Tarzan and his friends.

There was a wide path in the jungle. Tarzan guided the beast down close to the ground, and they sped along the trail, which proved man-made. He saw a break in the trees, and he went off the main trail, down that. This was a path made by animals, most likely in pursuit of water. The reptile's wings beat at the edges of the trees. Leaves came loose and went fluttering about in the dark. Tarzan didn't believe he could stay hidden, but if he could merely confuse their pursuers for a time, they might have a chance.

Peeking back, he saw a flock of dragons flying low along the wide man-made trail adjacent to the path he had taken with his beast. He saw the last of them pass. In a few moments they would realize they had been duped and would double back, but for now Tarzan flew on, low as possible to the ground.

Then things changed. Ahead the trail was too narrow for their flying mount, so Tarzan had no choice but to rein the creature up and into the moonlight.

"They have spotted us," said Zamona.

Tarzan flew on, realizing their combined weight was slowing them. He flew over the great lake where the broken men bobbed like lily pads. He flew over great patches of jungle.

"They are falling back," Zuppner said.

Tarzan took a look. They were indeed falling back. He had gained quite a gap between them and himself. The little venture down that narrow trail had given them just enough of a break, and even after being discovered, they were too far ahead to make it worth the warriors' efforts. They already had their meals, broken and secure, tenderizing slowly in the river of the great lake. What were three more?

Zuppner laughed out loud. "We have beaten them, Tarzan."

"Seems that way," Tarzan said.

The great winged beast flapped on.

They reached the great inland sea by morning and skirted the edge of it, stopping once to rest their mount. Tarzan tied the reins of the beast to a stout tree near the shore of the sea, left Zuppner and Zomona, took a spear from the sheath strapped to the monster, and trekked toward the deeper woods to hunt. Two hours later he returned with a deer over his shoulders.

Zuppner and Zamona had built a fire from dead wood, because the sea air had turned surprisingly cool. Tarzan had lost his knife somewhere during their capture by the jungle men, so he broke one of the spears off near the blade to make a new knife. He was grateful that the knife he lost had not been the one he normally carried: his father's knife from long ago. It was safe at his plantation in Africa. He skinned the deer with the makeshift knife, gutted it, made a wooden rack for the body, and cooked it over the fire.

Tarzan gave a raw leg of the deer to their flying stallion of sorts, and then he and his friends sat down to eat.

"That flying thing is quite amazing," said Zuppner.

"For his size he is astonishingly light," Tarzan said. "His bones must be hollow. And yet, it is strong."

"I think we should name him," Zuppner said.

"I never name anything I might have to eat," said Tarzan.

Once they were filled with food, fresh water, and rested, they took to the air again, flew over the great inland sea. It took some time, but they finally reached the opposite shore. They rested again for a while, and come morning they flew on with no set destination, just making sure they were putting space between themselves and the cannibals.

After a few days of travel and stops to hunt and eat, they came to the great, rock wall that surrounded the land that time forgot. Tarzan landed the beast. There was jungle and plenty of game along the edge of the wall. They made a good camp there. When the mist that surrounded the strange world thinned, they could see the ocean raging against the rock barrier below.

"How do we go home?" Zuppner said.

"Swimming won't do," Tarzan said.

Zuppner laughed. "I suppose not."

Zamona turned and looked back at the jungle and said nothing.

They built a fine hut that housed them comfortably and had plenty of room left over. They left a gap at the top of it to let out the smoke. They built a well-made corral with a roof for the flying creature, and kept it fed with game, of which they found plenty. From time to time they flew in trio on the back of the beast, looking to see what they could find, but never traveling too far from camp.

After many days, the three of them walked to their spot on the wall, the place where they liked to look out at the ocean. As they stood there, watching the pounding waves break against the blockade of stone, Tarzan said, "When we were first carried off by the winged things, I saw below us a place with wooden walls, like a fort, with buildings inside of it. It looked to me that it might be a kind of civilized settlement. I thought I might try and go there. It will take many days, and I would have to stop to find water and food, but perhaps there might be someone there who could help us, or assist us. If so, I will come back for you. They might be enemies. On this world that seems more likely. But I thought I might try. I must find a way to go home. I must see my wife, Jane."

Zuppner looked at Zamona, then back at Tarzan.

"This may sound odd, Tarzan," Zuppner said, "but Zamona and I, we want to stay. Right here. Where the game is thick and there seem to be fewer dangerous predators. Most importantly, we have each other. This is a world not too unlike the one from which she came, and I have nothing to go back to. And to be honest, I have learned to love this life. All that I need is right here, with her. We talked it over and decided a few days back. We have wanted to tell you for quite some time, and now we must."

Tarzan almost smiled. "I have suspected. And I understand. If Jane were with me, I might stay. If she is by my side, I can be anywhere in the world and find happiness."

Tarzan clamped Zuppner on the shoulder and smiled at Zamona. "Have your life and your love, but I must go. I must find a way to leave and go home to Jane."

When the morning light came, the mist was heavy. Tarzan and Zuppner and Zamona were all at the corral. Tarzan saddled up and reined the beast, guided it out through the open gate. It walked with a hobbling motion on its slightly bent legs. By the time he led the creature clear of the corral, the sun had started to penetrate the mist, but still they could not see the sky.

Tarzan had made himself a bow and arrows and a quiver of wood, and he had fashioned fresh spears with flint points to replace the broken ones from the quiver that was strapped to the reptile's saddle. He still had the knife he had made from one of the spears, the broken part of the shaft now wrapped in hide and strapped to his side in a sheath he had made from wild boar skin. He wore a loin cloth of spotted antelope hide. He arranged his weapons, the bow over his shoulder, the quiver strapped to his back, the knife at his side, the spears tucked tight into the sheath next to the saddle. He climbed on top of the beast and looked down at Zuppner and Zamona.

"Make a life," he said.

"We will," said Zamona, looking beautiful in the gossamer-veiled light. "We still live."

Tarzan tugged at the reins. The dragon flapped its wings, lifted into the air, and finally high into the mist where it was swallowed up, wrapped tight in white. Zuppner and Zamona could hear the monster's wings beating for a while, and then there was only silence, leaving them to their life, and Tarzan to further adventure.

 END

Story Notes

(1) Tarzan's adventure on the lost world would have taken place about 1929, when planes were nowhere as advanced or as able of flying long ranges. Besides, it's very likely that Tarzan's universe is an alternate universe that only crisscrosses ours from time to time.

(2) The sun of Pellucidar, the world inside our world, is always central and always bright. Pellucidar is a world of constant daylight.

(3) Although Tarzan could not discern the purpose of the pools, they are part of the evolutionary process of The Land That Time Forgot. When humans of a certain evolutionary scale are ready and prepared to move to a higher form, they enter the pools, and come out transformed. For more information on these pools, check out THE LAND THAT TIME FORGOT, THE PEOPLE TIME FORGOT, and OUT OF TIME'S ABYSS by Edgar Rice Burroughs.

(4) He's looking down on Ft. Dinosaur, built by previous adventurers. Again, see the books in the LAND THAT TIME FORGOT series by Burroughs.

✦ Authors Bios ✦

Kevin J. Anderson

Kevin J. Anderson has published one hundred twenty books, more than fifty of which have been national or international bestsellers. He has written numerous novels in the *Star Wars, X-Files,* and *Dune* universes, as well as a groundbreaking steampunk fantasy novel, *Clockwork Angels,* based on the new album by legendary rock group Rush. His original works include the *Saga of Seven Suns* series, the *Terra Incognita* fantasy trilogy, and his humorous horror series featuring Dan Shamble, Zombie PI.

Matthew V. Clemens

Matthew V. Clemens has collaborated with Max Allan Collins as forensics researcher and co-plotter on eight *USA TODAY*-bestselling *CSI* novels, two *CSI: Miami* novels, as well as tie-in novels for the TV series *Dark Angel, Bones* and *Criminal Minds.* He and Collins have published over a dozen short stories together (some gathered in their collection *My Lolita Complex,* as well as the Thriller Award-nominated *You Can't Stop Me* and its sequel, *No One Will Hear You.* He is the co-author of the true-crime regional bestseller, *Dead Water.* He lives in Davenport, Iowa, with his wife, Pam, a teacher. He cites Tarzan as one of the major fictional creations of all time, ranking with Sherlock Holmes and Batman.

Max Allan Collins

✥⪢══⪡✥

Max Allan Collins is the author of the *New York Times* bestselling graphic novel *Road to Perdition*, made into the Academy Award-winning film starring Tom Hanks and Paul Newman. His other credits include such comics as *Batman*, *Dick Tracy* and his own *Ms. Tree*; film scripts for HBO and Lifetime TV; and the Shamus-award-winning Nathan Heller detective novels. His tie-in novels include the bestsellers *Saving Private Ryan*, *Air Force One* and *American Gangster*, and he is working with the Mickey Spillane estate to finish a number of works by Mike Hammer's creator. He lives in Muscatine, Iowa, with his wife Barb, with whom he writes the popular "Trash 'n' Treasures" mystery series (*Antiques Roadkill*). His novel *The Pearl Harbor Murders* features Edgar Rice Burroughs as an amateur sleuth, and he credits Burroughs as a major influence on his storytelling technique.

Peter David

✥⪢══⪡✥

Peter David still remembers being ten years old, standing in his parents' backyard at the end of some really bad days, and staring longingly at the red planet, Mars, hoping to be hauled magically to its surface so he could hang with Tharks. The fact that he was likely staring at the Washington, D.C. shuttle into LaGuardia was kind of irrelevant. In any event, not being hauled up to Mars, he settled for remaining on this world and conjuring up stories involving green skinned monsters, alien space travelers, and exotic women. He even had a chance to visit Barsoom in producing the four-issue *John Carter* limited series for Marvel Comics, a prequel to the live-action film.

Robert T. Garcia

✥⪢══⪡✥

Bob Garcia worked at *Cinefantastique* magazine, Mayfair Games, and First Comics (as Senior Editor) before founding Garcia Publishing Services with his wife Nancy. They won the World Fantasy Award in 1983 for *American Fantasy*™ magazine, which spun off into American Fantasy Press, with books by Moorcock, Gaiman & Wolfe, Resnick,

Etchison, and Zambreno. In 2000, AFP released the World Fantasy award-winning novella *The Man on the Ceiling,* by Steve Rasnic & Melanie Tem, which also went on to win the IHG and the Stoker awards, the only story ever to do so. He's edited the anthologies *Temporary Walls* (with Greg Ketter), *Chilled to the Bone, Unrepentant: A Celebration of the Writings of Harlan Ellison®,* and edited/packaged the first US edition of Vargo Statten's *Creature From the Black Lagoon*™. It was the great Joe Kubert Tarzan adaptations for DC Comics which introduced him to the worlds of ERB, and he has kept on visiting them all his life, with a special fondness for the savage world of Pellucidar.

Sarah A. Hoyt

Sarah A. Hoyt cut her teeth on her grandfather's library of Dumas and Burroughs. The leatherbound volumes would never be the same again. But having acquired a taste for books, she went on to write them herself. Now she lives in Colorado and has close to thirty books to her credit. Her most recent work is a space opera from Baen Books: *Darkship Renegades,* sequel to the award-winning *Darkship Thieves.* There is also *A Few Good Men,* the first in the Earth Revolution, a sister series to the Darkship series.

Mercedes Lackey

Mercedes Lackey was born in Chicago, Illinois, on June 24, 1950. The very next day, the Korean War was declared. It is hoped that there is no connection between the two events. In 1985 her first book was published. In 1990 she met artist Larry Dixon at a small Science Fiction convention in Meridian, Mississippi, on a television interview organized by the convention. They moved to their current home, the "second weirdest house in Oklahoma," also in 1992. She has many pet parrots and "the house is never quiet." She is a *New York Times* bestselling fantasy author with over eighty books in print.

Joe R. Lansdale

Joe R. Lansdale is the author of over thirty novels and two hundred short pieces including fiction and non-fiction. His work has been adapted to film and comics and stage plays. He has written for *Batman: The Animated Series*, and is the recipient of numerous awards and recognitions, including the Edgar, two *New York Times* Notable Books, nine Bram Stoker Awards, the Grinzani Cavou Prize for Literature, and many others. He also was given the opportunity to finish *Tarzan: The Lost Adventure*, an unfinished novel by Edgar Rice Burroughs.

Richard A. Lupoff

Richard A. Lupoff became a leading figure in the Burroughs Revival of the 1960s when he was appointed Editor-in-Chief of Canaveral Press. He was responsible for the editing and publication of many posthumous Burroughs works, including *Tales of Three Planets, Tarzan and the Madman, Tarzan and the Castaways,* and *John Carter of Mars.* His studies of Burroughs and his creations, *Edgar Rice Burroughs: Master of Adventure* and *Barsoom: Edgar Rice Burroughs and the Martian Vision,* have become standard works of scholarship and criticism. His many other books include *The Great American Paperback* and *Writer at Large,* as well as many science fiction and mystery novels, and more than 100 short stories. In recent years he has held editorial posts at Canyon Press and Surinam Turtle Press, and on magazines including *Organ, Ramparts, Science Fiction Eye,* and *Locus.*

Todd McCaffrey

Todd Johnson McCaffrey wrote his first science-fiction story when he was twelve and has been writing on and off ever since. Including the *New York Times* bestselling *Dragon's Fire*, he has written eight books in the Pern universe both solo and in collaboration with his mother, Anne McCaffrey. His short stories have appeared in numerous anthologies. He is currently working on a Scottish steampunk alternate history. Visit his website at *http://www.toddmccaffrey.org*

Mike Resnick

Mike Resnick is, according to *Locus,* the all-time leading award-winner, living or dead, for short fiction. He is the winner of five Hugos, a Nebula, and other major awards in the USA, France, Japan, Poland, Croatia, and Spain. Mike is the author of seventy-one novels, more than two hundred fifty short stories, and three screenplays, and the editor of more than forty anthologies. His work has been translated into twenty-seven languages. He was the Guest of Honor at the 2012 World Science Fiction Convention.

Ralph Roberts

Edgar Rice Burroughs and Ralph Roberts have several things in common—they're both writers, they both like Tarzan and John Carter of Mars and they both served in the same army unit, the 7th Cavalry, Custer's old outfit. ERB served in the 1890s, out in Arizona territory, which explains the birth of Shoz-Dijiji, War Chief of the *Be-don-ko-he* Apaches, son of Geronimo. Ralph was with the unit in a later time of war, Vietnam. After the 7th Cav, ERB began writing Tarzan and John Carter novels, while Ralph worked with NASA during the Apollo moon-landing program, then proceeded to write more computer books than Burroughs, something over one hundred. With "Apache Lawman," Roberts and ERB come back together again, old cavalry brothers of different mothers and separate times . . . but of one mind about that noble savage, Shoz-Dijiji—and, thus, the Black Bear lives and loves his white goddess, Wichita Billings, once more.

Kristine Kathryn Rusch

Kristine Kathryn Rusch read her first Tarzan novel in the summer of her twelfth year. That year she also discovered Andre Norton, Victoria

Holt, and boys. It was a good year. Since then, she's become a bestselling author whose novels have been published in fifteen languages. Her short fiction has won numerous awards, including the Hugo, which she also won for editing. For more information, please go to her website at *www.kristinekathrynrusch.com.*

F. Paul Wilson

F. Paul Wilson is the award-winning, *New York Times* bestselling author of forty-plus books and many short stories spanning medical thrillers, sf, horror, adventure, and virtually everything between. More than nine million copies of his books are in print in the US, and his work has been translated into twenty-four languages. He also has written for the stage, screen, and interactive media. He was introduced to the worlds of Edgar Rice Burroughs in high school via the Ace reprints with the cool Frazetta and Krenkel covers and devoured each new title as soon as it was released. His latest thriller, *Cold City*, stars the notorious urban mercenary Repairman Jack, and is the first of *The Early Years Trilogy*. *Dark City* follows soon. He currently resides at the Jersey Shore and can be found on the Web at *www.repairmanjack.com.*